Cartographies

CONTEMPORARY AMERICAN ESSAYS

Cartographies

CONTEMPORARY AMERICAN ESSAYS

Edited by Diana Young

Bedford Books of *St. Martin's Press*

BOSTON

For Bedford Books

Publisher: Charles H. Christensen
Associate Publisher/General Manager: Joan E. Feinberg
Managing Editor: Elizabeth M. Schaaf
Developmental Editor: Jane Betz
Production Editor: Ann Sweeney
Copyeditor: Adaya Henis
Text Design: Melinda Grosser for *silk*
Cover Design: Steve Snider

Library of Congress Catalog Card Number: 93–73653

Manufactured in the United States of America.

8 7 6 5 4
f   e   d   c   b   a

For information, write: St. Martin's Press, Inc.
175 Fifth Avenue, New York, NY 10010

Editorial Offices: Bedford Books *of* St. Martin's Press
29 Winchester Street, Boston, MA 02116

ISBN: 0–312–09495–7

Acknowledgments

Terry Castle, "First Ed." From *The Apparitional Lesbian* by Terry Castle. Copyright 1994 © by Columbia University Press, New York. Reprinted by permission of the publisher. First published in *The Kenyon Review.*
Joan Didion, "*El Exilio* and the Melting Pot." From *Miami* by Joan Didion. Copyright © 1987 by Joan Didion. Reprinted by permission of Simon & Schuster, Inc.
Annie Dillard, "Total Eclipse." From *Teaching a Stone to Talk* by Annie Dillard. Copyright © 1982 by Annie Dillard. Reprinted by permission of HarperCollins Publishers, Inc.
Michael Dorris, "Life Stories." Copyright ©1989 by Michael Dorris. Reprinted by permission of the author.
Gerald Early, "Waiting for Miss America: Stand Up and Cheer." Copyright © 1989 by Gerald Early. From *Tuxedo Junction* by Gerald Early. Reprinted by permission of The Ecco Press.
Gretel Ehrlich, "Architecture." From *Islands, the Universe, Home* by Gretel Ehrlich. Copyright © 1991 by Gretel Ehrlich. Reprinted by permission of Viking Penguin, a division of Penguin Books USA, Inc.
Nora Ephron, "A Few Words About Breasts." From *Crazy Salad: Some Things About Women* by Nora Ephron. Copyright © 1972 by Nora Ephron. Reprinted by permission of International Creative Management, Inc.
Norma Field, "In the Realm of a Dying Emperor." From *In the Realm of a Dying Emperor* by Norma Field. Copyright © 1991 by Norma Field. Reprinted by permission of Pantheon Books, a division of Random House, Inc.
Frances FitzGerald, "Sun City—1983." From *Cities on a Hill.* Copyright © 1986 by Frances FitzGerald. Reprinted by permission of Simon & Schuster, Inc.
George Garrett, "*Whistling in the Dark.*" From *Whistling in the Dark: True Stories and Other Fables.* Copyright ©1992 by George Garrett. Reprinted by permission of Harcourt Brace & Company.

Acknowledgments and copyrights are continued at the back of the book on page 343, which constitutes an extension of the copyright page.

Preface

Essays and maps might be said to share the same enterprise. Paul Theroux believes that in "a sense, the world was once blank . . . and . . . cartography made it visible and glowing with detail." Eudora Welty circles around the same idea when she tells of seeing Mammoth Caves as a child: without interpretation, she writes, life is just the darkness of those vast caverns. Like maps, essays plot pathways through uncharted tracts, trying to bring something into being where there used to be nothing. Essays attempt to transform experience into knowledge.

The essays in *Cartographies* certainly do. Today's understanding of the essay has been molded by reportage, by the newspaper article, which has familiarized students with a narrowly descriptive mode. This collection offers a rich expository mode, in which the essays exhibit the *how* of a narrative, the way a mind focuses on and revolves around its subject. All the writers here are interested in analysis, which demands room to work. This collection offers students models of subtle, sophisticated, and powerful thought — of the sort that provokes the most articulate inquiry, and the most vivid and compelling writing.

These essays are great examples of the genre, but are not intended to stand like dead monuments to the essay. These voices are seldom interested in alluding to lyrical moments in literature, are not most centrally concerned with ideas embedded in the world of classical learning. That world — with its texts and experiences shared by a small population — is gone forever. But although the world is different, the genre itself is elastic enough to encompass the enormous changes.

Today's essay seems full of juice. First, universal education has allowed many more people to share in it. Second, a range of voices — women's, minorities', gays' — that was once all but silenced is now heard as having legitimate claims on our common life. Third, perhaps, the shrinking resources and the burgeoning violence in the world make

v

life more perilous, make it more urgent to provoke a response. *Cartographies* collects essays that take on the big hard subjects the world offers now: they show us the connection between the destruction of the rain forest and AIDS; they consider immigration in this politically rewritten global map; they talk about alcoholism, transsexuality, apocalyptic sects, pit bulls, supercomputers, and Miss America. The maps we need today are different from those the ancients needed; instead of filling in the blanks, we need maps to guide us through the congestion of political, social, and moral life. We need to hear from people who have thought deeply about difficult issues, and who can show us the possible pathways through the maze.

The essays have been arranged thematically in chapters whose titles encourage students to rethink ideas they might take for granted, and to reconsider the cultural construction of the ideas one might deploy to impose order on the world, including the world of words.

The anthology begins with a topic that concerns all students, that requires them to know nothing but their own autobiographies. The opening chapter, "Becoming," contains essays that are propelled by the dynamics of self-exploration and self-identity. In the next, "Embodying Identities," the writers establish a relationship with the body as a means of asserting or denying that identity, so that the body itself becomes a newly understood site of meaning. The essays in "Constructing Nature" encourage students to see nature as it is perceived and shaped by our expectations of it and of ourselves, rather than as it exists in itself. Nature is a cultural construction, and these essays, unlike classic nature essays, expose the logic of that construction. "Traveling" gathers together pieces that use the mode of traveling to explore the relationship between seeing and determining the truth of what is seen. Concomitantly, "Reading Cultures" contains essays that imply that it is the interplay between writing and watching that is responsible for producing the idea of a culture. From the first to the final chapter, the student has moved from the self out into the wider world, from the individual story to stories of whole groups of people.

So that each student is prepared to begin discussing the essay at the beginning of every class, I have included after each selection two questions designed to be "big" enough to start a general conversation on what the essay is about, but "small" enough so that students must marshal evidence to support their positions.

I have written a discussion on each question in the "Editor's Notes," which offer more questions and discussion topics for every essay. The notes were designed to enable most of the important aspects of each essay to be discussed within a regular classroom hour; they vary considerably in their focus. Each essay sets the course for the editor's investigations, which are as varied as is each essay itself. While the notes also suggest writing assignments and critical, theoretical, and literary sources that students might turn to in their research, they might also just be used as jumping-off points for your own class discussion.

Each essay is introduced by a biographical headnote, which presents a context for the authors' work and, often, their writing histories. Many of the essayists address the connections between their autobiographies and their writing, which can be used as another way to start the class thinking about methods of, and reasons for, shaping experience.

ACKNOWLEDGMENTS

John McPhee and Gerald Early were generous enough to write with thoughtful suggestions for writers who might be included in this anthology. For their gracious openhandedness, I thank them.

I want to thank Norma Field and Terry Castle for their belief that autobiography and rigorous intellectual analysis can coexist, and that, moreover, they strengthen fields of academic inquiry. The accessibility and power of their writing can only make the further reaches of academe available to students who might otherwise not discover an entryway.

Other thanks are owed to Karen Ravn, without whom the headnotes would be poor things. Andrea Goldman provided meticulous assistance; Beth Chapman turned her persuasive talents to negotiating permissions. Adaya Henis copyedited with a light hand and a gimlet eye, and Ann Sweeney, best of production editors, flattered me into my deadlines.

To my editor, Jane Betz, I owe an enormous debt; her intelligence, tenacity, and equanimity make all things possible.

Chuck Christensen and Joan Feinberg put out a list characterized by their willingness to support the ideas that people are grappling with, and their respect and perspicacity inform every title.

Bill Brown turned his powerful and precise mind to my every sentence; his interest in the project never wavered. Madeleine Lucy Fraser Brown, though less interested, taught me how to make more efficient use of my time.

Contents

Four

TRAVELING 193

Five

READING CULTURES 245

Cartographies

CONTEMPORARY AMERICAN ESSAYS

One

BECOMING

Barbara Grizzuti Harrison, GROWING UP APOCALYPTIC

N. Scott Momaday, THE HORSE

Michael Dorris, LIFE STORIES

George Garrett, WHISTLING IN THE DARK

Norma Field, IN THE REALM OF A DYING EMPEROR

*L*ike maps, essays are records. They are records that people make of the journeys through their own lives. They turn the unknown into the known, chaos into cosmos. As maps, essays are infinitely various, able to chart the psychological as well as the physical. In this chapter, the essayists examine familiar terrain, searching for landmarks of the transformational moments in their lives.

Barbara Grizzuti Harrison's landmark—converting to the Jehovah's Witnesses—is monumental, towering over any other experience of her life. This "fierce, messianic sect" practices divine cartography, mapping the state of the world and seeing everywhere in it signs of the great apocalypse to come: "There is a kind of ruthless glee in the way in which Jehovah's Witnesses point to earthquakes, race riots, heroin addiction, the failure of the United Nations, divorce, famine, and liberalized abortion laws as proof of the nearest Armageddon."

In the end, unable to share their reading of the world, Harrison leaves the Witnesses and leaves us at another transformational moment, ending the essay as she walks into an uncharted future.

N. Scott Momaday explores that kind of uncharted country in "The Horse." With Pecos, he is given a new vantage point: "On the back of my horse I had a different view of the world. I could see more of it, how it reached away beyond all the horizons I had ever seen." His essay shows how "the bright legend" of his youth shapes his adult self, just as the first words of a story do its end: "You cannot begin with the second word and tell the story, for the telling of the story is a cumulative process, a chain of becoming, at last of being."

Michael Dorris also sees the moments that determined his adulthood as being connected, but for him they are less linear, more like "overlapping stairs, unfolding a particular pattern at once haphazard and inevitable." Given greater freedom than Harrison, he has been able to taste more and varied experiences; given more time than his nineteenth-century Native American ancestors, his adult self has incorporated something from all his different experiences.

The essays in this chapter insist that the maps that are made depend upon the cartographer's point of view. In "Whistling in the Dark," George Garrett looks back to see himself as a young soldier in Europe during World War II, trying to make sense of the enormous and malevolent mystery of Hitler's "final solution," straining to understand his own place in the world. What he discovers is that, wherever he is, he is caught up in "his share of this world's woe and joy, the lament and celebration of all living things."

Norma Field shares Garrett's distance from youth; separated from her home in Tokyo by her biracialism, by time, by her life in the United States, she returns home to "become, again, daughter, granddaughter, and even niece, a process akin to regenerating amputated limbs." And what she rediscovers is that the learning lies in the telling, so that the map she draws of Japan—in which the past and the present share the same room—bears "witness against the indifference of time and the hostility of space."

All these essayists partake of this same effort to bear witness against time and space. These essays are drawn from their journeys; they have plotted their own psychic terrain, drawn the boundaries between the *is* and the *was*, tried to fix on those elusive coordinates that marked where they turned into themselves.

Barbara Grizzuti Harrison

GROWING UP APOCALYPTIC

Barbara Grizzuti Harrison was born in 1934 in Brooklyn, New York, where she still lives. A writer of both fiction and nonfiction, Harrison is perhaps best known as a practitioner of personal journalism. An article she wrote about her own child's school led to her first book, *Unlearning the Lie: Sexism in School* (1969). And, as its title suggests, her next book, *Vision of Glory: A History and a Memory of Jehovah's Witnesses* (1978), drew greatly upon experiences she had as an adolescent and a young woman. Harrison credits a "marvelous" high school English teacher and Doris Lessing's *The Golden Notebook* as important early influences on her writing career.

"The trouble with you," Anna said, in a voice in which compassion, disgust, and reproach fought for equal time, "is that you can't remember what it was like to be young. And even if you could remember—well, when you were my age, you were in that crazy Jehovah's Witness religion, and you probably didn't even play spin the bottle."

Anna, my prepubescent eleven-year-old, feels sorry for me because I did not have "a normal childhood." It has never occurred to her to question whether her childhood is "normal" . . . which is to say, she is happy. She cannot conceive of a life in which one is not free to move around, explore, argue, flirt with ideas and dismiss them, form passionate alliances and friendships according to no imperative but one's own nature and volition; she regards love as unconditional, she expects nurturance as her birthright. It fills her with terror and pity that anyone—especially her mother—could have grown up any differently—could have grown up in a religion where love was conditional upon rigid adherence to dogma and established practice . . . where approval had to be bought from authoritarian sources . . . where people did not fight openly and love fiercely and forgive generously and make decisions of their own and mistakes of their own and have adventures of their own.

"Poor Mommy," she says. To have spent one's childhood in love with/tyrannized by a vengeful Jehovah is not Anna's idea of a good time—nor is it her idea of goodness. As, in her considered opinion, my having been a proselytizing Jehovah's Witness for thirteen years was about as good a preparation for real life as spending a commensurate

3

amount of time in a Skinner box on the North Pole, she makes allowances for me. And so, when Anna came home recently from a boy-girl party to tell me that she had kissed a boy ("interesting," she pronounced the experiment), and I had heard my mouth ask that atavistic mother-question, "And what else did you do?" Anna was inclined to be charitable with me: "Oh, for goodness' sake, what do you think we did, screw? The trouble with you is . . . " And then she explained to me about spin the bottle.

I do worry about Anna. She is, as I once explained drunkenly to someone who thought that she might be the better for a little vigorous repression, a teleological child. She is concerned with final causes, with ends and purposes and means; she would like to see evidence of design and order in the world; and all her adventures are means to that end. That, combined with her love for the music, color, poetry, ritual, and drama of religion, might, I think, if she were at all inclined to bow her back to authority—and if she didn't have my childhood as an example of the perils thereof—have made her ripe for conversion to an apocalyptic, messianic sect.

That fear may be evidence of my special paranoia, but it is not an entirely frivolous conjecture. Ardent preadolescent girls whose temperament tends toward the ecstatic are peculiarly prone to conversion to fancy religions.

I know. My mother and I became Jehovah's Witnesses in 1944, when I was nine years old. I grew up drenched in the dark blood-poetry of a fierce messianic sect. Shortly after my conversion, I got my first period. We used to sing this hymn: "Here is He who comes from Eden / all His raiment stained with blood." My raiments were stained with blood, too. But the blood of the Son of Man was purifying, redemptive, cleansing, sacrificial. Mine was filthy—proof of my having inherited the curse placed upon the seductress Eve. I used to "read" my used Kotexes compulsively, as if the secret of life—or a harbinger of death —were to be found in that dull, mysterious effluence.

My brother, at the time of our conversion, was four. After a few years of listlessly following my mother and me around in our door-to-door and street-corner proselytizing, he allied himself with my father, who had been driven to noisy, militant atheism by the presence of two female religious fanatics in his hitherto patriarchal household. When your wife and daughter are in love with God, it's hard to complete— particularly since God is good enough not to require messy sex as proof or expression of love. As a child, I observed that it was not extraordinary for women who became Jehovah's Witnesses to remove themselves from their husband's bed as a first step to getting closer to God. For women whose experience had taught them that all human relationships were treacherous and capricious and frighteningly volatile, an escape from the confusions of the world into the certainties of a fundamentalist religion provided the illusion of safety and of rest. It is not too simple to say that the reason many unhappily married and sexually embittered women fell in love with Jehovah was that they didn't have to go to bed with Him.

Apocalyptic religions are, by their nature, antierotic. Jehovah's Witnesses believe that the world—or, as they would have it, "this evil system under Satan the Devil"—will end in our lifetime. After the slaughter Jehovah has arranged for his enemies at Armageddon, say the Witnesses, this quintessentially masculine God—vengeful in battle, benevolent to survivors—will turn the earth into an Edenic paradise for true believers. I grew up under the umbrella of the slogan. "Millions Now Living Will Never Die," convinced that 1914 marked "the beginning of the times of the end." So firmly did Jehovah's Witnesses believe this to be true that there were those who, in 1944, refused to get their teeth filled, postponing all care of their bodies until God saw to their regeneration in His New World, which was just around the corner.

Some corner.

Despite the fact that their hopes were not immediately rewarded, 10 Jehovah's Witnesses have persevered with increasing fervor and conviction, and their attitude toward the world remains the same: Because all their longing is for the future, they are bound to hate the present— the material, the sexual, the flesh. It's impossible, of course, truly to savor and enjoy the present, or to bend one's energies to shape and mold the world into the form of goodness, if you are only waiting for it to be smashed by God. There is a kind of ruthless glee in the way in which Jehovah's Witnesses point to earthquakes, race riots, heroin addiction, the failure of the United Nations, divorce, famine, and liberalized abortion laws as proof of the nearest Armageddon.

The world will end, according to the Witnesses, in a great shaking and rending and tearing of unbelieving flesh, with unsanctified babies swimming in blood—torrents of blood. They await God's Big Bang— the final orgasmic burst of violence, after which all things will come together in a cosmic orgasm of joy. In the meantime, they have disgust and contempt for the world; and freedom and spontaneity, even playfulness, in sex are explicitly frowned upon.

When I was ten, it would have been more than my life was worth to acknowledge, as Anna does so casually, that I knew what *screwing* was. (Ignorance, however, delivered me from that grave error.) Once, having read somewhere that Hitler had a mistress, I asked my mother what a mistress was. (I had an inkling that it was some kind of sinister superhousekeeper, like Judith Anderson in *Rebecca*.) I knew from my mother's silence, and from her cold, hard, and frightened face, that the question was somehow a grievous offense. I knew that I had done something terribly wrong, but as usual, I didn't know what. The fact was that I never knew how to buy God's—or my mother's—approval.

There were sins I consciously and knowingly committed. That was bad, but it was bearable. I could always pray to God to forgive me, say, for reading the Bible for its "dirty parts" (to prefer the Song of Solomon to all the begats of Genesis was proof absolute of the sinfulness of my nature). But the offenses that made me most cringingly guilty were those I had committed unconsciously; as an imperfect human being descended from the wretched Eve, I was bound—so I had been taught— to offend Jehovah seventy-seven times a day without my even knowing what I was doing wrong.

I knew that good Christians didn't commit "unnatural acts"; but I didn't know what "unnatural acts" were. I knew that an increase in the number of rapes was one of the signs heralding the end of the world, but I didn't know what rape was. Consequently, I spent a lot of time praying that I was not committing unnatural acts or rape.

My ignorance of all things sexual was so profound that it frequently led to comedies of error. Nothing I've ever read has inclined me to believe that Jehovah has a sense of humor, and I must say that I consider it a strike against Him that He wouldn't find this story funny: One night shortly after my conversion, a visiting elder of the congregation, as he was avuncularly tucking me in bed, asked me if I were guilty of performing evil practices with my hands under the covers at night. I was puzzled. He was persistent. Finally, I thought I understood. And I burst into wild tears of self-recrimination: What I did under the covers at night was bite my cuticles—a practice which, in fact, did afford me a kind of sensual pleasure. I didn't learn about masturbation—which the Witnesses call "idolatry" because "the masturbator's affection is diverted away from the Creator and is bestowed upon a coveted object . . . his genitals"—until much later. So, having confessed to a sin that I didn't even know existed, I was advised of the necessity of keeping one's body pure from sin; cold baths were recommended. I couldn't see the connection between cold baths and my cuticles, but no one ever questioned the imperatives of an elder. So I subjected my impure body, in midwinter, to so many icy baths that I began to look like a bleached prune. My mother thought I was demented. But I couldn't tell her that I'd been biting my cuticles, because to have incurred God's wrath— and to see the beady eye of the elder steadfastly upon me at every religious meeting I went to—was torment enough. There was no way to win.

One never questioned the imperatives of an elder. I learned as a very small child that it was my primary duty in life to "make nice." When I was little, I was required to respond to inquiries about my health in this manner: "Fine and dandy, just like sugar candy, thank you." And to curtsy. If that sounds like something from a Shirley Temple movie, it's because it is. Having been brought up to be the Italian working-class Shirley Temple from Bensonhurst, it was not terribly difficult for me to learn to "make nice" for God and the elders. Behaving well was relatively easy. The passionate desire to win approval guaranteed my conforming. But behaving well never made me feel good. I always felt as if I were a bad person.

I ask myself why it was that my brother was not hounded by the obsessive guilt and the desperate desire for approval that informed all my actions. Partly, I suppose, luck, and an accident of temperament, but also because of the peculiarly guilt-inspiring double message girls received. Girls were taught that it was their nature to be spiritual, but paradoxically that they were more prone to absolute depravity than were boys.

In my religion, everything beautiful and noble and spiritual and good was represented by a woman; and everything evil and depraved and monstrous was represented by a woman. I learned that "God's organization," the "bride of Christ," or His 144,000 heavenly co-rulers were represented by a "chaste virgin." I also learned that "Babylon the Great," or "false religion," was "the mother of the abominations or the 'disgusting things of the earth.' . . . She likes to get drunk on human blood. . . . Babylon the Great is . . . pictured as a woman, an international harlot."

Young girls were thought not to have the "urges" boys had. They were not only caretakers of their own sleepy sexuality but protectors of boys' vital male animal impulses as well. They were thus doubly responsible, and, if they fell, doubly damned. Girls were taught that, simply by existing, they were provoking male sexuality . . . which it was their job then to subdue.

To be female, I learned, was to be Temptation; nothing short of death—the transformation of your atoms into a lilac bush—could change that. (I used to dream deliciously of dying, of being as inert— and as unaccountable—as the dust I came from.) Inasmuch as males naturally "wanted it" more, when a female "wanted it" she was doubly depraved, unnatural as well as sinful. She was the receptacle for male lust, "the weaker vessel." If the vessel, created by God for the use of males, presumed to have desires of its own, it was perforce consigned to the consuming fires of God's wrath. If then, a woman were to fall from grace, her fall would be mighty indeed—and her willful nature would lead her into that awful abyss where she would be deprived of the redemptive love of God and the validating love of man. Whereas, were a man to fall, he would be merely stumbling over his own feet of clay.

(Can this be accident? My brother, when he was young, was always falling over his own feet. I, on the other hand, to this day sweat with terror at the prospect of going down escalators or long flights of stairs. I cannot fly; I am afraid of the fall.)

I spent my childhood walking a religious tightrope, maintaining a difficult dizzying balance. I was, for example, expected to perform well at school, so that glory would accrue to Jehovah and "His organization." But I was also made continually aware of the perils of falling prey to "the wisdom of this world which is foolishness to God." I had constantly to defend myself against the danger of trusting my own judgment. To question or to criticize God's "earthly representatives" was a sure sign of "demonic influence"; to express doubt openly was to risk being treated like a spiritual leper. I was always an honor student at school; but this was hardly an occasion for unqualified joy. I felt, rather, as if I were courting spiritual disaster: While I was congratulated for having "given a witness" by virtue of my academic excellence, I was, in the next breath, warned against the danger of supposing that my intelligence could function independently of God's. The effect of all this was to convince me that my intelligence was like some kind of tricky, predatory animal, which, if it were not kept firmly reined, would surely spring on and destroy me.

"Vanity, thy name is woman." I learned very early what happened to women with "independent spirits" who opposed the will and imperatives of male elders. They were disfellowshipped (excommunicated) and thrown into "outer darkness." Held up as an example of such perfidious conduct was Maria Frances Russell, the wife of Charles Taze Russell, charismatic founder of the sect.

Russell charged his wife with "the same malady which has smitted others—*ambition*." Complaining of a "female conspiracy" against the Lord's organization, he wrote: "The result was a considerable stirring up of slander and misrepresentation, for of course it would not suit (her) purposes to tell the plain unvarnished truth, that Sister Russell was ambitious. . . . When she desired to come back, I totally refused, except upon a promise that she should make reasonable acknowledgment of the wrong course she had been pursuing." Ambition in a woman was, by implication, so reprehensible as to exact from Jehovah the punishment of death.

(What the Witnesses appeared less eager to publicize about the Russells' spiritual-cum-marital problems is that in April 1906, Mrs. Russell, having filed suit for legal separation, told a jury that her husband had once remarked to a young orphan woman the Russells had reared: "I am like a jellyfish. I float around here and there. I touch this one and that one, and if she responds I take her to me, and if not I float on to others." Mrs. Russell was unable to prove her charge.)

I remember a line in *A Nun's Story*: "Dear God," the disaffected Bel- 25
gian nun anguished, "forgive me. I will never be able to love a Nazi." I, conversely, prayed tormentedly for many years, "Dear God, forgive me, I am not able to hate what you hate. I love the world." As a Witness I was taught that "friendship with the world" was "spiritual adultery."

The world was crawling with Satan's agents. But Satan's agents—evolutionists, "false religionists," and all those who opposed, or were indifferent to, "Jehovah's message"—often seemed like perfectly nice, decent, indeed lovable people to me. (They were certainly interesting.) As I went from door to door, ostensibly to help the Lord divide the "goats" from the "sheep," I found that I was more and more listening to *their* lives; and I became increasingly more tentative about telling them that I had *The* Truth. As I grew older, I found it more and more difficult to eschew their company. I entertained fantasies, at one time or another, about a handsome, ascetic Jesuit priest I had met in my preaching work and about Albert Schweitzer, J. D. Salinger, E. B. White, and Frank Sinatra; in fact, I was committing "spiritual adultery" all over the place. And then, when I was fifteen, I fell in love with an "unbeliever."

If I felt—before having met and loved Arnold Horowitz, English 31, New Utrecht High School—that life was a tightrope, I felt afterward that my life was perpetually being lived on a high wire, with no safety net to catch me. I was obliged, by every tenet of my faith, to despise him: to be "yoked with an unbeliever," an atheist and an intellectual . . . the pain was exquisite.

He was the essential person, the person who taught me how to love, and how to doubt. Arnold became interested in me because I was smart; he loved me because he though I was good. He nourished me. He nurtured me. He paid me the irresistible compliment of totally comprehending me. He hated my religion. He railed against the sect that would rather see babies die than permit them to have blood transfusions, which were regarded as unscriptural; he had boundless contempt for my overseers, who would not permit me to go to college—the "Devil's playground," which would fill my head with wicked, ungodly nonsense; he protested mightily, with the rage that springs from genuine compassion, against a religion that could tolerate segregation and apartheid, sneer at martyred revolutionaries, dismiss social reform and material charity as "irrelevant," a religion that—waiting for God to cure all human ills—would act by default to maintain the status quo, while regarding human pain and struggle without pity and without generosity. He loathed the world view that had been imposed on me, a black-and-white view that allowed no complexities, no moral dilemmas, that disdained metaphysical or philosophical or psychological inquiry; he loathed the bloated simplicities that held me in thrall. But he loved *me*. I had never before felt loved unconditionally.

This was a measure of his love: Jehovah's Witnesses are not permitted to salute the flag. Arnold came, unbidden, to sit with me at every school assembly, to hold my hand, while everyone else stood at rigid salute. We were very visible; and I was very comforted. And this was during the McCarthy era. Arnold had a great deal to lose, and he risked it all for me. Nobody had ever risked anything for me before. How could I believe that he was wicked?

We drank malteds on his porch and read T. S. Eliot and listened to Mozart. We walked for hours, talking of God and goodness and happiness and death. We met surreptitiously. (My mother so feared and hated the man who was leading me into apostasy that she once threw a loaf of Arnold bread out the window; his very name was loathsome to her.) Arnold treated me with infinite tenderness; he was the least alarming man I had ever known. His fierce concentration on me, his solicitous care uncoupled with sexual aggression, was the gentlest — and most thrilling — love I had ever known. He made me feel what I had never felt before — valuable, and good.

It was very hard. All my dreams centered around Arnold, who was 30
becoming more important, certainly more real to me, than God. All my dreams were blood-colored. I would fantasize about Arnold's being converted and surviving Armageddon and living forever with me in the New World. Or I would fantasize about my dying with Arnold, in fire and flames, at Armageddon. I would try to make bargains with God — my life for his. When I confessed my terrors to the men in charge of my spiritual welfare — when I said that I knew I could not rejoice in the destruction of the "wicked" at Armageddon — I was told that I was presuming to be "more compassionate than Jehovah," the deadliest sin against the holy spirit. I was reminded that, being a woman and therefore weak and sentimental, I would have to go against my sinful nature and listen to their superior wisdom, which consisted of my never seeing Arnold again. I was also reminded of the perils of being over-smart: If I hadn't been such a good student, none of this would have happened to me.

I felt as if I were leading a double life, as indeed I was. I viewed the world as beautifully various, as a blemished but mysteriously wonderful place, as savable by humans, who were neither good nor bad but imperfectly wise; but I *acted* as if the world were fit for nothing but destruction, as if all human efforts to purchase happiness and goodness were doomed to failure and deserving of contempt, as if all people could be categorized as "sheep" or "goats" and herded into their appropriate destinies by a judgmental Jehovah, the all-seeing Father who knew better than His children what was good for them.

As I had when I was a little girl, I "made nice" as best I could. I maintained the appearance of "goodness," that is, of religiosity, although it violated my truest feelings. When I left high school, I went into the full-time preaching work. I spent a minimum of five hours a day ringing doorbells and conducting home Bible studies. I went to three religious meetings a week. I prayed that my outward conformity would lead to inner peace. I met Arnold very occasionally, when my need to see him overcame my elders' imperatives and my own devastating fears. He was always accessible to me. Our meetings partook equally of misery and of joy. I tried, by my busyness, to lock all my doubts into an attic of my mind.

And for a while, and in a way, it "took." I derived sustenance from communal surges of revivalist fervor at religious conventions and from the conviction that I was united, in a common cause, with a tiny minority of persecuted and comradely brothers and sisters whose approval became both my safety net and the Iron Curtain that shut me off from the world. I felt that I had chosen Jehovah, and that my salvation, while not assured, was at least a possibility; perhaps He would choose me. I vowed finally never to see Arnold again, hoping, by this sacrifice, to gain God's approval for him as well as for me.

I began to understand that for anyone so obviously weak and irresponsible as I, only a life of self-sacrifice and abnegation could work. I wanted to be consumed by Jehovah, to be locked so closely into the straitjacket of His embrace that I would be impervious to the devilish temptations my irritable, independent intelligence threw up in my path.

I wished to be eaten up alive; and my wish was granted. When I was nineteen, I was accepted into Bethel, the headquarters organization of Jehovah's Witnesses, where I worked and lived, one of twelve young women among two hundred and fifty men, for three years. "Making nice" had paid off. Every minute of my waking life was accounted for; there was no leisure in which to cultivate vice or reflection. I called myself happy. I worked as a housekeeper for my brothers, making thirty beds a day, sweeping and vacuuming and waxing and washing fifteen rooms a day (in addition to proselytizing in my "free time"); I daily washed the bathtub thirty men had bathed in. In fact, the one demurral I made during those years was to ask—I found it so onerous—if perhaps the brothers, many of whom worked in the Witnesses' factory, could not clean out their own bathtub (thirty layers of grease is a lot of grease). I was told by the male overseer who supervised housekeepers that Jehovah had assigned me this "privilege." And I told myself I was lucky.

I felt myself to be even luckier—indeed, blessed—when, after two years of this servant's work, one of Jehovah's middlemen, the president of the Watch Tower Bible and Tract Society, told me that he was assigning me to proofread Watch Tower publications. He accompanied this benediction with a warning: This new honor, I was told, was to be a test of my integrity—"Remember in all things to defer to the brothers; you will have to guard your spirit against pride and vanity. Satan will try now to tempt you as never before."

And defer I did. There were days when I felt literally as if my eternal destiny hung upon a comma: If the brother with whom I worked decided a comma should go out where I wanted to put one in, I prayed to Jehovah to forgive me for that presumptuous comma. I was perfectly willing to deny the existence of a split infinitive if that would placate my brother. I denied and denied — commas, split infinitives, my sexuality, my intelligence, my femaleness, my yearning to be part of the world — until suddenly with a great silent shifting and shuddering, and with more pain than I had ever experienced or expect to experience again, I broke. I woke up one morning, packed my bags, and walked out of that place. I was twenty-two; and I had to learn how to begin to live. It required a great deal of courage; I do not think I will ever be capable of that much courage again.

The full story of life in that institution and the ramifications of my decision to leave it is too long to tell here; and it will take me the rest of my life to understand fully the ways in which everything I have ever done since has been colored and informed by the guilt that was my daily bread for so many dry years, by the desperate need for approval that allowed me to be swallowed up whole by a devouring religion, by the carefully fostered desire to "make nice" and to be "a good girl," by the conviction that I was nothing and nobody unless I served a cause superior to that of my own necessities.

Arnold, of course, foresaw the difficulty; when I left religion, he said, "Now you will be just like the rest of us." With no guiding passion, he meant; uncertain, he meant, and often muddled and confused, and always struggling. And he wept.

Questions

1. Barbara Grizzuti Harrison connects being female with fundamentalism, claiming that "ardent preadolescent girls whose temperament tends toward the ecstatic are peculiarly prone to conversion to fancy religions" (para. 5), and that "love for the music, color, poetry, ritual, and drama of religion" draws them toward apocalyptic, messianic sects (para. 4). Yet Harrison's own representation of the Jehovah's Witnesses does not seem to center on this music, color, poetry, and ritual. How does she explain why women, in particular, are drawn to messianic religions?

2. How does Arnold figure in this essay? How would you describe Harrison's relationship with him? Does it parallel, in any ways, her relationship with the religious patriarchy?

N. Scott Momaday

THE HORSE

Born in Lawton, Oklahoma, in 1934, and raised on Indian reservations in the Southwest, N. Scott Momaday has a rich and complex cultural heritage. His father was a Kiowa Indian. His mother was descended from Anglo-American pioneers, although she also had a Cherokee great-grandmother and, like her son, identified closely with her Native American background. Momaday is an artist, as was his father; a writer, as was his mother; and a teacher, as they both were. He has won awards for his poetry, fiction, and nonfiction, including the Pulitzer Prize for his novel *House Made of Dawn* (1969). In *The Names: A Memoir* (1976), from which this selection is taken, he explores and embraces the diversity of his roots.

The first word gives origin to the second, the first and second to the third, the first, second, and third to the fourth, and so on. You cannot begin with the second word and tell the story, for the telling of the story is a cumulative process, a chain of becoming, at last of being.

Oh, it is summer in New Mexico, in the bright legend of my youth. I want you to see the very many deep colors of the distance. I want you to live, to be for an hour or a day more completely alive in me than you have ever been. There are moments in that time when I live so intensely in myself that I wonder how it is possible to keep from flying apart. I want you to feel that, too, the vibrant ecstasy of so much being —to know beyond any doubt that it is only the merest happy accident that you can hold together at all in the exhilaration of such wonder. The wonder: I want to tell you of it; I want to speak and to write it all out for you.

I sometimes think of what it means that in their heyday—in 1830, say—the Kiowas owned more horses per capita than any other tribe on the Great Plains, that the Plains Indian culture, the last culture to evolve in North America, is also known as "the horse culture" and "the centaur culture," that the Kiowas tell the story of a horse that died of shame after its owner committed an act of cowardice, that I am a Kiowa, that therefore there is in me, as there is in the Tartars, an old, sacred notion of the horse. I believe that at some point in my racial life, this notion must needs be expressed in order that I may be true to my nature.

It happened so: I was thirteen years old, and my parents gave me a horse. It was a small nine-year-old gelding of that rare, soft color that is called strawberry roan. This my horse and I came to be, in the course of our life together, in good understanding, of one mind, a true story and history of that large landscape in which we made the one entity of whole motion, one and the same center of an intricate, pastoral composition, evanescent, ever changing. And to this my horse I gave the name Pecos.

On the back of my horse I had a different view of the world. I could see more of it, how it reached away beyond all the horizons I had ever seen; and yet it was more concentrated in its appearance, too, and more accessible to my mind, my imagination. My mind loomed upon the farthest edges of the earth, where I could feel the full force of the planet whirling into space. There was nothing of the air and light that was not pure exhilaration, and nothing of time and eternity. Oh, Pecos, *un poquito mas!*[1] Oh, my hunting horse! Bear me away, bear me away!

It was appropriate that I should make a long journey. Accordingly I set out one early morning, traveling light. Such a journey must begin in the nick of time, on the spur of the moment, and one must say to himself at the outset: Let there be wonderful things along the way; let me hold to the way and be thoughtful in my going; let this journey be made in beauty and belief.

I sang in the sunshine and heard the birds call out on either side. Bits of down from the cottonwoods drifted across the air, and butterflies fluttered in the sage. I could feel my horse under me, rocking at my legs, the bobbing of the reins to my hand; I could feel the sun on my face and the stirring of a little wind at my hair. And through the hard hooves, the slender limbs, the supple shoulders, the fluent back of my horse I felt the earth under me. Everything was under me, buoying me up; I rode across the top of the world. My mind soared; time and again I saw the fleeting shadow of my mind moving about me as it went winding upon the sun.

When the song, which was a song of riding, was finished, I had Pecos pick up the pace. Far down on the road to San Ysidro I overtook my friend Pasqual Fragua. He was riding a rangy, stiff-legged black and white stallion, half wild, which horse he was breaking for the rancher

___

[1]*un poquito mas*: A little bit more (Spanish).

Cass Goodner. The horse skittered and blew as I drew up beside him. Pecos began to prance, as he did always in the company of another horse. "Where are you going?" I asked in the Jemez language. And he replied, "I am going down the road." The stallion was hard to manage, and Pasqual had to keep his mind upon it; I saw that I had taken him by surprise. "You know," he said after a moment, "when you rode up just now I did not know who you were." We rode on for a time in silence, and our horses got used to each other, but still they wanted their heads. The longer I looked at the stallion the more I admired it, and I suppose that Pasqual knew this, for he began to say good things about it: that it was a thing of good blood, that it was very strong and fast, that it felt very good to ride it. The thing was this: that the stallion was half wild, and I came to wonder about the wild half of it; I wanted to know what its wildness was worth in the riding. "Let us trade horses for a while," I said, and, well, all right, he agreed. At first it was exciting to ride the stallion, for every once in a while it pitched and bucked and wanted to run. But it was heavy and raw-boned and full of resistance, and every step was a jolt that I could feel deep down in my bones. I saw soon enough that I had made a bad bargain, and I wanted my horse back, but I was ashamed to admit it. There came a time in the late afternoon, in the vast plain far south of San Ysidro, after thirty miles, perhaps, when I no longer knew whether it was I who was riding the stallion or the stallion who was riding me. "Well, let us go back now," said Pasqual at last. "No. I am going on; and I will have my horse back, please," I said, and he was surprised and sorry to hear it, and we said goodbye. "If you are going south or east," he said, "look out for the sun, and keep your face in the shadow of your hat. *Vaya con Dios*[2]" And I went on my way alone then, wiser and better mounted, and thereafter I held on to my horse. I saw no one for a long time, but I saw four falling stars and any number of jackrabbits, roadrunners, and coyotes, and once, across a distance, I saw a bear, small and black, lumbering in a ravine. The mountains drew close and withdrew and drew close again, and after several days I swung east.

Now and then I came upon settlements. For the most part they were dry, burnt places with Spanish names: Arroyo Seco, Las Piedras, Tres Casas. In one of these I found myself in a narrow street between high adobe walls. Just ahead, on my left, was a door in the wall. As I approached the door was flung open, and a small boy came running out, rolling a hoop. This happened so suddenly that Pecos shied very sharply, and I fell to the ground, jamming the thumb of my left hand. The little boy looked very worried and said that he was sorry to have caused such an accident. I waved the matter off, as if it were nothing;

[2]*Vaya con Dios*: Go with God (Spanish).

but as a matter of fact my hand hurt so much that tears welled up in my eyes. And the pain lasted for many days. I have fallen many times from a horse, both before and after that, and a few times I fell from a running horse on dangerous ground, but that was the most painful of them all.

In another settlement there were some boys who were interested 10 in racing. They had good horses, some of them, but their horses were not so good as mine, and I won easily. After that, I began to think of ways in which I might even the odds a little, might give some advantage to my competitors. Once or twice I gave them a head start, a reasonable head start of, say, five or ten yards to the hundred, but that was too simple, and I won anyway. Then it came to me that I might try this: we should all line up in the usual way, side by side, but my competitors should be mounted and I should not. When the signal was given I should then have to get up on my horse while the others were breaking away; I should have to mount my horse during the race. This idea appealed to me greatly, for it was both imaginative and difficult, not to mention dangerous; Pecos and I should have to work very closely together. The first few times we tried this I had little success, and over a course of a hundred yards I lost four races out of five. The principal problem was that Pecos simply could not hold still among the other horses. Even before they broke away he was hard to manage, and when they were set running nothing could hold him back, even for an instant. I could not get my foot in the stirrup, but I had to throw myself up across the saddle on my stomach, hold on as best I could, and twist myself into position, and all this while racing at full speed. I could ride well enough to accomplish this feat, but it was a very awkward and inefficient business. I had to find some way to use the whole energy of my horse, to get it all into the race. Thus far I had managed only to break his motion, to divert him from his purpose and mine. To correct this I took Pecos away and worked with him through the better part of a long afternoon on a broad reach of level ground beside an irrigation ditch. And it was hot, hard work. I began by teaching him to run straight away while I ran beside him a few steps, holding on to the saddle horn, with no pressure on the reins. Then, when we had mastered this trick, we proceeded to the next one, which was this: I placed my weight on my arms, hanging from the saddle horn, threw my feet out in front of me, struck them to the ground, and sprang up against the saddle. This I did again and again, until Pecos came to expect it and did not flinch or lose his stride. I sprang a little higher each time. It was in all a slow process of trial and error, and after two or three hours both Pecos and I were covered with bruises and soaked through with perspiration. But we had much to show for our efforts, and at last the moment came when we must put the whole performance together. I had not yet leaped into the saddle, but I was quite confident that I could now do so; only I must be sure to get high enough. We began this dress rehearsal then from a standing position. At my signal Pecos lurched and was running at once, straight away and smoothly. And at the same time I sprinted forward two steps and gathered myself up, placing my weight precisely at my wrists, throwing my feet out and together, perfectly. I brought my feet down sharply to the ground and sprang up hard, as hard as I could, bringing my legs astraddle of my horse—and everything was just right, except that I sprang too high. I vaulted all the way over my horse, clearing the saddle by a considerable margin, and came down into the irrigation ditch. It was a good trick, but it was not the one I had in mind, and I wonder what Pecos thought of it after all. Anyway, after a while I could mount my horse in this way and so well that there was no challenge in it, and I went on winning race after race.

I went on, farther and farther into the wide world. Many things happened. And in all this I knew one thing: I knew where the journey was begun, that it was itself a learning of the beginning, that the beginning was infinitely worth the learning. The journey was well undertaken, and somewhere in it I sold my horse to an old Spanish man of Vallecitos. I do not know how long Pecos lived. I had used him hard and well, and it may be that in his last days an image of me like thought shimmered in his brain.

Questions

1. Momaday's opening passage seems to be drawing a parallel between stories and human beings, between a narrative history and a personal history:

   > The first word gives origin to the second, the first and second to the third, the first, second, and third to the fourth, and so on. You cannot begin with the second word and tell the story, for the telling of the story is a cumulative process, a chain of becoming, at last of being.

   In this essay, how does Momaday focus on the idea of becoming?
2. Describe the relationship between Momaday and his horse. To what kinds of understandings does Pecos give his rider access? Why is Pecos so closely associated with Momaday's story of becoming?

Michael Dorris

LIFE STORIES

Michael Dorris was born into the Modoc Indian tribe in 1945. After taking a rather circuitous route through English, classics, and theater history departments, he arrived at his present position as professor of anthropology and Native American studies at Dartmouth College. In 1987 Dorris won wide acclaim for *The Broken Cord*, a nonfiction book about his adopted son in which he called attention to the dangers of fetal alcohol syndrome. Dorris is also the author of a novel, *A Yellow Raft in Blue Water* (1987), and often writes in collaboration with his wife, the novelist Louise Erdrich.

*I*n most cultures, adulthood is equated with self-reliance and responsibility, yet often Americans do not achieve this status until we are in our late twenties or early thirties—virtually the entire average lifespan of a person in a traditional non-Western society. We tend to treat prolonged adolescence as a warm-up for real life, as a wobbly suspension bridge between childhood and legal maturity. Whereas a nineteenth-century Cheyenne or Lakota teenager was expected to alter self-conception in a split-second vision, we often meander through an analogous rite of passage for more than a decade—through high school, college, graduate school.

Though he had never before traveled alone outside his village, the Plains Indian male was expected at puberty to venture solo into the wilderness. There he had to fend for and sustain himself while avoiding the menace of unknown dangers, and there he had absolutely to remain until something happened that would transform him. Every human being, these tribes believed, was entitled to at least one moment of personal, enabling insight.

Anthropology proposes feasible psychological explanations for why this flash was eventually triggered: Fear, fatigue, reliance on strange foods, the anguish of loneliness, stress, and the expectation of ultimate success all contributed to a state of receptivity. Every sense was quickened, alerted to perceive deep meaning, until at last the interpretation of an unusual event—a dream, a chance encounter, or an unexpected vista—reverberated with metaphor. Through this unique prism, abstractly preserved in a vivid memory or song, a boy caught foresight of both his adult persona and of his vocation, the two inextricably entwined.

Today the best approximations that many of us get to such a heady sense of eventuality come in the performance of our school vacation jobs. Summers are intermissions, and once we hit our teens it is during these breaks in our structured regimen that we initially taste the satisfaction of remuneration that is earned, not merely doled. Tasks defined as *work* are not only graded, they are compensated; they have a worth that is unarguable because it translates into hard currency. Wage labor —and in the beginning, this generally means a confining, repetitive chore for which we are quickly over-qualified—paradoxically brings a sense of blooming freedom. At the outset, the complaint to a peer that business supersedes fun is oddly liberating—no matter what drudgery requires your attention, it is by its very required nature serious and adult.

At least that's how it seemed to me. I come from a line of people   5 hard hit by the Great Depression. My mother and her sisters went to work early in their teens—my mother operated a kind of calculator known as a comptometer while her sisters spent their days, respectively, at a peanut factory and at Western Union. My grandmother did piecework sewing. Their efforts, and the Democratic Party, saw them through, and to this day they never look back without appreciation for their later solvency. They take nothing for granted. Accomplishments are celebrated, possessions are valuable, in direct proportion to the labor entailed to acquire them; anything easily won or bought on credit is suspect. When I was growing up we were far from wealthy, but what money we had was correlated to the hours some one of us had logged. My eagerness to contribute to, or at least not diminish, the coffer was countered by the arguments of those whose salaries kept me in school: My higher education was a sound group investment. The whole family was adamant that I have the opportunities they had missed, and no matter how much I objected, they stinted themselves to provide for me.

Summer jobs were therefore a relief, an opportunity to pull a share of the load. As soon as the days turned warm I began to peruse the classifieds, and when the spring semester was done, I was ready to punch a clock. It even felt right. Work in June, July, and August had an almost Biblical aspect: In the hot, canicular weather your brow sweated, just as God had ordained. Moreover, summer jobs had the luxury of being temporary. No matter how bizarre, how onerous, how off my supposed track, employment terminated with the falling leaves and I was back on neutral ground. So, during each annual three-month leave from secondary school and later from the university, I compiled an eclectic résumé: lawn cutter, hair sweeper in a barber shop, lifeguard, delivery boy, temporary mail carrier, file clerk, youth program coordinator on my Montana reservation, ballroom dance instructor, theater party promoter, night-shift hospital records keeper, human adding machine in a Paris bank, encyclopedia salesman, newspaper stringer, recreation bus manager, salmon fisherman.

The reasonable titles disguise the madness of some of these occupations. For instance, I seemed inevitably to be hired to trim the yards of the unconventional. One woman followed beside me, step by step, as I traversed her yard in ever tighter squares, and called my attention to each missed blade of grass. Another client never had the "change" to pay me, and so reimbursed my weekly pruning with an offering culled from his library. I could have done without the *Guide to Artificial Respiration* (1942) or the many well-worn copies of Reader's Digest Condensed Books, but sometimes the selection merited the wait. Like a rat lured repeatedly back to the danger of mild electric shock by the mystique of intermittent reenforcement, I kept mowing by day in hopes of turning pages all night.

The summer I was eighteen a possibility arose for a rotation at the post office, and I grabbed it. There was something casually sophisticated about work that required a uniform, about having a federal ranking, even if it was GS-1 (Temp/Sub), and it was flattering to be entrusted with a leather bag containing who knew what important correspondence. Every day I was assigned a new beat, usually in a rough neighborhood avoided whenever possible by regular carriers, and I proved quite capable of complicating what would normally be fairly routine missions. The low point came on the first of August when I diligently delivered four blocks' worth of welfare checks to the right numbers on the wrong streets. It is no fun to snatch unexpected wealth from the hands of those who have but moments previously opened their mailboxes and received a bonus.

After my first year of college, I lived with relatives on an Indian reservation in eastern Montana and filled the only post available: Coordinator of Tribal Youth Programs. I was seduced by the language of the announcement into assuming that there existed Youth Programs to be coordinated. In fact, the Youth consisted of a dozen bored, disgruntled kids—most of them my cousins—who had nothing better to do each day than to show up at what was euphemistically called "the gym" and hate whatever Program I had planned for them. The Youth ranged in age from fifteen to five and seemed to have as their sole common ambition the determination to smoke cigarettes. This put them at immediate and on-going odds with the Coordinator, who on his first day naively encouraged them to sing the "Doe, a deer, a female deer" song from *The Sound of Music*. They looked at me, that bleak morning, and I looked at them, each boy and girl equipped with a Pall Mall behind an ear, and we all knew it would be a long, struggle-charged battle. It was to be a contest of wills, the hearty and wholesome vs. prohibited vice. I stood for dodge ball, for collecting bugs in glass jars, for arts and crafts; they had pledged a preternatural allegiance to sloth. The odds were not in my favor and each waking dawn I experienced the lightheadedness of anticipated exhaustion, that thrill of giddy dissociation in which nothing seems real or of great significance. I went with the flow and learned to inhale.

The next summer, I decided to find work in an urban setting for 10 a change, and was hired as a general office assistant in the Elsa Hoppenfeld Theatre Party Agency, located above Sardi's restaurant in New York City. The Agency consisted of Elsa Hoppenfeld herself, Rita Frank, her regular deputy, and me. Elsa was a gregarious Viennese woman who established contacts through personal charm, and she spent much of the time courting trade away from the building. Rita was therefore both my immediate supervisor and constant companion; she had the most incredible fingernails I had ever seen— long, carefully shaped pegs lacquered in cruel primary colors and hard as stone—and an attitude about her that could only be described as zeal.

The goal of a theater party agent is to sell blocks of tickets to imminent Broadway productions, and the likely buyers are charities, B'nai Briths, Hadassahs, and assorted other fund-raising organizations. We received commissions on volume, and so it was necessary to convince a prospect that a play—preferably an expensive musical—for which we had reserved the rights to seats would be a boffo smash hit.

The object of our greatest expectation that season was an extravaganza called *Chu Chem*, a saga that aspired to ride the coattails of *Fiddler on the Roof* into entertainment history. It starred the estimable Molly Picon and told the story of a family who had centuries ago gone from Israel to China during the diaspora, yet had, despite isolation in an alien environment, retained orthodox culture and habits. The crux of the plot revolved around a man with several marriageable daughters and nary a kosher suitor within 5,000 miles. For three months Rita and I waxed eloquent in singing the show's praises. We sat in our little office, behind facing desks, and every noon while she redid her nails I ordered out from a deli that offered such exotic (to me) delicacies as fried egg sandwiches, lox and cream cheese, pastrami, *tongue*. I developed of necessity and habit a telephone voice laced with a distinctly Yiddish accent. It could have been a great career. However, come November, *Chu Chem* bombed. Its closing was such a financial catastrophe for all concerned that when the following January one Monsieur Dupont advertised on the Placement Board at my college, I decided to put an ocean between me and my former trusting clientele.

M. Dupont came to campus with the stated purpose of interviewing candidates for teller positions in a French bank. Successful applicants, required to be fluent in *français*, would be rewarded with three well-paid months and a rent-free apartment in Paris. I headed for the language lab and registered for an appointment.

The only French in the interview was *Bonjour, ça va?*, after which M. Dupont switched into English and described the wonderful deal on charter air flights that would be available to those who got the nod. Round-trip to Amsterdam, via Reykjavik, leaving the day after exams and returning in mid-September, no changes or substitutions. I signed up on the spot. I was to be a *banquier*, with *pied-à-terre* in Montparnasse!

Unfortunately, when I arrived with only $50 in travelers' checks in   15
my pocket—the flight had cleaned me out, but who needed money since my paycheck started right away—no one in Paris had ever heard of M. Dupont.

Alors.

I stood in the Gare du Nord and considered my options. There weren't any. I scanned a listing of Paris hotels and headed for the cheapest one: the Hotel Villedo, $10 a night. The place had an ambiance that I persuaded myself was antique, despite the red light above the sign. The only accommodation available was "the bridal suite," a steal at $20. The glass door to my room didn't lock and there was a rather continual floor show, but at some point I must have dozed off. When I awoke the church bells were ringing, the sky was pink, and I felt renewed. No little setback was going to spoil my adventure. I stood and stretched, then walked to a mirror that hung above the sink next to the bed. I leaned forward to punctuate my resolve with a confident look in the eye.

The sink disengaged and fell to the floor. Water gushed. In panic I rummaged through my open suitcase, stuffed two pair of underwear into the pipe to quell the flow, and before the dam broke, I was out the door. I barreled through the lobby of the first bank I passed, asked to see the director, and told the startled man my sad story. For some reason, whether from shock or pity, he hired me at $1.27 an hour to be a cross-checker of foreign currency transactions, and with two phone calls found me lodgings at a commercial school's dormitory.

From eight to five each weekday my duty was to sit in a windowless room with six impeccably dressed people, all of whom were totaling identical additions and subtractions. We were highly dignified with each other, very professional, no *tutoyer*ing.[1] Monsieur Saint presided, but the formidable Mademoiselle was the true power; she oversaw each of our columns and shook her head sadly at my American-shaped numbers.

My legacy from that summer, however, was more than an endur-   20
ing penchant for crossed 7s. After I had worked for six weeks, M. Saint asked me during a coffee break why I didn't follow the example of other foreign students he had known and depart the office at noon in order to spend the afternoon touring the sights of Paris with the *Alliance Française*.

---

[1] *tutoyer*ing: Addressing each other with informal pronouns and verb forms.

"Because," I replied in my halting French, "that costs money. I depend upon my full salary the same as any of you." M. Saint nodded gravely and said no more, but then on the next Friday he presented me with a white envelope along with my check.

"Do not open this until you have left the Société Générale," he said ominously. I thought I was fired for the time I had mixed up krøners and guilders, and, once on the sidewalk, I steeled myself to read the worst. I felt the quiet panic of blankness.

"Dear Sir," I translated the perfectly formed script. "You are a person of value. It is not correct that you should be in our beautiful city and not see it. Therefore we have amassed a modest sum to pay the tuition for a two-week afternoon program for you at the *Alliance Française*. Your wages will not suffer, for it is your assignment to appear each morning in this bureau and reacquaint us with the places you have visited. We shall see them afresh through your eyes." The letter had thirty signatures, from the Director to the janitor, and stuffed inside the envelope was a sheaf of franc notes in various denominations.

I rushed back to the tiny office. M. Saint and Mademoiselle had waited, and accepted my gratitude with their usual controlled smiles and precise handshakes. But they had blown their Gallic cover, and for the next ten days and then through all the days until I went home in September, our branch was awash with sightseeing paraphernalia. Everyone had advice, favorite haunts, criticisms of the *Alliance*'s choices or explanations. Paris passed through the bank's granite walls as sweetly as a June breeze through a window screen, and ever afterward the lilt of overheard French, a photograph of *Sacré Coeur* or the Louvre, even a monthly bank statement, recalls to me that best of all summers.

I didn't wind up in an occupation with any obvious connec- 25 tion to the careers I sampled during my school breaks, but I never altogether abandoned those brief professions either. They were jobs not so much to be held as to be weighed, absorbed, and incorporated, and, collectively, they carried me forward into adult life like overlapping stairs, unfolding a particular pattern at once haphazard and inevitable.

Questions

1. Why might Dorris have titled his piece "Life Stories"? What is the connection between the opening three paragraphs, the closing paragraph, and the title? What metaphor is sustained throughout these framing paragraphs?

2. What techniques does Dorris use to gain the comic effect in his narrative in paragraph 9?

George Garrett

WHISTLING IN THE DARK

The versatile and prolific George Garrett published his first book, a collection of poems, in 1957. Since then, he has published numerous novels,
short stories, and essays, as well as more poetry collections. In further
proof of his wide-ranging talents, he has also written scripts for television
and motion pictures, while maintaining his academic career as a professor of English and writer-in-residence at universities throughout the
country, where he's had a profound influence on young writers. Born in
1929, and a Princeton graduate in 1952, Garrett has said that after all his
years as a professional writer, he still feels "like a beginner. . . . because
one is always beginning, always challenged to learn newly."

1.

*T*wo men dressing. They are wearing GI undershorts and shiny dog
tags like necklaces. They are freshly shaved and showered. Their hair is
cut short on top and sidewalled. They are flat-stomached and hard-
muscled. Two American soldiers in a large high-ceilinged room located
in the heart of an old Luftwaffe barracks a little to the south of the city
of Linz. It's a fine stone, permanent barracks, the best these two soldiers
have lived or will live in. Waxed and shiny hardwood floors, high clear
windows overlooking a grassy parade ground. In this room there are
maybe half a dozen cots, neat and tight, perfectly made up, shiny green
footlockers with names and serial numbers painted on the lids of each.
There are large, ample wooden wall lockers that the Krauts left behind,
left open now with GI uniforms, khaki at this season, the ODs recently
packed away, hanging perfectly in strict proscribed rows.

The two soldiers are carefully and awkwardly dressing, their twin
cigarettes casting shimmying veils of pale smoke from a butt can. Awkwardly because they do not wish to sit on and muss up their beds while
dressing. If they sit, to lace up boots for example, they will have to use
a footlocker for a chair. Their khakis are tailored snug and crisp from
starched ironing, creases as straight and keen as a razor's edge. Their
brass, collar brass and belt buckles, glitters. They have put their buckles
on backward to save them from scratches, for the soldiers will be wearing pistol belts, too. Their cordovan-dyed jump boots are spit-shined
and glossy. They have put in white laces and will be wearing white

gloves, too, and white chin straps on their simonized helmet liners. Red artillery scarves instead of neckties. The blue-and-white TRUST patches, worn on the left shoulders and proudly set off with flashy white cross-stitching, that show they come from the old 351st Regimental Combat Team in Trieste, have now been removed and replaced by some bland patch or other. (Whose shape and color and meaning I have long since forgotten.) Indicating that they are serving in Austria. But anyone with a trained eye and any interest would know right away that they come from somewhere else. Most likely TRUST, but maybe from the 6th Infantry in Berlin, which affects some of the same singular style: dyed black-web equipment; pistol belts (in this case, with each and every one of their tiny brass eyelets buffed to remove the paint and grit to the metal and give it a high, bright shine, confirmed with clear nail polish); first-aid pouches hung on the left hip; and ammo pouches, holding two full clips of forty-five-caliber cartridges, worn up front just to the right — two eyelets over, I seem to recall — of the belt buckle. On the right hip they hang gleaming dark leather holsters holding the .45 pistols that they have been issued for today. Last of all, each puts on a brass whistle on a chain, attached to the left shirt-pocket button, and an arm band — *MP* for Military Police. There is no MP unit up here near Linz. Which, except for the Four Power City of Vienna, deep in the Russian Zone, is as far forward as Americans are. Just across the river, the dirty old Danube, from the Russkies. There are said to be about forty thousand of them over there. Over here we have a reconnaissance battalion, an old outfit that has been here a good while, an infantry battalion, and ourselves, the 12th Field Artillery Battery (Separate). In theory we have come here in response to the fact that they have suddenly, and for no discernible reason, moved those forty thousand combat troops into advance positions on the other side of the river. Should they decide to come across, to attack, that is, it is our function in this post to try to delay them for a period of between fifteen minutes and half an hour. That will give the main body of American forces in Salzburg, and farther west in Germany, time enough to take their defensive positions.

These two men have drawn MP duty on a quiet Saturday in springtime. Fully dressed and ready, they will be briskly inspected by somebody or other, the officer of the day most likely, or maybe the sergeant of the guard; then they will pick up a Jeep at the motor pool and drive into the city.

It is a clear bright day. And now these two, coming outside from the barracks, are jointly astonished to see a ring of distant snow-capped mountains all around. It has been so gray and close, wet and foggy since they got here that they never knew there were mountains within sight until this minute. They don't say anything. What is there to say? They are old-timers, short timers in the U.S. Army now. It is not that they are not surprised. It is that they are continually astonished by everything. They don't speak, but they stop in midstride. They stand there and just look around. The young corporal allows himself to whistle softly between his teeth.

"Let's go," the sergeant says then. "We're fixing to be late."   5

They move off side by side, in step. I can't remember the corporal's name for the life of me. The sergeant, of course, is myself.

2.

They pass by the gate guards and turn left on the highway heading for Linz. You can be sure that, without a word, a glance, or a nudge, they are both smiling for at least a moment. They sit in the front seats of the Jeep, the corporal driving, very straight, both of them feeling almost fragile as they seek to keep every crease and part of their uniforms crisply unwrinkled. They want to be sharp-looking downtown. They like to show the local girls, whores and shack-jobs, and hamburger bandits that Americans in uniform can look every bit as sharp as (everybody says) the Krauts did. Going out of the gate and turning left and north, they both smile into the breeze.

They are thinking about the moment they first arrived at that same gate maybe a month or so ago. How they left Trieste secretly by night. Went first to a staging area in pine woods near Pisa. Rumor was they were going to Greece, somewhere like that. Who knew? Anyway, they painted over all the unit numbers on all the vehicles. Got rid of patches and anything identifying them as coming from Trieste. They were loaded on trucks with all the canvas laced tight and sent off in small convoys, a few at a time, up north through the high Brenner Pass and into Austria. Nobody, except ranking officers, knew where they were headed until they actually got there. Except, of course (as ever and always), somebody goofed. Somebody forgot or maybe never knew that the vehicles of the Austrian command, alone of all commands in the U.S. Army, did not use a large white star, on each side of the vehicle and on top of the hood, as an identifying marker. For all our care and secrecy we were known at once, at first sight, as convoys coming from elsewhere by our gleaming white stars. Every spy between Pisa and Linz would have noted our coming and going. So that when we arrived at the old Luftwaffe camp and some guy in the outfit turned on his battery-powered portable radio, we picked up, from the Russian side, in good English, "Greetings to the men of the Twelfth Field Artillery on their safe arrival at Linz."

But that is not worth the kind of smile the two GIs are smiling. What has them grinning is the subject of women. When we pulled out of Trieste suddenly, the group had to say good-bye to their girlfriends (and semipermanent shack-jobs). Some of these couples had been to-gether for years. Some of them had children, illegitimate, of course, because it was an extremely difficult and complex process for a GI to marry a Triestene woman. It was not encouraged. Nevertheless, leaving was a wrench for all of them. A time of tears and gloom. Promises to write. Promises to meet again, somehow, someday. The gloom lasted for a few days over in the tent camp near Pisa, until it gradually began to dawn on all the guys that wherever they went next—to Greece or North Africa or the freaking South Pole—they would be starting over. A new deal. All-new girls. So by the time we were loaded, that was all the guys (especially the bona fide, certified lover boys) could think and talk about—the new and improved stuff, *strange nookie!* they were going to be enjoying very soon.

Try to imagine their crestfallen surprise, surprise for all of us, when   10
we pulled up at the main gate of the new camp and found a whole big bunch of women from Trieste just standing there, waving their hand-kerchiefs (Yoo-hoo!). Somehow, and easily enough, they had found out our Top Secret destination and, overcoming all obstacles and boundaries, beaten us there. I'm telling you there were some long faces and faint smiles in the trucks.

3.

Barring some major crime involving American GIs, and even in that case they will work mainly as liaison with and for the local Austrian police, the actual duties of these two soldiers are more in the line of courtesy patrol than anything else. They will patrol the town, check various well-known bars and public places, looking for GIs who are drunk or disorderly. Most of these, if any and if possible, they will not arrest but will simply carry back to the barracks. They will correct uni-form violations. They may spot-check for ID cards, passes, and papers. Mostly they will be a visible and symbolic presence of the American intention to maintain some kind of good order. Mostly, except for the boredom, it is good, clean duty and not a bad way to pass the time.

Once in town they check in on the basic radio network, linking themselves, more or less and depending on the equipment, to the camp, to the local Austrian police, and to the other patrols. They stop briefly at the station of the local police. Who are friendly enough and who are not, at this time, holding any GI under arrest for anything. These would have to be taken back to the camp and the stockade there.

Now they can take a turn or two slowly driving up and down some of the main streets, then they will go down to the bridge across the

Danube and the checkpoint on our side. There are two conventional checkpoints, one on each side, American and Russian.

The 12th Field has drawn the duty, for this month, of manning the American checkpoint, so our pair on patrol stop by to say hello to some guys from the outfit. Theoretically there is, by treaty, free access for troops both ways. We can go across the Russian zone into the Four Power City of Vienna on the train, the Mozart Express, with American flags painted on the cars and with soldiers armed with grease guns guarding each car. And, with a proper pass, American soldiers can cross the bridge and pass through the Russian checkpoint and vice versa. Every day or so this right is tested. A vehicle of some kind will be sent across to the other side. After passing the checkpoint the vehicle, having scored its legal point, will turn around and come back. The two soldiers in the Jeep might be asked to do this by the lieutenant on duty. But they are not; a truck went over and back this morning. They are relieved. It can be a . . . touchy situation. The Russians are, to us, very strange sometimes. Once, not long ago, for whatever reason, they suddenly closed the checkpoint and barred an American military truck at gunpoint. Because the bridge is narrow, the driver had to back his way to our side again. Our lieutenant called in, according to his strict instructions, to his commanding officer. And the news went all the way up the mysterious chain of command. After a while a Russian Jeep came roaring up to their checkpoint: driver, Russian officer, two enlisted men in the back. Out jumped the officer, who conferred briefly with the other Russian officer on duty there. They drew their pistols and shot the two soldiers who were guarding the checkpoint. At which point the two enlisted men jumped out of the Jeep, removed the weapons and equipment from the dead guards, and—one, two, three, heave-ho!—threw their bodies off the bridge and into the Danube. Whereupon the new guards took up positions at the barrier.

The funny part (can you believe there is a funny part?) is this. When the young and green American lieutenant saw what was happening he drew his pistol, shouted at his own men to follow him, and raced across the bridge to . . . to do what? He had just witnessed a crime, no question. But, pistol or no pistol, outrage or not, it was a double murder well outside his jurisdiction. The Russian officers were sympathetic to his feelings but nonetheless amused. In halting English they tried to explain that somebody had to be punished for the mistake of closing the checkpoint to our right of access. They pointed out that the two soldiers, whose bodies had long since vanished in the flow of the river, were only Mongols (as were the two new replacements) and wouldn't be missed by anyone. Anyway, there were millions more where they came from.

My own firsthand experience came from having to instruct my unit

15

in the Russian use of land mines and booby traps. It was supposed to be an area of my expertise. I knew a little, mostly self-taught, but not much. But nothing had prepared me for the chaotic and totally irrational ways and means of the Russian army with land mines. Every other army in the world (for many good reasons) makes and uses mines for specific purposes. For example, an antitank mine won't go off when a man walks over one. Maybe they have changed now, and I hope so, but in those days a cat, probably a mouse, could set off any Russian land mine. That's kind of crazy. Then there is the matter of the big bang. Every other army in the world uses mines that contain enough explosives, and no more, to do the job they are intended for. The Russkies had mines that, stepped on by one man (or one mouse), would blow up a whole football field. To what purpose? Terror, I reckon. Except that a combat soldier with any experience at all is not going to be terrified by a bigger bang. It's the death he fears, not the noise of it. Another example. In every other army in the world only fairly high-ranking officers, usually of field grade, can authorize laying down a mine field. It must be mapped and is usually clearly marked. The danger of it to one's own troops outweighs any value of intense secrecy. In the Russian army, in those days at least, a squad leader, a corporal or a sergeant, could lay mines anywhere without telling anyone and without mapping or marking them. In combat they often had to leave them right where they were, unseen or unknown, when they advanced or fell back. This didn't slow up the Germans much, but nobody will venture a guess as to how many Russians were blown up in World War II by their own mines. Huge numbers. No matter. Plenty more where they came from.

Today experts sometimes wonder why the Russians have built missiles with huge, "dirty" warheads, many megatons beyond any remotely conceivable destructive value or purpose. Counterproductive in the sense that they will create enormous dangers for their own people in the fallout. It makes no sense, but it is the same philosophy they had with land mines and Mongols.

We shoot the breeze with the guys at the checkpoint for a few minutes. Then we head back into Linz.

"Hey, let's get something to eat," the corporal says.

"Suits me."   20

4.

Everywhere the 12th Field went we had our special hideouts. In Trieste we had a hole in the wall called the Poker Bar. Here we found and laid claim to the *Gasthaus* of the little farm village of Leonding, a few miles outside of Linz and close by the rifle range, an old one going back to the bright and colorful Austro-Hungarian Empire days. Which is how we found it in the first place, marching out there to fire qualification on our M-1s and carbines. A big, sprawling place (large for such a small village), quiet, dark, low-ceilinged, a kind of cave with a long wooden bar and with huge round waxed oak tables. Here we held our battery party a couple of weeks ago — plenty of booze, a show all the way from Germany with a stripper, a couple of female acrobats, a magician, and a trained-dog act.

Some of us did skits for the show, too. Mine was the only one that called for a costume. Just before we did our little skit, I was to slip back to the room the Germans were using as a dressing room and change into my homemade clown costume. When the moment for me to go and get ready arrived, I was more than slightly drunk and bitterly disappointed, too, that I was going to have to miss the striptease.

For a moment it seemed to me that I had been waiting patiently for that particular striptease for my whole life. You know how a drunk thinks. I had done my duty, but nonetheless I was going to have to miss the whole thing. Saddened to the marrow of my bones, profoundly pissed off, I went back and found the room where everybody (with no privacy at all) was busily dressing and undressing, putting on makeup, etc.

Somehow I let everyone there know how bitterly disappointed I was to have to miss the stripteaser's performance. I may even have told her, for she was just leaving the dressing room when I came in — a tiny, dark-haired woman of indeterminate age (not young), layered in a gauzy, sequined black costume.

Inside the dressing room we could hear the bump-and-grind music   25 playing, hear also the shouts and cheers of the battery, while I put on my clown costume and makeup, then sat, disconsolate, on a stool, refusing to be cheered up by the young and amazingly attractive female acrobats. Who were lively and sympathetic and who were also (though I wouldn't even notice this at the time; only hours later, back at the barracks, would it dawn on me) as sleekly naked as golden apples on a bough. More so than the exotic dancer ever allowed herself to be. Nothing they said or did could cheer me up much. Not even when they slipped on their bathrobes and came out to watch my own amateur clown act. And then applauded and were wonderfully supportive. Even helping me out of my costume and makeup.

I remember this with mild embarrassment, but mostly for what it tells me about male (my own) psychology. How much of it, the dancing life of Eros, is in the head. How much even memory can be fantasy.

Here, though, out of the brightness of the spring afternoon we stand at the bar eating Holstein *Schnitzel*s, the ones with a couple of fried eggs on top, and drinking frosty steins of beer. The *Schnitzel*s are fine here and so is the venison the Austrians serve with a wine sauce. We are standing, trying to preserve our khakis from wrinkles. There are a few old guys playing cards at one table, nothing more going on.

We bullshit with the owner, who is really not much older than we are, though he looks a generation older. He speaks good English. He fought the Russians in the East and then was a prisoner in Siberia. We swap army stories. Our guys have mixed feelings about the Krauts, but everybody respects them as soldiers. He is telling us about how his father, who is still alive, and even some of these old card players still remember Hitler, who lived in Leonding as a child. Hitler's father was a customs officer who had owned a farm and lost it and moved into the village when Hitler was about six years old. The boy would come to the *Gasthaus* in the evening and get a bucket of draft for his father's supper. They can remember that. They remember, too, how he used to whistle, coming and going. He could whistle tunes very well, they say.

He would come into this same room and stand, right here in the same place where we are standing, waiting to get his bucket of beer. A funny feeling for us now.

We like this *Gasthaus* because they treat the guys from the 12th 30 Field well here. Even our very few black soldiers in the only-newly integrated American army. Other places, especially in the city, are not so friendly to black soldiers. Once they go to a place it gets a name and none of the locals will go back there. And they shun the whores who go with black soldiers. We don't care one way or the other what the locals do. Except where it concerns our own outfit. There is no color line in the 12th Field.

While we stand there eating, stuffing our faces with good food, he tells us how (he believes) he survived in the labor camp in Siberia. By counting calories and judging and doling out energy. Most of the time they lived on soup. The whole trick was to try to gain energy from the soup, not to spend more getting it than a serving of soup contained. It was always a matter of energy, not hunger. People who didn't know any better ran and jostled and wrestled each other for extra helpings when there were any, using up far more energy in the process than they would ever gain. They filled their bellies and they died sooner than the rest.

We nod with straight-faced understanding as we wolf the veal and eggs and swallow the rich, sweet, delicious local beer.

It is not that we are utterly insensitive. But we are young and strong and (as yet) undefeated. We cannot seriously imagine surrendering to anybody.

5.

More than thirty years later the sergeant, now a professor pushing on toward retirement, will write a poem about that very afternoon in that *Gasthaus*. It will, inevitably, being a part of memory and recollection, be slightly different, at least in focus and emphasis, from what I have already been telling you. But, nevertheless, it is part of the picture. The *moving picture*, if memory is a kind of movie.

Here is the poem: 35

Some Enormous Surprises

Not many may now remember,
fewer and fewer remember,
most because they never knew
in the first place, being lucky
or too young, and others
because they are too few and too old
already, but anyway, I remember

the three reasons most often advanced
in those innocent days before the War
as strong and self-evident argument
that Adolf Hitler was crazy.
First, that he was a strict vegetarian.
Second, that he did not smoke or permit
any smoking around him, being convinced

that smoking cigarettes was somehow
linked to lung cancer.
Third, because he went around saying
that the Volkswagen, laughable beetle,
was a car of the future.
Maybe God, in all His power and majesty,
can still enjoy the irony of it.

Miles later, young man, old soldier, I
stand at the bar of a *Gasthaus*
in Leonding, country village near Linz,
lean against the dark, smooth, polished wood,
drinking and listening to very old men
remembering the days of the Austro-Hungarian Empire.
Happens that Hitler's father lived here then.

And they can remember him and his son, too,
who every evening came to this *Gasthaus*
for a bucket of beer for his father's supper.
Would stand there patiently waiting where
you are standing now, then, pail in hand,
set off under early stars along a lane
toward the lights of home, whistling in the dark.

Everyone who knew agrees that then and later
he was a wonderful whistler, worth listening to.
I lean back against the bar to picture
how he was then, lips puckered,
whistling tunes I do not know,
beer rich and foamy, sloshing in the pail,
smells of wood smoke, cooking meat, and cabbage.

And, invisible and implacable, always
the wide smile of God upon His creatures, one and all,
great and small, among them this little pale-faced boy,
for whom He has arranged some enormous surprises,
beyond any kind of imagining, even myself,
drunk in this place, years from home, imagining it.

6.

Now then, full of good food and beer and full of goodwill toward humankind, one and all, our two soldiers have driven into town, parked
their Jeep in a reserved space, and are taking a stroll around the
Bahnhof. They will check the papers of a few GIs who are arriving and
departing. They will caution a soldier or two to button up a shirt pocket
or tighten up a necktie. And they will watch the trains come and go.
The weather is really fine and dandy, couldn't be better. Nice and warm
and getting warmer with the afternoon. The air is scented with springtime. Or is it the little bouquets of flowers so many people seem to be
carrying? The girls are in their light dresses already. Splendid, if a little
pale from winter. Sap stirs in the limbs of the sergeant and the corporal.

Unusually crowded today. They are separated by the crowds. No
matter. They will meet up sooner or later on one of the platforms or
back at the Jeep.

Alone, I stroll, not strut, out of the great barn of a building (most
GIs call it the Barnhof) into the sunlight on a platform. People, crowds
of them, smiling and jabbering, waiting for a train. Even if my German
were good enough to understand more than a few rudimentary
phrases, I could not hear what they are saying. Somewhere nearby,
though I can't yet see it, a brass band is playing cheerful oompah music.
Deafening and delightful.

Must be a local holiday of some kind. Now I am closer to the band.
I see the middle-aged musicians, their cheeks chipmunking as they
play. I am standing close by the huge bass drum. Which keeps a steady
rhythm.

This band is of an age that would allow them to have played all   40
through the war. I wonder if they did that.

Now, even as I hear the shrill scream of the whistle, I see all the
faces in the crowd turn toward the track where the train is coming
slowly, with sighs of steam, easing into the station. To my amazement
I see their faces, all of them, change entirely in a wink of time. A moment ago they were animated, smiling. Now each mask of flesh is anxious and searching. And, as if at an order, they all begin to cry. I have
never been among a huge crowd of weeping people before. Sobs and
tears all around me. Stunned and lost, I feel; out of empathy (and per-

haps out of a military reflex), tears well up in my own eyes. I am one of them, I am one with them, though I do not know why.

Now many in the crowd are holding up enlarged photographs, placards with names printed large on them. Like some kind of grotesque parody of a political rally.

The doors open, and out of the train, helped by porters, many of them with crude canes and crutches, here come, one after another, a ragged company of dazed, shabby, skinny scarecrows. They are weeping also, some of them. Others study the crowd, searching with hard looks and dry eyes for familiar faces. The band is deafening. Next to me the bass drum pounds and pounds in tune and in time with my heart.

In time, very soon, in fact, I will learn that they are the latest contingent of Austrian veterans from the Eastern Front, returning home from Siberia. The Russians are moving slowly, in their own inexorable, patient, glacial fashion, toward a treaty here in Austria (as I will learn much later), if not a war first. Part of that movement is to let some of the scarecrows who have somehow managed to survive until now come home.

But here and now I know nothing of that and care less. I see a   45 homecoming of the defeated and the wounded. Some greeted with great joy, with flowers and embracing. Some, as always, alone now even at home—though I see schoolchildren have been assigned the duty of making sure that everyone gets a greeting and some flowers.

I stand there knowing one thing for certain—that I am seeing our century, our time, close and truly. Here it is and, even among strangers, I am among them, sharing the moment of truth whether I want to or not.

An American sergeant stands in the swirling crowd with tears rolling down his cheeks. He will be gone from here soon, first miles, then years and years away. But he will not, because he cannot, forget this moment or himself in it, his share of this world's woe and joy, the lament and celebration of all living things.

Questions

1. In this essay you don't find out who the soldiers are until the final line of Part One. Discuss how Garrett uses pronouns in the opening segment of his essay to create particular effects. What do you make of the first line? What are the differences and similarities between it and the first line of the second paragraph?

2. *Whistling in the Dark* is also the title of the collection from which this essay was taken. It is also, of course, part of a line from the poem "Some Enormous Surprises." How do you understand it in the poem? In the essay?

Norma Field

IN THE REALM
OF A DYING EMPEROR

Born in 1947 in Tokyo, Norma Field grew up in a completely Japanese family, except for the "enormous exclamation point" of her six-foot-tall father, who invariably frightened away all her friends. Being driven in a khaki occupation bus to a base school every day made her "a real connoiseur and master of self-disguise"; she could be taken as American at school and as Japanese at home—or at least she thought she could. This early experience with the protean possibilities of representation has a lot to do with her obsession with words. Field received her B.A. in European studies in 1969, while living in France during the Paris uprisings. When she moved to the United States, she decided to connect herself formally with Japan and to dwell in classical Japanese poetry and prose, which resulted in a Ph.D. from Princeton, followed by the publication of *The Splendor of Longing in the Tale of Genji* (1987). But as Field found contemporary Japanese society more and more troubling, she emerged from her aesthetic retreat. In *In The Realm of a Dying Emperor: A Portrait of Japan at Century's End* (published in 1991, and winner of the American Book Award), she addresses the transformation both of Japan and of herself. Field is a professor of East Asian Languages and Civilizations at the University of Chicago and, in addition to publishing many scholarly works, has been involved in translation, journalism, and radio.

*A*ugust in Japan. The skies are brilliant, the air is heavy with the souls of the dead. The New Tokyo International Airport heaves with its own ghostly hordes straining for the beaches of Guam and Waikiki and the shops of San Francisco, Los Angeles, and New York, where everything is cheap, from paper napkins to Vuitton bags. Those who cannot participate in this rite of self-confirmation as members of the newly internationalized breed of Japanese may still join the exodus to the countryside that leaves Tokyo in a sun-blasted silence four or five days of the year. For this is O-bon: time to welcome the souls of ancestors, feast, and then encourage them to return whence they came so that the living can proceed with the business of the living. Less refreshed than their forebears, families struggle home, laden with gifts received in exchange for offerings dragged from Tokyo but a few days earlier. Increased efficiency in the dissemination and satisfaction of taste means that the goods traveling to and from the ancestral home are increasingly indistinguishable. Nature, for its part, gallops in flight from this meeting of city and countryside.

It isn't only folk custom that makes August the haunted month. First the sixth, then the ninth, and finally the fifteenth: Hiroshima, Nagasaki, and surrender. So many souls to be appeased. Television coverage of memorial rites in the two cities has declined precipitously since I was a child. In fact, second city Nagasaki barely makes it to the morning and evening news. Every year, however, in both cities there are still the black-clad representatives of the bereaved, the white-gloved officials, speeches, wreaths, and doves. A scant minority insist on calling August 15 the Anniversary of Defeat rather than, more reassuringly, the Anniversary of the End of the War. (Just across the Japan Sea, in Korea, August 15 is the Return of Light Day, marking the joyous dissolution of the Japanese Empire.) In 1988 a dying Hirohito officiated as usual in the ceremonies held at the giant hall for martial arts constructed for the Tokyo Olympics. He was flown in by helicopter from his summer villa to alight as a frail embodiment of the war, still nullifying all possibility of its discussion. The era closed with his life; does changing a name guarantee the obliteration of memory?

In 1989 it was the new emperor, nasal-voiced and distinctly uncharismatic, and doubtless the more useful for it. He was too long the diligent son waiting in the wings. I don't know how he did on the fifteenth. Since boldly announcing his resolve to protect the Constitution "together with all of you" on his first public appearance after the death of his father—a statement noteworthy not only for its sentiment but for its startling and eloquent use of the second person—he has receded into a predictable cautiousness.

Blistering August has its geographical and temporal role in my own perpetual calendar: birthday month for a biracial child ("one of them war babies!" as the father of a prospective student put it when I guided him and his daughter around the college of my choice in California) bused to school on an American base far from home. Which meant, of course, that there were no schoolmates around to celebrate with me. It would have been reckless anyway to invite those delicate sensibilities into a Japanese household. Ephemerally transplanted, pampered by the novel services of maids and chauffeurs, the American children of the Occupation and its aftermath were singularly respectful of such dictates as don't drink their water, don't eat their candy. It was better to leave my classmates out, even if my mother could and did produce birthday cakes from *Betty Crocker* or the *Joy of Cooking*, volumes worn with the effort to please her American husband. She invited her second cousins from across the street—three brothers who were closer to me in age—and the girl next door, my best and only friend until our families feuded over six inches of land. That was comfortable enough as long as my father wasn't around to scare them off.

August was also the last month of endless summer vacations, when I reread the same dozen books (especially a bilingual edition of *Little Women* and a battered Modern Library *Jane Eyre*), because I couldn't read enough Japanese, because it was too much trouble for the adults to take me to the school library, and because there was no money to take me anywhere else. Since my father's departure from the family, whether by choice or under duress, my grandparents' business of making and selling black-and-white postcard-sized pictures of American and European movie stars was faltering under the pressures of television and the growing popularity of color posters.

It was the August sun that saw me off when I finally left Japan after high school. It was hot in Los Angeles, too, where my father had been living for some years with his Scottish-immigrant mother under the barbarous palm trees. I met my American relatives for the first time: what d'you want to see first—Disneyland, college, or Forest Lawn? Eager to please, I went to them all, cemetery first and college last.

Since then, August has been the time for leave-taking. After a crammed yet timeless stay in my grandmother's house, the morning comes for the silent ride to the airport, followed by that endless flight over the Pacific and the Alaskan peaks to the American metropolises that have become my home. Then the walled skies of Manhattan or the vastness of Lake Michigan recover their cold unreality, and I am suspended between worlds equally remote.

In August of 1988, I reversed tracks and arrived, daughter and son in tow with husband to follow, to take over the two upstairs rooms of my grandparents' house for a year. The house stands on the plot of land where I was born, delivered by the same midwife who had delivered my mother. This one was built with savings my grandmother had managed from the successes in the 1960s of Robert Fuller and Eric Fleming (of *Laramie* and *Rawhide*, respectively, television and my grandparents' business having reconciled themselves by then) and above all, of Zeffirelli's *Romeo and Juliet*. It is the house to which my mother and grandmother had hoped to welcome me upon my graduation from college, until they learned that their worst fears had come true: letting me go off to America had meant, inevitably, the emergence of an American son-in-law.

The house strains to accommodate the four of us with our mostly American bodies. The three of them—mother, grandmother, and grandfather, whose combined ages exceed 230, as my mother is fond of pointing out—help by shrinking their already modest selves into a yet more concentrated diminution. We settle in.

I remind myself that this is necessarily an artificial homecoming. I must become, again, daughter, granddaughter, and even niece, a process akin to regenerating amputated limbs. I know that I will have to shed these same limbs at the end of the year, when my resuscitated capacity to lunch with family while conversing amiably about the noonday women's show and reporting on the obligatory reception attended the previous evening will be superfluous. My grandmother doesn't even like me to do the dishes—ostensibly on the grounds that I do it badly, but in fact because she wants to unburden me of all daily tasks. You have to do everything by yourself over *there*; we might be getting a little slow, and we're not much good for anything ("a mended lid for a broken pot"), but at least we're two women *here*. Before her determined generosity I am helpless. I am paralyzed by thoughts of finality. There never will be time to return such unmeasured generosity, let alone time to share again so extravagantly in the garden-sheltered house.

Experts declare that the surge of speculation in land and stocks will turn Japan into a more American-style, visibly antagonistic society. My grandmother blames Nakasone, the prime minister who flattered Reagan and other Americans with resemblance. Though she will not admit it, she broods over how much longer she will be able to stay on the land where she has spent most of her life. Like many Tokyoites, my grandparents own their house, but not the land on which it stands. Current regulations provide renters an uncertain blessing whereby they are entitled to 70 percent of the proceeds from the sales of rental rights. Not unreasonably, with her husband entering his tenth decade, my grandmother worries that when the time comes for title change, the temple owning her corner lot will raise the rent to the dizzying heights of market value and then, driven to selling her rights, she will be hard-pressed to pay the taxes on the proceeds.

Already across the street, next to my granduncle's house (now quiet, with the three brothers who dutifully attended my birthday parties grown up and gone), a bulldozer has come in to clear out an old neighbor's house. The lot is modest, about the size of my uncle's. His house has three rooms, not counting kitchen and bath. The developer who bought the adjacent lot is putting up an eight-unit condo, known technically as a "mansion" in Japan. Such multiple-unit dwellings are being squeezed between the sober one-and two-story houses that used to line the streets of this old neighborhood. Taxes make it impossible for most sons to stay on the land inherited from their fathers. They sell to developers and try to buy in places within a two-hour commute of Tokyo, taking with them not only their families but the rising prices of their old neighborhoods. All over Japan, land prices spiral, advancing suburban sprawl. Where can people go on this mountain-crowded, typhoon- and earthquake-prone archipelago? What hubris to send those towers soaring into the sky in Shinjuku, in the heart of the capital, or on the land reclaimed, as it is said, by dumping garbage into an already suffocating Tokyo Bay.

The bulldozer across the street transmits its vibrations to the desk I share with my daughter. My grandmother knows every shrub and wildflower in her garden: that camellia planted when your aunt in Nagasaki graduated from high school, this strawberry geranium from the time we all went climbing in Hakone, do you remember? Her trees give off oxygen for the neighborhood. Her flowers are anticipated by passersby. When her garden is gone, where will the glance alight to find respite from asphalt?

The clichéd expense of subsistence in Tokyo still delivers an initial jolt. For many years the stability of life was ensured by the simple, if computationally awkward, equation of $1 = ¥ 360$. It has already been two decades since that equation, symbol of a seemingly eternal American world order, was dismantled. No numerical fixity has replaced it. This time it takes me a month or more to lose the instinct for instant conversion. Dejected by movie tickets at twelve dollars a person or five apples on sale for four, I would seize upon cotton T-shirts for three dollars each—made, of course, in an Asia that Japan has cast off—and, in a burst of rebellion against austerity, end up with an unusable dozen. I try to settle into the fringes of what is surely historically fabulous middle-class existence.

It is a spectacle quite distinct from that earlier American paradise of 15 pastel houses fringed with Astroturf-anticipating lawn and enticing gape of pool set discreetly in the rear. Fin-de-siècle Tokyo has no more room for houses of any color. But there are marvelous compensations. The vegetables are unfailingly perfect. The Chinese radishes are pearly white and crisp, the corn full-kerneled and candy sweet, the tomatoes soft vermilion, flavorful but firm. As for the fruit! Now, at the onset of a Chicago autumn, I picture sadly the fruit and vegetable stands of my birthplace with four varieties of delicately green, succulent pears nestling against figs lingering on as their purple deepens. They will be followed by ten varieties of apple; sweet persimmon, rich in vitamin C and thought to lower blood pressure; and finally the mandarin oranges, juicy, easy to peel, and seedless, obstacle to the California orange in bilateral trade negotiations. The mandarin orange reigns through the winter. Spring brings a spell of loneliness, inadequately assuaged by domestic citruses and Florida grapefruit, until the procession of summer fruits begins again with strawberries, loquats, grapes, and peaches.

But at what cost! I don't mean simply that one small melon costs anywhere from twenty dollars (in my grandparents' low-cost neighborhood) to fifty. It doesn't take a farmer to imagine the chemical investment required to maintain such unvarying perfection. I have heard that by some measures, pesticide use in Japan is ten times per capita what it is in the United States. But whatever the hidden threats to health, there are other risks to living in a society where consumers are told that it is they, with their discriminating taste coupled with selfless discipline, who demand, deserve, and receive the best that modern life has to offer.

In Japan, as elsewhere, the allure of late capitalism comes saturated with irony. In Japan, as elsewhere, the citizenry seem not to care. Perhaps it is easier to suspend doubts where general prosperity reinforces an apparent homogeneity, where there are neither obvious oppressors nor unsightly victims. Nature, that trusty aide, is pressed into ever more ingenious service. On television, scenes from the Swiss Alps, the Sahara, or unnameable native ponds sheltering plump birds serve as background, or in more subtle cases as foreground, for the promotion of life insurance, sports cars, and soft drinks. Where can those ponds be, I ask myself, recalling a conversation between a movie director and a publisher of fishing books who agreed it was no longer possible to film such scenes in Japan. Pristine images proliferate as coastlines are paved over and national and local preserves converted into golf courses and ski resorts with governmental blessing. And as if to capture and transcend this process, commercials flaunt the biotechnological successors to the vegetables now bulging my mother's shopping bag: exquisite baby carrots grow from lush broccoli forest.

Several years ago, soaring land prices effectively terminated the dream of a minuscule home of one's own for most workers in the capital region. Relief from the regimen of work and commute comes at the same time for everyone in a country with more than half the population of the United States, a good part of which is squeezed into the nonmountainous, habitable 2 percent of the land, whose total mass approximates that of the state of California. On holidays (increasing in number as international opinion deems Japanese work habits unfair and duplicitous) and vacations (coming at New Year's and O-bon), there is a national migration in pursuit of a change of scene from the cramped apartment or even the modest house that enthralls its owners in "loan hell." No wonder that work comes to seem preferable to enforced recreation, not to mention familial intimacy. Everyday life in Japan compresses itself toward implosion.

It is unseemly for junior employees to leave before their seniors. In any case, the journey from workplace as office to workplace as bar is much shorter than the train ride sour with the exhalations of besotted men and OL (for "office lady," meaning the young women increasingly college- and junior college-educated who amass savings and spread their wings before leaving the work force for marriage in their mid-twenties).

The compulsory socializing dictated by work, in the form of drink- 20 ing on weekdays for most men and golf on weekends for the supervisory class, absorbs all "free" time. No wonder, then, that there are children who literally do not recognize the men who are their fathers; and men, who, because of habitual or prolonged absence, find that there is no more room for them at home. A noontime television show posits a father's "home refusal" syndrome, so named after the long-established "school refusal" syndrome of children who take to their rooms, if not to their beds, and absent themselves from school for months and even years. The men described as suffering from "home refusal" syndrome have had their places usurped by their children, especially those preparing for entrance examinations, who therefore command the unremitting devotion of their mothers. In acute cases the husbands begin to hallucinate, to commute to work from hospitals, and eventually, to renounce the gesture of homecoming altogether.

At present this phenomenon exists chiefly in the Harlequin sociology realm of the women's television show ("Checklist: Are You Driving Your Husband to Home Refusal Syndrome?"), but Japanese housewives indisputably manage their homes with an efficiency even less disrupted by the presence of infantilized husbands than was that of their American counterparts of the fifties, who mostly stayed home except for church, PTA, or scouting. Today a reasonably ambitious Japanese woman will have her children in cram school by fourth grade in order to position them for entrance into a desirable junior high school; if she is only mildly driven, or if her children are already deemed unpromising, the process will be delayed until junior high to prepare for high school entrance.

The process is arduous for both mother and child. The most dedicated mothers, those with children lucky enough to have won entrance to a prestigious cram school, attend their own study sessions on the Saturday afternoons or Sundays when their children are being tested on material engorged during the week. These mothers are told, and they learn to accept, that it is not unusual for children to stop eating altogether until they become habituated to the routine, a process that takes at least one month. Less privileged mothers contribute as they can, meeting their children with hot snacks before driving them to lessons if they are in the suburbs, staying up with them, preparing midnight snacks, and generally servicing them. (Incredulous, I try out on friends the suggestion that mother-son incest, widely acknowledged to be the more prevalent form in Japan, is associated with entrance-examination study. They say it isn't impossible.)

The sole expectation of children is that they study. This fact, and the nature of the study that is so inexorably imposed, have produced a host of side effects ranging from the disturbing (school refusal syndrome) to the terrifying (extreme bullying, tacitly condoned by insensitive or weary teachers, at times culminating in death). In compensation, children are showered with fantastically elaborate toys from birth, and when they get into university, if they work at all it is in order to travel to Canada, the United States, or Switzerland, that perdurable home of nature. Like Japanese adults, Japanese children accumulate savings: by sixth grade, many have all the material goods they can conceive of wanting. They therefore embark on the regimen of the passbook.

In the society they are growing into, the most significant and the only reliable freedom is the freedom to buy ever more refined commodities: exotic vegetables from Belgium or China to supplement the perfected domestic supplies; individual servings of sugar for coffee, sugar for tea in increasingly fanciful packaging; brand-name clothes, watches, and pens from Europe; and lately, a luxury car for the very rich who can't afford to buy homes. Presumably, satiation lies in an unforeseeable future, inasmuch as the yearning for a space to call one's own will go unfulfilled, and the subjection to discipline and the exercise of freedom will continue to meet in a useful confusion in the domain of consumption. For, on the one hand, the extraordinary, ever-intensifying daily sacrifices are justified by the abundance they evidently make possible, which also means there must be a perpetual escalation in the level and quality of abundance. On the other hand, the austere regimen imposed on men, women, and children is necessary precisely to maintain discipline in the face of voluptuous plenty, to ensure the continued production of the unnecessary. Recently, consumption as discipline has found its ideal expression in the exaltation of bodily hygiene to heights as yet unmatched even in the United States. Consequently, an ever-growing choice of sinks especially designed for the daily shampoo and electronic bidets (in a culture historically addicted to bathing) must be fitted into already bursting domestic spaces.

I retrace old patterns in the hopes of making myself at home. Most often, that means a trip to a shopping arcade in the neighborhood my grandparents occupied before evacuating to the countryside under intensified American bombing in 1945. The arcade, now covered with fancy plastic roofing with sliding partitions for air and sunshine, is lined with mom-and-pop stores, the inevitable McDonald's, always bustling, and the occasional franchise of a chain claiming lower prices for televisions, rice cookers, camcorders, and batteries than Akihabara, fabled electronics capital of the world. To the strains of "Three Coins in a Fountain," I wander past the gift shop with nested Lucite boxes, glass rocks, and other tempting baubles; glance at the kimono stores for items suggestive of tradition to serve as Christmas gifts to America; make my way through the miraculously low-priced children's shorts, pajamas, and socks to select a pair of pants bearing the words, "If your heart belongs to Daddy . . . Delicious, my dear! You've discovered my pet spread for cold cuts! *Celebrity* BRILLO. It works! And a 100%" My addiction to this form of shopping, with the clapping and calling of brash male clerks, samples of dumpling, aroma of roasting tea—so much celebration of buying and selling, living proof of the arcane distribution system contributing to the U.S. trade deficit—revives slowly but steadily.

I nurture this nascent sense of belonging by bringing back tokens of the arcade world to my grandmother and mother. My mother needs refreshment from her chief preoccupation, the administration of her father's existence. My grandfather is a man who broke a tray on his wife's head when he came home at two in the morning to find that she had let his rice burn (she was pregnant with my aunt next door, her third child, yet had no relief from her routine of cooking and cleaning, without running water or gas, for five live-in employees in addition to managing the business); who ran from the house with a five-thousand-yen bill clenched in his teeth, which he had squirreled away when family fortunes were at an ebb; who, in more prosperous days, outfitted a mistress with a set of false teeth and was foolish enough to record the same in a diary subsequently discovered by his wife. I should note, however, that he is also a man who was decorated in his early eighties for having "dedicated sixty years to the promotion of Western cinema in Japan."

Acute symptoms of high blood pressure in his fifties gave my mother and grandmother the first opportunity to encroach upon my grandfather's autonomy. The family doctor pronounced him a "drunk teetering on a rooftop whose fall should surprise no one." My grandmother promptly formulated an unvarying breakfast of peanut butter toast, powdered skim milk, and fresh fruit, reinforced by a draconian reduction in the use of soy sauce, principal source of flavor in Japanese cuisine, and in the absolute quantity of food intake. There were other challenges, however; for if it was one thing to ban domestic smoking, it was quite another to enforce it on my grandfather's daily rounds to the offices of MGM and Warner Brothers, the editors of movie magazines, the middlemen and retailers in the crammed and exquisitely tawdry entertainment district downtown. It was decided that he should be followed. These missions were usually undertaken by my mother and occasionally by my as yet unmarried aunt in Nagasaki. Lacking resources, they simply disguised themselves with glasses and struggled to keep up with my grandfather's prodigious pace, except, of course, as he paused at train stations or corner tobacco shops for a cigarette. Drinking was a similarly intractable problem.

Perhaps it was inevitable that efforts should eventually be redirected to monitoring his paper fetish, even though it involved no expense and the health risks were presumably negligible. My grandfather hoarded napkins from department store restaurants, posters from movie companies, envelopes and bags of all sizes from publishers.

These were brought home to be piled in aggressively precarious stacks. Today, four decades later, along with his toothpaste and soap, my grandfather has his toilet and tissue paper rationed. Keeping her father from paper theft occupies a considerable portion of my mother's waking and even sleeping energies. (One night she clocked him asking to blow his nose at 1:32 and 2:05 A.M.) My mother, beginning to suffer from osteoporosis, is convinced that forty years' worth of calcium from the powdered skim milk has left the old man indecently strong. I try to distract her with sweets and sweaters from the arcade.

It is several years since I have spoken to my grandfather. What seemed several decades ago to be a willfully selective loss of hearing has grown into a massive imperviousness to the world. Other than through fierce gesticulation, communication entails writing. When confronted with the furious traces of his wife's black magic marker, he maintains a stony silence, except when impelled by rage to denunciation. The circumference of his activities has been vastly reduced since the days of his imperious forays into the vigorous chaos of Tokyo. Every Sunday, my mother draws up his exercise chart for the week. It is the same chart each week, with the days of the week written horizontally above a vertical column of prescribed hours. He himself draws loops in the empty blocks to indicate completion, four times a day, of the course leading from his room through the corridor filled with our spillover books and coats, past the kitchen, through the television room, then back to his room. He takes a good ten minutes for each circuit, a distance the rest of us traverse in twenty seconds.

Even this world is further reduced on those occasions of physical 30 deterioration when he takes to his bed, moaning and even shrieking over back pain, provoking my grandmother's constant ministrations. These bouts are new, and come as a surprise after so many years of unwavering, reassuringly nasty activity. I should have guessed at changes in the dusty body when, during one of its exercise rounds, it struck out, without glance or pause, at its daughter, my mother. The combination of randomness and malicious accuracy was startling. During the bad spells, the randomness gains ground, and the intentionality of malice recedes behind whimpers. The progression is clear: he will eventually lose the desire, then the will, and finally the capacity to convert sounds into words. In the meanwhile, between bouts he is still able to harass his great-grandson, my son. By the end of our stay, my grandmother resorts to taping a purple ribbon down the center of the table between them. There will still be territorial skirmishes, with such instruments as drawing pads, markers, and speeding toy cars on the one side, stacks of old astrological calendars and hearing aid with long-dead batteries on the other. During cease-fires my grandfather watches his favorite TV show, a period piece in which a hero arrested in handsome old age wisely solves mysteries and lays swords to rest all over Japan.

This series, tirelessly rerun, was the favorite of the late Emperor Showa as well.

When that figure collapsed on September 19, 1988, my grandmother was sympathetic. In age Hirohito was midway between her and my grandfather. (I should note that to write *Hirohito* is an awkward gesture. The monarch is never so intimately referred to in Japanese, yet this use of the first name is standard and therefore seemingly neutral in English. "His Majesty the Emperor," the Japanese newspaper mode of reference, suggests a bureaucratic reverence; "Hirohito" carries simultaneous reverberations of wartime vituperation and friendly postwar condescension.) After the unprecedented surgery of the previous year, performed only after much debate over the propriety of piercing the jeweled body with a knife, my grandmother thought the old man was finally being left to indulge his botanical and marine-biological fancies at the imperial villa. Like many others in a country where patients are not normally informed of terminal conditions, she believed the benign diagnoses assiduously disseminated by the media. She made no attempt to reconcile her sympathy with the tenets of an antimilitarist socialism she had innocently and passionately espoused since winning the vote after the war.

In the days, weeks, and then months after September 19, the citizens of Japan were treated to daily reports on the input and output of blood from the emperor's body. Two relatively unfamiliar words entered the national vocabulary: *toketsu* and *geketsu*. As terms, these occupy an ambiguous zone, more forbidding than "vomiting blood" and "rectal bleeding," less clinical than "hematemesis" or "melena." Throughout the fall, after the initial drama of *toketsu*, every newspaper carried a box indicating the detection of a slight amount of *geketsu*, the quantity of compensatory transfusion, and the reassuringly homely readings of temperature and pulse. By the time of his death three and a half months later, the emperor had received 31,000 cc, or approximately thirty liters, of blood in transfusion. I heard, but couldn't confirm, that it cost about $170 per cc. Vampire jokes began to circulate. Later, journalists assessing media coverage of the emperor's illness and death observed that use of the word *geketsu* was tantamount to a second human declaration. (The first took place in January of 1946 under American supervision.)

For the modern emperor of Japan, the name of his reign is the name by which he will be known posthumously. The birth and death dates of every Japanese citizen, as well as of all events, national and international, are expressed as a combination of reign name and year. The emperor himself lives namelessly ("His Majesty the Emperor") but intimately with the name of his death. Thus, he who was known in the West as Hirohito became Emperor Showa on January 7, 1989, and ba-

bies born on January 8 were celebrated for arriving with the dawn of
Heisei, which is the name by which the present emperor will be known
after he dies.

The death of the human being now safely remembered as Emperor
Showa—"Shining Peace"—was surely one of the best prepared in history. The only unforeseen complication was the length of time the
dying was to take. Hirohito was the first Japanese emperor to die under
the postwar Constitution stipulating that sovereignty rests with the
people. From the instant of his death to the staging of his burial some
forty days later, the state choreographed an elaborate dance representing constitutionality and mystery, Western modernity and Eastern tradition. This dance had to suggest a history at once progressive and alluring, glossing adroitly over the interlude of war to elaborate the forty
years of postwar prosperity. Above all, it had to imperceptibly accommodate the realities facing the world's leading economy. For even the
temporality of the emperor is comprehended within the temporality of
contemporary capitalism. How many days could the stock exchange be
closed? banks? government offices? Still, even if the banks had to close,
their computers would keep running, maintaining the blood supply of
the world.

Hirohito's collapsing without dying meant that these ingenuities 35
had to be sustained over a far longer period than intended. Daily reverential reporting on the body of the emperor throughout the island nation both provoked and reinforced a massively orchestrated exercise in
"self-restraint," or *jishuku*, a newly popularized word. Some of the
losses—the expunging of felicitous wording such as "nice day" from
commercials, and of alcohol from political fund-raisers—were not regrettable in themselves. But autumn is a time of renewed vigor, commercial and otherwise, of recovery from brutal July and August. So it
was with a certain regret that neighborhood festivals were canceled one
after another, along with weddings in November, the preferred month
for matrimony. On field days at school, races began limply without the
pistol shot. Not surprisingly, the costs of abstemious behavior were
borne unevenly, by the makers and vendors of plastic masks, costume
jewelry, and goldfish for scooping at carnival stalls; by caterers for weddings and other festivities; by taxi drivers who transported merrymakers and entertainers who kept them happy once they got there. Like the
vampire jokes, the frustration of such people occupying the extensive
periphery of prosperity circulated beneath the surface of official reporting.

In addition to the national promotion of "self-restraint," numerous
preparations were made for the day of the unthinkable itself: movie theaters consulted department stores about whether to close, and for how
many days, or how to stay open and still convey mourning. Athletic facilities consulted movie theaters. Decisions were made about supervising au-

dience conduct at the instant of the announcement, about the status of the game, depending on the inning. Television stations, led by the government-owned NHK, wrangled only slightly over the number of days to be set aside for special programming: other than documentaries chronicling his late majesty's achievements, to be followed by documentaries chronicling the prolonged but altogether promising crown princeship of his son the new emperor, nature programs were to be the principal fare. FM stations stocked up on subdued recordings of Bach and Beethoven. Most of these arrangements had been in place for several years. In the course of "self-restraint" they were refined and often augmented.

Most of the measures other than media programming proved superfluous. Emperor Showa lingered well beyond baseball season into the new year. His death was announced early on January 7, a Saturday morning. Schools were in winter recess until the following Monday. The holiday rush was safely over for the stores. It was the last day of New Year's week, the crucial revenue-gathering period for Shinto shrines. The shrines, to be sure, had not altogether abandoned themselves to fate, for the national Shinto headquarters had discreetly announced in late 1988 that in the event of the unthinkable, worshipers would still be received for the customary New Year's observations. Like many religions, Shinto abhors pollution by blood and death. The emperor of Japan is the chief Shinto priest in his private capacity as the direct descendant of the sun goddess Amaterasu. Still, the shrines could not forgo the income to be generated by the sale of felicitous arrows and amulets appropriate for the forthcoming Year of the Snake.

So, on the crucial day, "self-restraint" amounted to minimizing the incessant announcements on public transport and operating stores with neon signs turned off and clerks wearing black arm bands moving to the notes of a Bach fugue. In his passing, the emperor of shining peace granted his nation respite from the incessant aural and visual stimuli of its fabulous economy. Rectal bleeding as sign of humanity.

Journalists, in reporting on the emperor's demise, were still under the spell of the "chrysanthemum taboo," so-called after the imperial crest, that crystallized in the 1960s through several episodes of right-wing attack on writers and publishers deemed guilty of transgressing imperial honor. Journalistic language used throughout Hirohito's illness and death revealed the continuing force of the taboo. Hirohito's death was reported as a *hōgyo* by every newspaper in the country except for the two dailies of Okinawa Prefecture and the *Red Flag*, the organ of the Japan Communist Party. According to standard dictionaries, only four Japanese can have this special word for death applied to their passing: the emperor, the empress, the dowager empress, and the grand dowager empress. All other Japanese, all other human beings for that matter, die ordinary deaths, linguistically speaking. There was considerable debate in journalistic circles as to whether Hirohito's death should be thus absolutely distinguished.

The issue was whether journalistic prose should be uniquely dis- 40 rupted by honorific markers for actions and objects associated with the emperor and his immediate family. Japanese, like many languages, is extensively developed for the expression of social hierarchy. Prefixes, personal pronouns, and verbal endings vary according to whether speaker and addressee are mother and daughter, mother and daughter-in-law, father and son, employees separated by one year in seniority, teacher and parents, or seller and buyer (whether butcher and house-wife, restaurant manager and diner, or banker and company president). That there are, of course, provisions for speakers and addressees of the same sex, age, and status reinforces, rather than denies, the hier-archical marking of every utterance. I was once reluctant to address adults, typically teachers, in English because "you" sounded too baldly intrusive, being so flattening, so equalizing. Now, on visits to Japan, I fall prey to something like a sickness, as if table legs had lost their metaphoricity, before the oppressive, formulaic humility or arrogance I must assume in my daily dealings, all the while recognizing that the very possibility of intimacy is embedded in the tyranny of the language. The luxury of addressing my grandmother without honorifics is insep-arable from the obligation to use them with her brother's wife, my grandaunt.

One of the achievements of modern Japanese writing was the de-velopment of a seemingly neutral mode that minimized such status and gender distinctions, effacing both distance and intimacy. In the instance of the emperor's death, the stylistic objectivity of journalistic Japanese had been irredeemably compromised by the repeated use of honorifics in reporting his illness. No wonder that, for all their soul-searching, journalists uniformly produced the event as a *hōgyo*.

Not that they were alone in their abjection. There were the masses of nonbelieving practitioners of "self-restraint," for instance; there were nonbelievers who even thronged to the palace to sign their names dur-ing the bleeding and after the dying because everyone was doing it, because they might get on television, because they—the young ones—thought of the emperor as a sweet, vulnerable old man who reminded them of a teenage idol who had recently committed suicide. There were also the cynics who emptied the shelves at rental video stores be-cause they knew the emperor had nothing to do with them and they found the reverential programming insufferably dull.

I fear the nonbelieving observers of social custom and the confident cynics more than the believers who embarrassed their cosmopolitan compatriots by kneeling and touching their heads in grief on the ground outside the palace, and more than the right-wing extremists with their blaring trucks. I am fearful of the latter, too, because rarely,

but memorably, they have killed and maimed, and their terrorizing behavior all but obliterates the fragile impulse to dissent. The sophisticated cynics do not see that they cannot disengage by choice: in their
submission to an education that robbed them of their childhood, that
holds their own children hostage through secret records passed from
school to school, reinforcing an ever more tyrannical regimen of competition, in their surrender to a crushing routine of work and commute,
they are participants in a compulsory game in which the emperor card
will turn up as the joker.

This is not to say that the emperor, or even the emperor system, as
intellectuals would more chastely put it, is to be held solely responsible
for the state of affairs in Japan today. Contrary to propaganda, the
foundations of the contemporary system are hardly ancient. The nineteenth-century statesman Itō Hirobumi lamented the absence of an indigenous belief system adequate to providing the psychic fuel and discipline necessary to hurtle society into a Western-style modernity
overnight. The solution, at that point, was to snatch the young Emperor Meiji from the shadowy court life of Kyoto and transform him
into a monarch in Western military costume for deployment in the
new capital city of Tokyo and throughout the nation. The image of this
emperor, who died in 1912, is still familiar in Japan. Heavy eyebrows
and braided uniform suggest a warrior in commanding stillness. This
was in fact a photograph of a painting, for even the image of a god-king
could not be exposed to ordinary eyes. There we have it: modern technology in the service of mystery in the service of a ruthless rationalization and industrial capability. The mystery makes the rationalization
palatable, hence feasible; the rationalization ensures a continual hunger for mystery—for transcendence of the economic through an un-
calculated leap into a past that never was.

Hirohito's funeral in February of 1989 was a celebration of the suc- 45
cesses of Japanese capitalism. How else explain the unseemly media
preoccupation with the number of heads of state in attendance, reminiscent of an Olympic medals count? In spite of strenuous precautions,
the long-repressed question of war guilt had resurfaced during
Hirohito's dying. The gathering of world leaders made that question
moot by bearing witness to the stunning achievements of Japanese modernity. Not only was the dead man not guilty, but the Japanese economic miracle was subtly but ineluctably linked to a culture that re-
veres emperors and provides them with ancient, august burial.

The equation of economic success with kingly presence is of course
a venerable one, detectable even in myths of archaic rulers as the embodiment of cosmic order, most crucially demonstrated by agricultural
abundance. In the Japanese nineteenth century, an imperial system re-
furbished to serve as potent symbol for unchanging tradition was

harnessed to an economic transformation envisioned initially without but subsequently within a cosmos defined by the terms of Western modernity. After World War II the American Occupation sent Hirohito on a tour of the war-ravaged land, above all to be seen by his people (American republicanism being willing to subscribe to royal magic where expedient), and occasionally to inspirit them with the bisyllabic utterance that became his trademark: *ah sō*, "is that right," delivered when, for example, the man in the crowd whom he had favored with conversation indicated that he had lost his house and all his family in the firebombing of Tokyo. Visibility was incomparably expanded in 1959 when his son Akihito, now emperor, married Michiko, miller's daughter or princess of the flour industry according to one's perspective, before the eyes of all Japan, for virtually every household had purchased a television set for the occasion.

The domestic style of the new couple, Akihito and Michiko, was widely disseminated through television and women's magazines. It was an appealing household, blossoming under the gaze of the benevolently aging emperor and empress. The image called out to the youth of Japan: work hard and you, too, may one day have a living room where children play musical instruments and read books at your knee. Erstwhile student activists who had joined the staffs of such magazines thought they could still undermine imperial ideology by displaying the once-sacred images on pages to be tossed into train station rubbish bins or traded in for toilet paper. Twenty years later, the same magazines would carry portraits of the now middle-aged couple in elegant mourning to complement chronicles of the human side, so-called, of Hirohito's life.

One month after the funeral, it was a thing of the remote past. The passage of a thousand years is as nothing compared to the power of the media to make births, deaths, earthquakes, famine, and genocide fade into a dusty past. As it happened, the media did not have to strain to distract the public during the spring and summer of 1989. Pursuit of a major bribery scandal, which had been disrupted by the imperial dying, was restored to the limelight, to be fortified by disclosures of sexual indiscretion and the imposition of a hated sales tax. As the majority of the print and visual media relentlessly converted controversy into entertainment, some citizens insisted on contesting the general presumption that they neither could nor would choose to see, to think, or to care about the world in which they lived. Thus, the great Socialist victory in the upper house elections of July 1989 created a painfully hopeful moment when it almost seemed as if one-party rule, which had already blanketed four decades, did not have to stretch into infinity.

I left, once again, in spirit-haunted August. I wish I could have stayed, not to witness the wasteful anachronism of the making of a monarch but to savor awhile longer the rupture of smugness by Social-ist chairwoman Doi Takako and her cohort of women. I wish I could have stayed to hear the new stories being told about the war, stories newly introspective about Japanese aggression in Asia, which render more compelling the old stories about Japanese victimization by Amer-ica in 1945. I wish I could have stayed to follow my grandmother's garden into autumn: the merely reliable phlox growing brilliant, the chrysanthemums in wild abundance, the osmanthus sweetening the sharp dusk air.

I would have stayed, but I couldn't, so I content myself with my 50 mother's letters, filled with suggestions for taking the bitterness out of eggplant and recipes for replenishing my repertoire, luxuriously de-pleted after a year of my grandmother's indulgence; tinged with angry sorrow over the distraction produced by media flutter over the prospect of princely marriage and anxious watchfulness over the inevitable bick-ering, slander, and even serious discussion as the Socialists imagine tak-ing power after forty years of abstract opposition. From across the Pa-cific and half a continent, I sense an autumnal cooling of those impulses to question the conditions of membership in the world's most orderly and prosperous society. My mother's letters grow dispirited. I force myself to read on, knowing she doesn't have the luxury of de-nunciation, dismissal, and departure.

Questions

1. Consider the degree to which Field has had to become someone other than she was to be able to see her subject in this essay. In what ways is she distanced from Japan, from her family, from herself? To what other forms of distance does she allude?

2. Field is not alone in the changes she has to make; she is consider-ing a society that has transformed itself since the end of World War II. Yet it is also a country that observes rituals. "My grand-mother knows every shrub and wildflower in her garden: that ca-mellia planted when your aunt in Nagasaki graduated from high school, this strawberry geranium from the time we all went climbing in Hakone, do you remember?" In this passage, the gar-den becomes a memory, in which, every year, the plants mark the anniversay of particular events. Discuss how ritual—from the memory garden to O-bon and the emperor system—holds the threat of change at bay.

Two

EMBODYING IDENTITIES

*M*ost of us are so used to our own bodies that we forget their enormous power to exchange information between what is inside us and what is outside us. For various reasons, the essayists in this chapter all have bodies that insistently demand their attention; these essays all bring to the foreground the self's relationship with the world as it is mediated through the body. The body is both the point of separation and the point of contact, both boundary and border. From many different viewpoints, these essays address the same question that William James asked about bodies: "Are they simply ours, or are they *us*"?

In "A Few Words about Breasts," Nora Ephron answers emphatically that her body *is* herself; it is, in fact, responsible for creating the Nora Ephron who constructs the essay. "If I had had them," she writes, "I would have been a completely different person. I honestly, believe that." Her essay demonstrates how the discrepancy between the shape of the stereotypical ideal woman and the shape of her own body has mapped the outline of her psyche. American Breast Worship has charted the boundaries of her identity.

Judy Ruiz, on the other hand, in taking her brother as her subject, takes the opposite point of view. Her brother is a transsexual, someone who feels trapped in the wrong body altogether. Now, technology allows us to make our bodies conform to our own internal maps. Ruiz is "stunned to learn that someone with an obsession of the mind can have parts of the body surgically removed." Ruiz's essay carries the idea of the strangeness of one's own body to its furthest logical extension.

Natalie Kusz's "Vital Signs" sees her body as the medium through which she learned lessons of morality and of mortality. Savaged by dogs as a child, Kusz's long and tenuous recovery "bred in [her] understandings that [she] would not relinquish now." Her body's wounds become the fissures through which she—and we—get to glimpse a spiritual map.

This long gaze is focused in another direction in Terry Castle's "First Ed." She looks back at herself as a little girl in the YWCA's "children's evening swim program," with its "delicious orchestrated flutterings of breast, elbow, and ankle." Gradually narrowing its focus to the object of her childhood gaze, the essay demonstrates how looking at a woman's body begins to reveal to Castle the truth of her own sexuality, letting her know "what tumult lay ahead." In this essay, another's body becomes the point against which the writer locates herself.

Scott Russell Sanders is also able to trace his adult self back to his childhood being; he understands the connection in a spatial metaphor: "Life with [my father] and the loss of him twisted us into shapes that will be familiar to other sons and daughters of alcoholics." Alcoholism is heritable, but the genetic code mapped out by the invisible double helix is opaque to anyone's view, hidden even from a son's knowledge. Sanders, unable to trust his own body, must "listen for the turning of a key" in his brain, listen for the moment when the dormant father might awaken.

In some ways, Sanders lives inside a body that could be a time bomb. All the essayists in this chapter inhabit their own skin uneasily. Although the body's outline can change, or one's own demands on the body's outline can change, we are all, inexorably, trammeled within our skins. These pages testify to the effects of this most personal of all maps; there is no way to efface the body itself.

Nora Ephron

A FEW WORDS ABOUT BREASTS

Born in 1941, Nora Ephron experienced her first taste of authorial success when her parents turned her letters home from Wellesley College into a play, *Take Her, She's Mine*. Soon after that, Ephron began her writing career in earnest as a reporter and later a columnist for the *New York Post*, *Esquire* magazine, and *New York* magazine. Her professional life took a turn in 1983 with the publication of her highly autobiographical novel *Heartburn* and the production of her screenplay *Silkwood*, written with Alice Arlen. *Silkwood* received an Oscar nomination for best original screenplay, and since that time Ephron has written primarily for motion pictures. Her many successes include an adaptation of *Heartburn* (1986), the popular comedy *When Harry Met Sally* (1989), and, most recently, *Sleepless in Seattle* (1993), which she directed and cowrote with David S. Ward and Jeff Arch.

I have to begin with a few words about androgyny. In grammar school, in the fifth and sixth grades, we were all tyrannized by a rigid set of rules that supposedly determined whether we were boys or girls. The episode in *Huckleberry Finn* where Huck is disguised as a girl and gives himself away by the way he threads a needle and catches a ball — that kind of thing. We learned that the way you sat, crossed your legs, held a cigarette and looked at your nails, your wristwatch, the way you did these things instinctively was absolute proof of your sex. Now obviously most children did not take this literally, but I did. I thought that just one slip, just one incorrect cross of my legs or flick of an imaginary cigarette ash would turn me from whatever I was into the other thing; that would be all it took, really. Even though I was outwardly a girl and had many of the trappings generally associated with the field of girldom — a girl's name, for example, and dresses, my own telephone, an autograph book — I spent the early years of my adolescence absolutely certain that I might at any point gum it up. I did not feel at all like a girl. I was boyish. I was athletic, ambitious, outspoken, competitive, noisy, rambunctious. I had scabs on my knees and my socks slid into my loafers and I could throw a football. I wanted desperately not to be that way, not to be a mixture of both things but instead just one, a girl, a definite indisputable girl. As soft and as pink as a nursery. And nothing would do that for me, I felt, but breasts.

I was about six months younger than everyone in my class, and so for about six months after it began, for six months after my friends had begun to develop—that was the word we used, *develop*—I was not particularly worried. I would sit in the bathtub and look down at my breasts and know that any day now, any second now, they would start growing like everyone else's. They didn't. "I want to buy a bra," I said to my mother one night. "What for?" she said. My mother was really hateful about bras, and by the time my third sister had gotten to that point where she was ready to want one, my mother had worked the whole business into a comedy routine, "Why not use a Band-Aid instead?" she would say. It was a source of great pride to my mother that she had never even had to wear a brassiere until she had her fourth child, and then only because her gynecologist made her. It was incomprehensible to me that anyone would ever be proud of something like that. It was the 1950s, for God's sake. Jane Russell. Cashmere sweaters. Couldn't my mother see that? *"I am too old to wear an undershirt."* Screaming. Weeping. Shouting. "Then don't wear an undershirt," said my mother. "But I want to buy a bra." "What for?"

I suppose that for most girls, breasts, brassieres, that entire thing, has more trauma, more to do with the coming of adolescence, of becoming a woman, than anything else. Certainly more than getting your period, although that too was traumatic, symbolic. But you could *see* breasts; they were there; they were visible. Whereas a girl could claim to have her period for months before she actually got it and nobody would ever know the difference. Which is exactly what I did. All you had to do was make a great fuss over having enough nickels for the Kotex machine and walk around clutching your stomach and moaning for three to five days a month about The Curse and you could convince anybody. There is a school of thought somewhere in the women's lib/women's mag/gynecology establishment that claims that menstrual cramps are purely psychological, and I lean toward it. Not that I didn't have them finally. Agonizing cramps, heating-pad cramps, go-down-to-the-school-nurse-and-lie-on-the-cot cramps. But unlike any pain I had ever suffered, I adored the pain of cramps, welcomed it, wallowed in it, bragged about it. "I can't go. I have cramps." "I can't do that. I have cramps." And most of all, gigglingly, blushingly: "I can't swim. I have cramps." Nobody ever used the hard-core word. Menstruation. God, what an awful word. Never that. "I have cramps."

The morning I first got my period, I went into my mother's bedroom to tell her. And my mother, my utterly-hateful-about-bras mother, burst into tears. It was really a lovely moment, and I remember it so clearly not just because it was one of the two times I ever saw my mother cry on my account (the other was when I was caught being a six-year-old kleptomaniac), but also because the incident did not mean to me what it meant to her. Her little girl, her firstborn, had finally become a woman. That was what she was crying about. My reaction to the event, however, was that I might well be a woman in some scientific, textbook sense (and could at least stop faking every month and stop wasting all those nickels). But in another sense—in a visible sense —I was as androgynous and as liable to tip over into boyhood as ever.

I started with a 28AA bra. I don't think they made them any 5 smaller in those days, although I gather that now you can buy bras for five year olds that don't have any cups whatsoever in them; trainer bras they are called. My first brassiere came from Robinson's Department Store in Beverly Hills. I went there alone, shaking, positive they would look me over and smile and tell me to come back next year. An actual fitter took me into the dressing room and stood over me while I took off my blouse and tried the first one on. The little puffs stood out on my chest. "Lean over," said the fitter (to this day I am not sure what fitters in bra departments do except to tell you to lean over). I leaned over, with the fleeting hope that my breasts would miraculously fall out of my body and into the puffs. Nothing.

"Don't worry about it," said my friend Libby some months later, when things had not improved. "You'll get them after you're married."

"What are you talking about?" I said.

"When you get married," Libby explained, "your husband will touch your breasts and rub them and kiss them and they'll grow."

That was the killer. Necking I could deal with. Intercourse I could deal with. But it had never crossed my mind that a man was going to touch my breasts, that breasts had something to do with all that, petting, my God they never mentioned petting in my little sex manual about the fertilization of the ovum. I became dizzy. For I knew instantly —as naive as I had been only a moment before—that only part of what she was saying was true: the touching, rubbing, kissing part, not the growing part. And I knew that no one would ever want to marry me. I had no breasts. I would never have breasts.

My best friend in school was Diana Raskob. She lived a block from 10 me in a house full of wonders. English muffins, for instance. The Raskobs were the first people in Beverly Hills to have English muffins for breakfast. They also had an apricot tree in the back, and a badminton court, and a subscription to *Seventeen* magazine, and hundreds of games like Sorry and Parcheesi and Treasure Hunt and Anagrams. Diana and I spent three or four afternoons a week in their den reading and playing and eating. Diana's mother's kitchen was full of the most colossal assortment of junk food I have ever been exposed to. My house was full of apples and peaches and milk and homemade chocolate-chip cookies—which were nice, and good for you, but-not-right-before-dinner-or-you'll-spoil-your-appetite. Diana's house had nothing in it that was good for you, and what's more, you could stuff it in right up until dinner and nobody cared. Bar-B-Q potato chips (they were the first in them, too), giant bottles of ginger ale, fresh popcorn with melted butter, hot fudge sauce on Baskin-Robbins jamoca ice cream, powdered-sugar doughnuts from Van de Kamps. Diana and I had been best friends since we were seven; we were about equally popular in school (which is to say, not particularly), we had about the same success with boys (extremely intermittent), and we looked much the same. Dark. Tall. Gangly.

It is September, just before school begins. I am eleven years old, about to enter the seventh grade, and Diana and I have not seen each other all summer. I have been to camp and she has been somewhere like Banff with her parents. We are meeting, as we often do, on the street midway between our two houses and we will walk back to Diana's and eat junk and talk about what has happened to each of us that summer. I am walking down Walden Drive in my jeans and my father's shirt hanging out and my old red loafers with the socks falling into them and coming toward me is . . . I take a deep breath . . . a young woman. Diana. Her hair is curled and she has a waist and hips and a bust and she is wearing a straight skirt, an article of clothing I have been repeatedly told I will be unable to wear until I have the hips to hold it up. My jaw drops, and suddenly I am crying, crying hysterically, can't catch my breath sobbing. My best friend has betrayed me. She has gone ahead without me and done it. She has shaped up.

Here are some things I did to help:
Bought a Mark Eden Bust Developer.
Slept on my back for four years.
Splashed cold water on them every night because some French actress said in *Life* magazine that that was what *she* did for her perfect bustline.   15
Ultimately, I resigned myself to a bad toss and began to wear padded bras. I think about them now, think about all those years in high school I went around in them, my three padded bras, every single one of them with different sized breasts. Each time I changed bras I changed sizes: one week nice perky but not too obtrusive breasts, the next medium-sized slightly pointed ones, the next week knockers, true knockers; all the time, whatever size I was, carrying around this rubberized appendage on my chest that occasionally crashed into a wall and was poked inward and had to be poked outward—I think about all that and wonder how anyone kept a straight face through it. My parents, who normally had no restraints about needling me—why did they say nothing as they watched my chest go up and down? My friends, who would periodically inspect my breasts for signs of growth and reassure me—why didn't they at least counsel consistency?

And the bathing suits. I die when I think about the bathing suits. That was the era when you could lay an uninhabited bathing suit on the beach and someone would make a pass at it. I would put one on, an absurd swimsuit with its enormous bust built into it, the bones from the suit stabbing me in the rib cage and leaving little red welts on my body, and there I would be, my chest plunging straight downward absolutely vertically from my collarbone to the top of my suit and then suddenly, wham, out came all that padding and material and wiring absolutely horizontally.

Buster Klepper was the first boy who ever touched them. He was my boyfriend my senior year of high school. There is a picture of him in my high-school yearbook that makes him look quite attractive in a Jewish, horn-rimmed glasses sort of way, but the picture does not show the pimples, which were air-brushed out, or the dumbness. Well, that isn't really fair. He wasn't dumb. He just wasn't terribly bright. His mother refused to accept it, refused to accept the relentlessly average report cards, refused to deal with her son's inevitable destiny in some junior college or other. "He was tested," she would say to me, apropos of nothing, "and it came out 145. That's near-genius." Had the word underachiever been coined, she probably would have lobbed that one at me, too. Anyway, Buster was really very sweet—which is, I know, damning with faint praise, but there it is. I was the editor of the front page of the high-school newspaper and he was editor of the back page; we had to work together, side by side, in the print shop, and that was how it started. On our first date, we went to see *April Love* starring Pat Boone. Then we started going together. Buster had a green coupe, a 1950 Ford with an engine he had handchromed until it shone, dazzled, reflected the image of anyone who looked into it, anyone usually being Buster polishing it or the gas-station attendants he constantly asked to check the oil in order for them to be overwhelmed by the sparkle on the valves. The car also had a boot stretched over the back seat for reasons I never understood; hanging from the rearview mirror, as was the custom, was a pair of angora dice. A previous girlfriend named Solange who was famous throughout Beverly Hills High School for having no pigment in her right eyebrow had knitted them for him. Buster and I would ride around town, the two of us seated to the left of the steering wheel. I would shift gears. It was nice.

There was necking. Terrific necking. First in the car, overlooking Los Angeles from what is now the Trousdale Estates. Then on the bed of his parents' cabana at Ocean House. Incredibly wonderful, frustrating necking, I loved it, really, but no further than necking, please don't, please, because there I was absolutely terrified of the general implications of going-a-step-further with a near-dummy and also terrified of his finding out there was next to nothing there (which he knew, of course; he wasn't that dumb).

I broke up with him at one point. I think we were apart for about   20
two weeks. At the end of that time I drove down to see a friend at a
boarding school in Palos Verdes Estates and a disc jockey played "April
Love" on the radio four times during the trip. I took it as a sign. I drove
straight back to Griffith Park to a golf tournament Buster was playing in
(he was the sixth-seeded teenage golf player in Southern California)
and presented myself back to him on the green of the 18th hole. It was
all very dramatic. That night we went to a drive-in and I let him get his
hand under my protuberances and onto my breasts. He really didn't
seem to mind at all.

"Do you want to marry my son?" the woman asked me.

"Yes," I said.

*I was nineteen years old, a virgin, going with this woman's son, this big
strange woman who was married to a Lutheran minister in New Hampshire
and pretended she was Gentile and had this son, by her first husband, this total
fool of a son who ran the hero-sandwich concession at Harvard Business School
and whom for one moment one December in New Hampshire I said — as much
out of politeness as anything else — that I wanted to marry.*

*"Fine," she said. "Now, here's what you do. Always make sure you're on
top of him so you won't seem so small. My bust is very large, you see, so I always
lie on my back to make it look smaller, but you'll have to be on top most of the
time."*

I nodded. "Thank you," I said.   25

*"I have a book for you to read," she went on. "Take it with you when you
leave. Keep it." She went to the bookshelf, found it, and gave it to me. It was a
book on frigidity.*

"Thank you," I said.

That is a true story. Everything in this article is a true story, but I
feel I have to point out that that story in particular is true. It happened
on December 30, 1960. I think about it often. When it first happened, I
naturally assumed that the woman's son, my boyfriend, was responsible. I invented a scenario where he had had a little heart-to-heart with
his mother and confessed that his only objection to me was that my
breasts were small; his mother then took it upon herself to help out.
Now I think I was wrong about the incident. The mother was acting on
her own, I think: That was her way of being cruel and competitive
under the guise of being helpful and maternal. You have small breasts,
she was saying; therefore you will never make him as happy as I have.
Or you have small breasts; therefore you will doubtless have sexual
problems. Or you have small breasts; therefore you are less woman
than I am. She was, as it happens, only the first of what seems to me to
be a never-ending string of women who have made competitive remarks to me about breast size. "I would love to wear a dress like that,"

my friend Emily says to me, "but my bust is too big." Like that. Why do women say these things to me? Do I attract these remarks the way other women attract married men or alcoholics or homosexuals? This summer, for example. I am at a party in East Hampton and I am introduced to a woman from Washington. She is a minor celebrity, very pretty and Southern and blonde and outspoken and I am flattered because she has read something I have written. We are talking animatedly, we have been talking no more than five minutes, when a man comes up to join us. "Look at the two of us," the woman says to the man, indicating me and her. "The two of us together couldn't fill an A cup." Why does she say that? It isn't even true, dammit, so why? Is she even more addled than I am on this subject? Does she honestly believe there is something wrong with her size breasts, which, it seems to me, now that I look hard at them, are just right? Do I unconsciously bring out competitiveness in women? In that form? What did I do to deserve it?

As for men.

There were men who minded and let me know they minded. There were men who did not mind. In any case, I always minded. 30

And even now, now that I have been countlessly reassured that my figure is a good one, now that I am grown up enough to understand that most of my feelings have very little to do with the reality of my shape, I am nonetheless obsessed by breasts. I cannot help it. I grew up in the terrible Fifties—with rigid stereotypical sex roles, the insistence that men be men and dress like men and women be women and dress like women, the intolerance of androgyny—and I cannot shake it, cannot shake my feelings of inadequacy. Well, that time is gone, right? All those exaggerated examples of breast worship are gone, right? Those women were freaks, right? I know all that. And yet, here I am, stuck with the psychological remains of it all, stuck with my own peculiar version of breast worship. You probably think I am crazy to go on like this: Here I have set out to write a confession that is meant to hit you with the shock of recognition and instead you are sitting there thinking I am thoroughly warped. Well, what can I tell you? If I had had them, I would have been a completely different person. I honestly believe that.

After I went into therapy, a process that made it possible for me to tell total strangers at cocktail parties that breasts were the hang-up of my life, I was often told that I was insane to have been bothered by my condition. I was also frequently told, by close friends, that I was extremely boring on the subject. And my girlfriends, the ones with nice big breasts, would go on endlessly about how their lives had been far more miserable than mine. Their bra straps were snapped in class. They couldn't sleep on their stomachs. They were stared at whenever the word *mountain* cropped up in geography. And *Evangeline*, good God what they went through every time someone had to stand up and re-cite the Prologue to Longfellow's *Evangeline*: "... *stand like druids of eld* .../ *With beards that rest on their bosoms.*" It was much worse for them, they tell me. They had a terrible time of it, they assure me. I don't know how lucky I was, they say.

I have thought about their remarks, tried to put myself in their place, considered their point of view. I think they are full of shit.

Questions

1. Ephron introduces her subject by addressing the theme of transformation. The young Ephron thinks that breasts will transform her from her liminal state into a more definite being. What is she afraid of? Of what will breasts be the visible sign?
2. At the end of the essay, Ephron worries that we will think she is "thoroughly warped" about the subject of breasts. But she's not the sole character in her work. It's no longer the fifties, and Jane Russell and cashmere sweaters are no longer the feminine ideal, yet who makes it plain that breasts are still central to Western culture's ideals of the female?

Judy Ruiz

ORANGES AND SWEET SISTER BOY

Judy Ruiz has taught English at the University of Arkansas in Fayette-ville. While in Fayetteville, she also taught creative writing in a commu-nity education program and directed a performance art group. She now teaches at Southwest Missouri State University in Springfield. Her first book of poems, *Talking Razzmatazz*, was published in 1991. "Oranges and Sweet Sister Boy" first appeared in *Iowa Woman* in 1988.

I am sleeping, hard, when the telephone rings. It's my brother, and he's calling to say that he is now my sister. I feel something fry a little, deep behind my eyes. Knowing how sometimes dreams get mixed up with not-dreams, I decide to do a reality test at once. "Let me get a cigarette," I say, knowing that if I reach for a Marlboro and it turns into a trombone or a snake or anything else on the way to my lips that I'm still out in the large world of dreams.

The cigarette stays a cigarette. I light it. I ask my brother to run that stuff by me again.

> It is the Texas Zephyr at midnight — the woman in a white suit, the man in a blue uniform; she carries flowers — I know they are flowers. The petals spill and spill into the aisle, and a child goes past this couple who have just come from their own wedding — goes past them and past them, going always to the toilet but really just going past them; and the child could be a horse or she could be the police and they'd not notice her any more than they do, which is not at all — the man's hands high up on the woman's legs, her skirt up, her stockings and garters, the petals and finally all the flowers spilling out into the aisle and his mouth open on her. My mother. My father. I am conceived near Dallas in the dark while a child passes, a young girl who knows and doesn't know, who witnesses, in glimpses, the creation of the universe, who feels an odd hurt as her own mother, fat and empty, snores with her mouth open, her false teeth slipping down, snores and snores just two seats behind the Creators.

News can make a person stupid. It can make you think you can do something. So I ask The Blade question, thinking that if he hasn't had the operation yet that I can fly to him, rent a cabin out on Puget Sound. That we can talk. That I can get him to touch base with reality.

"Begin with an orange," I would tell him. "Because oranges are mildly intrusive by nature, put the orange somewhere so that it will not bother you — in the cupboard, in a drawer, even a pocket or a handbag will do. The orange, being a patient fruit, will wait for you much longer than say a banana or a peach."

I would hold an orange out to him. I would say, "This is the one   5 that will save your life." And I would tell him about the woman I saw in a bus station who bit right into her orange like it was an apple. She was wild looking, as if she'd been outside for too long in a wind that blew the same way all the time. One of the dregs of humanity, our mother would have called her, the same mother who never brought fruit into the house except in cans. My children used to ask me to "start" their oranges for them. That meant to make a hole in the orange so they could peel the rind away, and their small hands weren't equipped with fingernails that were long enough or strong enough to do the job. Sometimes they would suck the juice out of the hole my thumbnail had made, leaving the orange flat and sad.

> The earrings are as big as dessert plates, filigree gold-plated with thin dangles hanging down that touch her bare shoulders. She stands in front of the Alamo while a bald man takes her picture. The sun is absorbed by the earrings so quickly that by the time she feels the heat, it is too late. The hanging dangles makes small blisters on her shoulders, as if a centipede had traveled there. She takes the famous river walk in spiked heels, rides in a boat, eats some Italian noodles, returns to the motel room, soaks her feet, and applies small band-aids to her toes. She is briefly concerned about the gun on the nightstand. The toilet flushes. She pretends to be sleeping. The gun is just large and heavy. A .45? A .357 magnum? She's never been good with names. She hopes he doesn't try to. Or that if he does, that it's not loaded. But he'll say it's loaded just for fun. Or he'll pull the trigger and the bullet will lodge in her medulla oblongata, ripping through her womb first, taking everything else vital on the way.

In the magazine articles, you don't see this: "Well, yes. The testicles have to come out. And yes. The penis is cut off." What you get is tonsils. So-and-so has had a "sex change" operation. A sex change operation. How precious. How benign. Doctor, just what do you people do with those penises?

News can make a person a little crazy also. News like, "We regret to inform you that you have failed your sanity hearing."

The bracelet on my wrist bears the necessary information about me, but there is one small error. The receptionist typing the information asked me my religious preference. I said, "None." She typed, "Neon."

> Pearl doesn't have any teeth and her tongue looks weird. She says, "Pumpkin pie." That's all she says. Sometimes she runs her hands over my bed sheets and says pumpkin pie. Sometimes I am under the sheets. Marsha got stabbed in the chest, but she tells everyone she fell on a knife. Elizabeth — she's the one who thinks her shoe is a baby — hit me in the back with a tray right after one of the cooks gave me extra toast. There's a note on the bulletin board about a class for the nurses: "How Putting A Towel On Someone's Face Makes Them Stop Banging Their Spoon/OR Reduction of Disruptive Mealtime Behavior By Facial Screening — 7 P.M. — Conference Room." Another note announces the topic for remotivation class: "COWS." All the paranoid schizophrenics will be there.

> Here, in the place for the permanently bewildered, I fit right in. Not because I stood at the window that first night and listened to the trains. Not because I imagined those trains were bracelets, the jewelry of earth. Not even because I imagined that one of those bracelets was on my own arm and was the Texas Zephyr where a young

couple made love and conceived me. I am eighteen and beautiful and committed to the state hospital by a district court judge for a period of one day to life. Because I am a paranoid schizophrenic.

I will learn about cows.

So I'm being very quiet in the back of the classroom, and I'm peeling an orange. It's the smell that makes the others begin to turn around, that mildly intrusive nature. The course is called "Women and Modern Literature," and the diaries of Virginia Woolf are up for discussion except nobody has anything to say. I, of course, am making a mess with the orange; and I'm wanting to say that my brother is now my sister.

Later, with my hands still orangey, I wander in to leave something on a desk in a professor's office, and he's reading so I'm being very quiet, and then he says, sort of out of nowhere, "Emily Dickinson up there in her room making poems while her brother was making love to her best friend right downstairs on the dining room table. A regular thing. Think of it. And Walt Whitman out sniffing around the boys. Our two great American poets." And I want to grab this professor's arm and say, "Listen. My brother called me and now he's my sister, and I'm having trouble making sense out of my life right now, so would you mind not telling me any more stuff about sex." And I want my knuckles to turn white while the pressure of my fingers leaves imprints right through his jacket, little indentations he can interpret as urgent. But I don't say anything. And I don't grab his arm. I go read a magazine. I find this:

> "I've never found an explanation for why the human race has so many languages. When the brain became a language brain, it obviously needed to develop an intense degree of plasticity. Such plasticity allows languages to be logical, coherent systems and yet be extremely variable. The same brain that thinks in words and symbols is also a brain that has to be freed up with regard to sexual turn-on and partnering. God knows why sex attitudes have been subject to the corresponding degrees of modification and variety as language. I suspect there's a close parallel between the two. The brain doesn't seem incredibly efficient with regard to sex."

John Money said that. The same John Money who, with surgeon Howard W. Jones, performed the first sex change operation in the United States in 1965 at Johns Hopkins University and Hospital in Baltimore.

Money also tells about the *hijra* of India who disgrace their families because they are too effeminate: "The ultimate stage of the *hijra* is to get up the courage to go through the amputation of penis and testicles. They had no anesthetic." Money also answers anyone who might think that "heartless members of the medical profession are forcing these poor darlings to go and get themselves cut up and mutilated," or who think the medical profession should leave them alone. "You'd have lots of patients willing to get a gun and blow off their own genitals if you don't do it. I've had several who got knives and cut themselves trying to get rid of their sex organs. That's their obsession!"

Perhaps better than all else, I understand obsession. It is of the mind. And it is language-bound. Sex is of the body. It has no words. I am stunned to learn that someone with an obsession of the mind can have parts of the body surgically removed. This is my brother I speak of. This is not some lunatic named Carl who becomes Carlene. This is my brother.

So while we're out in that cabin on Puget Sound, I'll tell him about LuAnn. She is the sort of woman who orders the in-season fruit and a little cottage cheese. I am the sort of woman who orders a double cheeseburger and fries. LuAnn and I are sitting in her car. She has a huge orange, and she peels it so the peel falls off in one neat strip. I have a sack of oranges, the small ones. The peel of my orange comes off in hunks about the size of a baby's nail. "Oh, you bought the *juice* oranges," LuAnn says to me. Her emphasis on the word *juice* makes me want to die or something. I lack the courage to admit my ignorance, so I smile and breathe "yes," as if I know some secret, when I'm wanting to scream at her about how my mother didn't teach about fruit and my own blood pounds in my head wanting out, out.

> There is a pattern to this thought as there is a pattern for a jumpsuit. Sew the sleeve to the leg, sew the leg to the collar. Put the garment on. Sew the mouth shut. This is how I tell about being quiet because I am bad, and because I cannot stand it when he beats me or my brother.

"The first time I got caught in your clothes was when I was four years old and you were over at Sarah what's-her-name's babysitting. Dad beat me so hard I thought I was going to die. I really thought I was going to die. That was the day I made up my mind I would *never* get caught again. And I never got caught again." My brother goes on to say he continued to go through my things until I was hospitalized. A mystery is solved.

He wore my clothes. He played in my makeup. I kept saying, back 15
then, that someone was going through my stuff. I kept saying it and saying it. I told the counselor at school. "Someone goes in my room when I'm not there, and I *know* it—goes in there and wears my clothes and goes through my stuff." I was assured by the counselor that this was not so. I was assured by my mother that this was not so. I thought my mother was doing it, snooping around for clues like mothers do. It made me a little crazy, so I started deliberately leaving things in a certain order so that I would be able to prove to myself that someone, indeed, was going through my belongings. No one, not one person,

ever believed that my room was being ransacked; I was accused of just making it up. A paranoid fixation.

And all the time it was old Goldilocks.

So I tell my brother to promise me he'll see someone who counsels adult children from dysfunctional families. I tell him he needs to deal with the fact that he was physically abused on a daily basis. He tells me he doesn't remember being beaten except on three occasions. He wants me to get into a support group for families of people who are having a sex change. Support groups are people who are in the same boat. Except no one has any oars in the water.

I tell him I know how it feels to think you are in the wrong body. I tell him how I wanted my boyfriend to put a gun up inside me and blow the woman out, how I thought wearing spiked heels and low-cut dresses would somehow help my crisis, that putting on an ultrafeminine outside would mask the maleness I felt needed hiding. I tell him it's the rule, rather than the exception, that people from families like ours have very spooky sexual identity problems. He tells me that his sexuality is a birth defect. I recognize the lingo. It's support-group-for-transsexuals lingo. He tells me he sits down to pee. He told his therapist that he used to wet all over the floor. His therapist said, "You can't aim the bullets if you don't touch the gun." Lingo. My brother is hell-bent for castration, the castration that started before he had language: the castration of abuse. He will simply finish what was set in motion long ago.

I will tell my brother about the time I took ten sacks of oranges into a school so that I could teach metaphor. The school was for special students—those who were socially or intellectually impaired. I had planned to have them peel the oranges as I spoke about how much the world is like the orange. I handed out the oranges. The students refused to peel them, not because they wanted to make life difficult for me— they were enchanted with the gift. One child asked if he could have an orange to take home to his little brother. Another said he would bring me ten dollars the next day if I would give him a sack of oranges. And I knew I was at home, that these children and I shared something that *makes* the leap of mind the metaphor attempts. And something in me healed.

A neighbor of mine takes pantyhose and cuts them up and sews 20
them up after stuffing them. Then she puts these things into Mason jars and sells them, you know, to put out on the mantel for conversation. They are little penises and little scrotums, complete with hair. She calls them "Pickled Peters."

A friend of mine had a sister who had a sex change operation. This young woman had her breasts removed and ran around the house with no shirt on before the stitches were taken out. She answered the door one evening. A young man had come to call on my friend. The sex-changed sister invited him in and offered him some black bean soup as if she were perfectly normal with her red surgical wounds and her black stitches. The young man left and never went back. A couple years later, my friends's sister/brother died when s/he ran a car into a concrete bridge railing. I hope for a happier ending. For my brother, for myself, for all of us.

My brother calls. He's done his toenails: Shimmering Cinnamon. And he's left his wife and children and purchased some nightgowns at a yard sale. His hair is getting longer. He wears a special bra. Most of the people he works with know about the changes in his life. His voice is not the same voice I've heard for years; he sounds happy.

My brother calls. He's always envied me, my woman's body. The same body I live in and have cursed for its softness. He asks me how I feel about myself. He says, "You know, you are really our father's first-born son." He tells me he used to want to be me because I was the only person our father almost loved.

The drama of life. After I saw that woman in the bus station eat an orange as if it were an apple, I went out into the street and smoked a joint with some guy I'd met on the bus. Then I hailed a cab and went to a tattoo parlor. The tattoo artist tried to talk me into getting a nice bird or butterfly design; I had chosen a design on his wall that appealed to me — a symbol I didn't know the meaning of. It is the Yin-Yang, and it's tattooed above my right ankle bone. I suppose my drugged, crazed consciousness knew more than I knew: that yin combines with yang to produce all that comes to be. I am drawn to androgyny.

Of course three is the nagging possibility that my brother's dilemma is genetic. Our father used to dress in drag on Halloween, and he made a beautiful woman. One year, the year my mother cut my brother's blond curls off, my father taped those curls to his own head and tied a silk scarf over the tape. Even his close friends didn't know it was him. And my youngest daughter was a body builder for a while, her lean body as muscular as a man's. And my sons are beautiful, not handsome: they look androgynous.

Then there's my grandson. I saw him when he was less than an hour old. He was naked and had hiccups. I watched as he had his first bath, and I heard him cry. He had not been named yet, but his little crib had a blue card affixed to it with tape. And on the card were the words "Baby Boy." There was no doubt in me that the words were true.

When my brother was born, my father was off flying jets in Korea. I went to the hospital with my grandfather to get my mother and this new brother. I remember how I wanted a sister, and I remember looking at him as my mother held him in the front seat of the car. I was certain he was a sister, certain that my mother was joking. She removed his diaper to show me that he was a boy. I still didn't believe her. Considering what has happened lately, I wonder if my child-skewed consciousness knew more than the anatomical proof suggested.

I try to make peace with myself. I try to understand his decision to alter himself. I try to think of him as her. I write his woman name, and I feel like I'm betraying myself. I try to be open-minded, but something in me shuts down. I think we humans are in big trouble, that many of us don't really have a clue as to what acceptable human behavior is. Something in me says no to all this, that this surgery business is the ultimate betrayal of the self. And yet, I want my brother to be happy.

It was in the city of San Antonio that my father had his surgery. I rode the bus from Kansas to Texas and arrived at the hospital two days after the operation to find my father sitting in the solarium playing solitaire. He had a type of cancer that particularly thrived on testosterone. And so he was castrated in order to ease his pain and to stop the growth of tumors. He died six months later.

Back in the sleep of the large world of dreams, I have done surgeries under water in which I float my father's testicles back into him, and he—the brutal man he was—emerges from the pool a tan and smiling man, parting the surface of the water with his perfect head. He loves all the grief away.

I will tell my brother all I know of oranges, that if you squeeze the orange peel into a flame, small fires happen because of the volatile oil in the peel. Also, if you squeeze the peel and it gets into your cat's eyes, the cat will blink and blink. I will tell him there is no perfect rhyme for the word *orange*, and that if we can just make up a good word we can be immortal. We will become obsessed with finding the right word, and I will be joyous at our legitimate pursuit.

I have purchased a black camisole with lace to send to my new sister. And a card. On the outside of the card there's a drawing of a woman sitting by a pond and a zebra is off to the left. Inside are these words: "The past is ended. Be happy." And I have asked my companions to hold me and I have cried. My self is wet and small. But it is not dark. Sometimes, if no one touches me, I will die.

Sister, you are the best craziness of the family. Brother, love what you love.

Questions

1. The first interruption to the body of this essay begins: "It is the Texas Zephyr at midnight—the woman in a white suit, the man in a blue uniform; she carries flowers—I know they are flowers. The petals spill and spill into the aisle. . . . " Who is the narrator of these passages? What relationship do they bear to the body of the text?
2. Throughout this essay, Ruiz seems to be attempting to locate exactly when and where things went wrong for her and her brother. What do you make of the competing theories each sibling offers to explain his transsexuality?

Natalie Kusz

VITAL SIGNS

Natalie Kusz won a Whiting Writer's Award in 1989 and a General Electric Award for Younger Writers in 1990. This success was soon followed by the publication of her first book, the autobiographical *Road Song* (1990), from which "Vital Signs" is taken. Kusz teaches creative writing at Bethel College in St. Paul, Minnesota.

I. IN HOSPITAL

I was always waking up, in those days, to the smell of gauze soaked with mucus and needing to be changed. Even when I cannot recall what parts of me were bandaged then, I remember vividly that smell, a sort of fecund, salty, warm one like something shut up and kept alive too long in a dead space. Most of the details I remember from that time are smells, and the chancest whiff from the folds of surgical greens or the faint scent of ether on cold fingers can still drag me, reflexively, back to that life, to flux so familiar as to be a constant in itself. Years after Children's Hospital, when I took my own daughter in for stitches in her forehead, and two men unfolded surgical napkins directly under my nose, I embarrassed us all by growing too weak to stand, and had to sit aside by myself until all the work was over.

It seems odd that these smells have power to bring back such horror, when my memories of that time are not, on the whole, dark ones. Certainly I suffered pain, and I knew early a debilitating fear of surgery itself, but the life I measured as months inside and months outside the walls was a good one and bred in me understandings that I would not relinquish now.

There was a playroom in the children's wing, a wide room full of light, with colored walls and furniture, and carpets on the floor. A wooden kitchen held the corner alongside our infirmary, and my friends and I passed many hours as families, cooking pudding for our dolls before they were due in therapy. Most of the dolls had amputated arms and legs, or had lost their hair to chemotherapy, and when we put on our doctors' clothes we taught them to walk with prostheses, changing their dressings with sterile gloves.

We had school tables, and many books, and an ant farm by the window so we could care for something alive. And overseeing us all was Janine, a pink woman, young even to seven-year-old eyes, with yellow, cloudy hair that I touched when I could. She kept it long, parted in the middle, or pulled back in a ponytail like mine before the accident. My hair had been blond then, and I felt sensitive now about the coarse brown stubble under my bandages. Once, on a thinking day, I told Janine that if I had hair like hers I would braid it and loop the pigtails around my ears. She wore it like that the next day, and every day after for a month.

Within Janine's playroom, we were some of us handicapped, but   5
none disabled, and in time we were each taught to prove this for ourselves. While I poured the flour for new play dough, Janine asked me about my kindergarten teacher: what she had looked like with an eye patch, and if she was missing my same eye. What were the hard parts, Janine said, for a teacher like that? Did I think it was sad for her to miss school sometimes, and did she talk about the hospital? What color was her hair, what sort was her eye patch, and did I remember if she was pretty? What would I be, Janine asked, when I was that age and these surgeries were past? Over the wet salt smell of green dough, I wished to be a doctor with one blue eye, who could talk like this to the sick, who could tell them they were still real. And with her feel for when to stop talking, Janine turned and left me, searching out volunteers to stir up new clay.

She asked a lot of questions, Janine did, and we answered her as we would have answered ourselves, slowly and with purpose. When called to, Janine would even reverse her words, teaching opposite lessons to clear the mist in between; this happened for Thomas and Nick in their wheelchairs, and I grew as much older from watching as they did from being taught. Both boys were eleven, and though I've forgotten their histories, I do remember their natures, the differences that drew them together.

They were roommates and best friends, and their dispositions reverberated within one another, the self-reliant and the needy. Thomas was the small one, the white one, with blue veins in his forehead and pale hair falling forward on one side. He sat always leaning on his elbows, both shoulders pressing up around his ears, and he rested his head to the side when he talked. He depended on Nick, who was tight-shouldered and long, to take charge for him, and he asked for help with his eyes half open, breathing out words through his mouth. And Nick reached the far shelves and brought Thomas books, and proved he could do for them both, never glancing for help at those who stood upright. His skin was darker than Thomas's, and his eyes much lighter, the blue from their centers washing out into the white.

When they played together, those boys, Thomas was the small center of things, the thin planet sunken into his wheelchair, pulling his friend after him. It must not have seemed to Nick that he was being pulled, because he always went immediately to Thomas's aid, never expecting anyone else to notice. Janine, of course, did. When Thomas wanted the television switched, and Nick struggled up to do it, she said, "Nick, would you like me to do that?"

"I can do it," he said.

"But so can I," Janine said, and she strode easily to the television 10 and turned the knob to *Sesame Street*. "Sometimes," she said to Nick, "you have to let your friends be kind; it makes them feel good." She went back to sit beside Thomas, and she handed him the Erector set. How would he turn the channel, she said, if no one else was here? What could he do by himself? And as the TV went unnoticed, Thomas imagined a machine with gears and little wheels, and Janine said she thought it could work. After that, Thomas was always building, though he still asked for help, and he still got it. Nick never did ask, as long as I knew him, but in time he managed to accept what was offered, and even, in the end, to say thanks.

In this way and in others, Janine encouraged us to change. When we had new ideas, they were outstanding ones, and we could count almost always on her blessing. We planned wheelchair races, and she donated the trophy—bubble-gum ice cream all around. When she caught us blowing up surgical gloves we had found in the trash, she swiped a whole case of them, conjuring a helium bottle besides; that afternoon the playroom smelled of synthetic, powdery rubber, and we fought at the tables over colored markers, racing to decorate the brightest balloon. Janine's was the best—a cigar-smoking man with a four-spiked mohawk—and she handed it down the table to someone's father.

She always welcomed our parents in, so long as they never interfered, and they respected the rule and acted always unsurprised. When Sheldon's mother arrived one day, she found her son—a four-year-old born with no hands—up to his elbows in orange fingerpaints. She stood for a moment watching, then offered calmly to mix up a new color.

We children enjoyed many moments like these, granted us by adults like Janine and our parents, and these instants of contentment were luxuries we savored, but on which, by necessity, we did not count. I've heard my father, and other immigrant survivors of World War II, speak of behavior peculiar to people under siege, of how they live in terms not of years but of moments, and this was certainly true of our lives. That time was fragmentary, allowing me to remember it now only as a series of flashes, with the most lyrical event likely at any moment to be interrupted. We children were each at the hospital for critical reasons, and a game we planned for one day was likely to be missing one or two players the next, because Charlie hemorrhaged in the night, Sarah was in emergency surgery, or Candice's tubes had pulled out. I myself missed many outings on the lawn because my bone grafts rejected or because my eye grew so infected that I had to be quarantined. At these times, I would watch the others out the closed window, waiting for them to come stand beyond the sterile curtain and shout to me a summary of the afternoon.

In the same way that the future seemed—because it might never arrive—generally less important than did the present, so too was the past less significant. Although each of us children could have recited his own case history by heart, it was rare that any of us required more than a faint sketch of another child's past; we found it both interesting and difficult enough to keep a current daily record of who had been examined, tested, or operated on, and whether it had hurt, and if so, whether they had cried. This last question was always of interest to us, and tears we looked on as marks not of cowards but of heroes, playmates who had endured torture and lived to testify. The older a child was, the greater our reverence when her roommate reported back after an exam; we derived some perverse comfort from the fact that even twelve-year-olds cracked under pressure.

Those of us who did choose to abide vigorously in each instant   15
were able to offer ourselves, during the day, to one another, to uphold that child or parent who began to weaken. If her need was to laugh, we laughed together; if to talk, we listened, and once, I remember, I stood a whole morning by the chair of a fifteen-year-old friend, combing her

hair with my fingers, handing her Kleenex and lemon drops, saying nothing. At night, then, we withdrew, became quietly separate, spoke unguardedly with our families. We spent these evening hours regrouping, placing the days into perspective, each of us using our own methods of self-healing. My mother would read to me from the Book of Job, about that faithful and guiltless man who said, "The thing that I so greatly feared has come upon me," and she would grieve, as I learned later, for me and for us all. Or she would sit with me and write letters to our scattered family—my father at work in Alaska, my younger brother and sister with an aunt in Oregon. Of the letters that still exist from that time, all are full of sustenance, of words like "courage" and "honor." It should have sounded ludicrous to hear a seven-year-old speaking such words, but I uttered them without embarrassment, and my parents did not laugh.

For most of us, as people of crisis, it became clear that horror can last only a little while, and then it becomes commonplace. When one cannot be sure that there are many days left, each single day becomes as important as a year, and one does not waste an hour in wishing that that hour was longer, but simply fills it, like a smaller cup, as high as it will go without spilling over. Each moment, to the very ill, seems somehow slowed down and more dense with importance, in the same way that a poem is more compressed than a page of prose, each word carrying more weight than a sentence. And though it is true I learned gentleness, and the spareness of time, this was not the case for everyone there, and in fact there were some who never embraced their mortality.

I first saw Darcy by a window, looking down into her lap, fingering glass beads the same leafy yellow as her skin. She was wearing blue, and her dress shifted under her chin as she looked up, asking me was I a boy, and why was my hair so short. Behind us, our mothers started talking, exchanging histories, imagining a future, and Darcy and I listened, both grown accustomed by now to all this talk of ourselves. Darcy was ten, and she was here for her second attempted kidney transplant, this time with her father as donor. The first try had failed through fault, her mother said, of the surgeons, and Washington State's best lawyer would handle the suit if anything went wrong this time. This threat was spoken loudly and often as long as I knew Darcy, and it was many years before I realized that her parents were afraid, and that they displayed their fear in anger and those thousand sideways glances at their daughter.

As a playmate, Darcy was pleasant, and she and I made ourselves jewelry from glitter and paste, and dressed up as movie stars or as rich women in France. We played out the future as children do, as if it were sure to come and as if, when it did, we would be there. It was a game we all played on the ward, even those sure to die, and it was some time before I knew that to Darcy it was not a game, that she believed it all. We were holding school, and Nick was the teacher, and Darcy was answering that when she grew up she would own a plane and would give us free rides on the weekends.

"What if," Nick said to her, "what if you die before then?"

Darcy breathed in and out once, hard, and then she said, "I'm tell- 20
ing my mother you said that." Then she stood and left the playroom and did not come back that day. Later, her father complained to Nick's, called him foolish and uncaring, and demanded that such a thing not happen again.

After that, Darcy came to play less often, and when she did, her parents looked on, even on days when Janine took us outside to look at the bay. Darcy grew fretful, and cried a good deal, and took to feeling superior, even saying that my father didn't love me or he wouldn't be in Alaska. When I forgave her, it was too late to say so, because I was gone by then and didn't know how to tell her.

Darcy's absence was a loss, not just to her but to us other children as well. Just as we had no chance to comfort her, to offer our hands when she was weak, we could not count on her during our worst times, for she and her family suffered in that peculiar way that admits no fellowship. I don't remember, if I ever knew, what became of Darcy, because I came down with chicken pox and was discharged so as not to jeopardize her transplant. I like to think she must have lived, it was so important to her, and as I think this, I hope she did survive, and that one day she grew, as we all did in some way, to be thankful.

One of my smallest teachers during this time was a leukemia patient, just three years old, who lived down the hall. Because of his treatments, Samuel had very little hair, and what he did have was too blond to see. There were always, as I remember, deep moons under his eyes, but somehow, even to us other children, he was quite beautiful. His teeth were very tiny in his mouth, and he chuckled rather than laughed out loud; when he cried, he only hummed, drawing air in and out his nose, with his eyes squeezed shut and tears forming in the cracks where there should have been lashes. Most children's wards have a few favorite patients, and Samuel was certainly among ours. Those few afternoons when his parents left the hospital together, they spent twenty minutes, on their return, visiting every room to find who had taken off with their son. More often than not, he was strapped to a lap in a wheelchair, his IV bottle dangling overhead like an antenna, getting motocross rides from an amputee.

Samuel possessed, even for his age, and in spite of the fact that he was so vulnerable, an implicit feeling of security, and it was partly this sense of trust that lent him that dignity I have found in few grown people. His mother, I remember, was usually the one to draw him away from our games when it was time for treatments, and, although he knew what was coming, he never ran from it; when he asked his mother, "Do I have to?" it was not a protest but a question, and when she replied that yes, this was necessary, he would accept her hand and leave the playroom on his feet.

I have heard debate over whether terminally ill children know they are going to die, and I can't, even after knowing Samuel, answer this question. We all, to some extent, knew what death was, simply because each of us had been friends with someone who was gone, and we realized that at some point many of us were likely to die; this likelihood was enough certainty for us, and made the question of time and date too insignificant to ask. I remember the last day I spent with Samuel, how we all invited him for a picnic on the lawn, though he could not eat much. He had had treatments that morning, which made him weak, made his smile very tired, but this was the same vulnerability we had always found charming, and I can't recall anything about that afternoon that seemed unusual. The rest of us could not know that Samuel would die before we woke up next morning, and certainly some things might have been different if we had; but I tend to think we would still have had the picnic, would still have rubbed dandelion petals into our skin, would still have taught Samuel to play slapjack. And, for his part, Samuel would, as he did every day, have bent down to my wrist and traced the moon-shaped scar behind my hand.

II. ATTACK

Our nearest neighbors through the trees were the Turners, two cabins of cousins whose sons went to my school. Both families had moved here, as we had, from California, escaping the city and everything frightening that lived there. One of the women, Ginny, had a grown son who was comatose now since he was hit on the freeway, and she had come to Alaska to get well from her own mental breakdown, and to keep herself as far away as she could from automobiles.

Brian and Jeff Turner were my best friends then, and we played with our dogs in the cousins' houses or in the wide snowy yard in between. On weekends or days off from school, my parents took us sledding and to the gravel pit with our skates. Sometimes, if the day was long enough, Brian and Jeff and I followed rabbit tracks through the woods, mapping all the new trails we could find, and my mother gave me orders about when to be home. Bears, she said, and we laughed, and said didn't she know they were asleep, and we could all climb trees anyway. We were not afraid, either, when Mom warned of dog packs. Dogs got cabin fever, too, she said, especially in the cold. They ran through the woods, whole crowds of them, looking for someone to gang up on.

That's okay, I told her. We carried pepper in our pockets in case of dogs: sprinkle it on their noses, we thought, and the whole pack would run away.

In December, the day before my birthday, when the light was dim and the days shorter than we had known before, Dad got a break at the union hall, a job at Prudhoe Bay that would save us just in time, before the stove oil ran out and groceries were gone. Mom convinced us children that he was off on a great adventure, that he would see foxes and icebergs, that we could write letters for Christmas and for New Year's, and afford new coats with feathers inside. In this last I was not much interested, because I had my favorite already—a red wool coat that reversed to fake leopard—but I would be glad if this meant we could get back from the pawn shop Dad's concertina, and his second violin, and mine, the half-size with a short bow, and the guitar and mandolin and rifles and pistol that had gone that way one by one. Whether I played each instrument or not, it had been good to have them around, smelling still of campfires and of songfests in the summer.

It was cold after Dad left, cold outside and cold in our house. Ice on 30
the trailer windows grew thick and shaggy, and my sister and I melted handprints in it and licked off our palms. There had been no insulation when the add-on went up, so frost crawled the walls there, too, and Mom had us wear long johns and shoes unless we were in our beds. Brian and Jeff came for my birthday, helped me wish over seven candles, gave me a comb and a mirror. They were good kids, my mother said, polite and with good sense, and she told me that if I came in from school and she was not home, I should take Hobo with me and walk to their house. You're a worrywart, Mommy, I said. I'm not a baby, you know.

On January 10, only Hobo met me at the bus stop. In the glare from the school bus headlights his blue eye shone brighter than his brown, and he watched until I took the last step to the ground before tackling me in the snow. Most days, Hobo hid in the shadow of the spruce until Mom took my book bag, then he erupted from the dark to charge up behind me, run through my legs and on out the front. It was his favorite trick. I usually lost my balance and ended up sitting in the road with my feet thrown wide out front and steaming dog tongue all over my face.

Hobo ran ahead, then back, brushing snow crystals and fur against my leg. I put a hand on my skin to warm it and dragged nylon ski pants over the road behind me. Mom said to have them along in case the bus broke down, but she knew I would not wear them, could not bear the plastic sounds they made between my thighs.

No light was on in our house.

If Mom had been home, squares of yellow would have shown through the spruce and lit the fog of my breath, turning it bright as I passed through. What light there was now came from the whiteness of snow and from the occasional embers drifting up from our stovepipe. I laid my lunchbox on the top step and pulled at the padlock, slapping a palm on the door and shouting. Hobo jumped away from the noise and ran off, losing himself in darkness and in the faint keening dog sounds going up from over near the Turners' house. I called, "Hobo. Come back here, boy," and took to the path toward Brian's, tossing my ski pants to the storage tent as I passed.

At the property line, Hobo caught up with me and growled, and I   35 fingered his ear, looking where he pointed, seeing nothing ahead there but the high curve and long sides of a quonset hut, the work shed the Turners used also as a fence for one side of their yard. In the fall, Brian and Jeff and I had walked to the back of it, climbing over boxes and tools and parts of old furniture, and we had found in the corner a lemming's nest made from chewed bits of cardboard and paper, packed under the curve of the wall so that shadows hid it from plain sight. We all bent close to hear the scratching, and while Brian held a flashlight I took two sticks and parted the rubbish until we saw the black eyes of a mother lemming and pink naked bodies of five babies. The mother dashed deeper into the pile and we scooped the nesting back, careful not to touch the sucklings for fear that their mama would eat them if they carried scent from our fingers.

The dogs were loud now beyond the quonset, fierce in their howls and sounding many more than just three. Hobo crowded against my legs, and as I walked he hunched in front of me, making me stumble into a drift that filled my boots with snow. I called him a coward and said to quit it, but I held his neck against my thigh, turning the corner into the boys' yard and stopping on the edge. Brian's house was lit in all its windows, Jeff's was dark, and in the yard between them were dogs, new ones I had not seen before, each with its own house and tether. The dogs and their crying filled the yard, and when they saw me they grew wilder, hurling themselves to the ends of their chains, pulling their lips off their teeth. Hobo cowered and ran and I called him with my mouth, but my eyes did not move from in front of me.

There were seven. I knew they were huskies and meant to pull dogsleds, because earlier that winter Brian's grandfather had put on his glasses and shown us a book full of pictures. He had turned the pages with a wet thumb, speaking of trappers and racing people and the ways they taught these dogs to run. They don't feed them much, he said, or they get slow and lose their drive. This was how men traveled before they invented snowmobiles or gasoline.

There was no way to walk around the dogs to the lighted house.

The snow had drifted and been piled around the yard in heaps taller than I was, and whatever aisle was left along the sides was narrow and pitted with chain marks where the animals had wandered, dragging their tethers behind. No, I thought, Jeff's house was closest and out of biting range, and someone could, after all, be sitting home in the dark.

My legs were cold. The snow in my boots had packed itself around my ankles and begun to melt, soaking my socks and the felt liners under my heels. I turned toward Jeff's house, chafing my thighs together hard to warm them, and I called cheerfully at the dogs to shut up. Oscar said that if you met a wild animal, even a bear, you had to remember it was more scared than you were. Don't act afraid, he said, because they can smell fear. Just be loud—stomp your feet, wave your hands—and it will run away without even turning around. I yelled "Shut up" again as I climbed the steps to Jeff's front door, but even I could barely hear myself over the wailing. At the sides of my eyes, the huskies were pieces of smoke tumbling over one another in the dark.

The wood of the door was solid with cold, and even through deer- 40
skin mittens it bruised my hands like concrete. I cupped a hand to the window and looked in, but saw only black—black, and the reflection of a lamp in the other cabin behind me. I turned and took the three steps back to the ground; seven more and I was in the aisle between doghouses, stretching my chin far up above the frenzy, thinking hard on other things. This was how we walked in summertime, the boys and I, escaping from bad guys over logs thrown across ditches: step lightly and fast, steady on the hard parts of your soles, arms extended outward, palms down and toward the sound. That ditch, this aisle, was a river, a torrent full of silt that would fill your clothes and pull you down if you missed and fell in. I was halfway across. I pointed my chin toward the house and didn't look down.

On either side, dogs on chains hurled themselves upward, choking themselves to reach me, until their tethers jerked their throats back to earth. I'm not afraid of you, I whispered; this is dumb.

I stepped toward the end of the row and my arms began to drop slowly closer to my body. Inside the mittens, my thumbs were cold, as cold as my thighs, and I curled them in and out again. I was walking past the last dog and I felt brave, and I forgave him and bent to lay my mitten on his head. He surged forward on a chain much longer than I thought, leaping at my face, catching my hair in his mouth, shaking it in his teeth until the skin gave way with a jagged sound. My feet were too slow in my boots, and as I blundered backward they tangled in the chain, burning my legs on metal. I called out at Brian's window, expecting rescue, angry that it did not come, and I beat my arms in front of me, and the dog was back again, pulling me down.

A hole was worn into the snow, and I fit into it, arms and legs drawn up in front of me. The dog snatched and pulled at my mouth, eyes, hair; his breath clouded the air around us, but I did not feel its heat, or smell the blood sinking down between hairs of his muzzle. I watched my mitten come off in his teeth and sail upward, and it seemed unfair then and very sad that one hand should freeze all alone; I lifted the second mitten off and threw it away, then turned my face back again, overtaken suddenly by loneliness. A loud river ran in my ears, dragging me under.

My mother was singing. *Lu-lee, lu-lay, thou little tiny child*, the song to the Christ child, the words she had sung, smoothing my hair, all my life before bed. Over a noise like rushing water I called to her and heard her answer back, Don't worry, just sleep, the ambulance is on its way. I drifted back out and couldn't know then what she prayed, that I would sleep on without waking, that I would die before morning.

She had counted her minutes carefully that afternoon, sure that   45
she would get to town and back, hauling water and mail, with ten minutes to spare before my bus came. But she had forgotten to count one leg of the trip, had skidded up the drive fifteen minutes late, pounding a fist on the horn, calling me home. On the steps, my lunchbox had grown cold enough to burn her hands. She got the water, the groceries, and my brother and sisters inside, gave orders that no one touch the wood stove or open the door, and she left down the trail to Brian's whistling Hobo in from the trees.

I know from her journal that Mom had been edgy all week about the crazed dog sounds next door. Now the new huskies leaped at her and Hobo rumbled warning from his chest. Through her sunglasses, the dogs were just shapes, indistinct in window light. She tried the dark cabin first, knocking hard on the windows, then turned and moved down the path between doghouses, feeling her way with her feet, kicking out at open mouths. Dark lenses frosted over from her breath, and she moved toward the house and the lights on inside.

"She's not here." Brian's mother held the door open and air clouded inward in waves. Mom stammered out thoughts of bears, wolves, dogs. Ginny grabbed on her coat. She had heard a noise out back earlier—they should check there and then the woods.

No luck behind the cabin and no signs under the trees. Wearing sunglasses and without any flashlight, Mom barely saw even the snow. She circled back and met Ginny under the window light. Mom looked that way and asked about the dogs. "They seem so hungry," she said.

Ginny said, "No. Brian's folks just got them last week, but the boys play with them all the time." All the same, she and Mom scanned their eyes over the kennels, looking through and then over their glasses. Nothing seemed different. "Are you sure she isn't home?" Ginny said. "Maybe she took a different trail."

Maybe. Running back with Ginny behind her, Mom called my   50 name until her lungs frosted inside and every breath was a cough. The three younger children were still the only ones at home, and Mom handed them their treasure chests, telling them to play on the bed until she found Natalie. Don't go outside, she said. I'll be back right soon.

Back at the Turners', Ginny walked one way around the quonset and Mom the other. Mom sucked air through a mitten, warming her lungs. While Ginny climbed over deeper snow, she approached the sled dogs from a new angle. In the shadow of one, a splash of red—the lining of my coat thrown open. "I've found her," she shouted, and thought as she ran, Oh, thank God. Thank, thank God.

The husky stopped its howling as Mom bent to drag me out from the hole. Ginny caught up and seemed to choke. "Is she alive?" she said.

Mom said, "I think so, but I don't know how." She saw one side of my face gone, one red cavity with nerves hanging out, scraps of dead leaves stuck on to the mess. The other eye might be gone, too; it was hard to tell. Scalp had been torn away from my skull on that side, and the gashes reached to my forehead, my lips, had left my nose ripped wide at the nostrils. She tugged my body around her chest and carried me inside.

III. VITAL SIGNS

I had little knowledge of my mother's experience of the accident until many months afterward, and even then I heard her story only after I had told mine, after I had shown how clearly I remembered the dogs, and their chains, and my own blood on the snow—and had proven how little it bothered me to recall them. When I said I had heard her voice, and named for her the songs she had sung to me then, my mother searched my face, looking into me hard, saying, "I can't believe you remember." She had protected me all along, she said, from her point of view, not thinking that I might have kept my own, and that mine must be harder to bear. But after she knew all this, Mom felt she owed me a history, and she told it to me then, simply and often, in words that I would draw on long after she was gone.

She said that inside the Turners' cabin, she laid me on Ginny's 55 couch, careful not to jar the bleeding parts of me, expecting me to wake in an instant and scream. But when I did become conscious, it was only for moments, and I was not aware then of my wounds, or of the cabin's warmth, or even of pressure from the fingers of Brian's grandfather, who sat up close and stroked the frozen skin of my hands.

Ginny ordered Brian and Jeff to their room, telling them to stay there until she called them, and then she stood at Mom's shoulder, staring down and swaying on her legs.

Mom looked up through her glasses and said, "Is there a phone to call an ambulance?"

Ginny was shaking. "Only in the front house, kid, and it's locked," she said. "Kathy should be home in a minute, but I'll try to break in." She tugged at the door twice before it opened, and then she went out, leaving my mother to sing German lullabies beside my ear. *When morning comes,* the words ran, *if God wills it, you will wake up once more.* My mother sang the words and breathed on me, hoping I would dream again of summertime, all those bright nights when the music played on outside, when she drew the curtains and sang us to sleep in the trailer. Long years after the accident, when she felt healed again and stronger, Mom described her thoughts to me, and when she did she closed her eyes and sat back, saying, "You can't know how it was to keep singing, to watch air bubble up where a nose should have been, and to pray that each of those breaths was the last one." Many times that night she thought of Job, who also had lived in a spacious, golden land, who had prospered in that place, yet had cried in the end, "The thing that I so greatly feared has come upon me." The words became a chant inside her, filling her head and bringing on black time.

The wait for the ambulance was a long one, and my mother filled the time with her voice, sitting on her heels and singing. She fingered my hair and patted my hands and spoke low words when I called out. Brian's grandfather wept and warmed my fingers in his, and Mom wondered where were my mittens, and how were her other children back home.

Ginny came back and collapsed on a chair, and Kathy, her sister-in-   60
law, hurried in through the door. Ginny began to choke, rocking forward over her knees, telling Kathy the story. Her voice stretched into a wail that rose and fell like music. "It's happening again," she said. "No matter where you go, its always there."

Kathy brought out aspirin, then turned and touched my mother's arm. She said that as soon as Ginny was quiet, she would leave her here and fetch my siblings from the trailer.

"Thank you," Mom told her. "I'll send someone for them as soon as I can." She looked at Ginny then, wishing she had something to give her, some way to make her know that she was not to blame here; but for now Mom felt that Ginny had spoken truth when she said that sorrow followed us everywhere, and there was little else she could add.

The ambulance came, and then everything was movement. I drifted awake for a moment as I was lifted to a stretcher and carried toward the door. I felt myself swaying in air, back and forth and back again. Brian's whisper carried over the other voices in the room, as if blown my way by strong wind. "Natalie's dying," he said; then his words were lost among other sounds, and I faded out again. A month later, when our first-grade class sent me a box full of valentines, Brian's was smaller than the rest, a thick, white heart folded in two. Inside it read, "I love you, Nataly. Pleas dont die." When I saw him again, his eyes seemed very big, and I don't remember that he ever spoke to me anymore.

It was dark inside the ambulance, and seemed even darker to my mother, squinting through fog on her sunglasses. She badgered the medic, begging him to give me a shot for pain. Any minute I would wake up, she said, and I would start to scream. The man kept working, taking my pulse, writing it down, and while he did, he soothed my mother in low tones, explaining to her about physical shock, about the way the mind estranges itself from the body and stands, unblinking and detached, on the outside. "If she does wake up," he said, "she'll feel nothing. She won't even feel afraid." When Mom wrote this in her journal, her voice was filled with wonder, and she asked what greater gift there could be.

At the hospital there were phone calls to be made, and Mom placed 65 them from outside the emergency room. First she called Dick and Esther Conger, two of the only summertime friends who had stayed here over winter. We had met this family on the way up the Alcan, had been attracted to their made-over school bus with its sign, "Destination: Adventure," and to the Alaskan license plates bolted to each bumper. Sometime during the drive up, or during the summer when we shared the same campfires, the children of our families had become interchangeable; Toni and Barry were in the same age group as we were, and discipline and praise were shared equally among us all. It was never shocking to wake up in the morning and find Toni and Barry in one of our beds; we just assumed that the person who belonged there was over sleeping in their bus. Now, as my mother explained the accident to Dick, our friend began to cry, saying, "Oh, Verna. Oh, no," and Esther's voice in the background asked, "What's happened? Let me talk to her." Mom asked the Congers to drive out for my brother and sisters, to watch them until my father came.

Leaning her head to the wall, Mom telephoned a message to the North Slope. She spoke to Dad's boss there, explaining only that "our daughter has been hurt." Just now, she thought, she couldn't tell the whole story again, and besides, the worst "hurt" my father would imagine could not be this bad. The crew boss said a big snowstorm was coming in, but they would try to fly my father out beforehand; if not, they would get him to the radio phone and have him call down. A nurse walked up then and touched Mom's shoulder, saying, "Your daughter is awake, and she's asking for you." A moment before, Mom had been crying, pressing a fist to her teeth, but now she closed up her eyes like a faucet and walked after the nurse, pulling up her chin and breathing deeply in her chest. She had trembled so that she could hardly wipe her glasses, but when she moved through the door and saw the white lights and me lying flat on a table, she was suddenly calm, and the skin grew warmer on her face.

Mom positioned herself in front of my one eye, hoping as she stood there that she wasn't shaking visibly, that her face was not obviously tense. She need not have bothered; as I lay staring right to where my eye veered off, the room was smoky gray, and I was conscious only of a vicious thirst that roughened the edges of my tongue, made them stick to my teeth. I was allowed no water, had become fretful, and when my mother spoke to me, I complained that the rag in my mouth had not been damp enough, and that these people meant to cut my favorite coat off of me. I have to think now that my mother acted courageously, keeping her face smooth, listening to me chatter about school, about the message I had brought from my teacher, that they would skip me to the second grade on Monday. Mom's answers were light, almost vague, and before she left the pre-op room, she told me to listen to the nurses, to let them do all they needed to; they were trying to help me, she said. A little later, after I was wheeled into surgery, a nurse handed her the things they had saved: my black boots and the Alice in Wonderland watch Mom had given me for Christmas.

My mother made more phone calls, to churches in town and to ones in California that we'd left behind, telling the story over again, asking these people to pray. Old friends took on her grief, asking did she need money, telling her to call again when she knew more. These people knew, as my mother did, that money was not so much the question now, but it was something they could offer, and so they did. And for months and years after this they would send cards and letters and candy and flowers and toys, making themselves as present with us as they could. For now, on this first night, they grieved with my mother, and they said to go lie down if she could, they would take over the phones. And each of these people made another call, and another, until, as my mother walked back to the waiting room, she knew she was lifted up by every friend we had ever made.

The Turners had arrived, and for a little while they all sat along the waiting room walls, stuffing fists into their pockets and closing their eyes. None of them wanted to talk about the accident, or to wonder about the progress in surgery, and when my mother said to Kathy, "I just talked to some people in California who would never *believe* the way we live here," her words seemed terribly funny, and started the whole room laughing. It wasn't so much, she said later, that they were forgetting why they were there; in fact, they remembered very well— so well that, compared to that fact, everything else was hilarious. And they could not possibly have continued for as long as they had been, she said, pressing their backs to the walls and waiting. So for hours after Mom's joke, and far into the night, the adults invented names for our kind—"the outhouse set," "the bush league"—and they contributed stories about life in Alaska that would shock most of the people Outside. They joked about Styrofoam outhouse seats—the only kind that did not promote frostbite—about catalogues that no one could afford to buy from, but whose pages served a greater purpose, about the tremendous hardship of washing dishes from melted snow and then tossing the gray water out the door. From time to time, Ginny got up from her seat to walk alone in the hall, but when she came back in she was ready again to laugh.

My father arrived about midnight, dressed in a week's growth of beard and in an army surplus parka and flight pants. Mom met him in the hall and stood looking up; Dad dropped his satchel to the floor, panting, and he watched my mother's face, the eyes behind her glasses. He spoke first, said his was the last plane out in a heavy snowstorm. Then: "How did it happen," he said. "Did she fall out the door?"   70

My mother waited a beat and looked at him. "It wasn't a car accident, Julius," she said. She started telling the story again, and my father looked down then at the blood crusted on her sweater, and he closed his eyes and leaned into the wall. My mother told him, "You can't appreciate how I feel, because you haven't seen her face. But I wish that when you pray you'd ask for her to die soon."

Dad opened his eyes. "That must seem like the best thing to ask," he said. "But we don't make decisions like that on our own. We never have, and we can't start now."

Sometime after two A.M., my three surgeons stepped in. My mother said later that, had they not still worn their surgical greens, she would not have recognized them; during the night she had forgotten their faces.

The men sagged inside their clothes, three sets of shoulders slumped forward under cloth. I was still alive, they said, but only barely, and probably not for long. I had sustained over one hundred lacerations from the shoulders up, and had lost my left cheekbone along with my eye. They'd saved what tissue they could, filling the bulk of the cavity with packings, and what bone fragments they had found were now wired together on the chance that some of them might live.

My father groped for a positive word. "At least she doesn't have   75 brain damage. I heard she was lucid before surgery."

Dr. Butler brushed the surgical cap from his head and held it, twisting it in his hands. His eyes were red as he looked up, explaining as kindly as it seemed he could. A dog's mouth, he said, was filthy, filthier than sewage, and all of that impurity had passed into my body. They had spent four hours just cleaning out the wounds, pulling out dirt and old berry leaves and dog feces. Even with heavy antibiotics, I would likely have massive infections, and they would probably spread into my brain. His voice turned hoarse and he looked across at Dr. Earp, asking the man to continue.

Dr. Earp rubbed hard at the back of his head and spoke softly, working his neck. For now, Dr. Earp said, they had been able to reconstruct the eyelids; that would make the biggest visible difference.

On my parents' first hourly visit to Intensive Care, Mom stopped at the door and put her hand to my father's chest. "No matter how she looks," she said, "don't react. She'll be able to tell what you're thinking."

The nurse at the desk sat under a shaded lamp, the only real light in the room. She stood and whispered that mine was the first bed to the left. "She wakes up for a minute or so at a time," she said. "She's been asking for you."

"First one on the left," my father said after her, a little too loud for   80 that place, and from somewhere inside a great rushing river I heard him and called out. At my bed, Mom watched him as he stood looking down, and when the lines in his face became deeper, she turned from him, pinching his sleeve with her fingers. She walked closer to me and held the bedrail.

IV. THE FEAR

It had to happen eventually, that I found a mirror and looked in. For the first days after my accident, I had stayed mostly in bed, leaning my bandages back on the pillow and peeling frostbite blisters from my hands. The new skin was pink, and much thinner than the old, as sensitive to touch as the nail beds I uncovered by chewing down to them. I had taken to running two fingers over stitches standing up like razor stubble on my face, then over the cotton that covered the right side and the rest of my head. The whole surgical team came in daily to lift me into a chair and unwind the gauze, releasing into the room a smell like old caves full of bones. And all this time I had never seen myself, never asked what was under there, in the place where my eye belonged.

I had asked my mother once if I would again see out of that eye. It was an hour after my dressings had been changed, and the smell of hot ooze still hovered in my room. Mom stood up and adjusted my bedrail. "Do you want your feet a little higher?" she said. "I can crank them up if you like."

I said, "Mommy, my eye. Will I be able to see from it?"

"Hang on," she said. "I need to use the little girls' room." She started to the door and I screamed after her, "Mommy, you're not answering me." But she was gone, and after that I did not ask.

Later, when the light was out, I lay back and looked far right, then   85 left, concentrating hard, trying to feel the bandaged eye move. I thought I could feel it, rolling up and then down, ceiling to floor, matching its moves with my other eye. Even after I was grown, I could swear that I felt it blink when I pressed my two lids together.

Men from down the hall visited me during the day, rolling in on wheelchairs or walking beside their IV racks. They all wore two sets of pajamas, one wrong way forward so their backsides were covered. The hospital floor was old, its tiles starting to bubble, and the wheels on my friends' IV racks made rumbling sounds as they passed over. If a nurse passed by the door and looked in, the men waved her away, saying, "It's all right, dear. I'm visiting my granddaughter." For a kiss they gave me a sucker and a story about bears, or they carried me to a wheelchair and took me around to visit. In this way, I passed from room to room, brushing at the green curtains between beds, pouring water into plastic glasses, gathering hugs and learning to shake hands in the "cool" way. I signed plaster casts in big red letters, and I visited the baby room, pressing my chin to the glass.

On a day when I felt at my smallest and was in my bed still sleeping, one of my favorite men friends checked out, leaving on my nightstand a gift and a note that said he would miss me. The gift was a music box in pink satin, with a ballerina inside who pirouetted on her toes when I wound the key. And behind her inside the lid, a triangular looking glass not much bigger than she was.

My mother came in behind me as I was staring into the mirror, holding it first from one angle, then from another, and she stood by the bed for a moment, saying nothing. When I turned, she was looking at me with her shoulders forward, and she seemed to be waiting.

"My eye is gone, isn't it?" I said.

She kept looking at me. She said, "Yes it is." 90

I turned again and lifted the box to my face. "I thought so," I said. "Those dogs were pretty mean."

I didn't understand, or was too small to know, what my mother thought she was protecting me from. It must be something very bad, I thought, for her to avoid every question I asked her. "Mommy," I said once, "I don't *feel* like I'm going to die."

She looked up from her book and the light shone off her glasses. She said, "Oh, no. You're certainly not going to do anything like that."

"Then will I be blind?"

"Well," she said. "You can see now, can't you?" And when I 95 pressed her with more questions, she looked toward the door and said, "Shh. Here comes your lunch tray."

It all made me wonder if my wounds were much worse than everyone said—and of course they were, but there were long years of surgery still ahead, and no one wanted me to feel afraid. I was angry, too

—as angry as a seven-year-old can be—that Mom patted my cheek with her palm and said she'd be taking my malamute to the pound before I came home. I stared at her then with my head up and sputtered out a peevish tirade, telling her I didn't hate all dogs, or even most dogs, but just the ones who bit me. It didn't occur to me until my own daughter was seven, the same age I was when I was hurt, that Mom might have been sending my dog away for her own sake.

V. SMALL PURCHASE

I have bought a one-eyed fish. As he drifts around the tank near my desk, his skin ripples silver like well-pressed silk, and he moves under the light and hovers with his one bronze eye turned toward me, waiting to be fed. His body is smooth and flat, like a silver dollar but twice the size, and his fins are mottled gold. He is a relative of the piranha, a meat eater with a bold round mouth, but even when the smaller fish challenge him, swishing their tails at his eye, he leaves them alone and swims off. He has not eaten one of them.

I call him Max, because my sister said I should. She did not remind me, when I brought him home, that I had wanted no pets, nothing with a life span shorter than my own, nothing that would die or have to be butchered as soon as I had given it a name. She just looked up with her face very serious as if she knew well how one could become attached to a fish, and she said to me, Max. Yes, that should be his name.

I had told us both, when I bought the aquarium, that fish were low-maintenance animals, without personalities and incapable of friendliness, and if one of them died you just flushed it away and got another. And besides, I said, I needed a fish tank. I had begun to feel stale, inert. I needed the sounds of moving water in my house, and I needed, too, something alive and interesting to stare at when I stopped typing to think of a new sentence.

Last summer, when I was tired and the writing was going badly, I got superstitious about the sea and thought that the lurch and pull of waves would freshen my ears and bring on clean thoughts. So I packed some books and a portable typewriter, drove to Homer on the coast, and rented a cabin near the beach. Something about the place, or its fishy air, or my aloneness in the middle of it worked somehow, and I breathed bigger there in my chest and wrote more clearly on the page. I had forgotten about tides and about the kelp and dried crabs that came in with them, and every morning I shivered into a sweater, put combs in my hair, and walked out to wade and to fill my pockets with what I found. I liked it best when the wind was blowing and the sky was gray, and the sounds of seagulls and my own breathing were carried out with the water.

Kelp pods washed up around my feet, and I stomped on them with tennis shoes to find what was inside. I collected driftwood, and urchins, and tiny pink clam shells dropped by gulls, thin enough to see through and smaller than a thumbnail. When the tide had gone far out, I climbed the bluff back to my cabin and sat writing in front of the window, eating cheese on bread and drinking orange spritzers or tea. The walls and windows there had space in between, and they let in shreds of wind and the arguing of birds and the metal smell of seaweed drying out on the beach. When the tide started back in, I took pen and notebook and sat on a great barnacled rock, letting water creep up and surround me, then jumping to shore just in time. An hour later, the rock would be covered, three feet or more under the gray, and I would know where it lay only because of the froth and swirl of whirlpools just above it.

When I came home I threw my bags on the bed and unfastened them, and a thousand aromas opened up then into my face, drifting out from the folds of my clothes, the seams in my shoes, the pages of my notebook. I had carried them back with me, the smells of wet sand and fish fins, of eagle feathers floating in surf, of candle wax burned at midnight and filled with the empty bodies of moths. I had grieved on the drive home for that place I was leaving, and for the cold wind of that beach, and I had decided that somehow water should move in my house, should rush and bubble in my ears, should bring in the sound of the sea, and the wind and dark currents that move it.

So I bought an aquarium, and fish to go in it, and a water pump strong enough to tumble the surface as it worked. I bought plants for the tank, and waved their smell into the room, and when I thought I was finished I made one more trip to a pet store, just to see what they had.

The shop was a small one, in an old wooden building with low ceilings, and the fish room in back was dark and smelled submarine—humid and slippery and full of live things. All light in the place came from the fish tanks themselves, and the plants inside them absorbed the glow and turned it green, casting it outward to move in shadowed patterns on my skin. When I closed my eyes, the sound was of rivers running out to the coast to be carried away mixed with salt. And the fish inside waved their fins and wandered between the rocks, opening and closing their mouths.

I glanced, but didn't look hard at the larger fish, because I had found already that they were always very expensive. I browsed instead through tetras and guppies, gouramis and cichlids, trying to be satisfied with the small ones, because after all it was just the water and its motion that I really wanted. So when I saw the wide silver fish and a sign that said "$10," I assumed it was a mistake but decided to ask about it while I ordered some neons dipped out. With my neck bent forward, I watched as fifty neons swam fast away from the net that would always catch them anyway. Was that big fish back there really only ten? I said.

The clerk said, "You mean the Matinnis with one eye. He's such a mellow guy."

I swung my head to look at her. One eye?

The woman stared at my face for a moment and opened her mouth. Her cheeks grew pinker, but when she answered me, her voice stayed even. She said, "Yes, his former owners thought he was a piranha and put him in the tank with some. They ate out one eye before anyone could get him back up."

"They go for the eyes so their lunch will quit looking at them," I said. I told the woman I would take the Matinnis. I thought we were a match, I said.

And I was right. As absurd as I felt about my affinity with a one-eyed fish, I found myself watching him for the ways he was like me, and I did find many. Max had already learned, by the time I got him, to hold his body in the water so that whatever he was interested in lay always on the same side of him as his eye. In the same way that I situate myself in movie theaters so that my best friend sits on my right side, Max turns his eye toward the wall of his tank, watching for my arm to move toward the food box. When I drop a worm cube down to him, he shifts his eye up to look at it and then swims at it from the side so he never loses it from vision. If the smaller fish fight, or behave defiantly around him, he turns his dead eye against them and flicks himself away to a far corner of the tank.

I don't know if it is normal to befriend a fish. I think probably not. I do know that as I sit by Max's tank and write, I stop sometimes and look up, and I think then that he looks terribly dashing, swimming around with his bad eye outward, unafraid that something might attack him from his blind side. I buy him special shrimp pellets, and I feed them to him one at a time, careful always to drop them past his good eye. My friends like to feed him, too, and I teach them how, warning them to drop his food where he can see it. Now one of my friends wants to introduce me to his neighbor's one-eyed dog, and another wishes she still had her one-eyed zebra finch so she could give it to me.

That's just what I need, I think—a houseful of blind-sided pets. We could sit around together and play wink-um, wondering was that a wink or just a lid shut down over a dry eyeball. We could fight about who got to sit on whose good side, or we could make jokes about how it takes two of us to look both ways before crossing the street. I laugh, but still I intend to meet the one-eyed dog, to see if he reminds me of Max—or of me. I wonder if he holds himself differently from other dogs, if when he hears a voice he turns his whole body to look.

And I wonder about myself, about what has changed in the world. At first, I wanted fish only for the water they lived in, for the movement it would bring to my house, the dust it would sweep from my brain. I thought of fish as "safe" pets, too boring to demand much attention, soulless by nature and indistinguishable from their peers. Maybe this is true for most of them. But I know that when the smaller fish chase after Max, or push him away from the food, I find myself fiercely angry. I take a vicious pleasure in dropping down shrimp pellets too big and too hard for the small ones to eat, and I find pleasure, too, in the way Max gobbles the food, working it to bits in his mouth. When he is finished, he turns a dead eye to the others and swims away, seeking things more interesting to look at.

Questions

1. "Once, on a thinking day," Kusz slips in casually, "I told Janine that if I had hair like hers I would braid it and loop the pigtails around my ears." What does Kusz mean by "on a thinking day"? What's left unsaid in this phrase? Consider how Kusz uses time in this essay, both as a subject in itself, and as something she manipulates. For example, we learn she's in the hospital from the very first word of this essay—but we don't learn the reason why until Part Two.

2. Throughout "Vital Signs," Kusz holds up portraits of those people who "bred in [her] the understandings [she] would not relinquish now." Yet she ends the essay with the story of her attachment to her one-eyed fish, with her small links with one-eyed animals. What does she learn from her human exemplars? From her animal exemplars?

Terry Castle

FIRST ED

On both a personal and an intellectual level, Terry Castle has always been interested in dualities and ambiguities, in bringing together things that appear to be opposites. These issues, as they relate to sexual and social identities, lie at the heart of her latest book, *The Apparitional Lesbian:*

Female Homosexuality and Modern Culture (1993). But the themes are not new to her work. Less directly, and in very different frameworks, she began exploring forms of instability in two earlier books as well: *Clarissa's Ciphers: Meaning and Disruption in Richardson's Clarissa* (1982); and *Masquerade and Civilization: The Carnivalesque in Eighteenth-Century English Literature and Fiction* (1986). Castle calls the essay her favorite form. "I'm with Poe," she has said. "I think things that can be read in one sitting are very satisfying." Castle was born in 1953, graduated from the University of Puget Sound, and earned her Ph.D. from the University of Minnesota in 1980. She is a professor of English at Stanford University.

*F*irst, Ed — who, for all the sense of drama her memory evokes, is surrounded with a certain haze, a nimbus of uncertainty. Did our encounter, the one I remember, take place in 1963 or 1964? It must, I think, have been 1964, if only because the Dixie Cups' "Chapel of Love" (a crucial clue) was on the radio that summer, lilting out of dashboards all over San Diego, along with "Don't Worry Baby," "Pretty Woman," and "I Want to Hold Your Hand." It was the summer that my father's large brown and white Oldsmobile got a cracked block from the heat, and his hair, which had gone gray after my mother divorced him, went completely white, like Marie Antoinette's. A few months later the Dodgers, resplendent with Koufax, won the Series, and I and my fellow sixth-graders, transistors in hand, celebrated with loud huzzahs on the rough gravel playgrounds of Whittier Elementary School.

All during the long hot months of vacation, I went once a week for a swimming lesson at the old YWCA downtown at 10th and C Street. We had recently returned (my mother, my younger sister, and I) from two years on the English coast, where we had lived in a gloomy village near Dover. My British-born mother had taken us there — in a flurry of misguided nostalgia and emotional confusion — immediately after her divorce in 1961, and we had stayed on, in a strange state of immobility and shared melancholia, until mid-1963. In the summer of 1964, however, things seemed better. While my sister and I reaccustomed ourselves to the unfamiliar sunshine, my mother exulted in being back in California, in living as a "bachelorette" (with two children) in the pink Buena Vista apartments, and in the hope — not yet dashed by various Jamesian revelations — of her imminent marriage to the handsome Chuck, the mustachioed ensign in the Navy with whom she had committed the sweetest of adulteries before her divorce.

My mother had been a swimming instructor for the Y during the ten years she had been married to my father, and the organization kept her loyalty, being associated with water, freedom, light, pools, and "living in San Diego"—with everything, indeed, that she had dreamed of as a teenager working for the gasworks in St. Albans. She herself had taken a number of classes at the downtown Y: the intermediate and advanced swim course, synchronized swimming, and beginning and advanced lifeguard training, during which she learned to divest herself of numerous layers of clothing, including laced snow boots, while submerged in eight feet of water. Despite my mother's demonstrated aquatic skills, however, I adamantly refused to let her teach me any of them and remained, at the relatively advanced age of ten, a coy nonswimmer. After several abortive sessions at the bathroom sink, during which she tried to make me open my eyes under water, it became clear that I was not going to learn anything under her tutelage, but would require instruction from some more neutral party. Hence my introduction to the Y, the children's evening swim program, and the delicious orchestrated flutterings of breast, elbow, and ankle.

The YWCA was an antiquated building by southern California standards—Julia Morganish, from the teens or twenties, though not a work of her hand. It preserved the dowdy grandeur of turn-of-the-century California women's buildings, manifest in its square white facade, Mission-style touches, and cool, cavernous interior. Of the actual decor of the building, I remember little: only, vaguely, some seedy fifties leatherette furniture parked at odd angles in the reception area, peeling bulletin boards, the ancient candy machine expelling Paydays and Snickers with a frightful death rattle, and the small front office staffed—inevitably—by a middle-aged, short-haired woman in slacks. The place had an interesting air of desolation: various lost or ill-fitting souls lingered in the front area especially—off-duty sailors, people speaking Spanish, Negroes and Filipinas, mysterious solitary women. I never saw any of the guest rooms and did not know that they existed: it would not have occurred to me that anyone might actually live there.

The indoor pool was deep in the netherworld of the building,   5
seemingly underground—a greenish, Bayreuthian extravagance, reeking of chlorine and steam. Entering from the women's locker room, one found oneself immediately at one of the pool's deep-end corners. A wobbly diving board jutted out here in dangerous invitation, while at the opposite end a set of pale scalloped steps beckoned to the less adventurous. Running around the pool on all sides was an ornate white tile gutter, cheerfully decorated—by the same wayward deco hand, presumably, that had done the steps—with tiny mosaic flowers and swastikas. The water itself was cloudy, awash with dead moths and floating Band-Aids, but nonetheless, in its foggy Byzantine way, also warm-seeming and attractive. A slippery tiled walkway, inset with more flowers and swastikas and the imprinted words DO NOT RUN,

completed the scene. Along this elevated platform our blond-haired teacher, an athletic woman named Pam, would slap up and down in bathing suit and bare feet, calling out instructions in a plaintive Midwestern tongue.

We were five or six in all, a sprinkling of little girls in cotton suits with elastic waists, and one or two even smaller boys in minuscule trunks. Under Pam's guidance we soon mastered the basics: the dog paddle, a variety of elementary crawls and backstrokes, flapping sidestrokes, "sculling" and "treading water"—all with much gasping and excitement. It was on one of these occasions, while struggling to float on my back without inhaling water, that I must first have seen Ed. The ceiling over the pool was high up, some thirty or forty feet, with tall windows of opaque glass near the roof line, through which a few dim green rays of evening sunlight would sometimes penetrate to the fluorescent fug below. A dusty balcony overhung the pool at this level, stacked with seldom-used folding chairs for the spectators who came to observe the water ballet displays put on by the synchronized swimming class. Ed stood up there aloft, along with a few seamen in whites, waiting for the adult free swim hour which immediately followed our class.

Even from my unusual angle I could see that Ed was spectacularly good-looking—in a hoodish fifties way which had not yet, by mid-1964, been utterly superseded by the incoming styles of the era. I might grace my bedroom bulletin board with the toothy images of John, Paul, George, and Ringo, but Ed's "look" (as I knew even then) was far more compelling. Indeed I felt oddly giddy those times when she met my gaze—as though our positions had reversed, water and air had changed places, and I was the one looking down from above. She wore men's clothes of a decade earlier, Sears and Roebuck style, the tightest of black pants (with a discreet fly), a dark leather belt and white shirt, a thin striped tie, and, as I saw later, the same pointy-toed black dress shoes worn by the Mexican "bad boys" at Clairemont High School, down the street from the Buena Vista apartments. Her hair was excessively, almost frighteningly groomed into a narrow scandalous pompadour, and had been oiled with brilliantine to a rich black-brown, against which her face stood out with stark and ravishing paleness. She appeared to be in her late twenties or early thirties—definitely "old" to me—though something about the drastic formality of her costume also gave her the look of a teenage boy, one dressed up, perhaps, for a senior prom. She spoke to no one, smoked a cigarette, and seemed, despite her great beauty, consumed by sadness. She had a thin face of the sort I would later find irresistible in women.

One evening, more sultry than usual, my mother, who normally dropped me off and picked me up after class in the front foyer, was unable to collect me, owing to some sudden disorder in the radiator of our bulbous green Studebaker. My teacher Pam and her mother, the gamy old Peg, a short tanned woman who wore pants and also taught swimming classes at the Y, agreed to drive me home to Clairemont in their car. As soon as they had closed up the office we were to leave.

I had already finished changing and sat by myself in the locker room, waiting for my ride, when Ed came in. The other little girls were long gone. The floor was still wet with the footprints of the departed; the thick damp air hung about like a dream. At the same time everything seemed to open up, as if I—or she and I together—had suddenly entered a clearing in a forest. Ed said nothing, yet seemed, in some distant way, to recognize me. I sat still, not knowing where to go. She scrutinized me ambiguously for a few moments. Then, as if some complex agreement had been reached between us, she began to strip away, vertiginously, the emblems of her manhood.

Ed, Ed, my first, my only undressing. She moved gracefully, like a 10 Pierrot, her pallid face a mask in the dim light. She removed her jacket and unbuckled her belt first, laying them carefully on the bench next to me. Then she slipped off her shoes and socks. I gazed down at her bare feet. Her eyes met mine and looked away. Then she loosened her tie with one hand and pulled it off, followed by her heavy cuff links. Glancing again in my direction, she began to unbutton her shirt, twisting her torso in an uneasy fashion as she did so. She wore, heart-stoppingly, a woman's white brassiere. This she unhooked slowly from behind, and watching me intently now, let her breasts fall forward. Her breasts were full and had dark nipples. She stopped to flick back some wet-looking strands of hair that had come down, Dion-like, over her brow. Then rather more quickly, with a practiced masculine gesture, she began to undo her fly. She removed her trousers, revealing a pair of loose Jockey shorts. She hesitated a moment before uncovering the soft hairiness beneath—that mystery against which I would thrust my head, blindly, in years to come. I stared childishly at the curly black V between her legs. She took off her watch, a man's gold Timex, last of all.

Her transfiguration was not complete, of course: now she took out a rusty-looking woman's swimsuit from a metal locker and began, uncannily, stepping into it. She became a woman. Then she folded up her clothes neatly and put them away. Still she did not speak—nor, it seemed, did she ever remove her eyes from mine.

I am aware, too late, how almost painfully sexy Ed was—and perhaps, at the level of hallucination, intended to be. Even now I seem to see the disquieting movement of her chest and shoulders as she leaned over the bench between us, the damp pressed-in look of her thighs when she began to pull the resistant nylon swimsuit up her body, her breasts poignantly hanging, then confined, with the aid of diffident fingers, in the suit's stiff built-in cups. Indeed, I seem to be assisting her, leaning into her, even (slyly) inhaling her. She bends slightly at the knees, balances herself with one hand against the locker, begins to hold me around the neck—but this is a fantasy of the present. In that moment my feelings were of a far more polite, delicate, even sentimental nature. Astonishment gave way to, resolved into, embarrassment. When at last Ed drew on, over the dark crown of her head, a flowered Esther Williams-style bathing cap—the final clownish touch of femininity—I felt, obscurely, the pathos of her transformation: she had become somehow less than herself. But her eyes, with their mute, impassive challenge, never faltered. They seemed to say, I own you now. And I realized too, though I had no words for it at the time, how much I adored her, and what tumult lay ahead.

The other women came and got me soon enough—Ed must have gone—for the next thing I remember is sitting deep in the well of the backseat of my teacher's Plymouth, the warm night breeze blowing in my face, and the lights of downtown glinting in the background as we drove away. Pam and her mother talked in a desultory, friendly way in the front seat. They used slang with each other and swore softly—almost as if I weren't there, or were much older, which I enjoyed. I looked at the back of their heads, at Pam's blond nape and her mother's cropped gray thatch, while the sounds of the radio—KCBQ—wafted sweetly through the summer air:

We're going to the chapel
And we're
Gonna get ma-a-a-rried

Going to the Chapel of Love

Then, as we wound our way down 101 through Balboa Park, under the tall bridge by the zoo, the two of them began—as if to the music—to talk about Ed. They seemed to know her; they spoke almost tenderly, referring to her by name. Ed looked more like a guy than ever, my teacher remarked. The words hung about softly in the air. I began listening hard, as I did at school. Her mother, Peg, reflected for a moment, then glanced back and smiled at me in the dark, enigmatically, before murmuring in reply, "Yeah, but she don't have the superior plumbing system." And into the night we sped away.

Many years later, when I had just turned twenty-two, and lay in   15
bed with a much older woman with whom I was greatly in love, I told the story of Ed, this story, for the first time. I was already getting on Helen's nerves by that point; she tried to find the fastest way through my postcoital maunderings. Ed was, she concluded, "just an externalization." As she often reminded me, Helen had spent fifty thousand dollars a year for eight years of psychoanalysis in Chicago. She wore her hair in a long braid down her back to represent, she told me, her "missing part." She was thin and dark, and when she wasn't teaching wore a man's watch and lumberman's jacket. My mother, she said, "sounded like a hysteric." A lot of things happened later, and I finally got to resenting Helen back, but that's a winter, not a summer story.

Questions

1. Castle writes that Ed is "surrounded with a certain haze, a nimbus of uncertainty." In many ways, that phrase could be understood as the theme of this essay. What moments in "First Ed" (and why does the title have no comma; why does the opening phrase have one?) reinforce the idea of the uncertain, or, perhaps, subvert the idea of the certain?
2. Castle describes the YWCA minutely. What importance does the setting have to the event that takes place in it?

Scott Russell Sanders

UNDER THE INFLUENCE

The widely published Scott Russell Sanders has written in a multitude of forms and styles — everything from science fiction to folktales to personal essays, from children's stories to historical novels to a newspaper column. What holds all of his work together, he says, is his overarching attempt "to understand our place in nature, trace the sources of our violence, and speculate about the future of our species." Sanders was born in 1945 and educated at Brown University (B.A.) and Cambridge University (Ph.D.). Now a professor at Indiana University, where he teaches literature and intellectual history, he won the Penrod Award for *Stone Country* (1985) and the Associated Writing Programs Award for Creative Nonfiction for *The Paradise of Bombs* (1987).

*M*y father drank. He drank as a gut-punched boxer gasps for breath, as a starving dog gobbles food—compulsively, secretly, in pain and trembling. I use the past tense not because he ever quit drinking but because he quit living. That is how the story ends for my father, age sixty-four, heart bursting, body cooling and forsaken on the linoleum of my brother's trailer. The story continues for my brother, my sister, my mother, and me, and will continue so long as memory holds.

In the perennial present of memory, I slip into the garage or barn to see my father tipping back the flat green bottles of wine, the brown cylinders of whiskey, the cans of beer disguised in paper bags. His Adam's apple bobs, the liquid gurgles, he wipes the sandy-haired back of a hand over his lips, and then, his bloodshot gaze bumping into me, he stashes the bottle or can inside his jacket, under the workbench, between two bales of hay, and we both pretend the moment has not occurred.

"What's up, buddy?" he says, thick-tongued and edgy.

"Sky's up," I answer, playing along.

"And don't forget prices," he grumbles. "Prices are always up. And   5
taxes."

In memory, his white 1951 Pontiac with the stripes down the hood and the Indian head on the snout jounces to a stop in the driveway; or it is the 1956 Ford station wagon, or the 1963 Rambler shaped like a toad, or the sleek 1969 Bonneville that will do 120 miles per hour on straightaways; or it is the robin's-egg blue pickup, new in 1980, battered in 1981, the year of his death. He climbs out, grinning dangerously, unsteady on his legs, and we children interrupt our game of catch, our building of snow forts, our picking of plums, to watch in silence as he weaves past into the house, where he slumps into his overstuffed chair and falls asleep. Shaking her head, our mother stubs out the cigarette he has left smoldering in the ashtray. All evening, until our bedtimes, we tiptoe past him, as past a snoring dragon. Then we curl in our fearful sheets, listening. Eventually he wakes with a grunt, Mother slings accusations at him, he snarls back, she yells, he growls, their voices clashing. Before long, she retreats to their bedroom, sobbing—not from the blows of fists, for he never strikes her, but from the force of words.

Left alone, our father prowls the house, thumping into furniture, rummaging in the kitchen, slamming doors, turning the pages of the newspaper with a savage crackle, muttering back at the late-night drivel from television. The roof might fly off, the walls might buckle from the pressure of his rage. Whatever my brother and sister and mother may be thinking on their own rumpled pillows, I lie there hating him, loving him, fearing him, knowing I have failed him. I tell myself he drinks to ease an ache that gnaws at his belly, an ache I must have caused by disappointing him somehow, a murderous ache I should be able to relieve by doing all my chores, earning A's in school, winning baseball games, fixing the broken washer and the burst pipes, bringing in money to fill his empty wallet. He would not hide the green bottles in his tool box, would not sneak off to the barn with a lump under his coat, would not fall asleep in the daylight, would not roar and fume, would not drink himself to death, if only I were perfect.

I am forty-two as I write these words, and I know full well now that my father was an alcoholic, a man consumed by disease rather than by disappointment. What had seemed to me a private grief is in fact a public scourge. In the United States alone some ten or fifteen million people share his ailment, and behind the doors they slam in fury or disgrace, countless other children tremble. I comfort myself with such knowledge, holding it against the throb of memory like an ice pack against a bruise. There are keener sources of grief: poverty, racism, rape, war. I do not wish to compete for a trophy in suffering. I am only trying to understand the corrosive mixture of helplessness, responsibility, and shame that I learned to feel as the son of an alcoholic. I realize now that I did not cause my father's illness, nor could I have cured it. Yet for all this grown-up knowledge, I am still ten years old, my own son's age, and as that boy I struggle in guilt and confusion to save my father from pain.

Consider a few of our synonyms for *drunk*: tipsy, tight, pickled, soused, and plowed; stoned and stewed, lubricated and inebriated, juiced and sluiced; three sheets to the wind, in your cups, out of your mind, under the table; lit up, tanked up, wiped out; besotted, blotto, bombed, and buzzed; plastered, polluted, putrified; loaded or looped, boozy, woozy, fuddled, or smashed; crocked and shit-faced, corked and pissed, snockered and sloshed.

It is a mostly humorous lexicon, as the lore that deals with drunks 10 —in jokes and cartoons, in plays, films, and television skits—is largely comic. Aunt Matilda nips elderberry wine from the sideboard and burps politely during supper. Uncle Fred slouches to the table glassy-eyed, wearing a lamp shade for a hat and murmuring, "Candy is dandy but liquor is quicker." Inspired by cocktails, Mrs. Somebody recounts the events of her day in a fuzzy dialect, while Mr. Somebody nibbles her ear and croons a bawdy song. On the sofa with Boyfriend, Daughter giggles, licking gin from her lips, and loosens the bows in her hair. Junior knocks back some brews with his chums at the Leopard Lounge and stumbles home to the wrong house, wonders foggily why he cannot locate his pajamas, and crawls naked into bed with the ugliest girl in school. The family dog slurps from a neglected martini and wobbles to the nursery, where he vomits in Baby's shoe.

It is all great fun. But if in the audience you notice a few laughing faces turn grim when the drunk lurches on stage, don't be surprised, for these are the children of alcoholics. Over the grinning mask of Dionysus, the leering mask of Bacchus, these children cannot help seeing the bloated features of their own parents. Instead of laughing, they wince, they mourn. Instead of celebrating the drunk as one freed from constraints, they pity him as one enslaved. They refuse to believe *in vino veritas*, having seen their befuddled parents skid away from truth toward folly and oblivion. And so these children bite their lips until the lush staggers into the wings.

My father, when drunk, was neither funny nor honest; he was pathetic, frightening, deceitful. There seemed to be a leak in him somewhere, and he poured in booze to keep from draining dry. Like a torture victim who refuses to squeal, he would never admit that he had touched a drop, not even in his last year, when he seemed to be dissolving in alcohol before our very eyes. I never knew him to lie about anything, ever, except about this one ruinous fact. Drowsy, clumsy, unable to fix a bicycle tire, throw a baseball, balance a grocery sack, or walk across the room, he was stripped of his true self by drink. In a matter of minutes, the contents of a bottle could transform a brave man into a coward, a buddy into a bully, a gifted athlete and skilled carpenter and shrewd businessman into a bumbler. No dictionary of synonyms for *drunk* would soften the anguish of watching our prince turn into a frog.

Father's drinking became the family secret. While growing up, we children never breathed a word of it beyond the four walls of our house. To this day, my brother and sister rarely mention it, and then only when I press them. I did not confess the ugly, bewildering fact to my wife until his wavering walk and slurred speech forced me to. Recently, on the seventh anniversary of my father's death, I asked my mother if she ever spoke of his drinking to friends. "No, no, never," she replied hastily. "I couldn't bear for anyone to know."

The secret bores under the skin, gets in the blood, into the bone, and stays there. Long after you have supposedly been cured of malaria, the fever can flare up, the tremors can shake you. So it is with the fevers of shame. You swallow the bitter quinine of knowledge, and you learn to feel pity and compassion toward the drinker. Yet the shame lingers in your marrow, and, because of the shame, anger.

For a long stretch of my childhood we lived on a military reserva- 15 tion in Ohio, an arsenal where bombs were stored underground in bunkers, vintage airplanes burst into flames, and unstable artillery shells boomed nightly at the dump. We had the feeling, as children, that we played in a mine field, where a heedless footfall could trigger an explosion. When Father was drinking, the house, too, became a mine field. The least bump could set off either parent.

The more he drank, the more obsessed Mother became with stopping him. She hunted for bottles, counted the cash in his wallet, sniffed at his breath. Without meaning to snoop, we children blundered left and right into damning evidence. On afternoons when he came home from work sober, we flung ourselves at him for hugs, and felt against our ribs the telltale lump in his coat. In the barn we tumbled on the hay and heard beneath our sneakers the crunch of buried glass. We tugged open a drawer in his workbench, looking for screwdrivers or crescent wrenches, and spied a gleaming six-pack among the tools. Playing tag, we darted around the house just in time to see him sway on the rear stoop and heave a finished bottle into the woods. In his good night kiss we smelled the cloying sweetness of Clorets, the mints he chewed to camouflage his dragon's breath.

I can summon up that kiss right now by recalling Theodore Roethke's lines about his own father in "My Papa's Waltz":

> The whiskey on your breath
> Could make a small boy dizzy;
> But I hung on like death:
> Such waltzing was not easy.

Such waltzing was hard, terribly hard, for with a boy's scrawny arms I was trying to hold my tipsy father upright.

For years, the chief source of those incriminating bottles and cans was a grimy store a mile from us, a cinder block place called Sly's, with two gas pumps outside and a moth-eaten dog asleep in the window. A strip of flypaper, speckled the year round with black bodies, coiled in the doorway. Inside, on rusty metal shelves or in wheezing coolers, you could find pop and Popsicles, cigarettes, potato chips, canned soup, raunchy postcards, fishing gear, Twinkies, wine, and beer. When Father drove anywhere on errands, Mother would send us kids along as guards, warning us not to let him out of our sight. And so with one or more of us on board, Father would cruise up to Sly's, pump a dollar's worth of gas or plump the tires with air, and then, telling us to wait in the car, he would head for that fly-spangled doorway.

Dutiful and panicky, we cried, "Let us go in with you!"

"No," he answered. "I'll be back in two shakes."   20

"Please!"

"No!" he roared. "Don't you budge, or I'll jerk a knot in your tails!"

So we stayed put, kicking the seats, while he ducked inside. Often, when he had parked the car at a careless angle, we gazed in through the window and saw Mr. Sly fetching down from a shelf behind the cash register two green pints of Gallo wine. Father swigged one of them right there at the counter, stuffed the other in his pocket, and then out he came, a bulge in his coat, a flustered look on his red face.

Because the Mom and Pop who ran the dump were neighbors of ours, living just down the tar-blistered road, I hated them all the more for poisoning my father. I wanted to sneak in their store and smash the bottles and set fire to the place. I also hated the Gallo brothers, Ernest and Julio, whose jovial faces shone from the labels of their wine, labels I would find, torn and curled, when I burned the trash. I noted the Gallo brothers' address, in California, and I studied the road atlas to see how far that was from Ohio, because I meant to go out there and tell

Ernest and Julio what they were doing to my father, and then, if they showed no mercy, I would kill them.

While growing up on the back roads and in the country schools and   25 cramped Methodist churches of Ohio and Tennessee, I never heard the word *alcoholism*, never happened across it in books or magazines. In the nearby towns, there were no addiction treatment programs, no community mental health centers, no Alcoholics Anonymous chapters, no therapists. Left alone with our grievous secret, we had no way of understanding Father's drinking except as an act of will, a deliberate folly or cruelty, a moral weakness, a sin. He drank because he chose to, pure and simple. Why our father, so playful and competent and kind when sober, would choose to ruin himself and punish his family, we could not fathom.

Our neighborhood was high on the Bible, and the Bible was hard on drunkards. "Woe to those who are heroes at drinking wine, and valiant men in mixing strong drink," wrote Isaiah. "The priest and the prophet reel with strong drink, they are confused with wine, they err in vision, they stumble in giving judgment. For all tables are full of vomit, no place is without filthiness." We children had seen those fouled tables at the local truck stop where the notorious boozers hung out, our father occasionally among them. "Wine and new wine take away the understanding," declared the prophet Hosea. We had also seen evidence of that in our father, who could multiply seven-digit numbers in his head when sober, but when drunk could not help us with fourth-grade math. Proverbs warned: "Do not look at wine when it is red, when it sparkles in the cup and goes down smoothly. At the last it bites like a serpent, and stings like an adder. Your eyes will see strange things, and your mind utter perverse things." Woe, woe.

Dismayingly often, these biblical drunkards stirred up trouble for their own kids. Noah made fresh wine after the flood, drank too much of it, fell asleep without any clothes on, and was glimpsed in the buff by his son Ham, whom Noah promptly cursed. In one passage — it was so shocking we had to read it under our blankets with flashlights — the patriarch Lot fell down drunk and slept with his daughters. The sins of the fathers set their children's teeth on edge.

Our ministers were fond of quoting St. Paul's pronouncement that drunkards would not inherit the kingdom of God. These grave preachers assured us that the wine referred to during the Last Supper was in fact grape juice. Bible and sermons and hymns combined to give us the impression that Moses should have brought down from the mountain another stone tablet, bearing the Eleventh Commandment: Thou shalt not drink.

The scariest and most illuminating Bible story apropos of drunkards was the one about the lunatic and the swine. Matthew, Mark, and Luke each told a version of the tale. We knew it by heart: When Jesus climbed out of his boat one day, this lunatic came charging up from the graveyard, stark naked and filthy, frothing at the mouth, so violent that he broke the strongest chains. Nobody would go near him. Night and day for years this madman had been wailing among the tombs and bruising himself with stones. Jesus took one look at him and said, "Come out of the man, you unclean spirits!" for he could see that the lunatic was possessed by demons. Meanwhile, some hogs were conveniently rooting nearby. "If we have to come out," begged the demons, "at least let us go into those swine." Jesus agreed. The unclean spirits entered the hogs, and the hogs rushed straight off a cliff and plunged into a lake. Hearing the story in Sunday school, my friends thought mainly of the pigs. (How big a splash did they make? Who paid for the lost pork?) But I thought of the redeemed lunatic, who bathed himself and put on clothes and calmly sat at the feet of Jesus, restored—so the Bible said—to "his right mind."

When drunk, our father was clearly in his wrong mind. He became   30 a stranger, as fearful to us as any graveyard lunatic, not quite frothing at the mouth but fierce enough, quick-tempered, explosive; or else he grew maudlin and weepy, which frightened us nearly as much. In my boyhood despair, I reasoned that maybe he wasn't to blame for turning into an ogre. Maybe, like the lunatic, he was possessed by demons. I found support for my theory when I heard liquor referred to as "spirits," when the newspapers reported that somebody had been arrested for "driving under the influence," and when church ladies railed against that "demon drink."

If my father was indeed possessed, who would exorcise him? If he was a sinner, who would save him? If he was ill, who would cure him? If he suffered, who would ease his pain? Not ministers or doctors, for we could not bring ourselves to confide in them; not the neighbors, for we pretended they had never seen him drunk; not Mother, who fussed and pleaded but could not budge him; not my brother and sister, who were only kids. That left me. It did not matter that I, too, was only a child, and a bewildered one at that. I could not excuse myself.

On first reading a description of delirium tremens—in a book on alcoholism I smuggled from the library—I thought immediately of the frothing lunatic and the frenzied swine. When I read stories or watched films about grisly metamorphoses—Dr. Jekyll becoming Mr. Hyde, the mild husband changing into a werewolf, the kindly neighbor taken over by a brutal alien—I could not help seeing my own father's mutation from sober to drunk. Even today, knowing better, I am attracted by the demonic theory of drink, for when I recall my father's transformation, the emergence of his ugly second self, I find it easy to believe in possession by unclean spirits. We never knew which version of Father would come home from work, the true or the tainted, nor could we guess how far down the slope toward cruelty he would slide.

How far a man *could* slide we gauged by observing our back-road neighbors—the out-of-work miners who had dragged their families to our corner of Ohio from the desolate hollows of Appalachia, the tight-fisted farmers, the surly mechanics, the balked and broken men. There was, for example, whiskey-soaked Mr. Jenkins, who beat his wife and kids so hard we could hear their screams from the road. There was Mr. Lavo the wino, who fell asleep smoking time and again, until one night his disgusted wife bundled up the children and went outside and left him in his easy chair to burn; he awoke on his own, staggered out coughing into the yard, and pounded her flat while the children looked on and the shack turned to ash. There was the truck driver, Mr. Sampson, who tripped over his son's tricycle one night while drunk and got so mad that he jumped into his semi and drove away, shifting through the dozen gears, and never came back. We saw the bruised children of these fathers clump onto our school bus, we saw the abandoned children huddle in the pews at church, we saw the stunned and battered mothers begging for help at our doors.

Our own father never beat us, and I don't think he ever beat Mother, but he threatened often. The Old Testament Yahweh was not more terrible in his wrath. Eyes blazing, voice booming, Father would pull out his belt and swear to give us a whipping, but he never followed through, never needed to, because we could imagine it so vividly. He shoved us, pawed us with the back of his hand, as an irked bear might smack a cub, not to injure, just to clear a space. I can see him grabbing Mother by the hair as she cowers on a chair during a nightly quarrel. He twists her neck back until she gapes up at him, and then he lifts over her skull a glass quart bottle of milk, the milk running down his forearm; and he yells at her, "Say just one more word, one goddamn word, and I'll shut you up!" I fear she will prick him with her sharp tongue, but she is terrified into silence, and so am I, and the leaking bottle quivers in the air, and milk slithers through the red hair of my father's uplifted arm, and the entire scene is there to this moment, the head jerked back, the club raised.

When the drink made him weepy, Father would pack a bag and 35 kiss each of us children on the head, and announce from the front door that he was moving out. "Where to?" we demanded, fearful each time that he would leave for good, as Mr. Sampson had roared away for good in his diesel truck. "Someplace where I won't get hounded every minute," Father would answer, his jaw quivering. He stabbed a look at Mother, who might say, "Don't run into the ditch before you get there," or, "Good riddance," and then he would slink away. Mother watched him go with arms crossed over her chest, her face closed like the lid on a box of snakes. We children bawled. Where could he go? To the truck stop, that den of iniquity? To one of those dark, ratty flophouses in town? Would he wind up sleeping under a railroad bridge or on a park bench or in a cardboard box, mummied in rags, like the bums we had seen on our trips to Cleveland and Chicago? We bawled and bawled, wondering if he would ever come back.

He always did come back, a day or a week later, but each time there was a sliver less of him.

In Kafka's *The Metamorphosis*, which opens famously with Gregor Samsa waking up from uneasy dreams to find himself transformed into an insect, Gregor's family keep reassuring themselves that things will be just fine again, "When he comes back to us." Each time alcohol transformed our father, we held out the same hope, that he would really and truly come back to us, our authentic father, the tender and playful and competent man, and then all things would be fine. We had grounds for such hope. After his weepy departures and chapfallen returns, he would sometimes go weeks, even months without drinking. Those were glad times. Joy banged inside my ribs. Every day without the furtive glint of bottles, every meal without a fight, every bedtime without sobs encouraged us to believe that such bliss might go on forever.

Mother was fooled by just such a hope all during the forty-odd years she knew this Greeley Ray Sanders. Soon after she met him in a Chicago delicatessen on the eve of World War II and fell for his buttermelting Mississippi drawl and his wavy red hair, she learned that he drank heavily. But then so did a lot of men. She would soon coax or scold him into breaking the nasty habit. She would point out to him how ugly and foolish it was, this bleary drinking, and then he would quit. He refused to quit during their engagement, however, still refused during the first years of marriage, refused until my sister came along. The shock of fatherhood sobered him, and he remained sober through my birth at the end of the war and right on through until we moved in 1951 to the Ohio arsenal, that paradise of bombs. Like all places that make a business of death, the arsenal had more than its share of alcoholics and drug addicts and other varieties of escape artists. There I turned six and started school and woke into a child's flickering awareness, just in time to see my father begin sneaking swigs in the garage.

He sobered up again for most of a year at the height of the Korean War, to celebrate the birth of my brother. But aside from that dry spell, his only breaks from drinking before I graduated from high school were just long enough to raise and then dash our hopes. Then during the fall of my senior year—the time of the Cuban missile crisis, when it seemed that the nightly explosions at the munitions dump and the nightly rages in our household might spread to engulf the globe—Father collapsed. His liver, kidneys, and heart all conked out. The doctors saved him, but only by a hair. He stayed in the hospital for weeks, going through a withdrawal so terrible that Mother would not let us visit him. If he wanted to kill himself, the doctors solemnly warned him, all he had to do was hit the bottle again. One binge would finish him.

Father must have believed them, for he stayed dry the next fifteen   40 years. It was an answer to prayer, Mother said, it was a miracle. I believe it was a reflex of fear, which he sustained over the years through courage and pride. He knew a man could die from drink, for his brother Roscoe had. We children never laid eyes on doomed Uncle Roscoe, but in the stories Mother told us he became a fairy-tale figure, like a boy who took the wrong turning in the woods and was gobbled up by the wolf.

The fifteen-year dry spell came to an end with Father's retirement in the spring of 1978. Like many men, he gave up his identity along with his job. One day he was a boss at the factory, with a brass plate on his door and a reputation to uphold; the next day he was a nobody at home. He and Mother were leaving Ontario, the last of the many places to which his job had carried them, and they were moving to a new house in Mississippi, his childhood stomping grounds. As a boy in Mississippi, Father sold Coca-Cola during dances while the moonshiners peddled their brew in the parking lot; as a young blade, he fought in bars and in the ring, seeking a state Golden Gloves championship; he gambled at poker, hunted pheasants, raced motorcycles and cars, played semiprofessional baseball, and, along with all his buddies—in the Black Cat Saloon, behind the cotton gin, in the woods—he drank. It was a perilous youth to dream of recovering.

After his final day of work, Mother drove on ahead with a car full of begonias and violets, while Father stayed behind to oversee the packing. When the van was loaded, the sweaty movers broke open a six-pack and offered him a beer.

"Let's drink to retirement!" they crowed. "Let's drink to freedom! to fishing! hunting! loafing! Let's drink to a guy who's going home!"

At least I imagine some such words, for that is all I can do, imagine, and I see Father's hand trembling in midair as he thinks about the fifteen sober years and about the doctors' warning, and he tells himself *God damnit, I am a free man,* and *Why can't a free man drink one beer after a lifetime of hard work?* and I see his arm reaching, his fingers closing, the can tilting to his lips. I even supply a label for the beer, a swaggering brand that promises on television to deliver the essence of life. I watch the amber liquid pour down his throat, the alcohol steal into his blood, the key turn in his brain.

Soon after my parents moved back to Father's treacherous stomp-   45 ing ground, my wife and I visited them in Mississippi with our five-year-old daughter. Mother had been too distraught to warn me about the return of the demons. So when I climbed out of the car that bright July morning and saw my father napping in the hammock, I felt uneasy, for in all his sober years I had never known him to sleep in daylight. Then he lurched upright, blinked his bloodshot eyes, and greeted us in a syrupy voice. I was hurled back helpless into childhood.

"What's the matter with Papaw?" our daughter asked.

"Nothing," I said. "Nothing!"

Like a child again, I pretended not to see him in his stupor, and behind my phony smile I grieved. On that visit and on the few that remained before his death, once again I found bottles in the workbench, bottles in the woods. Again his hands shook too much for him to run a saw, to make his precious miniature furniture, to drive straight down back roads. Again he wound up in the ditch, in the hospital, in jail, in treatment centers. Again he shouted and wept. Again he lied. "I never touched a drop," he swore. "Your mother's making it up."

I no longer fancied I could reason with the men whose names I found on the bottles—Jim Beam, Jack Daniels—nor did I hope to save my father by burning down a store. I was able now to press the cold statistics about alcoholism against the ache of memory: ten million victims, fifteen million, twenty. And yet, in spite of my age, I reacted in the same blind way as I had in childhood, ignoring biology, forgetting numbers, vainly seeking to erase through my efforts whatever drove him to drink. I worked on their place twelve and sixteen hours a day, in the swelter of Mississippi summers, digging ditches, running electrical wires, planting trees, mowing grass, building sheds, as though what nagged at him was some list of chores, as though by taking his worries on my shoulders I could redeem him. I was flung back into boyhood, acting as though my father would not drink himself to death if only I were perfect.

I failed of perfection; he succeeded in dying. To the end, he considered himself not sick but sinful. "Do you want to kill yourself?" I asked him. "Why not?" he answered. "Why the hell not? What's there to save?" To the end, he would not speak about his feelings, would not or could not give a name to the beast that was devouring him.   50

In silence, he went rushing off the cliff. Unlike the biblical swine, however, he left behind a few of the demons to haunt his children. Life with him and the loss of him twisted us into shapes that will be familiar to other sons and daughters of alcoholics. My brother became a rebel, my sister retreated into shyness, I played the stalwart and dutiful son who would hold the family together. If my father was unstable, I would be a rock. If he squandered money on drink, I would pinch every penny. If he wept when drunk—and only when drunk—I would not let myself weep at all. If he roared at the Little League umpire for calling my pitches balls, I would throw nothing but strikes. Watching him flounder and rage, I came to dread the loss of control. I would go through life without making anyone mad. I vowed never to put in my mouth or veins any chemical that would banish my everyday self. I would never make a scene, never lash out at the ones I loved, never hurt a soul. Through hard work, relentless work, I would achieve something dazzling—in the classroom, on the basketball floor, in the science lab, in the pages of books—and my achievement would distract the world's eyes from his humiliation. I would become a worthy sacrifice, and the smoke of my burning would please God.

It is far easier to recognize these twists in my character than to undo them. Work has become an addiction for me, as drink was an addiction for my father. Knowing this, my daughter gave me a placard for the wall: WORKAHOLIC. The labor is endless and futile, for I can no more redeem myself through work than I could redeem my father. I still panic in the face of other people's anger, because his drunken temper was so terrible. I shrink from causing sadness or disappointment even to strangers, as though I were still concealing the family shame. I still notice every twitch of emotion in the faces around me, having learned as a child to read the weather in faces, and I blame myself for their least pang of unhappiness or anger. In certain moods I blame myself for everything. Guilt burns like acid in my veins.

I am moved to write these pages now because my own son, at the age of ten, is taking on himself the griefs of the world, and in particular the griefs of his father. He tells me that when I am gripped by sadness he feels responsible; he feels there must be something he can do to spring me from depression, to fix my life. And that crushing sense of responsibility is exactly what I felt at the age of ten in the face of my father's drinking. My son wonders if I, too, am possessed. I write, therefore, to drag into the light what eats at me — the fear, the guilt, the shame — so that my own children may be spared.

I still shy away from nightclubs, from bars, from parties where the solvent is alcohol. My friends puzzle over this, but it is no more peculiar than for a man to shy away from the lions' den after seeing his father torn apart. I took my own first drink at the age of twenty-one, half a glass of burgundy. I knew the odds of my becoming an alcoholic were four times higher than for the sons of nonalcoholic fathers. So I sipped warily.

I still do—once a week, perhaps, a glass of wine, a can of beer, 55 nothing stronger, nothing more. I listen for the turning of a key in my brain.

Questions

1. What does the title mean to you before you read this essay? What does it suggest after reading "Under the Influence"? How does the title comment on one of Sanders's major points?

2. In this essay, Sanders keeps returning to the theme of transformation. "No dictionary of synonyms for *drunk*," he writes, "would soften the anguish of watching our prince turn into a frog." Sanders reverses the fairy-tale ending here, so we see alcohol as the magic spell that ruins his father. Consider other passages—see paragraphs 30, 32, and 37 — that present various transformations and discuss how Sanders supports this theme throughout his piece.

Three

CONSTRUCTING NATURE

*T*he nature essays in this chapter disrupt the paradigm of what we might call the classic nature essay, in which the essayists, devoted to appreciating the beauty and bounty of the earth, render the natural world familiar. In that familiarity, nature reveals its truth to the writer—and it reveals truth about the writer. The new nature essay complicates these claims from the outset. In fact, most of the essayists here don't take nature itself head-on as their subject. Rather, they travel down quirky byroads, rummaging around in weedy and neglected patches. Although they take the setting for granted, they are self-conscious about the role the essayist has in creating the world on the page; they keep worrying at the relationship between nature and human nature. How do we make sense of the very idea of nature?

Where do we fit? In asking these questions, the essays in this chapter try to locate our proper place in the world of nature, attempt to make out the cartography of home.

Gretel Ehrlich, in "Architecture," understands nature as an idea that we build, not one that just is. She discards the old notion of the house, in which " 'inside' is equated with a static sort of security, a blockade against the commotions of nature, against the plurality of ourselves, while 'outside' has come to signify everything that is not human, everything inimical." Her essay suggests constructing a new kind of architecture, in which human beings are able to allow design "dictated by the unruliness of nature."

Like Ehrlich, Oliver Sacks, in "A Walking Grove," is interested in locating our proper place in the world of nature. Unlike Ehrlich, however, Sacks looks at human nature, a nature that reveals itself only in the proper cultural context. His subject, Martin, has become estranged from his essential self because he has lost that context. Without church and without music, Martin dwells only in the "small, petty, nasty, and dark" world of "the retardate," cut off from the path to humanity and divinity. Martin's return to church—to his "proper place" in the world—makes him "a different man": "The pseudo-persons—the stigmatised retardate, the snotty, spitting boy—disappeared." The music transforms him utterly, so that his human nature, hidden by defects and pathologies, is revealed intact, and Martin's real self appears in its "absorption and animation, wholeness and health."

In his investigation of human nature, Lewis Thomas stands the orthodoxies on their heads. Of the three orders of beings, animals, humans, and computers, only animals are missing the "splendid freedom" that defines the human—the freedom to make a mistake. And Thomas redefines a mistake as a positive virtue, a fresh beginning. Since computers are designed by the human mind, they carry that mind's rich possibility for error. The machine's ability to get things completely wrong is, then, a great chance; we may find our salvation comes from a place unimagined, as yet unmapped.

Vicki Hearne would disagree with Thomas's categories. Far from holding animals to be static in their infallibility, "Consider the Pit Bull" argues that dogs operate within a moral arena, in which they—like human beings—have freedom to act. Yet the stories we construct about dogs in general, and about pit bulls in particular, insist that they act "without decision in the matter," blindly following their inherently vicious natures. Her essay speculates about the reasons we construct horror stories about dogs, about what it is in our nature that causes us to be so frightened about theirs.

The total eclipse that Annie Dillard offers inspires such fear because it can obliterate human consciousness. The death of the light she witnesses conjures up not only the experience of her own death, but also the death of all her species. That mass death, of course, would bring the death of memory and of human history. A total eclipse is a natural phenomenon that is finite; it only suggests what death would be like. Yet this is enough to render its meaning to Dillard, to allow her to reevaluate "our complex and inexplicable caring for each other, and for our life together here."

Richard Preston considers our life together from another vantage point in "Crisis in the Hot Zone." Charting the path of a new virus that escapes when its host monkeys are imported from the rain forest into the United States, Preston connects the deforestation practiced so far away with our very survival. The vast reservoir of unknown viruses contained in the Amazon basin is just a plane flight away from the rest of the world. Because that same rain forest produced the HIV virus, we see with chilling clarity the link between ecology and AIDS, between conservation and the future of our species, between another part of the world and ourselves. Last time, the Ebola virus rose, "flashed its colors, replicated, and subsided into the forest"; next time, we may not be so lucky.

Rather than the abundance or sublimity that the nature essayist traditionally evokes, Preston makes us imagine scarcity or threat. Charting a change in the national psyche by tracing a change in dog stories, Hearne shows us that not only is our idea of nature culturally constructed, but our culture constructs itself partly in response to its unease with the natural world. On the one hand, finding a place for the human in a nature as vastly terrifying as Dillard's might be the work of the next century; on the other hand, the work might be finding a place for nature in the human world. Then again, one of Thomas's computers might remap the universe in such a way that the border between nature and culture is erased altogether.

Gretel Ehrlich

ARCHITECTURE

When she was thirty years old, Gretel Ehrlich transplanted herself from Manhattan, where she had been working as a documentary maker, to the barren Big Horn Basin of northern Wyoming, where she began to "cowboy." It was there, too, that she began to write, something she had always wanted to do, she has said, but not "before I knew anything." Her first book, *The Solace of Open Spaces* (1985), is a collection of essays about the land and the people of Wyoming, which she has come to consider her "real spiritual home." Ehrlich was born in 1946, grew up near Santa Barbara, California, and studied at Bennington College in Vermont, UCLA's film school, and the New School for Social Research in New York. Her books include a novel, *Heart Mountain*, and a collection from which this selection was taken, *Islands, the Universe, Home*, and she frequently publishes in periodicals. In 1987, she won a Whiting Writer's Award.

Late fall in Wyoming is the end of barefoot days, of nights under single cotton blankets, looking at stars; it is the end of carelessness. "Survive," my body calls out as the first blizzard whips by. No human shelter seems sturdy enough. Why didn't I fly south with my bachelor duck or dig into a steep mountain slope and sleep with the bears? The horses turn tail to oncoming storms and huddle in a clump of cottonwoods. The cattle go down-country, finding shelter in low-spreading junipers.

Walking home from hunting camp last week, my foot fell into a bear track. Not a perfect fit, but my heel pressed into the sow's heelprint as if I were her twin. Her tracks led up a hill into pine trees where I knew from other years, she'd had a den. Bears are particular about their winter quarters. They like a steep slope facing away from prevailing winds, and deep snow, and sometimes an overhanging boulder or log under which to dig. When denning time comes, a bear may travel hundreds of miles to return to a site that stuck in her mind months before as suitable winter quarters. My question is, what is it that brings a bear back? The sound of a waterfall, the scent of whortleberries, the way the breeze brushes her fur coat smooth?

Dens vary, as human houses do. There's an entryway, a long tunnel, sometimes straight, sometimes angled, then one or two sleeping rooms, small enough to trap the bear's body heat, and a sleeping platform laid with the soft tips of pine boughs. The bear smooths the walls with her paws, as if smoothing mortar. Because she bears her young inside the den, she's careful about disclosing her whereabouts. She'll wait to start digging until a good snow begins to fall, filling in her tracks. One biologist saw a bear actually back away from the den using her own tracks so whoever came along would think she was still there. Some sites are hidden, some so spectacularly precarious as to pique our imaginations, such as the den three quarters of the way up an almost vertical wall next to a three-hundred-fifty-foot waterfall.

Orientation, room shape, slope, wind direction, weather: what moves a bear to select a site? Does the idea stay firm in her mind all summer, or year after year? What does the idea look like? Is it a blueprint, a landscape description, a scent? Where in her mind do room designs evolve?

Wyoming has no indigenous architecture, unless it's the outlaw cave. The log cabin was an idea imported in the 1600s by Swedish immigrants in what is now Delaware, and it moved west along with the settlers. In the mountains I often come on trappers' cabins — tiny structures built close to the ground, with one window and a small door so low even I have to bend over to enter. Homesteaders who arrived just as winter was setting in made do with what they could find: some lived in wall tents or tipis, others in tiny one-room cabins made of logs or adobe, where husband, wife, children, and relatives could only have huddled.

No architectural legacy has taken hold. Housing has a temporary look: sheep wagons, section cars, trailer houses. As one old-timer said, "Everything from the old days has burned down at least once." Here and there are hermits' huts or a basement house whose presence is revealed only by the pickup trucks parked around the roof. New houses built from Boise Cascade kits are perched aboveground and face the highway with an unopenable picture window, so that a passerby can see the cool glow of the television screen at night, but the hermetically sealed residents can't reach out to the world. And throughout the state, there are hundreds of miles where there has never been any human habitation at all.

Warm days return. On the lake at the ranch, ice cracks and thaws in a wavy line across the middle, then a long chunk breaks out like a leg and floats alone in the water as if trying to stand, to make its escape before the arrival of winter. Elsewhere, imbricated plates of ice have thawed and refrozen and are layered like fish scales, while beneath in the mud, fish and frogs sleep.

Nearby I come on a grackle's nest suspended in the forked branch of a currant bush. Ingeniously placed, it uses the running water from a ditch as a moat to protect the eggs from ground predators. A nest is a cup of space and represents the transformation of the stochastic natural order to the social one. The sins of human architecture—the ways our houses barricade us from natural forces and all human feeling—send me to the dictionary to look for answers, and I find this: the German word for "building" is derived from a word, *bin*, that also means "to be," and the Japanese for "nest" can be read doubly as "to live."

The house should not be separate, a hollow sculpture conforming to an architect's ego. Rather, it should invoke something of how a human moves and breathes; it should be the flexible casing for metabolism. The first house is the uterus—or else, the neck: in one species of frog, tadpoles incubate in the throat of the father, and when they are big enough, they swim out of his mouth to freedom. All animals are natural builders. Ants of one genus use their bodies architectonically, functioning as both doors and doorkeepers. Flattened in front, with enlarged heads, they fit into the entrance of the anthill with a carpenter's precision. They're color coded to match the soil and savvy enough to allow entrance when secret knocks and smells are emitted.

How desultory most human shelters must seem: all padding and 10 armor, with wall-to-wall carpets, curtains, extraneous decor. I see houses, schools, hospitals built with windows that can't be opened. How can a child understand the rhythms of life if he or she is sealed away from seasons and weather? The new parts of our cities are mirrored and self-referential facades. How can I see into the soul of a building when it has no eyes? Everywhere, unforgiving materials are used, which can't absorb human sweat or hold warmth, or the drumlike beat of sobbing, singing, or laughter. Who wants to make love on the wrong side of mirrored glass?

After breakfast I ride my colt. He is tall and good-looking and likes to put his head down low and set out at a fast walk. Down in the valley, I ride by a field where the shadows of trees have turned white. The rising sun has burned away all the frost on the field except where tree trunks blocked the rays. All that is left are white images of trees lying flat on mown grass—ghostly apparitions—as if matter had borrowed from spirit, and spirit from matter. Later, when I ride home, the frost has melted and the shadows the trees made are black again.

I put my horse away and climb a low knob where I've often thought of building a house. Facing east, I can see up and down this long valley: eleven-thousand-foot peaks to the north, red mesas and another distant mountain range to the south. Directly below my feet, an irrigation ditch curves around the hill like a moat, and beyond are the island and the lake. I sit on a granite boulder sloughed off the face of the mountain who knows how many thousands of years ago. The lichen on its surface is green and black, and the ground is gruss—rotted granite—scoured down into pale red soil.

To start, but how? I think of the Lost Woman of San Nicolas Island, off my hometown in California, who wore cormorant-skin dresses and built a house of whale ribs. The ribs of a horse, cow, or buffalo would make a much smaller house, too small, in fact, but what a wonderful thought: to live in a shelter made from skeletal remains, a body inside a body—but then again, logs and rocks are another kind of bone. Frank Lloyd Wright says: "From nature inward; from within outward." I want to break down the dichotomy between inside and outside, interior and exterior, beauty and ugliness, form and function, because they are all the same.

In a deep bathtub I read about cosmic strings. Dense, invisible, high-energy threads, they unwound from the nuclear explosion at the moment of the Big Bang and function as cosmic two-by-fours, building matter into galactic neighborhoods. But unlike studs, cosmic strings, besides being invisible, are in constant, flexing motion. The physicist Alexander Vilenkin describes them: "Wiggling violently from tension, curved strings often cross themselves and one another. They break at the point of intersection and join again in different configurations. A closed loop splits when it twists on itself. Long coiled strings cross themselves many times over and closed loops get lopped off at intersections." A house is not an empty shell but a path that crosses itself.

It begins to snow. I'm in my own eighty-year-old house, which is 15 uninsulated and made of a poured gypsum block that is crumbling like aspirin. Cold rises through a thin pine floor and pours through the walls. Soon fat flakes will line the arms of trees. All is white except for the thawed circle at the center of the lake, a blowhole through which the planet breathes.

Cosmic strings are flaws that occurred in the featureless vacuum of space; they look like the cracks in lake ice as water freezes, or like fault lines in the earth. From the beginning, the universe was built on symmetries undoing themselves into asymmetries: from the symmetry of featurelessness to the asymmetry of texture and topography. Design is a form of imperfection. It comes from within, it is dictated by the unruliness of nature. A house is bent into shape by space, topography, and prevailing winds; in turn, its captured space reshapes what is beyond its walls.

Another blizzard comes. As I walk, I try to make out which is the lake and which is dry land. Blowing snow "vanishes" me. What I can see is only snow pouring through bronze reeds onto ice like snakes, and as I try to find my way, I think how much a house is like a body, trying to point its feet the right way, trying to see, trying to let in light. House building is a process of locating oneself on the planet, about reading landscape, bending branches down and lifting a structure back up.

When I finally reach the house, I sit on the veranda. Snow stings my face. The walls of traditional Japanese houses open onto verandas that face on gardens, streams, bamboo forests, mountains, or ocean. A house is a platform on which the transaction between nature and culture, internal and external, form and formlessness occurs. Too often "inside" is equated with a static sort of security, a blockade against the commotions of nature, against the plurality of ourselves, while "outside" has come to signify everything that is not human, everything inimical.

A blueprint should be a spiritual proposition: walls and windows become a form of discipline, an obstruction that liberates space and spirit by giving it form. Space is viscous and visceral. It can be held in the hand or in the mind; a body can curve around it, or a room. It starts right here at my lips. I gulp it in, and it oxygenates my blood. I swallow space; I wedge it into my psyche as a way of lifting the roof of the mind off the noise of thoughts, so that in the intervening silence, any kind of willful spirit can express itself.

I come up with this: If I built a house, a stream would trickle 20 through the main room, then continue on, threading together gardens, studies, bathrooms. A rock wall made from the granite strewn across the house site would bolster the house against prevailing northwesterly winds. A dense forest of bamboo or aspen would frame the twisted entrance, thinning out until it opened into a room. Walls, ceilings, floors jutting out beyond sliding doors, would be made of local materials: cottonwood, pine, fir, granite, willow branches braided with sage. Floor levels would change with topography, function, view, the way the basins of waterfalls do, catching pools of activity, then spilling them again. Rooms would not have common walls. Covered verandas or corridors would link bedrooms, bathrooms, studies, and on the way, an alcove might invite the passerby in to sit and look at a hill where swifts and swallows nest, or open onto a tiny garden. Passageways would lift me up or down, alter my pace, my sense of self. A granite boulder would burst through the wall of the main room to remind me that a wall, like a thought, is a flexible thing, that a house is not a defense *against* nature but a way of letting it in. In the kitchen, polished granite slabs would serve as counters. I might spread gruss under my feet near south-facing windows to absorb heat; I might have trees growing next to books. I'd let fault lines tell me where to elevate or drop a floor; clouds might shape the ceiling. The way the house moved over the contour of the land would be the way it speaks.

I'm on the knob again. The sun is out, and the hole in the center of the lake has thawed, though I don't know yet that this is the last time I'll see open water. If only my bachelor duck could see the lake's opening, would he return? At dusk the hole is a pot of gold-gilded ripples, a way of looking into the earth's belly, but in the morning winter sets in.

It snows: six inches, then seven more, until the white is continuous, day and night, lifting the level of the ground twenty, thirty, forty inches. The wind howls, and during interstices coyotes howl back. The light is flat, and the landscape is ever-changing: drifts curve down from buildings and fence lines; sagebrush, fence lines, roadbeds, and five-strand barb-wire fences have all disappeared.

How far away autumn seems now, and its many days of burnished ruddiness. Like a house built into a hill, winter is cantilevered over all that. I can no longer see the lake, distinguish the knob from the flat, though the lake ice groans, shifting under the muffle of snow. An Alaskan biologist who lives on pack ice at Resolute Bay and in the Chukchi and Beaufort seas four months of the year says, "Reading the landscape up there means watching a whole topography come into existence. Ice collides and forms pressure ridges. I watch entire mountains come into existence. And just when I'm getting to know my way around in this newly formed landscape, the ice melts, the formations are gone, and my intimacy with that place is over."

Matsuo Bashō writes, in the essay "Hut of the Phantom Dwelling": "The grebe attaches its floating nest to a single strand of reed, counting on the reed to keep it from washing away in the current." By what thin strands of luck we stay alive and know in which direction our feet are pointing!

The snow continues. I keep thinking of the Crow word for loneliness,   25 which translates literally as "I can't see myself." Perhaps the word was composed during a blizzard. Every morning my husband harnesses his team of black Percherons, and we make our way down what appears to have been a road — now mounded with drifts — to feed the cows. It's a twelve-mile round trip. The dogs, running ahead, vanish under the snow, then leap straight up into the air as if to say, "I'm still here."

Wind has carved the landscape into an impenetrable being, and worked snow down steep slopes into white whorls of brocade. When the storm ends, the sky clears fast, and at night it is thirty below zero. In the morning, sun hits the top of the mountain: light moving down the slope looks like cream being poured.

Winter solstice. How quickly the sun flies across the southern sky, ringed by a huge halo: a sun dog. At night constellations are blueprints, pointing the way between twists of cosmic strings. The winter night I flew out of Fairbanks, Alaska, a folding curtain of northern lights pulsed upward and pierced the Big Dipper, as if trying to follow an architect's plan, trying to unfold itself into rooms.

Questions

1. In passages like this one, Gretel Ehrlich defines what a house should not be, as well as what it should be: "The house should not be separate, a hollow sculpture conforming to an architect's ego. Rather, it should invoke something of how a human moves

and breathes; it should be the flexible casing for metabolism." Discuss the various definitions of the house that Ehrlich offers throughout this essay, concentrating especially on paragraphs 18–20.

2. What does Ehrlich consider the virtues of bears' dens, birds' nests, anthills, and toads' throats as various forms of homes? Why does she compare them to human shelters? How does she integrate the fact that these structures are deliberately made — at least, in the case of the bears' dens and the birds' nests — into her argument?

Oliver Sacks

A WALKING GROVE

A doctor from a family of doctors, Oliver Sacks was born in London in 1933 and studied medicine at Oxford before coming to the United States in 1960. He has always taken an interest in his patients as people, and this interest has transferred naturally, and felicitously, to his writing. In his many journal articles and books, he presents case histories that are much more than dry medical analyses. They are the life stories of real people with whom all readers can identify. In one of his most famous books, *Awakenings* (1973), Sacks tells of his work trying to arouse survivors of a sleeping sickness epidemic who had been "asleep" for more than forty years. In another, *The Man Who Mistook His Wife for a Hat* (1985), from which this essay was taken, Sacks deals with people suffering from varied forms of brain damage. Although his power as an author has been compared to that of a novelist or short-story writer, Sacks doesn't consider himself in those terms. But, he has said, "There's something about words, and the written word in particular, which is almost necessary for my own processes of thought."

Martin A., aged 61, was admitted to our Home toward the end of 1983, having become Parkinsonian and unable to look after himself any longer. He had had a nearly fatal meningitis in infancy, which caused retardation, impulsiveness, seizures, and some spasticity on one side. He had very limited schooling, but a remarkable musical education—his father was a famous singer at the Met.

He lived with his parents until their death, and thereafter eked out a marginal living as a messenger, a porter, and a short-order cook—whatever he could do before he was fired, as he invariably was, because of his slowness, dreaminess, or incompetence. It would have been a dull and disheartening life, had it not been for his remarkable musical gifts and sensibilities, and the joy this brought him—and others.

He had an amazing musical memory—"I know more than two thousand operas," he told me on one occasion—although he had never learned or been able to read music. Whether this would have been possible or not was not clear—he had always depended on his extraordinary ear, his power to retain an opera or an oratorio after a single hearing. Unfortunately his voice was not up to his ear—being tuneful, but gruff, with some spastic dysphonia.[1] His innate, hereditary musical gift had clearly survived the ravages of meningitis and brain-damage — or had it? Would he have been a Caruso if undamaged? Or was his musical development, to some extent, a "compensation" for brain-damage and intellectual limitations? We shall never know. What is certain is that his father not only transmitted his musical genes, but his own great love for music, in the intimacy of a father-son relationship, and perhaps the specially tender relation of a parent to a retarded child. Martin — slow, clumsy — was loved by his father, and passionately loved him in return; and their love was cemented by their shared love for music.

The great sorrow of Martin's life was that he could not follow his father, and be a famous opera and oratorio singer like him—but this was not an obsession, and he found, and gave, much pleasure with what he *could* do. He was consulted, even by the famous, for his remarkable memory, which extended beyond the music itself to all the details of performance. He enjoyed a modest fame as "walking encyclopedia," who not only knew the music of two thousand operas, but all the singers who had taken the roles in countless performances, and all the details of scenery, staging, dress and decor. (He also prided himself on a street-by-street, house-by-house, knowledge of New York—and knowing the routes of all its buses and trains.) Thus, he was an opera-buff, and something of an "idiot savant"[2] too. He took a certain child-like pleasure in all this—the pleasure of such eidetics[3] and freaks. But the real joy—and the only thing that made life supportable—was actual participation in musical events, singing in the choirs at local

[1] *spastic dysphonia*: Difficulty or pain in speaking due to contractions of the larynx.

[2] *idiot savant*: A developmentally disabled person who exhibits brilliance in a particular field.

[3] *eidetics*: People who have extraordinary and vivid recall, especially of visual images.

churches (he could not sing solo, to his grief, because of his dysphonia), especially in the grand events at Easter and Christmas, the *John* and *Matthew Passions*, the *Christmas Oratorio*, the *Messiah*, which he had done for fifty years, boy and man, in the great churches and cathedrals of the city. He had also sung at the Met and, when it was pulled down, at Lincoln Center, discreetly concealed amid the vast choruses of Wagner and Verdi.

At such times—in the oratorios and passions most of all, but also in   5
the humbler church choirs and chorales—as he soared up into the music Martin forgot that he was "retarded," forgot all the sadness and badness of his life, sensed a great spaciousness enfold him, felt himself both a true man and a true child of God.

Martin's world—his inner world—what sort of a world did he have? He had very little knowledge of the world at large, at least very little living knowledge, and no interest at all. If a page of an encyclopedia or newspaper was read to him, or a map of Asia's rivers or New York's subways shown to him, it was recorded, instantly, in his eidetic memory. But he had no relation to these eidetic recordings—they were "a-centric," to use Richard Wollheim's term, without him, without anyone, or anything, as a living centre. There seemed little or no emotion in such memories—no more emotion than there is in a street-map of New York—nor did they connect, or ramify, or get generalised, in any way. Thus his eidetic memory—the freak part of him—did not in itself form, or convey any sense of, a "world." It was without unity, without feeling, without relation to himself. It was physiological, one felt, like a memory-core or memory-bank, but not part of a real and personal living self.

And yet, even here, there was a single and striking exception, at once his most prodigious, most personal, and most pious deed of memory. He knew by heart Grove's *Dictionary of Music and Musicians*, the immense nine-volume edition published in 1954—indeed he was a "walking Grove." His father was ageing and somewhat ailing by then, could no longer sing actively, but spent most of his time at home, playing his great collection of vocal records on the phonograph, going through and singing all his scores—which he did with his now thirty-year-old son (in the closest and most affectionate communion of their lives), and reading aloud Grove's dictionary—all six thousand pages of it—which, as he read, was indelibly printed upon his son's limitlessly retentive, if illiterate, cortex. Grove, thereafter, was "heard" *in his father's voice*—and could never be recollected by him without emotion.

Such prodigious hypertrophies of eidetic memory, especially if employed or exploited "professionally," sometimes seem to oust the real self, or to compete with it, and impede its development. And if there is no depth, no feeling, there is also no pain in such memories—and so they can serve as an "escape" from reality. This clearly occurred, to a great extent, in Luria's Mnemonist, and is poignantly described in the last chapter of his book. It obviously occurred, to some extent, in Martin A., José, and the Twins but was *also*, in each case, used for reality, even "super-reality"—an exceptional, intense and mystical sense of the world. . . .

Eidetics apart, what of his world generally? It was, in many respects, small, petty, nasty, and dark—the world of a retardate who had been teased and left out as a child, and then hired and fired, contemptuously, from menial jobs, as a man: the world of someone who had rarely felt himself, or felt regarded as, a proper child or man.

He was often childish, sometimes spiteful, and prone to sudden   10
tantrums—and the language he then used was that of a child. "I'll throw a mudpie in your face!" I once heard him scream, and, occasionally, he spat or struck out. He sniffed, he was dirty, he blew snot on his sleeve—he had the look (and doubtless the feelings) at such times of a small, snotty child. These childish characteristics, allied to a certain lack of common warmth and kindness, and topped off by his irritating, eidetic showing off, endeared him to nobody. He soon became unpopular in the Home, and found himself shunned by many of the residents. A crisis was developing, with Martin regressing weekly and daily, and nobody was quite sure, at first, what to do. It was at first put down to "adjustment difficulties," such as all patients may experience on giving up independent living outside, and coming into a "Home." But Sister felt there was something more specific at work—"something gnawing him, a sort of hunger, a gnawing hunger we can't assuage. It's destroying him," she continued. "We have to *do* something."

So, in January, for the second time, I went to see Martin — and found a very different man: no longer cocky, showing off, as before, but obviously pining, in spiritual and a sort of physical pain.

"What is it?" I said. "What is the matter?"

"I've got to sing," he said hoarsely. "I can't live without it. And it's not just music—I can't pray without it." And then, suddenly, with a flash of his old memory: " 'Music, to Bach, was the apparatus of worship,' Grove, article on Bach, page 304. . . . I've never spent a Sunday," he continued, more gently, reflectively, "without going to church, without singing in the choir. I first went there, with my father, when I was old enough to walk, and I continued going after his death in 1955. *I've got to go,*" he said fiercely. "It'll kill me if I don't."

"And go you shall," I said. "We didn't know what you were missing."

The church was not far from the Home, and Martin was welcomed   15
back — not only as a faithful member of the congregation and the choir, but as the brains and adviser of the choir that his father had been before him.

With this, life suddenly and dramatically changed. Martin had resumed his proper place, as he felt it. He could sing, he could worship, in Bach's music, every Sunday, and also enjoy the quiet authority that was accorded him.

"You see," he told me, on my next visit, without cockiness, but as a simple matter of fact, "they know I know all Bach's liturgical and choral music. I know all the church cantatas—all 202 that Grove lists— and which Sundays and Holy Days they should be sung on. We are the only church in the diocese with a real orchestra and choir, the only one where all of Bach's vocal works are regularly sung. We do a cantata every Sunday—and we are going to do the *Matthew Passion* this Easter!"

I thought it curious and moving that Martin, a retardate, should have this great passion for Bach. Bach seemed so intellectual—and Martin was a simpleton. What I did not realise, until I started bringing in cassettes of the cantatas, and once of the *Magnificat*, when I visited, was that for all his intellectual limitations Martin's musical intelligence was fully up to appreciating much of the technical complexity of Bach; but, more than this—that it wasn't a question of intelligence at all. Bach lived for him, and he lived in Bach.

Martin did, indeed, have "freak" musical abilities—but they were only freak-like if removed from their right and natural context.

What was central to Martin, as it had been central for his father, and   20 what had been intimately shared between them, was always the *spirit* of music, especially religious music, and of the voice as the divine instrument made and ordained to sing, to raise itself in jubilation and praise.

Martin became a different man, then, when he returned to song and church—recovered himself, recollected himself, became real again. The pseudo-persons—the stigmatised retardate, the snotty, spitting boy—disappeared; as did the irritating, emotionless, impersonal eidetic. The real person reappeared, a dignified, decent man, respected and valued now by the other residents.

But the marvel, the real marvel, was to see Martin when he was actually singing—or in communion with music—listening with an intentness which verged on rapture—"a man in his wholeness wholly attending." At such times—it was the same with Rebecca when she acted, or José when he drew, or the Twins in their strange numerical communion—Martin was, in a word, transformed. All that was defective or pathological fell away, and one saw only absorption and animation, wholeness and health.

POSTSCRIPT

When I wrote this piece, and the two succeeding ones, I wrote solely out of my own experience, with almost no knowledge of the literature on the subject, indeed with no knowledge that there *was* a large literature (see, for example, the fifty-two references in Lewis Hill 1974). I only got an inkling of it, often baffling and intriguing, after "The Twins" was first published, when I found myself inundated with letters and offprints.

In particular, my attention was drawn to a beautiful and detailed case-study by David Viscott (1970). There are many similarities between Martin and his patient Harriet G. In both cases there were extraordinary powers—which were sometimes used in an "a-centric" or life-denying way, sometimes in a life-affirming and creative way: thus, after her father had read it to her, Harriet retained the first three pages of the Boston Telephone Directory ("and for several years could give any number on these pages on request"); but, in a wholly different, and strikingly creative, mode she could compose, and improvise in the style of any composer.

It is clear that both—like the Twins . . .—could be pushed, or   25
drawn, into the sort of mechanical feats considered typical of "idiot savants"—feats at once prodigious and meaningless; but that both also (like the Twins), when not pushed or drawn in this fashion, showed a consistent seeking after beauty and order. Though Martin has an amazing memory for random, meaningless facts, his real pleasure comes from order and coherence, whether it be the musical and spiritual order of a cantata, or the encyclopedic order of Grove. Both Bach and Grove communicate a *world*. Martin, indeed, has no world *but* music—as is the case with Viscott's patient—but this world is a real world, makes him real, can transform him. This is marvellous to see with Martin—and it was evidently no less so with Harriet G:

> This ungainly, awkward, inelegant lady, this overgrown five-year-old, became absolutely transformed when I asked her to perform for a seminar at Boston State Hospital. She sat down demurely, stared quietly at the keyboard until we all grew silent, and brought her hands slowly to the keyboard and let them rest a moment. Then she nodded her head and began to play with all the feeling and movement of a concert performer. From that moment she was another person.

Questions

1. To what does the title metaphor refer? Does Martin's knowledge of *Grove* have any meaning for him? How does his knowledge of *Grove* differ from his knowledge of Asia's rivers or New York's subways?
2. What are the three personalities that Martin exhibits? How are these personalities contingent on outside circumstances?

Lewis Thomas

TO ERR IS HUMAN

President Emeritus of the Sloan-Kettering Cancer Center in New York, Lewis Thomas was born in 1913 and has practiced and taught medicine for more than fifty years at some of the most prestigious institutes in the country. His distinguished career as a physician and scholar has been paralleled by a similarly noteworthy record as an essayist for both academic and lay audiences. Selections from "Notes of a Biology Watcher," a column Thomas writes for the *New England Journal of Medicine*, have been collected into four books. The first of these, *The Lives of a Cell: Notes of a Biology Watcher* (1979), won the American Book Award for science. Thomas believes that a symbiotic relationship must be maintained between humankind and the rest of nature. He writes in *The Lives of a Cell* that the idea of an "autonomous, independent, isolated island of a Self—is a myth."

*E*veryone must have had at least one personal experience with a computer error by this time. Bank balances are suddenly reported to have jumped from $379 into the millions, appeals for charitable contributions are mailed over and over to people with crazy-sounding names at your address, department stores send the wrong bills, utility companies write that they're turning everything off, that sort of thing. If you manage to get in touch with someone and complain, you then get instantaneously typed, guilty letters from the same computer, saying, "Our computer was in error, and an adjustment is being made in your account."

These are supposed to be the sheerest, blindest accidents. Mistakes are not believed to be part of the normal behavior of a good machine. If things go wrong, it must be a personal, human error, the result of fingering, tampering, a button getting stuck, someone hitting the wrong key. The computer, at its normal best, is infallible.

I wonder whether this can be true. After all, the whole point of computers is that they represent an extension of the human brain, vastly improved upon but nonetheless human, superhuman maybe. A good computer can think clearly and quickly enough to beat you at chess, and some of them have even been programmed to write obscure verse. They can do anything we can do, and more besides.

It is not yet known whether a computer has its own consciousness, and it would be hard to find out about this. When you walk into one of those great halls now built for the huge machines, and stand listening,

it is easy to imagine that the faint, distant noises are the sound of thinking, and the turning of the spools gives them the look of wild creatures
rolling their eyes in the effort to concentrate, choking with information. But real thinking, and dreaming, are other matters.

On the other hand, the evidences of something like an *unconscious*,   5
equivalent to ours, are all around, in every mail. As extensions of the
human brain, they have been constructed with the same property of
error, spontaneous, uncontrolled, and rich in possibilities.

Mistakes are at the very base of human thought, embedded there,
feeding the structure like root nodules. If we were not provided with the
knack of being wrong, we could never get anything useful done. We think
our way along by choosing between right and wrong alternatives, and the
wrong choices have to be made as frequently as the right ones. We get
along in life this way. We are built to make mistakes, coded for error.

We learn, as we say, by "trial and error." Why do we always say
that? Why not "trial and rightness" or "trial and triumph"? The old
phrase puts it that way because that is, in real life, the way it is done.

A good laboratory, like a good bank or a corporation or government, has to run like a computer. Almost everything is done flawlessly,
by the book, and all the numbers add up to the predicted sums. The
days go by. And then, if it is a lucky day, and a lucky laboratory, somebody makes a mistake: the wrong buffer, something in one of the
blanks, a decimal misplaced in reading counts, the warm room off by a
degree and a half, a mouse out of his box, or just a misreading of the
day's protocol. Whatever, when the results come in, something is obviously screwed up, and then the action can begin.

The misreading is not the important error; it opens the way. The
next step is the crucial one. If the investigator can bring himself to say,
"But even so, look at that!" then the new finding, whatever it is, is
ready for snatching. What is needed, for progress to be made, is the
move based on the error.

Whenever new kinds of thinking are about to be accomplished, or   10
new varieties of music, there has to be an argument beforehand. With two
sides debating in the same mind, haranguing, there is an amiable understanding that one is right and the other wrong. Sooner or later the thing is
settled, but there can be no action at all if there are not the two sides, and
the argument. The hope is in the faculty of wrongness, the tendency toward error. The capacity to leap across mountains of information to land
lightly on the wrong side represents the highest of human endowments.

It may be that this is a uniquely human gift, perhaps even stipulated
in our genetic instructions. Other creatures do not seem to have DNA
sequences for making mistakes as a routine part of daily living, certainly not for programmed error as a guide for action.

We are at our human finest, dancing with our minds, when there
are more choices than two. Sometimes there are ten, even twenty different ways to go, all but one bound to be wrong, and the richness of

selection in such situations can lift us onto totally new ground. This process is called exploration and is based on human fallibility. If we had only a single center in our brains, capable of responding only when a correct decision was to be made, instead of the jumble of different, credulous, easily conned clusters of neurones that provide for being flung off into blind alleys, up trees, down dead ends, out into blue sky, along wrong turnings, around bends, we could only stay the way we are today, stuck fast.

The lower animals do not have this splendid freedom. They are limited, most of them, to absolute infallibility. Cats, for all their good side, never make mistakes. I have never seen a maladroit, clumsy, or blundering cat. Dogs are sometimes fallible, occasionally able to make charming minor mistakes, but they get this way by trying to mimic their masters. Fish are flawless in everything they do. Individual cells in a tissue are mindless machines, perfect in their performance, as absolutely inhuman as bees.

We should have this in mind as we become dependent on more complex computers for the arrangement of our affairs. Give the computers their heads, I say; let them go their way. If we can learn to do this, turning our heads to one side and wincing while the work proceeds, the possibilities for the future of mankind, and computerkind, are limitless. Your average good computer can make calculations in an instant which would take a lifetime of slide rules for any of us. Think of what we could gain from the near infinity of precise, machine-made miscomputation which is now so easily within our grasp. We would begin the solving of some of our hardest problems. How, for instance, should we go about organizing ourselves for social living on a planetary scale, now that we have become, as a plain fact of life, a single community? We can assume, as a working hypothesis, that all the right ways of doing this are unworkable. What we need, then, for moving ahead, is a set of wrong alternatives much longer and more interesting than the short list of mistaken courses that any of us can think up right now. We need, in fact, an infinite list, and when it is printed out we need the computer to turn on itself and select, at random, the next way to go. If it is a big enough mistake, we could find ourselves on a new level, stunned, out in the clear, ready to move again.

Questions

1. In some ways, "To Err Is Human" is a study in the subversion of conventional wisdom. The basis for this whole essay is a new understanding of the concept of error. Compare Thomas's definition of a mistake with the orthodox definition.

2. Is this essay about human beings or about computers? If "to err is

human," then what does Thomas imply about computers? Discuss error as a "uniquely human gift," thanks to our DNA being coded for mistakes, and consider how that definition squares with his suggestion that human error is hard-wired into supercomputers.

Vicki Hearne

CONSIDER THE PIT BULL

Writer, philosopher, animal trainer—Vicki Hearne is all of these in remarkably equal, and stunningly complementary, measure. As the trainer teaches, it appears, the philosopher learns, and then it is the writer's turn to get it all down, to recount, as Hearne puts it, the stories the animals tell. Nowhere, perhaps, is the perfect blending of Hearne's diverse talents more evident than in *Adam's Task: Calling Animals by Name* (1986), a collection of essays providing rare insight into the minds of the animals that are its subjects. Hearne was born in 1946, graduated from University of California, Riverside, and studied creative writing on a Stegner Fellowship at Stanford University. Now teaching writing at Yale, she is the author of two books of poetry, *Nervous Horses* (1980) and *In the Absence of Horses* (1984); a second book of essays, *Bandit: Dossier of a Dangerous Dog* (1991); a novel, *The White German Shepherd* (1988); and numerous magazine essays.

Your goodness must have some edge to it—else it is none.

—Ralph Waldo Emerson

A disproportionately large number of pit bulls are able to climb trees.

—Richard Stratton

A few years back, when I was living in California, I happened to be looking for a working dog, by which I mean a dog bred to think and to do a job, not just to look pretty while the cameras snap. So I put the word out among the dog people I know. Poodles, bouviers des

Flandres, and the like were pretty low on my list, since I am not fond of grooming (though I should say that Airedales, which need a lot of grooming, are always high on my list). Doberman pinschers and boxers were pretty high on the list, as were English bull terriers. I was really just waiting for a dog with genuine class to show up. I would have looked at a cocker spaniel if someone reliable had told me of a good one.

I heard, eventually, of a litter of puppies in which there was a promising little bitch. They were pit bulls, or what are commonly called pit bulls, though pit bulls are often called by other names, and other breeds are often misidentified as pit bulls—all this a result of newspaper and television and word-of-mouth horror stories about pit bulls, which is what *this* story is about. Anyway, fighting breeds, of which the pit bull is one, were also high on my list, and the pups were within my price range. So I went to take a look. The bitch puppy looked as good in the flesh as she had been made to look in the story I had heard about her. I bought her and named her Belle, a name that may sound fancy to Yankee ears, but a good old down-home name for a nice bitch. In Belle's eyes there was (and is) a certain quiet gleam of mischief and joy; more than that, she had a general air that made it clear that I was going to be dealing with her on *her* terms—and that one of these might be an impulse to make a fool of me.

Belle is mostly white, with some reddish brindle here and there, including, over one eye, a patch that sometimes gives her a raffish air but at other times, when she has her dignity about her (which is about 99 percent of the time), makes her look like the queen of an exotic and powerful nation. Except for that gleam in her eye, she is fairly typical of her breed in that she is very serious about whatever she happens to be doing. I've had her going on three years now, and the most violent thing she has done is this: one day, when her pillows were in the wash, she went about the house appropriating everyone else's pillows. Not *all* of the pillows; only the newer, plumper, more expensive ones. She was quite young when she did this. Maturity has brought with it a sense of the importance of respecting the property rights of others.

In James Thurber's day there were a lot of horror stories around about bloodhounds, and he was exercised enough by these stories to write at least two pieces (including "Lo, Hear the Gentle Bloodhound!") defending these creatures. Of course no one these days believes bloodhounds eat up old ladies and nubile maidens. This, or something like it, is what people have come to believe about pit bulls, largely because of horror stories like the ones repeated on ABC's *20/20* one night last winter: "February 1984, Cleveland, Ohio. Police capture a pit bull terrier who attacked a two-year-old child at a bus stop. December 1984, Davie, Florida. This dog attacked a seven-week-old boy in his crib. The child later died. January 1985, Phoenix, Arizona. A fifty-year-old woman was attacked by her son's dogs when she tried to get into her own house."

These stories have a deceptively straightforward look about them;   5 here, at least, it seems that we know what we're talking about. But it isn't at all clear what the stories are about (or *who* they are about), and I am exercised about this, and want to talk about the stories and about pit bulls.

A word about names. The French philosopher Jacques Derrida once remarked in a lecture about memory and mourning that we never know—that we die without being quite sure—what our proper names are. This is not always obvious to us, except perhaps in the case of some newlyweds. We do not generally feel puzzled or at a loss for an answer when someone asks, "What's your name?" The uncertainty Derrida spoke of is obvious, though, when we turn to the pit bull. There are a number of breeds that are related to the pit bull and are often confused with it. Among these are:

American pit bull dogs	Jack Russell terriers
English bull terriers	Staffordshire bull terriers
French bulldogs	Colored bull terriers
English bulldogs	

Often, in the horror stories published and broadcast and passed along in conversation, other breeds wholly unrelated to the pit bull are accused of being pit bulls. These include:

Doberman pinschers	Rottweilers
Boxers	Collies
Airedales	

I actually read a story about a "pit bull" who turned out to be a collie. The dog was supposed to have hurt a baby; he had not, though he did snap at the infant. When I protested to the newspaper editor that the dog was plainly a collie, the reply was: "But it could have been a pit bull."

The dog I left off the list of genuine relatives of the pit bull is the American Staffordshire terrier, which some American Staffordshire fanciers say is the same breed as the pit bull, as do some serious pit bull people; other members of both groups argue that the breeds are separate. If you own a pit bull, or something like a pit bull, and are tired (as I am) of people clutching their purses and babies and shying away from you whenever they see your dog, just tell them that what you have is an American Staffordshire terrier. Almost no one, so far as I know, is afraid of American Staffordshire terriers.

As for the names of the actual dog under discussion, the possibili-   10
ties include:

Pit bull	American (pit) bull terrier
Pit bull terrier	American pit bull terrier
Bull terrier	American bulldog
American bull terrier	Bulldog

As to the history of the pit bull, it seems clear that at some point an
Englishman bred a terrier with what is often referred to as an English
bulldog. Involved in this history are bear baiting and bull baiting—
especially the latter, as bulls were often baited with dogs before being
killed as a way of tenderizing the meat for human consumption. Dog
fighting, to the death in the pit, also figures in this history. If you were
to try to write an actual history of the breed, you would have to find
out which if any of the following names is a past name for the pit bull
or an ancestor of the pit bull. Some of these are now the names of
definite breeds; others are *probably* names for the pit bull that have
passed out of use. Among these names are:

Irish pit terrier	Bandog
Catch dog	Hog dog
Bear biter	Southern hound
Boar hound	Neopolitan mastiff
Bull biter	Dogue de Bordeaux
Mastiff	Olde bulldogge
Bull mastiff	Argentine dogo
Molossian	Tosa-inu
Bear dog	Colored bull terrier

The United Kennel Club in Kalamazoo, Michigan, after much debating and many divorces, officially named the breed the American
(pit) bull terrier. Affectionate owners call the dog simply pit. What pit
bulls actually are, by the way, are bulldogs, though that is not the real
name of the breed. And those dogs that *are* called bulldogs (including
Handsome Dan, the mascot of the Yale football team) are not in fact
bulldogs at all. They couldn't get a bull to behave if heaven depended
on it for supper. (Still, I should say that Yale, in welcoming my pit bull,
has warmed my heart.)

It was in the early 1970s that the first of the horror stories about pit
bulls appeared. I didn't see the original one—a product of the inflamed
mind of a Chicago journalist, I am told—but as the story was passed
along and picked up and reprinted, polished, and "improved" by every
paper in the country, as far as I could tell (I was doing some traveling
then), I got to read it often. In its various versions, the tale ended to tell
of what natural people-haters pit bulls are—preferring the flesh of elderly women and infants—and of what dog-haters "pit men" are, pit

men being those who breed and handle dogs for organized pit fighting. (Staged dogfights are illegal in all fifty states, and moving dogs across state lines for the purpose of fighting is a federal offense. Fights are organized clandestinely throughout the country.)

At first, I was mildly amused and not especially worried by these stories; I have trained dogs professionally, I know many dog people, and at the time my life was in this world, in which there are no horror stories about pit bulls. Indeed, in this world, pit bulls are generally recognized as an amiable, easygoing lot. If pit bulls have a flaw in their relationship to people, it is that they sometimes show a tendency toward reserve, a kind of aloofness that is a consequence of their being prone to love above all else reflection and meditation. Pit bulls — not all of them, but some — often hang back in social situations they don't understand.

Pit men, who breed and train their dogs to kill others for sport —   15 the fighting-dog men who know what they are about, anyway — will tell you that a pit bull fighter is not a man-hating animal; in fact, a man-hating animal is not likely to survive in the pit, is apt to be a coward, a fear-biter rather than a tough, gamely fighter. In truth, there are very few biters among pit bulls.

You have to know this about fighting dogs, or hunting dogs who take on opponents like mountain lions — any dog in whom the quality called gameness matters: in a true fighting dog there is no ill temper, no petty resentment. I once had an Airedale who was a visionary fighter, a veritable incarnation of the holy Law of the Jaw. (Never let go.) You could tell that Gunner was going into his fight mode by a certain precise and friendly wagging of the tail, a happy pricking of the ears, and a cheerful sparkle in the eye that quickly progressed to an expression of high trance. He was, when he wasn't fighting or thinking about fighting (he didn't think about it all of the time, only when it was appropriate), a dog of enormous charm and wit who never minded playing the fool.

One of the things he liked to do was to climb up the ladders of playground slides and then slide down, with a goofy, droll look in his eyes and his ears flying out. (He looked like a child playing at being an airplane.) His charm was often an annoyance: he always insisted on making an entrance and looking around happily for the cheering section. The only time I knew him to menace a human being happened when he was about a year old. It was late at night, and a man attacked me with a knife, a rather puny sort of knife. That man lost part of his nose and cheek and I don't know what else (it was dark).

Richard Stratton, in *The World of the American Pit Bull Terrier* and elsewhere, writes about the development of the horror stories and their consequences, one of which has been the impounding and in some cases the destruction of pit bulls and other dogs. In San Diego not long ago the good citizens saw to it that an entire line of dogs, on whose development the owner had spent decades, was killed. Later, a court ruled that the killing of the dogs had been illegal, but the corpses of the dogs appear not to have been impressed by this development. Stratton writes of how this peculiar form of "humania" has caught on around the country:

> In each case the approach was the same: the same stories as before were told, to which was added that certain states have very effective laws. Each state was assured that it was the center of dog fighting in America, and wasn't that a shameful "honor"? A news-media blitz characteristically preceded attempts at putting through legislation. In some states, penalties as high as ten years in prison were specified.

One of the standard elements in the horror stories is a gleeful account of how pit bull puppies are trained to be killers by starting them off on declawed kittens. The interesting thing here is that an authentic and intelligent admirer of good fighting dogs would find this an insult to the dogs and to the men who train them to fight—partly because most lovers of pit bulls are saps about animals of all sorts (often they hate hunting), and partly because they have a kind of Nietzschean sense of what counts as a worthy opponent (and kittens, declawed or otherwise, clearly are not). Someone like Richard Stratton would have deep contempt for anyone who would set a pit bull against a *dog* who was not a match. What Stratton and those like him say is roughly this: Look. We're talking about a dog who can stay the round with a porcupine. This dog doesn't need to practice on kittens. Which is to say, the charge of cruelty to kittens is secondary to a more serious charge: the insult to the nobility and courage of a breed.

It wasn't long after I got Belle, my pit bull, that she began to take   20 an interest in the welfare and development of James, my year-old nephew. James would throw a plaything out of reach, and Belle would bring it back to him. James was entranced by this; soon he was spending most of his time throwing playthings out of reach. Belle, with a worried look about her, continued patiently to fetch them.

I must remind you of the seriousness of mind of this breed. It became clear after a short while that Belle was not just "playing fetch." Pit bulls are never just doing *anything*. Belle began bringing James her dumbbell, which I use in training her, and which is not a plaything in her mind; more than that, she began attempting to get him to handle it correctly. This was only natural: Belle's mother had been extremely devoted to the education of Belle and her litter-mates, and Belle takes her responsibilities seriously. She seems to feel that a necessary condition of fully developed humanhood is good dog-training skills; as I watched her trying to get James to hold the dumbbell properly, it dawned on me that she was trying to teach him to train *her*!

Belle's behavior with James is related to a standard pit bull trait, for that matter, standard to all gamely dogs. If purity of heart is to will one thing, as Kierkegaard said it was, then these dogs have purity of heart. A less generous way of putting it is to say that they have one-track minds. Bill Koehler, the father of my friend Dick Koehler and one of the grandest animal trainers the world will ever know, warns owners of such dogs not to play ball with them in the house except on the ground floor, because if the ball goes out the window, so does the dog.

I was talking to Dick Koehler one day about how nice it is to have Belle around, but how hard it is to explain *why*. Dick, a dog trainer like his father, said, "Yeah, it's hard to explain. They are so *aware*." And that's it, that's the quality Belle radiates quietly but unmistakably: awareness of all the shifting gestalts of the spiritual and emotional life around her. She spends a lot of her time just sitting and contemplating people and situations (which is one reason some people are afraid of her). Since in her case this awareness is coupled with a deep gentleness —no bull-in-the-china-shop routines once puppyhood was over— Dick has urged me not to have her spayed, for a while at least.

Dick thinks Belle might be a good "foundation dam" for a line of dogs bred to work with the handicapped. Which brings up another aspect of the horror stories: they tend to be told about just those breeds that are the best prospects for work with, say, the old, or those in wheelchairs. Some readers may remember the stories about German shepherds "turning on their masters"—dogs with whom the safety of the blind can be trusted! I think that the same qualities that make these breeds reliable companions for the more difficult-to-care-for members of our species inspire the horror stories. Belle's refusal to play with strangers who coo at her, which sometimes causes the strangers to fear her, is the quality that would make her reliable in a distracting situation if her quadriplegic master really needed her attentiveness.

Most dogs have an unusual amount of emotional courage in rela-   25
tionship to humans: they are willing and able to keep coming back; they have the heart to turn our emotional static back to us as clarity. But dogs who work with people with various disabilities, including the sort not always regarded as pathologies, such as an addiction to type-writers, need much more of this quality in order to do a proper job of being a dog. Someone who is, or who perceives himself to be, power-less will be querulous from time to time in his handling of a dog, and may occasionally be downright loony. The dog who can keep her cool and continue to do her job under such circumstances has to be more than just cuddly and agreeable, and certainly mustn't have any heart-tugging spookiness in her makeup; such a dog must be prepared to *think* and act in the absence of proper guidance from the master and (as

in the case of guide dogs) even in the face of wrong guidance. For such a dog, love doesn't make a whole lot of sense outside the context of a disciple, a discipline in the older, fuller sense of that word, in which the context is the cosmos and not the classroom. What I am trying to say is, Real love has teeth. A dog with such a capacity to love is able to give the moral law to herself when her master (who, of course, runs the universe from the dog's point of view) fails to act on the law of being.

Pit bulls will often give themselves the moral law. One afternoon, while I was abstractedly working on something, I was startled into consciousness by Belle suddenly giving out, in place of the wimpy puppy-bark I had so far heard (she was about five months old at the time), a full-fledged, grownup, I've-got-duties-around-here bark.

Investigation showed that the meter reader was going into the backyard by the side gate *without asking permission*. So I said, "What's up, Pup?" and put her on her leash and followed her outside to check the situation out. (This is part of the handling of a dog like Belle, a procedure designed to show respect for and encourage the dog's instinct to protect while making it clear that she must think and exercise judgment.) When we got outside I said, "Oh. That's just the meter reader, and you don't have to worry about him." Then, putting Belle on a "stand-for-examination"—an exercise in which the dog is not allowed to move toward or away from anyone or anything—I asked the meter reader to pet her.

He refused, saying that he was afraid of her. This worried me a bit, since Belle was only a puppy, and while it wasn't too early in her career for her to be barking at strangers who enter the premises without asking permission, she was too young to be seriously menacing anyone. So I asked if she had ever tried to bite him, or whatever.

He said that Belle had never bothered him, but that he carried liver treats with him on his rounds in order to "make friends" with the dogs, and the only dog who had refused his liver treats had been Belle. No, ma'am, she didn't growl or anything, just turned her head away.

I refrained from telling him how rapidly anyone who offers a bribe   30 to a pit bull sinks in the dog's estimation, really plummets; I simply suggested that in the future he knock on the front door when he came to read the meter and I would make sure the dog was in the house. After that Belle, understanding the situation, announced his arrival with two precise barks and otherwise seemed content to let him do his job—though she did keep an eye on him.

The meter reader incident filled me with dog-owner pride; but it also made me aware of the responsibility I had assumed in taking on a dog who needed no training to know a bribe when she saw one. I don't mean that I am afraid she is going to bite me, but that any unfairness or sloppiness in the way I handle her will be made known to me.

What Belle has is an ability to act with moral clarity, and this is a result of having qualities that have to do with real love, love with teeth. Do we tell horror stories about dogs because it is love that horrifies us?

Training Belle often seems astonishingly easy. This is not unusual with these dogs; I have friends with pit bulls who speak of having the sensation that they aren't so much training the dogs as reminding them of something. And yet there are people in other dog circles who wonder whether it is possible to train pit bulls (and dogs like them) at all. This is because these dogs are unresponsive to anything short of genuine training. Belle is as honest as daylight about her work, and because of that my training technique has had to improve a lot: she does not respond if I do something wrong. She is committed to her training, and she expects me to be; it is easy to mess these dogs up precisely because they know so much about how their training ought to go. Once I picked up Belle's leash and some other equipment, preparing to take her outside. But before I could get out the door, I got involved in a conversation—I got distracted. Belle barked three times, sharply, to remind me of my duties. It was a trivial conversation; she doesn't interrupt me when I'm giving my attention to something important.

When Belle was only a few months old I taught her that before she goes through any door to go outside, she must sit and wait for the release command. This was easy to do, as Belle takes to domestic order. Then I went out of town for a week, leaving Belle—with her new sit-and-wait discipline—in the care of a friend. My friend is a splendid woman, no two ways about it, but she never has seen the point of training the poor dogs (as she puts it), who would rather be left alone. When I got back I was told that Belle, no matter how full her bladder was, resisted going through the door. My friend would swing open the door and expect Belle to skip through—despite the fact that I had told her about Belle's command. My friend tried coaxing and cooing her through the door. Belle would lie down flat, ears and tail low and immobile—a melancholy imitation of the Rock of Gibraltar being her usual response to coaxing, flattery, and insults.

I didn't travel again until I felt Belle had a little more experience   35 under her belt; maturity makes all of us less vulnerable to the various inconsistencies life brings. While she was still young, it was possible to break her heart—and a broken-hearted pit bull was not something I wanted to have around. My decision to stay home with Belle, by the way, was less a comment on my temperament than on hers—and on the way pit bulls inspire devotion. And this is why the ladies and gentlemen who want to exterminate pit bulls may win some battles but will never win the war.

Belle was still a puppy, and not a very big one—three months old, maybe fifteen pounds—the first time I took her to the campus of the

University of California at Riverside, where I was teaching. I went into the department office with Belle at heel, and one of the secretaries was so struck with terror that she couldn't speak. It was the horror stories, of course. A friend came in, assessed the situation, and asked the secretary, "What's wrong, Frieda?"

"Tha . . . tha . . . that . . . *dog!*"

"But it's only a puppy."

"That doesn't matter with these dogs. They're born killers."

Belle was by now looking at the secretary in uneasy puzzlement; 40 just a puppy, she didn't know anything about the horror stories. But now she had had her first lesson. I suspect that some pit bulls, once they come to grips with the horror stories, do start biting people who send out the wrong signals. Belle, as it happens, didn't start biting, and very few pit bulls do, but I wouldn't have blamed her if she had.

Anyway, for months, whenever Frieda's path and mine crossed on campus she would sidle along a wall, as far from Belle as she could get, or duck into the nearest doorway until we were safely past. Frieda would behave, in short, like a guilty woman; and dogs, like people, figure that behavior of this sort is suspicious. So Belle, because of the damned horror stories, is more wary than she would otherwise have been.

Then there are the horror stories about me: Belle is plainly the outward sign of my inner viciousness. Some of the expressions of this get back to me: "Oh yes. Vicki Hearne. She has a very repressive ideology. She keeps a pit bull, you know." Also: "Vicki is a threat to the collegiate atmosphere, with that dog of hers." This may be true, since I don't know what a collegiate atmosphere is. And of course there is: "She *delights* in harboring vicious animals."

In time, though, Belle herself began effecting changes in these stories. The serenity and sweetness she radiates is so strong that it can't help but be felt by all but the most distant of the tale-tellers. So recently what I have started hearing is, "Vicki, I don't know where you get off thinking that's a vicious dog. That dog wouldn't hurt a butterfly; a real patsy if I ever saw one!" Or: "Vicki likes to think she's tough, but I'll bet she can't bring herself to give a grade lower than B+, and just look at that mushy dog of hers!"

It is this, the way the horror stories can so easily flip over, that suggests that we are on to something. "That dog wouldn't hurt a butterfly" and "born killer" are part of the same logical structure, the same story—an insight I owe largely to Stanley Cavell's *The Claim of Reason*, in which he writes:

> The role of Outsider might be played, say in a horror movie, by a
> dog, mankind's best friend. Then the dog allegorizes the escape from
> human nature (required in order to know of the existence of others)

in such a way that we see the requirement is not necessarily for greater (super-human) intelligence. The dog sniffs something, a difference, something in the air. And it is important that we do not regard the dog as honest; merely as without decision in the matter. He is obeying his nature, as he always does, must.

It is important to tellers of dog horror stories that "we do not regard the dog as honest; merely as without decision in the matter." The dog has no moral dimension: *that* is the hidden and stinging part of the logic of these stories.

Consider the falseness of "wouldn't hurt a butterfly." As it happens, 45 Belle would nail anyone who threatened me seriously, and right now. Notice that I said *seriously*—she wouldn't do anything to a guy who just grabbed my arm and wanted to talk. What I have been saying about this dog is that she has extraordinarily good judgment, which means that I do "regard the dog as honest," and not as "without decision in the matter." So, she is not obeying her nature in the way, say, that a falling stone is obeying its nature. She is not morally inert.

I would like to talk briefly about a painting titled *I'm Neutral, But Not Afraid of Any of Them*, dated 1914 and signed by Wallace Robinson. It depicts the heads of five dogs. From left to right are: English bulldog, German dachshund, American pit bull terrier, French bulldog, Russian wolfhound. Each dog is wearing the uniform of his country, and the pit bull, which not only is in the center but is also larger than the others, has an American flag tied sportively around his neck. It is the pit bull who is saying, "I'm neutral, but not afraid of any of them." This is plainly part of a story America was telling itself about the war in Europe. It was a story *about* Americans. In a tight spot, it was not such a bad story to be telling. The pit bull here, as in many other places (Thurber's tales and drawings, or Pete the Pup of *Our Gang*), is an emblem of what is used to be possible to think of as American virtues: independence, ingenuity, cooperation, a certain rakish humor, the refusal of the aristocratic pseudo-virtues of Europe.

These values and visions have failed; the new stories about pit bulls are also stories about Americans, about an America that seems to have gone out of its mind—about how skittish, and dangerously so, we have become. And it is not only in the "text" of the pit bull that this can be read. I am addicted to dog stories of all sorts—the most awful, sentimental children's tale will do. These stories have changed as radically as the stories about pit bulls. Most of the older dog stories were not written with Thurber's canny intelligence and humor, but in them there were generally children, and a dog, and the children learned from the dog's courage, loyalty, or wit how to clarify their own stances in the world. In the new sort of story, the initial situation is the same—the dog remains for the child the only point of emotional clarity in a shifting world. But today there is the possibility that halfway through the book the dog will be poisoned.

Dick Koehler and his father and hosts of other trainers, including the monks of New Skete, a Franciscan order (see their book, *How to Be Your Dog's Best Friend*), speak contemptuously of the "humaniacs" who babble about "affection training" and the dog "who only needs understanding." These trainers' contempt for kindness is a Nietzschean maneuver; it is not kindness itself that is being refused, but rather the word *kind*, because the word has become contaminated.

But *kind* is a good word, and I find myself wanting it back. I don't have room here to do a full job of reclaiming it, but I can at least recall that the word has a history. C. S. Lewis has more than once discussed the history of *kind*; this is from *The Discarded Image*:

> In medieval science the fundamental concept was that of certain sympathies, antipathies, and strivings inherent in matter itself. Everything has its right place, its home, the region that suits it, and, if not forcibly restrained, moves thither by a sort of homing instinct:
>
> > Every kindly thing that is
> > Hath a kindly stede there he
> > May best in hit conserved be
> > Unto which place everything
> > Through his kindly enclyning
> > Moveth for to come to.
> >   (Chaucer, *Hous of Fame*, II, 730 sq.)
>
> Thus, while every falling body for us illustrates the "law" of gravitation, for them it illustrated the "kindly enclyning" of terrestrial bodies to their "kindly stede" the Earth, the center of the Mundus.

What I would like to say is this: to be kind to a creature may mean being what we call harsh (though not cruel), but it always means respecting the *kind* of being the creature is, and the deepest kindness is the natural kind, in which your being is matched to the creature's, perhaps by a kindly inclining.

Understanding kindness in this way leads to an understanding that it is about as cruel to match pit bulls against each other in properly regulated matches as it is to take healthy greyhounds out for runs. In making that remark I do not imagine that I have settled the issue, only gestured at what a complicated matter it would be to raise it properly. And I don't intend to fight Belle, even though I understand that a breeding program managed by knowledgeable people who breed their fighters only from dogs showing gameness and stamina in properly managed pit fights can be as fine a thing as human beings are capable of.

Perhaps it is time for me to say emphatically that my praise of pit bulls should not be construed as advice that anyone should rush out and get one. They do like to fight other dogs, and they are, as you must realize by now, a tremendous spiritual responsibility. For example, once it turned out that I hadn't worked with Belle on retrieving for three days. I was lazing about, reading in bed, on the left side of the bed. Belle brought me her dumbbell and stared at me loudly. (Pit bulls can stare loudly without making a sound.) I said, "Oh, not now Belle. In a few minutes." She dumped the dumbbell on top of the book I was reading, put her paws upon the edge of the bed, and bit my hand, very precisely. She took the trouble to bite my *right* hand, even though my left one hung within easy reach. She bit, that is, the hand with which I throw the dumbbell when we are working. A gentle bite, I should say, but also just. An inherently excellent moment of exactitude: love with teeth.

Pit bulls give you the opportunity to know, should you want so terrible a knowledge, whether your relationships are coherent; whether your notion of love is a truncated, distorted, and free-floating bit of the debris of Romanticism or a discipline that can renew the resources of consciousness.

If you're ready for it, and can find a *real* dog trainer to help you figure out what you're doing, then go to. But be prepared. When these dogs are in motion, they are awesome. Still, for most people, this awesomeness is not the most hazardous trait. There is something more subtle. If, for example, your boss comes over for dinner and coos at your dog or perhaps offers her an hors d'oeuvre, and the dog regards him impassively or turns away, the boss's feelings will be hurt, and your job may be in jeopardy. Moreover, if the boss later gets tipsy and tries to insult your dog, he will get the same treatment. And, be sure your spouse or lover is not the sort of person whose feelings will be so hurt. The dog, remember, has the power to compel your loyalty.

Questions

1. Hearne passes along horror stories about pit bulls, but instead of transmitting those urban legends intact, she dismantles them: "I actually read a story about a 'pit bull' who turned out to be a collie," she writes. "The dog was supposed to have hurt a baby; he had not, though he did snap at the infant." Locate other instances in this essay where Hearne disputes the facts of the pit bull horror stories. Can you describe the elements of these stories? Does Hearne? Why might she be interested in their morphology? Consider her comments in paragraph 5 in your answer.

2. Hearne ushers in her subject by recounting her search for a good

working dog, which made her confront the "horror stories about pit bulls, which is what *this* story is about." She is conscious of the powers of narrative, of storytelling, in this essay, and she searches for reasons for why we might tell stories about pit bulls. She thinks these stories might reflect on our national character. Consider paragraphs 46 and 47 and analyze how Hearne makes the connection from characterizing a dog to characterizing a nation.

Annie Dillard

TOTAL ECLIPSE

Annie Dillard won the Pulitzer Prize in 1974 for her very first published prose, *Pilgrim at Tinker Creek*. Although Dillard maintains that her success was not quite as easy nor as instant as it might seem—it required long hours of work, not in an idyllic natural setting, but in the dull confines of a library carrel—still she was doing something she truly cared about. "It's all a matter of keeping my eyes open," Dillard writes, and in her subsequent work, too, she has continued to demonstrate a passion for learning to "see truly." Dillard was born in Pennsylvania in 1945 and earned a B.A. (1967) and M.A. (1968) from Hollins College. She is currently a contributing editor to *Harper's* magazine, and among her books are *Living by Fiction* (1982), *Teaching a Stone to Talk: Expeditions and Encounters* (1982), and *An American Childhood* (1987).

I

*I*t had been like dying, the sliding down the mountain pass. It had been like the death of someone, irrational, that sliding down the mountain pass and into the region of dread. It was like slipping into fever, or falling down that hole in sleep from which you wake yourself whimpering. We had crossed the mountains that day, and now we were in a strange place—a hotel in central Washington, in a town near Yakima.

The eclipse we had traveled here to see would occur early in the next morning.

I lay in bed. My husband, Gary, was reading beside me. I lay in bed and looked at the painting on the hotel room wall. It was a print of a detailed and lifelike painting of a smiling clown's head, made out of vegetables. It was a painting of the sort which you do not intend to look at, and which, alas, you never forget. Some tasteless fate presses it upon you; it becomes part of the complex interior junk you carry with you wherever you go. Two years have passed since the total eclipse of which I write. During those years I have forgotten, I assume, a great many things I wanted to remember—but I have not forgotten that clown painting or its lunatic setting in the old hotel.

The clown was bald. Actually, he wore a clown's tight rubber wig, painted white; this stretched over the top of his skull, which was a cabbage. His hair was bunches of baby carrots. Inset in his white clown makeup, and in his cabbage skull, were his small and laughing human eyes. The clown's glance was like the glance of Rembrandt in some of the self-portraits: lively, knowing, deep, and loving. The crinkled shadows around his eyes were string beans. His eyebrows were parsley. Each of his ears was a broad bean. His thin, joyful lips were red chili peppers; between his lips were wet rows of human teeth and a suggestion of a real tongue. The clown print was framed in gilt and glassed.

To put ourselves in the path of the total eclipse, that day we had driven five hours inland from the Washington coast, where we lived. When we tried to cross the Cascades range, an avalanche had blocked the pass.

A slope's worth of snow blocked the road; traffic backed up. Had the avalanche buried any cars that morning? We could not learn. This highway was the only winter road over the mountains. We waited as highway crews bulldozed a passage through the avalanche. With two-by-fours and walls of plywood, they erected a one-way, roofed tunnel through the avalanche. We drove through the avalanche tunnel, crossed the pass, and descended several thousand feet into central Washington and the broad Yakima valley, about which we knew only that it was orchard country. As we lost altitude, the snows disappeared; our ears popped; the trees changed, and in the trees were strange birds. I watched the landscape innocently, like a fool, like a diver in the rapture of the deep who plays on the bottom while his air runs out.

The hotel lobby was a dark, derelict room, narrow as a corridor, and seemingly without air. We waited on a couch while the manager vanished upstairs to do something unknown to our room. Beside us on an overstuffed chair, absolutely motionless, was a platinum-blond woman in her forties wearing a black silk dress and a strand of pearls. Her long legs were crossed; she supported her head on her fist. At the dim far end of the room, their backs toward us, sat six bald old men in their shirtsleeves, around a loud television. Two of them seemed asleep. They were drunks. "Number six!" cried the man on television. "Number six!"

On the broad lobby desk, lighted and bubbling, was a ten-gallon aquarium containing one large fish; the fish tilted up and down in its water. Against the long opposite wall sang a live canary in its cage. Beneath the cage, among spilled millet seeds on the carpet, were a decorated child's sand bucket and matching sand shovel.

Now the alarm was set for six. I lay awake remembering an article I had read downstairs in the lobby, in an engineering magazine. The article was about gold mining.

In South Africa, in India, and in South Dakota, the gold mines extend so deeply into the earth's crust that they are hot. The rock walls burn the miners' hands. The companies have to air-condition the mines; if the air conditioners break, the miners die. The elevators in the mine shafts run very slowly, down, and up, so the miners' ears will not pop in their skulls. When the miners return to the surface, their faces are deathly pale.

Early the next morning we checked out. It was February 26, 1979, 10 a Monday morning. We would drive out of town, find a hilltop, watch the eclipse, and then drive back over the mountains and home to the coast. How familiar things are here; how adept we are; how smoothly and professionally we check out! I had forgotten the clown's smiling head and the hotel lobby as if they had never existed. Gary put the car in gear and off we went, as off we have gone to a hundred other adventures.

It was dawn when we found a highway out of town and drove into the unfamiliar countryside. By the growing light we could see a band of cirrostratus clouds in the sky. Later the rising sun would clear these clouds before the eclipse began. We drove at random until we came to a range of unfenced hills. We pulled off the highway, bundled up, and climbed one of these hills.

II

The hill was five hundred feet high. Long winter-killed grass covered it, as high as our knees. We climbed and rested, sweating in the cold; we passed clumps of bundled people on the hillside who were setting up telescopes and fiddling with cameras. The top of the hill stuck up in the middle of the sky. We tightened our scarves and looked around.

East of us rose another hill like ours. Between the hills, far below, was the highway which threaded south into the valley. This was the Yakima valley; I had never seen it before. It is justly famous for its beauty, like every planted valley. It extended south into the horizon, a distant dream of a valley, a Shangri-la. All its hundreds of low, golden slopes bore orchards. Among the orchards were towns, and roads, and plowed and fallow fields. Through the valley wandered a thin shining river; from the river extended fine, frozen irrigation ditches. Distance blurred and blued the sight, so that the whole valley looked like a thickness or sediment at the bottom of the sky. Directly behind us was more sky, and empty lowlands blued by distance, and Mount Adams. Mount Adams was an enormous, snow-covered volcanic cone rising flat, like so much scenery.

Now the sun was up. We could not see it; but the sky behind the band of clouds was yellow, and, far down the valley, some hillside orchards had lighted up. More people were parking near the highway and climbing the hills. It was the West. All of us rugged individuals were wearing knit caps and blue nylon parkas. People were climbing the nearby hills and setting up shop in clumps among the dead grasses. It looked as though we had gathered on hilltops to pray for the world on its last day. It looked as though we had all crawled out of spaceships and were preparing to assault the valley below. It looked as though we were scattered on hilltops at dawn to sacrifice virgins, make rain, set stone stelae in a ring. There was no place out of the wind. The straw grasses banged our legs.

Up in the sky where we stood the air was lusterless yellow. To the   15 west the sky was blue. Now the sun cleared the clouds. We cast rough shadows on the blowing grass; freezing, we waved our arms. Near the sun, the sky was bright and colorless. There was nothing to see.

It began with no ado. It was odd that such a well-advertised public event should have no starting gun, no overture, no introductory speaker. I should have known right then that I was out of my depth. Without pause or preamble, silent as orbits, a piece of the sun went away. We looked at it through welders' goggles. A piece of the sun was missing; in its place we saw empty sky.

I had seen a partial eclipse in 1970. A partial eclipse is very interesting. It bears almost no relation to a total eclipse. Seeing a partial eclipse bears the same relation to seeing a total eclipse as kissing a man does to marrying him, or as flying in an airplane does to falling out of an airplane. Although the one experience precedes the other, it in no way prepares you for it. During a partial eclipse the sky does not darken—not even when 94 percent of the sun is hidden. Nor does the sun, seen colorless through protective devices, seem terribly strange. We have all seen a sliver of light in the sky; we have all seen the crescent moon by day. However, during a partial eclipse the air does indeed get cold, precisely as if someone were standing between you and the fire. And blackbirds do fly back to their roosts. I had seen a partial eclipse before, and here was another.

What you see in an eclipse is entirely different from what you know. It is especially different for those of us whose grasp of astronomy is so frail that, given a flashlight, a grapefruit, two oranges, and fifteen years, we still could not figure out which way to set the clocks for Daylight Saving Time. Usually it is a bit of a trick to keep your knowledge from blinding you. But during an eclipse it is easy. What you see is much more convincing than any wild-eyed theory you may know.

You may read that the moon has something to do with eclipses. I have never seen the moon yet. You do not see the moon. So near the sun, it is as completely invisible as the stars are by day. What you see before your eyes is the sun going through phases. It gets narrower and narrower, as the waning moon does, and, like the ordinary moon, it travels alone in the simple sky. The sky is of course background. It does not appear to eat the sun; it is far behind the sun. The sun simply shaves away; gradually, you see less sun and more sky.

The sky's blue was deepening, but there was no darkness. The sun 20 was a wide crescent, like a segment of tangerine. The wind freshened and blew steadily over the hill. The eastern hill across the highway grew dusky and sharp. The towns and orchards in the valley to the south were dissolving into the blue light. Only the thin river held a trickle of sun.

Now the sky to the west deepened to indigo, a color never seen. A dark sky usually loses color. This was a saturated, deep indigo, up in the air. Stuck up into that unworldly sky was the cone of Mount Adams, and the alpenglow was upon it. The alpenglow is that red light of sunset which holds out on snowy mountaintops long after the valleys and tablelands are dimmed. "Look at Mount Adams," I said, and that was the last sane moment I remember.

I turned back to the sun. It was going. The sun was going, and the world was wrong. The grasses were wrong; they were platinum. Their every detail of stem, head, and blade shone lightless and artificially distinct as an art photographer's platinum print. This color has never been seen on earth. The hues were metallic; their finish was matte. The hillside was a nineteenth-century tinted photograph from which the tints had faded. All the people you see in the photograph, distinct and detailed as their faces look, are now dead. The sky was navy blue. My hands were silver. All the distant hills' grasses were finespun metal which the wind laid down. I was watching a faded color print of a movie filmed in the Middle Ages; I was standing in it, by some mistake. I was standing in a movie of hillside grasses filmed in the Middle Ages. I missed my own century, the people I knew, and the real light of day.

I looked at Gary. He was in the film. Everything was lost. He was a platinum print, a dead artist's version of life. I saw on his skull the darkness of night mixed with the colors of day. My mind was going out; my eyes were receding the way galaxies recede to the rim of space. Gary was light-years away, gesturing inside a circle of darkness, down the wrong end of a telescope. He smiled as if he saw me; the stringy crinkles around his eyes moved. The sight of him, familiar and wrong, was something I was remembering from centuries hence, from the other side of death: yes, *that* is the way he used to look, when we were living. When it was our generation's turn to be alive. I could not hear him; the wind was too loud. Behind him the sun was going. We had all started down a chute of time. At first it was pleasant; now there was no stopping it. Gary was chuting away across space, moving and talking and catching my eye, chuting down the long corridor of separation. The skin on his face moved like thin bronze plating that would peel.

The grass at our feet was wild barley. It was the wild einkorn wheat which grew on the hilly flanks of the Zagros Mountains, above the Euphrates valley, above the valley of the river we called *River*. We harvested the grass with stone sickles, I remember. We found the grasses on the hillsides; we built our shelter beside them and cut them down. That is how he used to look then, that one, moving and living and catching my eye, with the sky so dark behind him, and the wind blowing. God save our life.

From all the hills came screams. A piece of sky beside the crescent 25 sun was detaching. It was a loosened circle of evening sky, suddenly lighted from the back. It was an abrupt black body out of nowhere; it was a flat disk; it was almost over the sun. That is when there were screams. At once this disk of sky slid over the sun like a lid. The sky snapped over the sun like a lens cover. The hatch in the brain slammed. Abruptly it was dark night, on the land and in the sky. In the night sky was a tiny ring of light. The hole where the sun belongs is very small. A thin ring of light marked its place. There was no sound. The eyes dried, the arteries drained, the lungs hushed. There was no world. We were the world's dead people rotating and orbiting around and around, embedded in the planet's crust, while the earth rolled down. Our minds were light-years distant, forgetful of almost everything. Only an extraordinary act of will could recall to us our former, living selves and our contexts in matter and time. We had, it seems, loved the planet and loved our lives, but could no longer remember the way of them. We got the light wrong. In the sky was something that should not be there. In the black sky was a ring of light. It was a thin ring, an old, thin silver wedding band, an old, worn ring. It was an old wedding band in the sky, or a morsel of bone. There were stars. It was all over.

III

It is now that the temptation is strongest to leave these regions. We have seen enough; let's go. Why burn our hands any more than we have to? But two years have passed; the price of gold has risen. I return to the same buried alluvial beds and pick through the strata again.

I saw, early in the morning, the sun diminish against a backdrop of sky. I saw a circular piece of that sky appear, suddenly detached, blackened, and backlighted; from nowhere it came and overlapped the sun. It did not look like the moon. It was enormous and black. If I had not read that it was the moon, I could have seen the sight a hundred times and never thought of the moon once. (If, however, I had not read that it was the moon—if, like most of the world's people throughout time, I had simply glanced up and seen this thing—then I doubtless would not have speculated much, but would have, like Emperor Louis of Bavaria in 840, simply died of fright on the spot.) It did not look like a dragon, although it looked more like a dragon than the moon. It looked like a lens cover, or the lid of a pot. It materialized out of thin air— black, and flat, and sliding, outlined in flame.

Seeing this black body was like seeing a mushroom cloud. The heart screeched. The meaning of the sight overwhelmed its fascination. It obliterated meaning itself. If you were to glance out one day and see a row of mushroom clouds rising on the horizon, you would know at once that what you were seeing, remarkable as it was, was intrinsically not worth remarking. No use running to tell anyone. Significant as it was, it did not matter a whit. For what is significance? It is significance for people. No people, no significance. This is all I have to tell you.

In the deeps are the violence and terror of which psychology has warned us. But if you ride these monsters deeper down, if you drop with them farther over the world's rim, you find what our sciences cannot locate or name, the substrate, the ocean or matrix or ether which buoys the rest, which gives goodness its power for good, and evil its power for evil, the unified field: our complex and inexplicable caring for each other, and for our life together here. This is given. It is not learned.

The world which lay under darkness and stillness following the closing of the lid was not the world we know. The event was over. Its devastation lay around about us. The clamoring mind and heart stilled, almost indifferent, certainly disembodied, frail, and exhausted. The hills were hushed, obliterated. Up in the sky, like a crater from some distant cataclysm, was a hollow ring.

You have seen photographs of the sun taken during a total eclipse. The corona fills the print. All of those photographs were taken through telescopes. The lenses of telescopes and cameras can no more cover the breadth and scale of the visual array than language can cover the breadth and simultaneity of internal experience. Lenses enlarge the sight, omit its context, and make of it a pretty and sensible picture, like something on a Christmas card. I assure you, if you send any shepherds a Christmas card on which is printed a three-by-three photograph of the angel of the Lord, the glory of the Lord, and a multitude of the heavenly host, they will not be sore afraid. More fearsome things can come in envelopes. More moving photographs than those of the sun's corona can appear in magazines. But I pray you will never see anything more awful in the sky.

You see the wide world swaddled in darkness; you see a vast breadth of hilly land, and an enormous, distant, blackened valley; you see towns' lights, a river's path, and blurred portions of your hat and scarf; you see your husband's face looking like an early black-and-white film; and you see a sprawl of black sky and blue sky together, with unfamiliar stars in it, some barely visible bands of cloud, and over there, a small white ring. The ring is as small as one goose in a flock of migrating geese — if you happen to notice a flock of migrating geese. It is one 360th part of the visible sky. The sun we see is less than half the diameter of a dime held at arm's length.

The Crab Nebula, in the constellation Taurus, looks, through binoculars, like a smoke ring. It is a star in the process of exploding. Light from its explosion first reached the earth in 1054; it was a supernova then, and so bright it shone in the daytime. Now it is not so bright, but it is still exploding. It expands at the rate of seventy million miles a day. It is interesting to look through binoculars at something expanding seventy million miles a day. It does not budge. Its apparent size does not increase. Photographs of the Crab Nebula taken fifteen years ago seem identical to photographs of it taken yesterday. Some lichens are similar. Botanists have measured some ordinary lichens twice, at fifty-year intervals, without detecting any growth at all. And yet their cells divide; they live.

The small ring of light was like these things — like a ridiculous lichen up in the sky, like a perfectly still explosion 4,200 light-years away: it was interesting, and lovely, and in witless motion, and it had nothing to do with anything.

It had nothing to do with anything. The sun was too small, and too 35
cold, and too far away, to keep the world alive. The white ring was not enough. It was feeble and worthless. It was as useless as a memory; it was as off kilter and hollow and wretched as a memory.

When you try your hardest to recall someone's face, or the look of a place, you see in your mind's eye some vague and terrible sight such as this. It is dark; it is insubstantial; it is all wrong.

The white ring and the saturated darkness made the earth and the sky look as they must look in the memories of the careless dead. What I saw, what I seemed to be standing in, was all the wrecked light that the memories of the dead could shed upon the living world. We had all died in our boots on the hilltops of Yakima, and were alone in eternity. Empty space stoppered our eyes and mouths; we cared for nothing. We remembered our living days wrong. With great effort we had remembered some sort of circular light in the sky—but only the outline. Oh, and then the orchard trees withered, the ground froze, the glaciers slid down the valleys and overlapped the towns. If there had ever been people on earth, nobody knew it. The dead had forgotten those they had loved. The dead were parted one from the other and could no longer remember the faces and lands they had loved in the light. They seemed to stand on darkened hilltops, looking down.

IV

We teach our children one thing only, as we were taught: to wake up. We teach our children to look alive there, to join by words and activities the life of human culture on the planet's crust. As adults we are almost all adept at waking up. We have so mastered the transition we have forgotten we ever learned it. Yet it is a transition we make a hundred times a day, as, like so many will-less dolphins, we plunge and surface, lapse and emerge. We live half our waking lives and all of our sleeping lives in some private, useless, and insensible waters we never mention or recall. Useless, I say. Valueless, I might add—until someone hauls their wealth up to the surface and into the wide-awake city, in a form that people can use.

I do not know how we got to the restaurant. Like Roethke, "I take my waking slow." Gradually I seemed more or less alive and already forgetful. It was now almost nine in the morning. It was the day of a solar eclipse in central Washington, and a fine adventure for everyone. The sky was clear; there was a fresh breeze out of the north.

The restaurant was a roadside place with tables and booths. The other eclipse-watchers were there. From our booth we could see their cars' California license plates, their University of Washington parking stickers. Inside the restaurant we were all eating eggs or waffles; people were fairly shouting and exchanging enthusiasms, like fans after a World Series game. Did you see . . . ? Did you see . . . ? Then somebody said something which knocked me for a loop. 40

A college student, a boy in a blue parka who carried a Hasselblad, said to us, "Did you see that little white ring? It looked like a Life Saver. It looked like a Life Saver up in the sky."

And so it did. The boy spoke well. He was a walking alarm clock. I myself had at that time no access to such a word. He could write a sentence, and I could not. I grabbed that Life Saver and rode it to the surface. And I had to laugh. I had been dumbstruck on the Euphrates River, I had been dead and gone and grieving, all over the sight of something which, if you could claw your way up to that level, you would grant looked very much like a Life Saver. It was good to be back among people so clever; it was good to have all the world's words at the mind's disposal, so the mind could begin its task. All those things for which we have no words are lost. The mind—the culture—has two little tools, grammar and lexicon: a decorated sand bucket and a matching shovel. With these we bluster about the continents and do all the world's work. With these we try to save our very lives.

There are a few more things to tell from this level, the level of the restaurant. One is the old joke about breakfast. "It can never be satisfied, the mind, never." Wallace Stevens wrote that, and in the long run he was right. The mind wants to live forever, or to learn a very good reason why not. The mind wants the world to return its love, or its awareness; the mind wants to know all the world, and all eternity, and God. The mind's sidekick, however, will settle for two eggs over easy.

The dear, stupid body is as easily satisfied as a spaniel. And, incredibly, the simple spaniel can lure the brawling mind to its dish. It is everlastingly funny that the proud, metaphysically ambitious, clamoring mind will hush if you give it an egg.

Further: while the mind reels in deep space, while the mind grieves 45 or fears or exults, the workaday senses, in ignorance or idiocy, like so many computer terminals printing out market prices while the world blows up, still transcribe their little data and transmit them to the warehouse in the skull. Later, under the tranquilizing influence of fried eggs, the mind can sort through this data. The restaurant was a halfway house, a decompression chamber. There I remembered a few things more.

The deepest, and most terrifying, was this: I have said that I heard screams. (I have since read that screaming, with hysteria, is a common reaction even to expected total eclipses.) People on all the hillsides, including, I think, myself, screamed when the black body of the moon detached from the sky and rolled over the sun. But something else was happening at that same instant, and it was this, I believe, which made us scream.

The second before the sun went out we saw a wall of dark shadow come speeding at us. We no sooner saw it than it was upon us, like thunder. It roared up the valley. It slammed our hill and knocked us out. It was the monstrous swift shadow cone of the moon. I have since read that this wave shadow moves 1,800 miles an hour. It was 195 miles wide. No end was in sight—you saw only the edge. It rolled at you across the land at 1,800 miles an hour, hauling darkness like plague behind it. Seeing it, and knowing it was coming straight for you, was like feeling a slug of anesthetic shoot up your arm. If you think very fast, you may have time to think, "Soon it will hit my brain." You can feel the deadness race up your arm; you can feel the appalling, inhuman speed of your own blood. We saw the wall of shadow coming, and screamed before it hit.

This was the universe about which we have read so much and never before felt: the universe as a clockwork of loose spheres flung at stupefying, unauthorized speeds. How could anything moving so fast not crash, not veer from its orbit amok like a car out of control on a turn?

Less than two minutes later, when the sun emerged, the trailing edge of the shadow cone sped away. It coursed down our hill and raced eastward over the plain, faster than the eye could believe; it swept over the plain and dropped over the planet's rim in a twinkling. It had clobbered us, and now it roared away. We blinked in the light. It was as though an enormous, loping god in the sky had reached down and slapped the earth's face.

Something else, something more ordinary, came back to me along 50 about the third cup of coffee. During the moments of totality, it was so dark that drivers on the highway below turned on their cars' headlights. We could see the highway's route as a strand of lights. It was bumper-to-bumper down there. It was eight-fifteen in the morning, Monday morning, and people were driving into Yakima to work. That it was as dark as night, and eerie as hell, an hour after dawn, apparently meant that in order to *see* to drive to work, people had to use their headlights. Four or five cars pulled off the road. The rest, in a line at least five miles long, drove to town. The highway ran between hills; the people could not have seen any of the eclipsed sun at all. Yakima will have another total eclipse in 2086. Perhaps, in 2086, businesses will give their employees an hour off.

From the restaurant we drove back to the coast. The highway crossing the Cascades range was open. We drove over the mountain like old pros. We joined our places on the planet's thin crust; it held. For the time being, we were home free.

Early that morning at six, when we had checked out, the six bald men were sitting on folding chairs in the dim hotel lobby. The televi-

sion was on. Most of them were awake. You might drown in your own
spittle, God knows, at any time; you might wake up dead in a small
hotel, a cabbage head watching TV while snows pile up in the passes,
watching TV while the chili peppers smile and the moon passes over
the sun and nothing changes and nothing is learned because you have
lost your bucket and shovel and no longer care. What if you regain the
surface and open your sack and find, instead of treasure, a beast which
jumps at you? Or you may not come back at all. The winches may jam,
the scaffolding buckle, the air conditioning collapse. You may glance up
one day and see by your headlamp the canary keeled over in its cage.
You may reach into a cranny for pearls and touch a moray eel. You
yank on your rope; it is too late.

Apparently people share a sense of these hazards, for when the
total eclipse ended, an odd thing happened.

When the sun appeared as a blinding bead on the ring's side, the
eclipse was over. The black lens cover appeared again, backlighted, and
slid away. At once the yellow light made the sky blue again; the black lid
dissolved and vanished. The real world began there. I remember now: we
all hurried away. We were born and bored at a stroke. We rushed down
the hill. We found our car; we saw the other people streaming down the
hillsides; we joined the highway traffic and drove away.

We never looked back. It was a general vamoose, and an odd one, 55
for when we left the hill, the sun was still partially eclipsed—a sight
rare enough, and one which, in itself, we would probably have driven
five hours to see. But enough is enough. One turns at last even from
glory itself with a sigh of relief. From the depths of mystery, and even
from the heights of splendor, we bounce back and hurry for the lati-
tudes of home.

Questions

1. "Total Eclipse" is divided into four parts. Can you describe those
   divisions? How does Part One function, for example, in relation
   to the rest of the essay?
2. Dillard begins her essay with the idea of death:

   > It had been like dying, the sliding down the mountain pass. It
   > had been like the death of someone, irrational, that sliding
   > down the mountain pass and into the region of dread. It was
   > like slipping into fever, or falling down that hole in sleep from
   > which you wake yourself whimpering.

   Analyze her rhetorical technique in the opening paragraph and
   consider why she might want to start "Total Eclipse" this way.

Richard Preston

CRISIS IN THE HOT ZONE

Richard Preston was born in Cambridge, Massachusetts, in 1954, and in 1972 he graduated from Wellesley High School, where he had the same English teacher as Sylvia Plath. After studying at Pomona College (B.A.) and Princeton University (Ph.D.), he became a professional writer, a decision he has described as taking "the easy way out" in a tough academic job market. For his first book, *First Light: The Search for the Edge of the Universe* (1987), he won the Science Writing Award in Physics and Astronomy from the American Institute of Physics. A frequent contributor to periodicals, including *The New Yorker* Preston says, "I try to see through people's faces into their minds, and listen through their words into their lives, and then I try to describe what I find there."

The main building of the United States Army Medical Research Institute for Infectious Diseases is an essentially windowless concrete block that covers several acres at Fort Detrick, an Army base in Frederick, Maryland, fifteen miles east of Antietam. Military people call the structure the Institute, or they call it by its acronym, USAMRIID, drawling it as You Sam Rid. Or they call the place RIID, as in getting rid of something. Vent stacks on its roof discharge filtered exhaust air from sealed biological laboratories inside the building. Fort Detrick, the envelope of USAMRIID, sits in rolling country on the eastern slope of the Appalachian Mountains, in the drainage of the Potomac River. The Potomac bends through oak-blanketed mountains at Harpers Ferry and enters farmland, and eventually passes near Reston, Virginia, a town outside the Washington Beltway where farms give way to business parks, and where in the eighties office buildings accreted like crystals.

The mission of USAMRIID is medical defense. The Institute conducts research into ways to protect soldiers against biological weapons and natural infectious diseases. It specializes in vaccines, drug therapy, and biocontainment. That is, the Institute knows methods for stopping a monster virus before it ignites an explosive chain of lethal transmission in the human race. The laboratory suites at USAMRIID are maintained at four levels of biological security. The levels go from Biosafety Level 1, which is the lowest, up to Biosafety Level 4, the highest. The Biosafety Level 4 rooms contain BL-4 agents, also known as hot agents. A BL-4 hot agent is a lethal virus for which, in most cases, there is no vaccine and no cure. It is in the nature of hot agents to travel through the air: they can become airborne. The hot agents live in the hot suites in blood serum and bits of meat, frozen at −70° Centigrade. All the biocontainment laboratories at USAMRIID are kept under negative air pressure, so that if a leak develops air will flow *into* the hot rooms and out of the normal world, rather than the other way around. The Army does not publish a list of the viruses it keeps in the hot suites at USAMRIID, but here is a list of BL-4 viruses: Junin. Lassa. Machupo. Tick-borne encephalitis virus complex. Guanarito. Crimean-Congo. Marburg. Ebola Sudan. Ebola Zaire. Ebola Reston. If you want to shake hands with one of these viruses, you had better wear a space suit. That's a federal rule. It holds equally at USAMRIID and at the Centers for Disease Control, in Atlanta, which are the only two laboratories in the United States that can handle BL-4 viruses.

To go inside a Biosafety Level 4 hot suite that contains life, first you have to strip naked. You put on surgical scrubs and then a space suit. You pull the helmet down over your head and close the suit. Then you enter an antechamber, a kind of air lock. It leads to Biosafety Level 4. Military people consider this air lock a gray zone, a place where two worlds meet. The air-lock doors are blazed with the international symbol for biohazard, a red trefoil that reminds me of a flower. I think it looks not unlike a red trillium, or toadshade. At USAMRIID, toadshades bloom in the gray zones.

Lieutenant Colonel Nancy Jaax is the chief of the pathology division of USAMRIID. She is a slender and rather beautiful woman, a doctor of veterinary medicine, forty-two years old, with curly auburn hair and green eyes. She has a brisk manner. On the job, Nancy Jaax wears a uniform consisting of green slacks and a green shirt with shoulder bars displaying the silver oak leaves of her rank. Or she wears a space suit. She is married to Colonel Gerald Jaax, who is the chief of the veterinary-medicine division at USAMRIID. The Army assigned Nancy Jaax and her husband to USAMRIID in 1979. She had just been awarded the rank of major, and she entered the pathology training program at USAMRIID as a veterinary-pathology resident. Pathologists at USAMRIID, who cut up hot tissue, are given vaccinations for lethal agents. Nancy Jaax said to me, "My vaccinations were for yellow fever, Q fever, Rift Valley—there were so many. The VEE, EEE, and WEE. complex, anthrax, and botulism. And, of course, rabies, since I'm a veterinarian." She had an underlying medical condition that caused her immune system to react badly to the shots: the shots made her sick. The Army therefore stopped her vaccinations and assigned her to work in a space suit in the Biosafety Level 4 suites. "There aren't any immunizations for most BL-4 agents, and that's why you work in a space suit," she explained.

In 1980, Nancy Jaax joined a group of military scientists who were performing experiments with Ebola virus on monkeys. They were infecting monkeys with Ebola and then treating them with interferon and other substances to see if the treatments stopped or weakened the disease. The purpose of the experiments was to find some chemical therapy for military personnel who might become infected with Ebola.

Ebola is one of a class of viruses known as the filoviruses. That means thread viruses. They look like spaghetti. As of this writing, the class comprises three subtypes of Ebola and a virus known as Marburg. Ebola virus is named for the Ebola River, a tributary of the Zaire (Congo) River which runs through northern Zaire. The first known emergence of Ebola Zaire—the hottest subtype of Ebola virus—happened in September, 1976, when the virus erupted simultaneously in fifty-five villages near the Ebola River. Ebola Zaire is a slate-wiper in humans. It killed eighty-eight percent of the people it infected. Apart from rabies and the human immunodeficiency virus, HIV, which causes AIDS, this was the highest rate of mortality that has been recorded for a human virus. Ebola was spread mainly among family members, through contact with bodily fluids and blood. Many of the people in Africa who came down with Ebola had handled Ebola-infected cadavers. It seems that one of Ebola's paths wends to the living from the dead.

Ebola victims died about a week after the onset of the first symptom, which was a headache. The Ebola patient soon breaks into a relentless fever, and then come the complications. Ebola triggers a paradoxical combination of blood clots and hemorrhages. The patient's bloodstream throws clots, and the clots lodge everywhere, especially in the spleen, liver, and brain. This is called DIC, or disseminated intravascular coagulation. DIC is a kind of stroke through the whole body. No one knows how Ebola triggers blood-clotting. As the strokelike condition progresses and capillaries in the internal organs become jammed with clots, the hemorrhaging begins: blood leaks out of the capillaries into the surrounding tissues. This blood refuses to coagulate. It is grossly hemolyzed, which means that its cells are broken. You are stuffed with clots, and yet you bleed like a hemophiliac who had been in a fistfight. Your skin develops bruises and goes pulpy, and tears easily, and becomes speckled with purple hemorrhages called petechiae, and erupts in a maculopapular rash that has been likened to tapioca pudding. Your intestines may fill up completely with blood. Your eyeballs may also fill with blood. Your eyelids bleed. You vomit a black fluid. You may suffer a hemispherical stroke, which paralyzes one whole side of the body and is invariably fatal in a case of Ebola. In the pre-agonal stage of the disease (the endgame), the patient leaks blood containing huge quantities of virus from the nose, mouth, anus, and eyes, and from rips in the skin. In the agonal-stage, death comes from hemorrhage and shock.

People seem unable to develop protective antibodies to Ebola. You can't fight off an Ebola infection the way you fight off a cold. Ebola seems to crush the immune system. The virus perhaps makes immuno-suppressant proteins. No one knows the nature of such proteins, since there aren't many virologists who care to study a virus for which there is no vaccine and no cure. (They don't want the virus to do research on them.) Immunosuppressive proteins—if, indeed, they exist—would act as molecular bombs that ruin parts of the immune system, enabling the virus to multiply without opposition.

Like all viruses, Ebola and its cousin Marburg are parasites. They can copy themselves only inside a cell. Viruses need to use a cell's equipment to reproduce. Ebola and Marburg grow promiscuously in human tissue, sprouting from cells like hair, forming tangled masses and braids and "g"s and "y"s and pigtails. Marburg-virus particles often roll up into tiny Cheerios. All filoviruses form semi-crystalline blocks inside cells, which are known as inclusion bodies. Some scientists call them bricks. The bricks may pack a cell until there's almost nothing left of the cell but bricks: the cell bloats into a sack of bricks. Then the bricks break apart into threads of virus, and the threads push through the cell wall like grass rising from seeded loam.

A classic sign of infection by Ebola or Marburg is a certain expres- 10 sion that invariably creeps over the patient's face as the infection progresses. The face becomes fixed and "expressionless," "masklike," "ghostlike" (in the words of doctors who have seen it), with wide, deadened, "sunken" eyes. The patient looks and sometimes behaves like a zombie. This happens because Ebola damages the brain in some way that isn't known. The classic masklike facial expression appears in all primates infected with Ebola, both monkeys and human beings. They act as if they were already embalmed, even though they are not yet dead. The personality may change: the human patient becomes sullen, hostile, agitated, or develops acute psychosis. Some have been known to escape from the hospital.

Disseminated clotting cuts off the blood supply to tissues, causing focal necrosis—dead spots in the liver, spleen, brain, kidneys, and lungs. In severe cases, Ebola kills so much tissue that after death the cadaver rapidly deteriorates. In monkeys, and perhaps in people, a sort of melting occurs, and the corpse's connective tissue, skin, and organs, already peppered with dead areas and heated with fever, begin to liquefy, and the slimes and uncoagulated blood that run from the cadaver are saturated with Ebola-virus particles. That may be one of Ebola's strategies for success.

Lieutenant Colonel Nancy Jaax's job during the Army's 1980 experiments with Ebola was to dissect and examine monkeys that had died of the virus. Her space suit had triple pairs of gloves. First, there was an inner latex surgical glove. Over that, the suit had attached to it a heavy rubber glove. Over the rubber glove she wore another latex surgical glove. Her space suit and gloves were often splashed with blood as she cut into dead monkeys, and she regularly dipped her gloves in a pan of Envirochem—a liquid disinfectant that the Army believes is effective on viruses—to rinse away the blood. They use a buddy system in BL-4. You don't work alone in a hot area. The buddies are trained to glance at each other's gloves for leaks. ("The weak link is your glove," Jaax told me. "You are handling needles, knives, and sharp pieces of bone.") One day, Jaax's buddy noticed a hole in Jaax's right outer latex glove. The glove was covered with Ebola-laden blood. Jaax rinsed the glove in Envirochem and took it off, and found monkey blood inside it: the blood had run through the hole and drenched the heavy rubber glove.

Then she felt something clammy *inside* the heavy glove. She wondered if it was a leaker.

She rinsed her bloody glove and went into the air lock. There, still wearing her space suit, she pulled a chain to start the decontamination, or "decon," cycle. The decon cycle took five minutes. First, a hot-water shower came on, and then came a mist of Envirochem, which washed away any blood from the exterior of her suit, while sterilizing it. She stepped into a tub of Envirochem, bent over, put her hands in the tub, and scrubbed her booties and gloves with a brush. (In the old days, the Army's air lock showers ran with Lysol. It kills germs, as advertised, but it made some people itch.) Then a final water shower came on and stopped. Nancy Jaax left the air lock and entered a staging area, where she stepped out of her space suit, withdrawing her latex-gloved hands from the suit's heavy gloves. As her right hand came out of the suit, she saw it was red—bloody. The suit's heavy glove had been a leaker.

The blood had smeared the inner-most latex glove, right against her skin. Her heart pounded, and her stomach turned over. "I got that *oogh* feeling. That feeling you sometimes get when you work with these agents," she said. "I went, 'Oh, shit. What now? Oh, *Jesus*. What do I have to do now?'" On her right hand, under the last glove, she had an open cut in her skin. She does all the cooking for her family; she had cut herself with a paring knife while slicing vegetables, and had covered the cut with a Band-Aid. The question was whether any blood had penetrated the last glove to the Band-Aid and the cut. If so, it would amount to a death warrant. Five or ten virus particles suspended in a microscopic droplet of blood could easily slip through a pinhole in a surgical glove, and that would probably be enough to start a fatal infection. At USAMRIID, there is a group of pressurized hospital rooms designed so that patients can be treated by nurses and doctors wearing space suits. The place is an isolation hospital, and they call it the Slammer. Nancy Jaax began to wonder if she would end up in the Slammer by nightfall. She and her husband have two children. She did not want to break with Ebola virus in the Slammer and never see her children again. She dipped her last, bloody glove in Envirochem, and went over to a sink, and removed the glove. She put it under a faucet and filled it with water, like a water balloon. It held. No leaks. "This incident came into the category of close call," she said to me.

Nancy Jaax continued with the experiment, and all the monkeys that had been infected with Ebola died; the drugs had no effect on the course of the disease. She kept two control monkeys—healthy monkeys—apart from the others, in separate cages inside the hot suite. Then both control monkeys died of Ebola. They had not been injected with virus, and their cages were on the far side of the room from those of the sick monkeys. "So the question is: How did they get it?" Lieutenant Colonel Nancy Jaax said to me. "They probably got it from aerosolized droplets from the sick monkeys. That was when I knew that Ebola could spread through the air."

A virus is a small capsule consisting of membranes and proteins. The capsule holds one or more strands of RNA or DNA that contain the software program for making a copy of the virus. The virus penetrates a cell wall, and the capsule breaks apart inside the cell, releasing the strands of genetic material, which take over the cell and force it to make copies of the virus. Eventually, the cell gets pigged with virus, and pops. Or viruses can bud through a cell wall like sweat coming off a drip hose. In either case, viruses tend to kill cells. If they kill enough cells, or if they kill a class of cell that the host needs for survival, then the host dies. Viruses that kill their hosts do not themselves survive. It is in the virus's best interest to let the host live, but accidents happen. Some biologists classify viruses as "life forms"—ambiguously alive. Bacteria and cells are always humming with activity, enzymatic processes. Viruses that are outside cells merely sit there; nothing happens. But when they get inside a cell they switch on and begin to replicate. Viruses can seem alive when they multiply, but in another sense they are molecular machines—obviously nonliving, strictly mechanical, no more alive than a jackhammer. Compact, logical, hard, engineered by the forces of evolution, and totally selfish, the viral machinery is dedicated to making copies of itself—which it can do on occasion with radiant speed.

Viruses are not easy to see, even with an electron microscope. Here is a way to imagine the size of a virus. Consider the island of Manhattan, shrunk to this size:

This shrunken Manhattan could easily hold nine million common-cold viruses. If you made an aerial reconnaissance of it with an electron microscope, you would see little figures milling like the lunch crowd on Fifth Avenue. Viruses can be purified and concentrated into crystals.

Packed in a crystalline layer, shoulder to shoulder and only one virus deep, a hundred million polio viruses could cover the period at the end of this sentence. There could be a thousand Giants Stadiums of viruses sitting on that period—two hundred and fifty Woodstocks of viruses, a third of the population of the United States, sitting on that period—but you wouldn't know it without a scope.

In 1892, a Russian scientist named Dimitry Ivanovsky studied a dis-   20
ease of tobacco leaves which gives them white spots. He passed the juice of sick leaves through extremely fine filters, and when he injected healthy plants with the filtered juice they got sick and developed white spots. Ivanovsky concluded that some very small agent was causing the disease, but he didn't know whether it was a toxic chemical or a living thing. In 1898, Martinus Beijerinck, a Dutch botanist, proved that Ivanovsky's virus was a replicative infectious agent. It has since come to be called tobacco-mosaic virus. In 1900, the United States Army discovered the first human virus—the yellow-fever agent. That was the work of Walter Reed and his team. The Army has tracked viruses from the beginning.

There is no fossil record in rocks to indicate that viruses existed before the late nineteenth century, when tobacco-mosaic virus was first noticed. Fossils of bacteria have turned up in rocks that are more than three billion years old, but no fossils of viruses have ever been found. Nevertheless, viruses are obviously ancient, and perhaps primeval. They are molecular sharks, a motive without a mind. They have sorted themselves into tribes, and they infect everything that lives.

The human immunodeficiency virus, or HIV, is a not very infectious but lethal Biosafety Level 2 or 3 agent, which most likely emerged from the rain forests of Central Africa. You don't need to wear a space suit while handling blood infected with HIV. During the nineteen-seventies, the virus fell like a shadow over the human population living along the east-west highway that links Kinshasa, in Zaire, with Mombasa, in Kenya. The emergence was subtle: the virus incubates for years in a human host before it kills the host.

A zoonotic virus is a virus that lives naturally in an animal and can infect human cells, perhaps mutating slightly in the course of passage, which enables the virus to start a chain of infection through human hosts. For example, HIV-2 (one of the two major strains of HIV) may be a mutant zoonotic virus that jumped into us from an African monkey known as the sooty mangabey, perhaps when monkey-hunters touched bloody tissue. No one really knows where HIV came from. HIV-1 (the other strain) may have jumped into us from chimpanzees, or it may be a human virus that has been in our species for ages, circulating in some isolated group of people in Central Africa. As outsiders came into the area, AIDS came out, and passed into the general human population.

The emergence of AIDS appears to be a natural consequence of the ruin of the tropical biosphere. Unknown viruses are coming out of the equatorial wildernesses of the earth and discovering the human race. It seems to be happening as a result of the destruction of tropical habitats. You might call AIDS the revenge of the rain forest. AIDS is arguably the worst environmental disaster of the twentieth century, so far. Some of the people who worry in a professional capacity about viruses have begun to wonder whether HIV isn't the only rain-forest virus that will sweep the world. The human immunodeficiency virus looks like an example rather than a culminating disaster. As lethal viruses go, HIV is by no means nature's preeminent display of power. The rain forest, being by far the earth's largest reservoir of both plant and animal species, is also its largest reservoir of viruses, since all living things carry viruses. Just how large the tropical reservoir of viruses is no one knows, but here is one way to consider the question. The earth is estimated to contain between three million and thirty million species of plants and animals. Most of the species are fungi, insects, and non-insect arthropods, such as ticks and mites, and the bulk of them live in tropical forests. Viruses often adapt to one or two species. For example, human beings carry more than a hundred different cold viruses that are adapted almost exclusively to the human host. If we suppose that every species carries one virus exclusively adapted to it, then there may be from three to thirty million strains of viruses. Possibly the number of virus strains is much larger than that—perhaps a hundred million—but nobody has ever tried to count them.

When an ecosystem suffers degradation, many species die out and 25
a few survivor-species have population explosions. Viruses in a damaged ecosystem can come under extreme selective pressure. Viruses are adaptable: they react to change and can mutate fast, and they can jump among species of hosts. As people enter the forest and clear it, viruses come out, carried in their survivor-hosts—rodents, insects, soft ticks— and the viruses meet *Homo sapiens*. Here are the names of some emerging viruses: Lassa. Rift Valley. Oropouche. Rocio. Q fever. VEE Guanarito. Ross River. Monkeypox. Dengue. Chikungunya. Hantaan. Machupo. Junin. The rabies-like strains Mokola and Duvenhage. Le Dantec. Human immunodeficiency virus—which might have been called Kinshasa Highway, if it had been noticed earlier—is considered an emerger, since its penetration of the human race is incomplete and is still happening explosively, with no end in sight. The Kyasanur Forest virus. The Semliki virus. Crimean-Congo. Sindbis. O'nyong-nynong. Marburg. Ebola. Most of them—but not all—come from tropical forests or tropical savannas. When a virus that lives in some nonhuman host is about to crash into the human species, the warning sign may be a spatter of breaks—disconnected emergences, at different times and places. I tend to think of rats leaving a ship. The presence of international airports puts every virus on earth within a day's flying time of the United States.

Reston, Virginia, is near Washington. The town has an active chamber of commerce and a visitors' center designed to lure high-technology businesses to the area. Along the Leesburg Pike, a commuter route that funnels traffic to Washington, you see developments of executive homes. The homes are pseudo-Victorians, with unused porches, and stick-built neo-Georgians, with false-brick fronts and a Baby Benz parked in a semicircular carriageway. You also see the occasional bungalow with cardboard stuffed in a broken window and a Harley in the driveway. The town of Reston is bisected by the Dulles Access and Toll Road, which connects Dulles Airport with Washington. Not far from the Dulles Access Road in Reston is a small business park. Until recently, a company called Hazleton Research Products had a monkey house in a one-story building in the business park. It was known as the Reston Primate Quarantine Unit. Hazleton Research Products sells animals for research; it is a division of Corning Incorporated. Hazleton was importing monkeys from the tropics and bringing them through J.F.K. International Airport to the Reston Primate Quarantine Unit. Each year, about sixteen thousand wild monkeys are imported into the United States, to be used as laboratory animals. Federal regulations require that imported monkeys be held in quarantine for at least thirty-one days before they are shipped anywhere else in the United States. This is to prevent the spread of infectious diseases that could kill other primates, including laboratory workers.

Dan Dalgard, doctor of veterinary medicine, is the principal scientist at Hazleton Washington, which has its offices on the Leesburg Pike, in Vienna, next to Reston. Dan Dalgard has an international reputation as a knowledgeable and skilled veterinarian who specializes in primate husbandry, and he understands monkey behavior and monkey diseases. He is a calm, blunt man in his late fifties. He wears glasses, and he has a square, pleasant face. On evenings and weekends, he repairs antique clocks as a hobby. He likes to use his hands and his mind to figure out how a broken complicated system can be fixed. Dalgard sometimes has longings to leave veterinary medicine and immerse himself in clocks.

On Wednesday, October 4, 1989, Hazleton accepted a shipment of a hundred wild monkeys from the Philippines. The shipment originated on the island of Mindanao, at a Philippine monkey-export company. The monkeys were macaques, and the species was *Macaca fascicularis*. Zookeepers call it the crab-eating macaque. It is a common monkey that lives along rivers and in mangrove swamps in Southeast Asia, and it is often used as a laboratory animal. It eats fruit, crabs, insects, and small pieces of clay. A crab-eating macaque will snatch a crab out of the water and quickly rip its claws off and throw them away before devouring the rest of the crab. Sometimes a crab-eating macaque isn't quick enough with the claws, and when the monkeys are on a feeding bout in a mangrove swamp at low tide you can occasionally hear shrieks when a crab fastens on a monkey. The crab-eating macaque has brown eyes, pointed ears, tawny fur, and a long tail. As monkeys go, crab-eating macaques have a calm temperament, provided that you don't stare at them. Any monkey thinks staring is rude, and the crab eater will respond on the same level, screaming *"Kra, kra!"* and hurling its feces at you.

The Philippine monkeys arrived at J.F.K. and were taken by truck to Hazleton's Reston Primate Quarantine Unit. The monkeys were kept in stainless-steel cages in windowless rooms, under artificial lights, and were fed monkey biscuits. The Reston quarantine rooms were designated by letters of the alphabet, from "A" through "L." The Philippine monkeys were put in Room F. The ventilation system recirculated some air in common through the rooms, so that the monkeys were breathing one another's air.

By the first of November, twenty-seven monkeys had died. That 30 was more than usual for a shipment of wild monkeys. Dan Dalgard performed necropsies on the ones that had died, and concluded that they were being killed by dysentery and pneumonia. These diseases are not uncommon in wild monkeys. A week later, on Monday, November 6th, another shipment of crab-eating macaques arrived, making a total of about five hundred monkeys in the quarantine unit, all crab-eating macaques from the Philippines. But by November 10th Dalgard had begun to suspect that some of his monkeys might be dying of simian hemorrhagic fever, or SHF, a virus that is lethal to monkeys but does not cause clinical disease in humans. (It infects people but doesn't make them sick.) The possibility worried Dalgard, because SHF is highly contagious in monkeys, and can wipe out a colony.

He began sacrificing monkeys that appeared sick, by injecting them with overdoses of an anesthetic, and then he opened them up. He found that their spleens were enlarged — a classic sign of simian hemorrhagic fever. But monkeys infected with SHF typically die sneezing blood or with other evidence of hemorrhaging, and Dalgard hadn't seen any of these signs in the monkeys that died before November 10th. The monkeys had simply stopped eating and died of shock. The focus of the infection was Room F, where most of the monkeys had perished. The disease gave Dalgard an eerie feeling, and prompted him to keep a diary. Of the monkeys that had died in Room F he wrote:

> Many of the animals were in prime condition and had more abdominal and subcutaneous fat than is customary for animals arriving from the wild. The diagnosis at this time was continuing to point more strongly toward S.H.F. but the slow progression [of the disease] and the lack of the hemorrhagic component confused the diagnosis.

He decided to take the mystery to the United States Army Medical Research Institute for Infectious Diseases, where he knew about a virologist named Peter Jahrling, who had done work on SHF. He described to Jahrling the illness that was burning through his monkeys, and he sent some blood and tissue samples to Jahrling. Some of the samples came from a monkey known as O53, which had lived in Room F. Jahrling froze some of the tissues and placed them in a Biosafety Level 3 containment room. This level is kept under negative pressure, but you don't need to wear a space suit inside it.

One way to identify a virus is to make it multiply inside living cells in a flask. You drop a very small sample of the virus into the cells, and as the virus spreads through the cells extraordinary numbers of virus particles are produced. You can then look at them under a microscope, or you can put different kinds of fluorescent antibodies—immunity proteins—in the virus culture. These antibodies attach themselves to infected cells and glow under ultraviolet light, and the antibody that makes cells glow tells you which particular virus you have in the flask.

A civilian technician named Joan Rhoderick cultured the unknown monkey virus from the liver of Monkey O53. She ground up a bit of the liver with a mortar and pestle, and dropped some of the resultant mush into flasks that contained a living strain of cells from the kidney of a green monkey. Joan Rhoderick wore a surgical mask and rubber gloves but not a space suit, and she worked with the samples kept in a safety cabinet that pulls air away from the samples and through a filter.

John Rhoderick and Peter Jahrling looked at slices of liver and spleen from Monkey O53, and Jahrling gave a presumptive diagnosis of simian hemorrhagic fever to Dan Dalgard. At this point, Dalgard felt that he had no choice but to sacrifice all the monkeys in Room F in order to halt the spreading disease. If those monkeys were infected with SHF, they would die anyway, and if they weren't sacrificed the disease could spread to other rooms, killing more monkeys. Dalgard and an assistant, wearing surgical masks and rubber gloves, euthanized all the monkeys in Room F on November 16th—some seventy monkeys in all. They gave the monkeys injections of an anesthetic. Dalgard opened ten of the corpses to see what he could see, and sent everything to an incinerator.

At the beginning of Thanksgiving week of 1989, when these events were taking place at the Reston Primate Quarantine Unit, Thomas Geisbert was a twenty-seven-year-old civilian researcher working at USAMRIID while he studied for a Ph.D. in microbiology. His specialty is the electron microscope. Geisbert is something of a loner, a tall man with blue eyes, brown hair, and arrestingly large ears. He grew up an only child in western Maryland, where he spent a lot of time camping in the woods alone or with his uncles, who taught him how to hunt and fish. Geisbert's boss at USAMRIID was Peter Jahrling. Tom Geisbert goes deer hunting in West Virginia every year around Thanksgiving. He planned to leave on Monday morning of that week, but something prompted him to stop by his lab at USAMRIID for a last look at the flasks of monkey cells that were incubating the virus from Reston. At nine in the morning, he put on a surgical mask and gloves and entered the BL-3 suite. There he met Joan Rhoderick, the technician who had started the Reston culture. She was looking at a flask under a microscope. The flask contained cells infected with virus from the Reston monkey O53. She said to Geisbert, "There's something flaky going on in this flask."

The flask was small — four inches long — and it was made of plastic and had a screw cap. Geisbert looked through the eyepieces of the microscope into the flask. Living cells ordinarily cling to the bottom of a flask in a carpet. This carpet looked eaten by moths. It was full of holes: dead and dying cells had detached from the flask and drifted into the fluid. Later, he described to me what he'd seen. "Cells that have been infected with SHF take on a spiderweb look. These cells didn't look like that. They were rounded and had a granular, pepperlike look. Some were dead. They were 'off the plastic,' as we say. It means they had floated away."

This didn't look like simian hemorrhagic fever. He went out and got Peter Jahrling, his boss. He said to Jahrling, "There's something very strange going on in that flask, but I'm not sure what."

Jahrling had worked at USAMRIID long enough to have seen some strange things in flasks. "The cells were blown away. They were *crud*," Jahrling recalled later. He thought that a wild strain of bacteria had invaded the cell culture. This is a common and annoying occurrence in cell cultures, and it wipes out the culture. Bacteria give off odors as they multiply, and Peter Jahrling had smelled enough bacterial contaminations so that he knew how to distinguish them by nose. Viruses, on the other hand, kill cells without releasing an odor. Jahrling guessed that the flask had been wiped out by a common soil bacterium named pseudomonas, which, he says, "smells like Welch's grape juice." He unscrewed the cap and waved his hand over it, and took a whiff, and said to Geisbert, "Have you ever smelled pseudomonas?" Geisbert accepted the flask from Jahrling and sniffed. He didn't smell any Welch's grape juice. There was no odor. Jahrling, who hadn't smelled anything, either, took back the flask and whiffed it again. Nothing. No smell. But the cells were blown away.

Geisbert poured some milky fluid out of the flask into a test tube 40 and spun it in a microcentrifuge. A small "button" of material collected at the bottom of the test tube — a pill of dead and dying cells. Geisbert removed the button with a wooden stick and soaked it in plastic resin. Then he went hunting in West Virginia. He planned to look at the button in his microscope when he returned, after Thanksgiving. When Ebola virus infects a human being, the incubation period is from seven to fourteen days, while the number of virus particles gradually climbs in the bloodstream. Then comes the headache.

The first known emergence of a filovirus happened in August, 1967, in Marburg, Germany. A shipment of green monkeys from Uganda had arrived in Frankfurt. Green-monkey kidney cells are useful for the production of vaccines, and these monkeys were going to be killed for their kidneys. Most of the monkeys were trucked from Frankfurt to a factory in Marburg that produced serum and vaccines, while a few monkeys from the same shipment stayed in Frankfurt, and a few others went to Belgrade, Yugoslavia. The first person known to be infected with the virus—the index case—was a man known as Klaus F., an animal-care technician at the serum factory in Marburg. He broke with fever and rash on August 8th, and died two weeks later.

So little is known about the Marburg agent that only one book has been published about it, "Marburg Virus Disease," edited by G. A. Martini and R. Siegert. In it we learn:

> The monkey-keeper HEINRICH P. came back from his holiday on August 13th 1967 and did his job of killing monkeys from August 14th–23rd. The first symptoms appeared on August 21st.

> The laboratory assistant RENATE L. broke a test-tube that was to be sterilized, which had contained infected material, on August 28th, and fell ill on September 4th 1967.

And so on. Thirty-one laboratory workers acquired the disease; seven died. In other words, the case-fatality rate of Marburg virus in hospitalized patients was twenty-two percent. That was terrifying. Yellow fever, which is considered a lethal virus, kills only five percent of the infected once they reach a hospital.

Marburg began with a splitting headache, focused behind the eyes and temples. That was followed by a fever. The characteristic diagnostic sign was a red speckled rash over the body which blistered into a sea of tiny white bubbles. "Most of the patients showed a sullen, slightly aggressive, or negativistic behavior," Martini wrote. "Two patients [had] a feeling as if they were lying on crumbs." One became deranged and psychotic. These mental signs were caused by the virus's having damaged the brain. The patient Hans O.-V. showed no signs of mental change, but he suffered a sudden, acute fall of blood pressure and died. At autopsy, his brain was found to be laced with hemorrhages, and there was a massive, fatal hemorrhage at the center. In Frankfurt, an animal attendant known as B. developed a high fever and eventually began bleeding from his mouth, nose, and gastrointestinal tract. He was given whole-blood transfusions, but then he developed uncontrollable hemorrhages at the sites of the IV punctures. He died with blood running from his mouth and his nipples. All the survivors lost their hair. During convalescence, the skin peeled off their faces, hands, feet, and genitals. It was a small, frightening emergence.

Marburg virus looks like rope, or it rolls up into the rings that resemble Cheerios. Virologists had never seen a ring-shaped virus, and couldn't figure out how to classify it. They thought that it might be a type of rabies. The rabies particle is shaped like a bullet, and if you stretch a bullet it becomes a rod, and the rod can be bent into a doughnut: Marburg. They started calling Marburg "stretched rabies." But it is not related to rabies.

The question was: What is the virus's natural history? In what animal or insect does Marburg hide? Marburg evidently does not circulate in monkeys. Monkeys die quickly of the disease, and if they were the reservoir, Marburg wouldn't wipe them out. The monkey's immune system would have learned to attack the virus, and the virus itself would have become better adapted to living in monkeys without killing them, since it is in the virus's best interest to let the host survive. The Marburg monkeys had been collected in Uganda by native trappers— apparently in forested habitat to the west of Mt. Elgon, an extinct volcano that straddles the border between Uganda and Kenya. Teams of epidemiologists combed Uganda, and especially the western slopes of Mt. Elgon, looking for some animal or insect that harbored Marburg virus; they found nothing.

In 1980, a French engineer who was employed by the Nzoia Sugar Company at a factory in Kenya within sight of Mt. Elgon developed Marburg and died. He was an amateur naturalist who spent time camping and hiking around Mt. Elgon, and he had recently visited a cavern on the Kenyan side of the mountain which was known as Kitum Cave. It wasn't clear where the Frenchman had picked up the virus, whether at the sugar factory or outdoors. Then, in the late summer of 1987, a Danish boy whose name will be given here as Peter Cardinal visited the Kenyan side of Mt. Elgon with his parents—the Cardinals were tourists —and the boy broke with Marburg and died.

Epidemiologists at USAMRIID became interested in the cases, and they traced the movements of the French engineer and the Danish boy in the days before their illnesses and deaths. The result was weird. The paths of the French engineer and the Danish boy had crossed only once —in Kitum Cave. Peter Cardinal had gone inside Kitum Cave. As for the Ugandan trappers who had collected the original Marburg monkeys, they might have poached them from the Kenyan side of Mt. Elgon. Those monkeys might have lived near Kitum Cave, and might even have occasionally visited the cave.

Mt. Elgon is a huge, eroded volcanic massif, fifty miles across—one of the largest volcanoes in East Africa. Kitum Cave is one of a number

45

of caverns that penetrate Mt. Elgon at an altitude of around eight thousand feet and open their mouths in a deep forest of podo trees, African junipers, African olives, and camphors. Kitum Cave descends into tight passages and underground pools that extend an unknown distance back into Mt. Elgon. The volcanic rock within Kitum Cave is permeated with mineral salts. Elephants go inside the cave to root out chunks of salty rock with their tusks and chew on them. Water buffalo also visit the cave to lick the rocks, and they may be followed into the cave by leopards. Fruit bats and insect-eating bats roost in the cave, filling the air with a sour smell. The animals drop their dung in the cave—an enclosed airspace—and they attract biting flies and carry ticks and mites. The volcanic rock contains petrified logs, the remains of trees that were enveloped in lava, and the logs are filled with sharp crystals. Peter Cardinal may have handled crystals inside the cave and scratched his hands. Possibly the crystals were tainted with animal urine or the remains of an insect. The Army keeps some of Peter Cardinal's tissues frozen in cryovials, and the Cardinal strain is viciously hot. It kills guinea pigs like flies. In February, 1988, a few months after Peter Cardinal died, the Army sent a team of epidemiologists to Kitum Cave.

The team wore Racal suits inside the cave. A Racal is a lightweight 50 pressurized suit with a filtered air supply, used for hot operations in the field. There is no vaccine for Marburg, and the Army people had come to believe that the virus could be spread through the air. Near and inside the cave they set out, in cages, guinea pigs and primates—baboons, green monkeys, and Sykes' monkeys—and they surrounded the cages with electrified wire to discourage predators. The guinea pigs and monkeys were sentinel animals, like canaries in a coal mine: they were placed there in the theory or the hope that some of them would develop Marburg. With the help of Kenyan naturalists, the Army team trapped as many different kinds of wild mammals as they could find, including rodents, rock hyraxes, and bats, and drew blood from them. They collected insects. Some local people, the il-Kony, had lived in some of the caves. A Kenyan doctor from the Kenya Medical Research Institute, in Nairobi, drew blood from these people and took their medical histories. At the far end of Kitum Cave, where it disappears in pools of water, the Army team found a population of sand flies. They mashed some flies and tested them for Marburg.

The expedition was a dry hole. The sentinel animals remained healthy, and the blood and tissue samples from the mammals, insects, arthropods, and local people showed no obvious signs of Marburg. To this day, the natural reservoir of Marburg is unknown. Marburg lives somewhere in the shadow of Mt. Elgon.

On July 6, 1976, five hundred miles northwest of Mt. Elgon, in the township of Nzara, Sudan, in densely wooded country at the edge of the African rain forest, a man referred to as YuG died of a hemorrhagic fever. He was a storekeeper in a cotton factory, and he was the index case of a new strain of filovirus. The clinical features of the disease were indistinguishable from those of Marburg—masklike facial expression, rash, bleeding, terminal shock. Two of YuG's co-workers also came down with the disease and died. No one knows how the virus got into the cotton factory. One of the dead men, a man known as PG, had a wide circle of friends and contacts, and he also had several mistresses. Most of the subsequent fatal cases of what later came to be known as the Sudan subtype of Ebola hemorrhagic fever can be traced back through chains of infection to PG, through as many as six generations of infection. The strain burned through the town of Nzara, and then reached eastward to the town of Maridi, where there was a large hospital, and it hit the hospital like a bomb. It killed nurses and aides, and it savaged patients and then radiated outward from the hospital through patients' families. (A characteristic of a lethal, highly transmissible, and incurable virus is that it kills medical people first. Frequently, as in this case, the medical-care system actually intensifies the outbreak, like a lens that focuses sunlight in a heap of tinder.) The Sudan virus was more than twice as lethal as Marburg—its case-fatality rate was fifty percent, the same as that of bubonic plague before antibiotics. And the death rate kept climbing, until by the third month of the Sudan outbreak mortality among the infected had hit seventy percent, as if perhaps the virus were mutating, getting hotter as it passed from generation to generation in humans. Then, for reasons that aren't clear, the outbreak subsided. The surviving staff of the Maridi hospital had panicked and run away, and that may have helped break the chain of infection. Or possibly the human hosts died too quickly to be efficient transmitters of the virus. Whatever the reason, the organism vanished.

In early September, 1976, two months after the beginning of the Sudan break, a similar yet more lethal strain emerged five hundred miles to the west, in the Bumba Zone of Zaire, an area of humid rain forest drained by the Ebola River. The Ebola River strain seemed to come out of nowhere, and popped up in the Yambuku Mission Hospital, an upcountry clinic run by Belgian nuns. The nuns and staff at Yambuku were using five needles a day to give injections of antibiotics and vitamins to hundreds of people in the hospital's outpatient and maternity clinics. The staff sometimes rinsed the needles in a pan of warm water between injections. The virus entered the cycle of dirty needles, and erupted in fifty-five villages around the hospital. It first killed people who had received injections, and then killed family members—particularly women, who in Africa prepare the dead for burial.

The virus also wiped out the Yambuku Hospital's medical staff.

(Medical people go first.) By the end of September, two-thirds of the staff were dead or dying, and the hospital closed down. A critically ill Belgian nun who was a nurse at the hospital, Sister M.E., was flown to Kinshasa, the capital of Zaire, with another nun, Sister E.R., who nursed her. Sister M.E. was admitted to the Ngaliema Hospital, and she died there shortly afterward. Sister E.R. then became ill and died. Then a Zairian nurse at Ngaliema Hospital, identified as M.N., developed fever and bleeding. She had cared for Sister M.E.; she herself would soon die. While M.N. was incubating the virus, she had had face-to-face contact with several dozen people in the city of Kinshasa. The virus seemed about to start an explosive chain of lethal transmission in Kinshasa, a poor, crowded city with a population of two million, where the virus might go off like a bonfire. This epidemiological possibility triggered a panic in European capitals. Kinshasa has direct air links to Europe, and European governments contemplated blocking flights from Kinshasa. The World Health Organization feared that the nurse M.N. might be the vector for a worldwide pandemic. The Zairian government ordered its army to seal off the Bumba Zone with roadblocks, and all radio contact with the province was lost. Bumba had dropped off the earth, into the silent heart of darkness.

Out of Bumba came some tubes of blood, and from Sudan came 55 some vials of serum. A few of the samples ended up in Atlanta, Georgia, at the Centers for Disease Control, where a team headed by Karl M. Johnson isolated the Ebola River virus for the first time. Key members of the team were Frederick A. Murphy, who is an expert in the electron microscope, and Patricia A. Webb, a virologist. (She was married to Karl Johnson at the time.) The team started to grow the virus in cultures of monkey cells, and Murphy began looking at the cells in his microscope. On October 13th, Webb telephoned her husband, Johnson, and said to him, "Karl, you'd better come quick to the lab. Fred has harvested some cells, and they've got *worms*." The virus looked like Marburg, but Johnson found that it didn't react to Marburg antibodies. Therefore it was a new virus. Karl Johnson and his team had performed what is known as the first isolation and characterization of the agent— they had got it to replicate, and they had proved it was something new. (Teams at the Microbiological Research Establishment in Porton Down, England, and at the Institute for Tropical Medicine in Antwerp, Belgium, had isolated the virus, too, but they didn't know what it was.) Johnson's team had earned the right to name the organism. They named it Ebola.

I learned that Johnson could be reached at a fax number in Big Sky, Montana, so I sent him a fax, in which I said that Ebola virus fascinated me. My fax machine emitted this reply:

Mr. Preston:

Unless you include the feeling generated by gazing into the eyes of a waving confrontational cobra, "fascination" is not what I feel about Ebola. How about shit scared?

The richest trout river in America may be the Bighorn, a green, muscular river in Montana that flows out of the Bighorn Mountains into grassland, and is lined with cottonwoods. One recent day in October, the brown trout were spawning in the Bighorn, and the cottonwoods had turned yellow and rattled in a south wind. Standing waist-deep in a mutable slick of the river, wearing sunglasses, with a cigarette hanging from the corner of his mouth and a fly rod in his hand, Karl Johnson ripped his line off the water and laid a cast upstream. Johnson is a great figure in the history of virology; he trained an entire generation of field virologists at a tropical laboratory called MARU, which he ran in Panama. "I'm so *glad* nature is not benign," he said. He studied the water, took a step downstream, and whipped another cast. "But on a day like today, we can pretend nature is benign—all monsters and beasts have their benign moments." Johnson was a member of a World Health Organization team that went to Kinshasa to try to contain the Ebola virus. "When we got to Kinshasa, the place was an absolute madhouse. There was no news coming out of Bumba province, no radio contact. We knew it was bad in there, and we knew we were dealing with something new. We didn't know if the virus could be spread by droplets in the air, somewhat like influenza. If Ebola *had* easily spread through the air, the world would be a very different place today."

"How so?"

"There would be a lot fewer of us. It would have been *exceedingly* difficult to contain that virus if it had had any major respiratory component."

"Were you afraid you wouldn't come out alive?"

60

"Yeah. But I'd been there before. In 1963, I led the investigation of the Machupo outbreak, named for a river that runs by a little town in the plains of eastern Bolivia. Same kind of thing. People bleeding and dying."

Karl Johnson performed the first isolation of the Machupo virus, a deadly emerger that belongs to a family known as the arenaviruses, because the virus particles are speckled with dots that look like sand. (*Arena* is Latin for "sand") Johnson came down with Machupo in Bolivia—he went into borderline shock in a hospital in the Canal Zone, after he'd been flown out of Bolivia, and he nearly died. Johnson also collaborated on the first isolation of the Hantaan virus, a lethal east-Asian organism (classified as a BL-3 agent), which happens to be another important emerger. A Hantaan relative now infects the rats of

Baltimore and Philadelphia; no obvious human epidemic has yet occurred in the United States. Johnson has therefore been credited with work that led to the discovery and classification of three major groups of emerging human hemorrhagic-fever viruses—the filoviruses, the arenaviruses, and the hantaviruses (named after Hantaan).

"I've seen young physicians run from these hemorrhagic viruses, literally," he said. "In the Zaire thing, we had a young doctor from the CDC who just couldn't get on the plane with me to Kinshasa. He admitted he was too afraid. We sent him home. I did figure that if Ebola was the Andromeda strain—incredibly lethal and spread by droplet infection—then there wasn't going to be any safe place in the world anyway. It was better to be working at the epicenter than to get the infection at the London opera."

The WHO team in Zaire wore fabric helmets with full-face respirators, and disposable gowns, gloves, and overshoes. They set up two containment pavilions at Ngaliema Hospital. Into one pavilion they shut thirty-seven people who had had face-to-face contact with M.N., the Zairian nurse who was then dying, and into the other pavilion they shut all medical staff who had had contact with the nuns who had already died. Doctors and nurses entered the containment areas through a double-doored antechamber, a gray zone. They wrapped the cadavers of the nuns and the nurse (when she died) in sheets soaked in a phenolic disinfectant, then double-bagged these mummies in plastic, put them in coffins that had screwdown lids, and issued instructions to the families of the deceased to bury the coffins immediately, with no wake. The rooms where the nuns had suffered their agonals were not pleasant to behold. The floors, furniture, and walls were stained with blood. The aspect of those rooms may have raised in some minds one or two questions about the nature of the Supreme Being, or, for persons not inclined to theology, the blood on the walls may have served as a reminder of the nature of Nature. The team washed everything with bleach and smoked the victims' rooms with formaldehyde vapor. No one in the containment pavilions or in the city fell ill with the virus. Somewhat to the team's surprise, and to its great relief, the Ebola agent seemed not to be contagious in face-to-face contacts.

"We got an advance party into the bush with a couple of Land Rovers," Johnson said. "They wore respirators and paper gowns and rubber gloves. It turned out that the epidemic was already in decline when the teams got there. The village elders had had the wisdom to institute procedures for dealing with smallpox, which has been a problem for centuries in Africa. An infected person was put in a hut by himself, and food and water were pushed through the doorway. If the person was able to care for himself, he'd eventually come out of the hut. Otherwise, they'd burn the hut down. It really worked with Ebola. But think what that does to a traditional culture. In order to stop an epidemic that way, you have to suspend all the normal cultural relations that surround death. You have to put a parent or a child into that hut and burn it down afterward. The African technique would *work* in the United States, but I don't think we'd do it."

During Thanksgiving week of 1989, Nancy Jaax's father was dying of cancer in Wichita, Kansas, and she and Jerry drove home. Nancy had grown up on a farm in Wichita. Her father had owned a small chain of hamburger restaurants called Dunn's Grills. They lived on a farm outside town, where they grew truck crops, such as tomatoes, cantaloupes, peppers, watermelons, and corn, for the restaurants. Nancy would get up at five in the morning to work in the fields with her father. Later, in high school, she moved in with her grandmother in Wichita, and in the evenings she would help run another restaurant owned by her father called the Plantation (her father had sold Dunn's Grills). Thanksgiving of 1989 was the most painful family reunion of her life. She said her farewell to her father. She didn't know whether she would see him again.

Tom Geisbert shot a buck in West Virginia, and returned home to spend Thanksgiving with his family. Dan Dalgard spent an uneasy Thanksgiving with his wife. He had not stopped the apparent course of simian hemorrhagic fever in his monkeys by sacrificing the monkeys in Room F. Dead monkeys appeared in Room H, two doors down the hall from Room F. After the holiday weekend, Dalgard performed necropsies on four monkeys, taking slices of spleen, liver, and kidney. He wrote in his diary, "Gut feeling after looking at the animals and tissues is that we are not seeing lesions compatible with SHF." He had no idea what was killing his monkeys.

At seven-thirty on Monday morning, November 27th, Tom Geisbert reported to work at his laboratory at USAMRIID. He wanted to get an early start with his electron microscope, looking at the button of dead cells he had harvested the previous Monday. Recently, I met with Geisbert in his office. The walls were plastered with photographs of the Ebola virus. Some of the viruses were ten inches long and resembled ballpark frankfurters. I asked him how he takes a photograph of a virus. He unlocked a filing cabinet and removed from it a metal object the size of a pocket pencil sharpener. "This is a diamond knife," he said. "These things cost about four grand apiece. See the diamond?" Hesitantly, he slid his treasure across his desk toward me, and I picked it up. A prism gleamed. "Please don't touch the edge," he said. "You'll completely trash it. You'll dull it, and your finger oils will stick to the edge. Four thousand dollars."

He showed me a button of cells. It was a dot the size of a toast crumb, embedded in a wedge of clear plastic. The cells—from a monkey's liver—were almost rotten with Ebola virus, but he'd sterilized the button with chemicals. He took the button into another room, where he mounted the button and the diamond knife in a machine and threw a switch. The machine worked like a deli slicer. It drew the diamond knife across the button, peeling off a slice, just like a slice of luncheon meat. The slice was this size:

.

It contained as many as ten thousand cells. Geisbert picked up the   70 slice with a tiny copper mesh, and carried the sample into a darkened room containing a metal tower taller than a person. That was his microscope. He put the sample in a chamber in the microscope, and pushed a button. A complicated image appeared on a viewing screen, showing a tiny corner of one cell—a cellscape of oxbow rivers and lakes that reminded me of an aerial view of jungle.

"I don't see any Ebola here," Geisbert declared, turning a knob, while the cellscape drifted across the field of view. We huddled over the viewing screen, and lakes and paths and specks went by almost without end, until I felt as if we were inside a starship, making a low-orbit pass over a huge, unexplored planet near Tau Ceti. "Sometimes the viruses are everywhere, or sometimes I have to look for six hours before I find a particle," Geisbert said. He was immutably patient, his eyes scanning the terrain. He could pick out patterns of sickness in a cell, subtle anomalies which, like footprints, would lead him to the horrible brood. In the case of Ebola, it is a brood. When Ebola replicates, the virus grows in blocks inside a cell, which are like nests. These are the inclusion bodies, or bricks. The bricks migrate toward the surface of the cell. As a brick reaches the cell wall, it disintegrates into hundreds of individual viruses, and the broodlings bud through the cell membrane and float away in the universe of the host. No one knows how the Ebola bricks are propelled toward the surface of the cell.

"That was quite a day," Geisbert said, sitting at the microscope in the darkened room. His face glowed in the light of the screen. "It's in the morning, around ten o'clock. The sample is cell culture from Monkey 053. I put the sample in the scope. I switch it on. I've looked at it for maybe fifteen seconds, and then—'Oh, *shit.*' The tissue was a mess, and it was *wall-to-wall* with filovirus." Some areas were so thick with virus that they looked like buckets of rope. "I almost lost it," he said. "The only filovirus I'd ever seen in the microscope was Marburg. I had worked with the Cardinal strain of Marburg—the strain from the Danish boy who got Marburg at Kitum Cave in Mt. Elgon—and I knew what that looked like. So I thought, Marburg. I knew that Pete Jahrling and I had sniffed those flasks. I thought, Oh, man, Pete and I have been handling this stuff in BL-3 conditions, and this is a BL-4 agent."

He developed a few photographs of the virus particles and hurried into the office of Peter Jahrling, his boss. Jahrling reacted calmly. It seemed to be a filovirus—Jahrling could see wormlike shapes. Jahrling and Geisbert could have breathed it into their lungs. They began counting days back to the time of their exposure. Seven days had passed since they inhaled from the flask. Well, they didn't have headaches yet.

Jahrling went to get his boss, Colonel Clarence James Peters—he goes by the name C. J.—who was then the chief of the disease-assessment division at USAMRIID. Colonel Peters came into Jahrling's office and looked at Geisbert's photographs. Peters feared that any public announcement of a Marburg-virus outbreak might cause a panic in Reston, once people had learned the history of Marburg. He wanted to get a definite positive identification of the strain before the Army made any announcement.

Tom Geisbert stayed up most of that night. He went into the BL-3 laboratory and found a plastic jug that contained sterilized pieces of liver from Monkey 053. He fished some liver out of the jug, clipped bits off it, and fixed the bits in plastic, preparatory to slicing them for viewing in his electron microscope. He left the plastic to cure and went home for a couple of hours to try to sleep. He returned to Fort Detrick while it was still dark, at five in the morning, and before the sun rose he had developed photographs of filovirus particles budding directly out of cells in the monkey's liver. It was a definite confirmation that the Reston monkeys were infected with a filovirus. But what strain was it? Everyone assumed that it was Marburg, which kills about one in four people it infects. All that day, in his laboratory, Peter Jahrling used a fluorescence test to try to nail down the strain. At five o'clock in the evening, he put some samples under an ultraviolet light and, to his shock, found that the stuff that glowed wasn't Marburg: it was Ebola, the slate-wiper, which kills almost nine out of ten people.

The news that Ebola virus had broken out near Washington, D.C., was not received casually at Fort Detrick. Shortly after five o'clock, minutes after Jahrling typed the strain, Colonel Peters notified the chain of command. First, Peters and Jahrling went to Colonel David Huxsoll, the head of USAMRIID. Picking up Huxsoll and then Nancy Jaax, the group then went to Major General Philip Russell, the commander of the Army Medical Research & Development Command at Fort Detrick. General Russell was himself a virologist, and when he saw Geisbert's glossy photographs he knew what he was looking at. The meeting became tumultuous. With people talking loudly in the background, General Russell picked up the telephone and called the Centers for Disease Control, and got Frederick Murphy on the line. Murphy is an expert on the Ebola virus—he had performed the first isolation of the virus with Karl Johnson, during the 1976 Zaire outbreak—and now, perhaps understandably, Murphy was skeptical when General Russell told him that the Army had isolated Ebola near Washington. Murphy is reported to have said to General Russell, "You can't fool me.

You have crud in your scope." Still, Murphy took it seriously. He said that a team from the CDC would fly to USAMRIID early the next morning to review the data. He advised Russell to notify Hazleton Research Products, so that the company's employees could be protected, and also to notify the Virginia State Department of Health.

Russell and Huxsoll put C. J. Peters in charge of any Army units that would be needed to deal with the Ebola outbreak. Next, Peters set up a conference call with Dan Dalgard, at his home. He told Dalgard that his monkeys had Ebola virus, probably in a mixed infection with simian hemorrhagic fever. Dalgard had heard of Marburg but never of Ebola.

The next morning—Wednesday, November 29th—seven dead monkeys turned up in Room H at the Reston Primate Quarantine Unit. It seemed that Room H had now become the hot spot.

Then Dalgard got another disturbing piece of news. An animal caretaker at the Reston monkey unit, who will here be called Jarvis Purdy, had suffered a heart attack and had been taken to Loudoun Hospital, near Reston. Dalgard wondered if Purdy's heart attack had been triggered by an Ebola infection. Had Purdy thrown an Ebola clot? Dalgard called the hospital and, without mentioning the word *Ebola*, left instructions for Purdy's doctor that if he saw any unusual signs in Purdy he should immediately notify Colonel C. J. Peters, of the United States Army. Dalgard also issued an order to the monkey caretakers at the Reston unit. As he recorded in his journal,

> All operations other than feeding, observation and cleaning were to be suspended. Anyone entering the rooms was to have full protection—Tyvek suit, respirator, and gloves. Dead animals were to be double-bagged and placed in a refrigerator.

That morning, Colonel Peters and Lieutenant Colonel Nancy Jaax 80 drove down to Hazleton Washington's headquarters, in Vienna, where Dalgard has his office and the company has a laboratory. Peters, in command of the Army groups that would respond to the Reston emergence in whatever way might be needed, sensed that the Army might have to act decisively to deal with the virus. As he drove to Vienna, he turned over in his mind the question of whether the Army would have to sterilize the Reston Primate Quarantine Unit, using military biohazard teams. There is a slang term in the Army for this type of action: the term is *nuke*. In the world of biocontainment, nuke has nothing to do with nuclear weapons. It has to do with neutralizing hot organisms: to nuke a place means to sterilize it. You go into the place in space suits and you isolate any infected hosts. If the hosts are animals, you kill them, bag them, and incinerate them. If the hosts are human, you put them in bubble stretchers and take them to the biocontainment hospital at USAMRIID—the Slammer. Then you sterilize the hot zone with biocides and formaldehyde gas.

C. J. Peters is not a hardboiled military type. He is a medical doctor and a field virologist of the old school, a jungle hand who got his training with Karl Johnson in Panama and worked with him during the Machupo outbreak in Bolivia. Peters has recently left the Army to become the chief of the Special Pathogens Branch of the Centers for Disease Control—a job that he landed at least partly because of the way he handled the Reston emergence. Peters is a chunky, affable man in his fifties, with a mustache, a round face, and what I think of as stingingly alert eyes.

Not wanting to attract attention, Peters and Lieutenant Colonel Jaax drove in separate civilian cars to the corporate office of Hazleton Washington. They were in uniform. At Hazleton, they talked with Dalgard and looked at slides of monkey tissue. They wanted to get samples, and perhaps some cadavers, and they wanted to see the monkeys at the monkey house face-to-face. Dalgard, perhaps fearful of losing control of the situation, would not allow them to visit the Reston Primate Quarantine Unit. Instead, the two Army officers drove four miles down the Leesburg Pike into Reston and parked in a cul-de-sac beside an Amoco station, near some pay telephones, waiting for someone from the Reston monkey house to bring them samples of monkey tissue. It was early afternoon. "We watched guys buying Cokes to drink, and housewives calling their boyfriends," Peters said to me. Eventually a windowless Hazleton van pulled up and parked beside the colonels, and a Hazleton employee swung heavily out of the driver's seat. "I've got 'em right back here," he said. He threw open the door of the van, and the colonels saw seven garbage bags.

"I said to myself, 'What *is* this?'" Peters recalled. The garbage bags held seven dead monkeys, and they were as hot as hell. Presumably lethal. They were the seven crab-eating macaques that had turned up dead that morning in Room H.

Jaax was getting that *oogh* feeling in the pit of her stomach. She turned to Peters. "I'm not putting that shit in the trunk of this car," she said. "As a veterinarian, I have certain responsibilities with regard to transportation of dead animals, sir. I can't just knowingly ship a dead animal with an infectious disease across state lines. You're a doc. You can get away with this." She nodded at his shoulder bars and said, "This is why you put on those big eagles, sir."

Nancy Jaax wanted to dissect the monkeys as soon as possible, 85 since she had noticed how Ebola-infected cadavers degenerate. ("If the animal has been dead for more than twenty-four hours, you have a bag of soup to look at.") Peters inspected the bags—it was a relief to see that the monkeys were triple-bagged, anyway—and he decided to take them to Fort Detrick and worry about health laws afterward. "If the guy drove them back to Reston, I felt there would be a certain added risk to the population just from his driving them around in the van, and there would also be a delay in diagnosing them," he said to me. "We felt that if we could quickly get a definite diagnosis of Ebola it would be in everyone's favor." They loaded the bags into the trunk of Peters' car, a red Toyota. The monkeys depressed the rear end of his car. Peters didn't see anything dripping. Nancy Jaax followed him to Fort Detrick.

When she arrived, she immediately suited up. First, she went into a locker room and put on a long-sleeved scrub suit and tucked her hair into a surgical cap. She put on a pair of white socks. Then she walked across the floor in her socks and waved a magnetic swipe-card across an entry sensor. A central computer at USAMRIID noted that Jaax, Nancy, was attempting entry into Containment Suite AA-5. Finding that she was cleared to enter the area, the computer beeped and unlocked the door. She went through the door into a negative-pressure Biosafety Level 3 staging area, the route into BL-4, the hot zone. There were two other pathologists in the staging area, and they and Nancy Jaax would work as buddies in the hot zone. She put on her inner surgical gloves and sealed them to the sleeves of her scrub suit with bands of sticky tape. Now she had one intact barrier between her and Nature. Her space suit was hanging on a peg, under ultraviolet lights. It was bright blue and was made of plastic. It had a soft plastic helmet with a clear faceplate. The suit had soft feet, like the feet in a bunny suit, and, attached at the wrists, rubber gloves. She stepped into the suit, fitted her hands into the gloves, and pulled the helmet over her head. She closed a steel zipper, followed by a Ziploc-type zipper. Her breath clouded the faceplate. Peering through condensation, she opened a supply air lock. Sitting in the air lock were the seven bagged monkeys. She picked up a couple of the bags and a box of necropsy tools, opened a door marked with a red toad-shade, and stepped into the gray-zone air lock leading to Biosafety Level 4. In this air lock was a chemical shower. She opened the far door and walked into Biosafety Level 4, the hot zone. As she closed the air lock behind her, she pulled a chain, and the air lock began a decon cycle: an Envirochem shower ran in the chamber. That was to stop any backflow of organisms from the hot zone through the air lock.

From the ceiling of the hot room dangled an array of yellow air hoses. Jaax plugged a hose into her suit, and dry air cleared her faceplate. It made a loud rushing noise. People in BL-4 can hardly hear each other shout, and they often communicate by hand signals, like scuba divers. When you were in BL-4, even with a buddy, you were essentially alone. Jaax thought that it was like going into outer space.

She opened a stainless-steel-lined closet which was flooded with ultraviolet light, and removed a pair of rubber boots and pulled them on. She collected her necropsy tools and specimen containers and laid them beside a stainless-steel table. She untied a bag, and laid a crab-eating macaque on the table. Unclouded brown eyes stared at her. Some animal behaviorists think that monkeys are an alien consciousness unto themselves, where human rules don't necessarily apply, and others think that monkeys' minds and emotions work much like ours, since we are all primates. She slit the monkey's abdomen with a scalpel, and then disposed of the scalpel in a sharps container. From this point on, she would use scissors. Scalpels are deadly instruments in a BL-4 hot suite. If you were to cut yourself with a hot scalpel, your boss would be filling out accident reports while you sat in the Slammer for the rest of your life—which might not be long.

The spleen was enlarged, but there were no obvious lesions inside this monkey. Then, at the base of the stomach, she found a ring of hemorrhages on the junction between the stomach and the small intestine—a lesion that is associated with simian hemorrhagic fever. She clipped samples of tissue and pressed them on glass slides. The slides were the only glass objects allowed in the hot zone. All laboratory beakers were plastic. A sliver of glass might pierce the suit and you, bringing into your bloodstream the replicative other. She worked slowly, rinsing her gloves often in Clorox. She was alone in a cocoon with the sound of her air.

While Nancy Jaax was in the hot room, a big meeting occurred in   90
a conference room at USAMRIID. The meeting turned into a power struggle, between the Centers for Disease Control and the Army, over which institution would manage the Reston outbreak. Representing the CDC were Dr. Joseph McCormick, who was then the chief of the Special Pathogens Branch at the CDC, and Dr. Frederick Murphy, who had first isolated Ebola. McCormick spoke for the CDC, and, according to the impression the USAMRIID people got, he said to them, in effect: Thanks for alerting us. The big boys are here now. You can turn this over to us. After all, the CDC has a mandate for protecting the American population from infectious disease.

Colonel Peters resisted a takeover by the CDC. He and McCormick personally disliked each other, and the clash of personalities rapidly became institutional head-butting between the CDC and the Army. At its heart, the argument concerned turf between doctors. Peters said to McCormick that the Army had appropriate containment suites for handling the organism and good tests that would reveal its presence in tissue. McCormick claimed that the CDC had a better, newer technique for testing for Ebola. Peters replied that an ongoing epidemic is not the time to try to field-test a new technique. Peters added that USAMRIID was closer to the outbreak than the CDC. Peters hardly needed to add that those seven dead monkeys, even as he spoke, were being dissected in a hot suite: possession is nine-tenths of the law, and the Army had the meat. The participants agreed, finally, that the CDC would manage the human-health aspects of the Ebola outbreak, while the Army would deal with the monkeys in Reston.

The next day, Peters walked into the office of Colonel Jerry Jaax, Nancy Jaax's husband, and put him in charge of the group that would go to Reston. Jerry Jaax, in turn, called a meeting of military people and civilians at USAMRIID, and asked for volunteers to terminate the monkeys in Room H, take clinical samples, and sterilize the room. It was going to be a limited operation. They would leave the rest of the monkey house alone.

At five-thirty in the morning on Friday, December 1st, an Army biohazard group—all volunteers, mixed civilians and soldiers (including both officers and enlisted people), led by Jerry Jaax—assembled in a parking lot next to USAMRIID. Everyone wore civilian clothes, and they drove their own cars, to avoid attracting attention. They had filled three unmarked vans with equipment. The vans contained, among other things, Racal suits—the same type of lightweight suit that the Army team had used inside Kitum Cave. The group moved out, soon got stuck in rush-hour traffic, and didn't arrive at the business park where the monkey house was situated until eight-thirty. They drove across a lawn and assembled in a secluded spot behind the monkey house, along a fringe of woods. The back side of the building presented a brick face, some narrow windows, and a glass door. The door was the insertion point.

It was a freezing, overcast day. From where they stood, they could see through the trees a day-care center with a playground, and they could hear shouts of children in the air. The operation would be carried out near children. Jerry Jaax had named Major Mark Haines, a veterinarian, the operational leader of the space-suited teams working inside the building. Haines, a Green Beret, had trained in the Green Berets' scuba-diving school. Haines' experience in underwater operations would prove helpful. A battery pack attached to each suit powered a blower that kept the suit pressurized with filtered air. The batteries had a life span of six hours, and people would have to be extracted from the hot area and decontaminated before their batteries failed, or they would be in trouble. Major Haines told the group that he wanted everyone to use the buddy system. Stick with your buddy and watch your buddy's suit for rips or holes, he told them. Two of the group members were dating each other: they worked separately, following Army policy. Almost none of the teams' members, including Haines and Jerry Jaax, had ever worn a Racal suit.

Nancy Jaax knew something about space suits, and she spoke to 95 some of the team members. "Your suits are under pressure," she said. "If you get a rip in your suit, you have to tape it shut right away, or you'll lose your pressure, and contaminated air could flow inside the suit." She held up a roll of brown sticky tape. "I wrap extra tape around my ankle, like this"—she demonstrated—"and then you can tear off a length of tape and use it to patch a hole in your suit. Be exquisitely careful. Know where your hands and body are at all times. If you get blood on your suit, stop and clean it off. Keep your gloves clean. With bloody gloves, you can't see a hole in the glove."

Suiting up proved to be difficult and embarrassing. You had to remove all your clothes, including your underwear, and then put on a surgical scrub suit. The teams rigged up a changing room inside one of the vans, screening it with sheets of plastic, but the women felt exposed. It was also bitterly cold. After you had put on your scrub suit, you went in through the insertion-point door to a staging area, and a support team there helped you put on your Racal suit.

The staging area led into a hallway deeper in the monkey house. They used this hallway as a makeshift air lock, or gray zone. It had doors at either end. One door led out to the staging area; the other door led into the monkey rooms. At no time were both doors to be opened simultaneously. The first two people to put on their suits and enter the air lock were Colonel Jerry Jaax and Major Mark Haines. They stood in the air lock for a moment, and then opened the door and entered the monkey area. Something had gone wrong with the heating system, and the temperature had soared above ninety in there. Jaax and Haines began to pour sweat—the Racal suits weren't insulated—and their plastic head bubbles fogged up. The monkeys were subdued and hungry. Jaax and Haines walked up and down the hallways, going into each monkey room and checking the cages for dead or sick monkeys. They fed the monkeys their monkey biscuits. The monkeys hooted with excitement every time Jaax got near a biscuit bin. They found some chairs in a lounge and carried them into a hallway, where the volunteers could sit and rest while they sorted tubes of blood and loaded syringes with drugs. Jaax wanted to be sure that no one would reach inside a cage with a hypodermic syringe and get bitten by a monkey infected with Ebola. He had devised a mop handle with a U-shaped attachment on the end that would pin a monkey down in its cage. Then someone could stick the monkey with a syringe on the end of a pole.

Each insertion of a pair of buddies took twenty minutes. As the pairs were coming in, Jaax and Haines loaded some syringes with double doses of ketamine, an anesthetic. Then they went into Room H, the focus of the outbreak, and ran the mop handle into one cage after another, sticking each nervous animal with the pole syringe, and reloaded the pole with a full syringe after each injection. The monkeys began to collapse in their cages. When a monkey was down, Jaax injected the animal with a sedative, Rompun, which put it in a deep sleep.

The bleed teams set up bleed tables in a hallway, outside the view of any monkeys. (Monkeys get upset when they see euthanasia going on.) Haines would put an unconscious monkey on a bleed table, stick a needle in its thigh, and draw samples of blood. He would pass the monkey to Major Nathaniel Powell, Jr., a veterinarian, at a euthanasia table. Powell would lay the monkey out and give it an injection of T-61, a euthanasia agent, which killed the monkey. When the monkey's breathing and heart had stopped, Powell would hand the monkey to Major Stephen Denny. He would open the monkey with scissors, snip out bits of spleen and liver, and put the samples in tubes. The other soldiers and the civilians put the monkeys in plastic biohazard bags, adding paper towels or kitty litter to soak up blood. They triple-bagged each monkey, washing the outside of each bag with Clorox, and then they loaded the bags into drums called hatboxes, which look like ice-cream containers but are blazed with biohazard symbols.

People grew tired and overheated in their suits, and some needed   100 to go to the bathroom. As the day wore on, they began coming out in pairs through the air lock. A gray team, also wearing Racal suits, stood in the air lock between the two worlds and sprayed each person's suit with Clorox. Then the person went into the staging area, where the support team peeled off the suit, and the person climbed into the van and stripped to the skin, a shivering tropical primate. The men and women put on their clothes and stood around on the grass, looking pale, weak, and thoughtful. By nightfall, all the monkeys in Room H had been put to death.

That weekend, Dan Dalgard caught up on his diary. "Retirement as a clock repairman looks better each day," he wrote. He worried that television crews would show up on Monday morning, and he ordered the Hazleton animal caretakers, who were still entering the Reston monkey unit to feed the surviving monkeys but were now wearing respirators and overalls, not to go outside the building with their protective equipment on. He did not want images of Hazleton monkey workers wearing what looked like gas masks to appear on the evening news.

He arrived at the monkey unit early on Monday morning, and was parking his car when he saw a Hazleton animal caretaker, who will here be called Francis Milton, standing out on the lawn by the main entrance wearing his respirator and suit. Dalgard was furious. He jumped out of his car. Suddenly, Milton pulled off his respirator, knelt in the grass, and vomited. Dalgard was "scared shitless," he told me later. Milton developed the dry heaves. Dalgard helped him to his feet, took him indoors, and had him lie down on a couch. They couldn't find a thermometer. Someone ran to a drugstore and bought one. Milton had a fever of a hundred and one. He was shaky and felt faint. He appeared to be breaking with Ebola. He did not seem afraid; he told people that he had been previously saved, and had put his life in the hands of Our Lord. They called an ambulance. Just as it showed up, so did television crews. The ambulance, chased by television vans, took Milton to Fairfax Hospital, where he was put into an isolation ward.

Dalgard now had two employees in the hospital—Purdy with a heart attack and Milton with a fever—and either of them could be breaking with Ebola. He decided that he must order the destruction of all the monkeys. The time had come to evacuate the building and turn it over to the Army. He called Colonel Peters at Fort Detrick. Peters asked Dalgard to send him a letter ceding control of the building to the Army. Dalgard sent it immediately by fax. Peters showed it to General Russell. Peters saw a need for clarity and speed. "You reach a point where you need to make a decision," Peters explained to me. Dalgard, in his letter, had asked the Army to assume responsibility for any liability that would arise after the Army took over. Peters refused to assume liability. Dalgard backed down; they signed the letter, Dalgard evacuated and locked the building; a Hazleton courier drove the keys to Fort Detrick; and the building fell under the control of the Army.

The next day—Tuesday—the biohazard teams returned, with their marked vans, and deployed in the grassy area behind the building. The teams began to suit up. Before they went inside, Major Haines, the Green Beret, gave them a talk. By his later account, his words went this way: "You are going to euthanize a whole building full of animals. This is not a fun operation. You must consider these animals as beings of a kind. Don't go in and play with the monkeys. I don't want to hear laughing and joking around the animals. I can be hard. Remember the veterinarian's creed: You have a responsibility to animals and you have a responsibility to science. These animals gave their lives to science. They were caught up in this thing; it's not their fault; they had nothing to do with it. Go in by twos. Never hand a used needle to another person. If a needle comes out of its cap, it goes straight into an animal, and then don't recap it, because you could stick yourself. Put the used syringe straight into a disposal container. If you get tired, tell your supervisor, and we'll decon you out."

It took three days to kill all the monkeys, and the teams did it room 105 by room. The most dangerous job fell to Jerry Jaax. That was to inject conscious monkeys with the first anesthetic, and not get bitten. A sergeant named Thomas Amen stayed at Jaax's side during most of the operation. He and Jaax took turns pinning the monkeys with the mop handle and giving them injections with the pole syringe. The lowest banks of cages were at floor level and were often dark. Jaax, who is a tall man, had to get down on his knees to peer inside them. He could hardly see anything through his head bubble. He would pick out the shape of a monkey in the back of a cage, pin it down, and then Sergeant Amen would ease the pole syringe into the cage, aiming for the thigh. There would be screeches and a wild commotion, the monkey shrieking *"Kra, kra!"* Jaax's knees hurt and he could hardly stand up after a day of injecting monkeys. He was one of the last to be deconned out at the end of each day, and Mark Haines remarked later that when Jerry Jaax took off his Racal suit he looked ten years older.

At Fort Detrick, Nancy Jaax stayed up late every night, dissecting monkeys and preserving their tissues. Nancy and Jerry didn't speak much about the job to their children—a son and a daughter, who were both in middle school. The children hardly saw their parents during the emergency. On December 7th, Nancy's father died, in Wichita. Jerry urged her to go home for the funeral. She flew home alone, reflecting that she had not been there to hold her father's hand.

Inside the Reston monkey facility, the bleed team set up a table in an empty monkey room, where there was a water faucet and a floor drain. The constant sampling of monkey blood and tissues generated much blood; they washed it down the drain with Clorox. As the nuking went on, by the second and third days you could see exhausted soldiers and civilians in suits, men and women, their head bubbles clouded with condensation, sitting in the chairs in the main hallway, loading syringes with T-61 and sorting boxes full of blood tubes. Some talked loudly, to be heard over the whine of their blowers, and others just stared at the walls.

When the monkeys were dead, the teams cleared out, and locked the building. They had collected a total of thirty-five hundred clinical samples, but nobody had stuck himself with a needle or received a bite. Then the decon team arrived. The rooms and halls were bloodstained and strewn with medical packaging, monkey biscuits, and monkey feces. Every object and surface had to be presumed lethally hot. The decon team wore Racal suits and worked slowly. They washed the walls with Clorox bleach. They bagged the medical debris, and washed feces out of corners with bleach and shoveled it into bags. The bagged monkeys were delivered to Dalgard's people, to be burned at a Hazleton incinerator. Using silver duct tape, the decon teams taped all the doors and windows shut and taped sheets of plastic over vent openings, first inside the building and then outside, until they had made the building airtight.

Finally, on December 18th, the decon team set out patches of paper saturated with spores of a harmless bacterium known as *Bacillus subtilis niger*, scattering them all around the monkey house. These spores are hard to kill. It is believed that a decon job that kills *niger* will kill anything. The team had brought thirty-nine Sunbeam electric frying pans. Sunbeam frying pans are the Army's tool of choice for a decon job. They plugged the frying pans into heavy-duty electrical outlets all around the monkey building, which were wired to a master switch. Into each Sunbeam they dropped a handful of paraformaldehyde crystals. They dialed the pans to "high." At 18:00 hours on December 18th, someone threw the master switch, and the Sunbeams began to cook, releasing formaldehyde gas. The building's doors, windows, and vents, having been taped, prevented the gas from escaping. Three days later, the decon team, again wearing Racal suits, went back inside the building and collected the spore samples. The Sunbeam treatment had killed the *niger*. Total, unequivocal sterilization of a room is difficult to achieve and nearly impossible to verify, but a Sunbeam cookout that exterminates *niger* implies success. The building had been nuked. For a short while, the Reston Primate Quarantine Unit was probably the only building in the world where nothing lived, nothing at all.

Tom Geisbert and Peter Jahrling, who had breathed Ebola Reston 110 virus from a flask, worked around the clock for weeks, testing monkey blood and tissues. As the days went by and they did not develop headaches, their worry subsided. They were encouraged by the fact that Dan Dalgard had not developed Ebola-virus infection. He had been dissecting hot monkeys weeks before the Army found Ebola in them, and he was fine. In the end, neither Geisbert nor Jahrling came down with Ebola, and neither showed immunological signs of having been exposed to the virus. As for Francis Milton, the Hazleton animal caretaker who had vomited on the lawn, he recovered quickly. It seemed that Milton had had influenza—or, possibly, an extremely mild case of Ebola Reston. Later, Milton developed antibodies to Ebola Reston. That means he had become infected with the strain. The virus had multiplied inside him, but he had not developed clinical disease, except, perhaps, nausea and fever—if, indeed, his illness came from Ebola rather than flu. Milton did not give Ebola to anyone else. As for Purdy, the animal caretaker who had had a heart attack, he recovered normally.

After the decon team left, Hazleton Research Products took the building back. In January, 1990, the company restocked the building with monkeys, which it had bought from the same Philippine exporter that supplied the earlier batches of sick monkeys. A few weeks after the restocking, Ebola Reston virus mixed with simian hemorrhagic fever again broke out in the monkey building. It seemed that the Ebola Reston virus had been circulating at the Philippine exporter's compound in Mindanao.

This time, Dan Dalgard did not turn the Reston monkey house over to the Army, but he did let the Army take samples back to USAMRIID. Since no human illness had resulted from the first outbreak, Dalgard decided to try to contain the disease room by room. When disease broke out in a room, he sacrificed all the monkeys in that room. But the virus began appearing in room after room, accompanied by respiratory signs, such as coughing, bloody sputum, and hemorrhagic pneumonia, and by March most of the monkeys were dead. Hazleton was renting the building from a commercial landlord. Not surprisingly, relations between Hazleton and the landlord did not improve during the Army nuking and the second outbreak of Ebola. Hazleton vacated the building after the second outbreak, and to this day it stands empty.

Perhaps the most surprising fact about the Reston emergence is that it has not resulted in any obvious human illness or death. There was, however, a subtle and perhaps sinister effect. Six Hazleton employees had close contact with the sick monkeys, including Dan Dalgard. Of those six men, four—all but Dalgard and a supervisor—developed antibodies to the virus in their bloodstream. That means that the virus replicated successfully in the four men's tissues. One of the four, a man who will here be called John Coleus, cut his finger with a scalpel while performing a necropsy on a monkey that had died of Ebola Reston. It happened during the second outbreak, in February, 1990. "We were frankly fearful that he had bought the farm," Peter Jahrling said to me. But John Coleus didn't even get sick. Why John Coleus didn't die of Ebola is one of the great mysteries of the Reston outbreak. He was certainly infected with Ebola—the virus had multiplied in him—yet he showed no ill effects. As for the three other men who caught Ebola Reston, it seems that they must have picked up the virus through the air. They were using water hoses to clean the cages, and they may have breathed droplets of monkey waste or monkey mucus into their lungs. To date, none of the four men have shown any clinical symptoms of illness. Ebola Reston virus infects human beings but apparently doesn't make them sick—or possibly it gives them a flu-like illness. Yet it appears to be absolutely deadly to monkeys.

Ebola Reston virus is an extremely close relative of Ebola Zaire, the hot strain. It may be that Ebola Reston is a variant of Ebola Zaire; perhaps a mutation rendered it harmless to human beings. It may be that Ebola Reston is a Southeast Asian cousin of Ebola Zaire. Epidemiologists visited the Philippine monkey-export facility in Mindanao and found that none of the employees there had suffered a serious unknown illness in the year preceding the Reston emergence. Ebola Reston and Ebola Zaire look the same in an electron microscope. A molecular biologist at the CDC named Anthony Sanchez has begun to analyze the Ebola virus's genetic sequences. He has found that Ebola Reston is, genetically, very close to Ebola Zaire. "I term them kissing cousins," he said to me. "But I can't put my finger on why Reston is apparently apathogenic in human beings and doesn't make us sick."

In March, 1990, right after the second Reston outbreak, the CDC   115 slapped a heavy set of restrictions on monkey importers, tightening the testing and quarantine procedures. The CDC also temporarily revoked the licenses of three companies—Hazleton Research Products, the Charles River Primates Corporation, and Worldwide Primates—charging those companies with violating quarantine rules. The CDC's actions effectively stopped the importation of monkeys into the United States for several months. The total loss to Hazleton ran into the millions of dollars. Monkeys are worth money. Crab-eating macaques fetched around five hundred dollars apiece before the Reston outbreak; since then, government regulations and a monkey shortage have driven the price to fifteen hundred dollars. Despite the CDC's action against Hazleton, scientists at USAMRIID, and even some at the CDC, give Dalgard and his company high praise for making the decision to hand the monkey facility over to the Army, which cost the company millions but seemed essential for the safety of the American population. "It was hard for Hazleton, but they did the right thing," Peter Jahrling said to me.

Jahrling, an inhaler of Ebola who lived to tell about it, is now the acting chief of virology at USAMRIID. He is also credited, along with Tom Geisbert, with having performed the first laboratory isolation and characterization of the Ebola Reston strain. This recognition gives Jahrling the right to name it; he hasn't decided on a name. One day, in his office, he showed me a photograph of some Ebola virus particles. They looked as if they had been cooked al dente and would make a tempting first course at a trattoria in Rome. "Look at this honker. Look at this long sucker here," Jahrling said, his finger tracing a spaghetto. "It's Res — Oh, I was about the say it's Reston, but it isn't. It's Zaire. The point is, you can't easily tell the difference between them by looking. It brings you back to a philosophical question: Why is the Zaire stuff hot? Why isn't Reston hot, when they're so close to each other? The Ebola Reston virus is almost certainly transmitted by some airborne route. Those Hazleton workers who developed antibodies to the virus—I'm pretty sure they got the virus through the air."

"Did we dodge a bullet?" I asked.

"I don't think we did," he said. "The bullet hit us. We were just lucky that the bullet we took was a rubber bullet from a .22 rather than a dumdum bullet from a .45. My concern is that people are saying, 'Whew, we dodged a bullet.' And the next time they see Ebola in a microscope they'll say, 'Aw, it's just Reston,' and they'll take it outside a containment facility. And we'll get whacked in the forehead when the stuff turns *not* to be Reston but its big brother."

Karl Johnson, the leader of the team that isolated and named the Ebola virus, is sitting in a swale of dry grass on the bank of the Bighorn River. Something screams on the opposite bank. "Hear that pheasant? That's what I like about the Bighorn," he says. He peers across the water, where insects are hatching from the river's surface. "Huh! We've got two different emergences going on here."

I look carefully and see two swarms of insects coming off the water. One type of insect is flying upstream, into the wind; the other type is being blown downstream. The clouds are passing through each other, two interpenetrative rivers of insects flowing above the river of water. "The ones that are flying upstream are little tiny mayflies called tricos," Johnson says. "The others are the baetises. They have really long tails. These insects spend a year or more at the bottom of the river as nymphs. Then they pupate and rapidly emerge from the water and fly away as adults. The adults molt into spinners, which is the egg-laying form, and the spinners lay their eggs on the surface of the river and die. The process from emergence to dying can happen fast—the whole thing might take a couple of hours. These hatchers are like emerging viruses. The viruses have been on the earth a long, long time. Invisible. In the river, you might say." Johnson tells me that the word *emerge* comes from the Latin word *emergere*. In Webster's unabridged dictionary, its first meaning is: "To rise from . . . an enveloping fluid." He says, "It means to come through another medium. Most of the emerging viruses are being transmitted to man from animals. Coming through another medium. There's been this incredible damned surge of people on our planet. There's been a human population explosion and human invasion of tropical habitats. There are just too many people entering too many ecosystems and violating them. People stumble into something and get sick."

Johnson stands up and knots to his line a tiny fly that looks like a dead spinner, a canapé for a trout. Bufflehead ducks are diving at the head of the pool, and a trout rises and flops, transmitting rings into the water that spread and die, absorbed in the filiations of the Bighorn.

"Do you find viruses beautiful?"

"Oh, yeah," he says softly. "Looking at Ebola under an electron microscope is like looking at a gorgeously wrought ice castle. The thing is so cold. So totally pure. In Bolivia, we found out that the reservoir of the Machupo virus is a wild mouse. Machupo is fundamentally a sexually transmitted infection in a mouse. These Bolivian mice live in demes, which are like villages. They copulate frequently. When the mouse population expands to the point where there is contact among the demes, you have a sexually transmitted plague of Machupo in the mice, and the population crashes. The Machupo virus is a force that keeps the mouse population from going out of control and using up its food supply. Machupo *benefits* the mouse as a species, because when the demes touch, the population gets thinned out. This is Nature. And I happen to think it is one of the loveliest biological structures I've ever seen."

"It sounds like AIDS," I say.

"You're damned right. AIDS is that way for us. As a biologist, from a deeply philosophical viewpoint, I don't think there's any difference. As a physician, of course, I can't turn my back on another human being." 125

This past week in Washington, the Institute of Medicine, which is chartered by the National Academy of Sciences, called a news conference and released a frightening report entitled "Emerging Infections." The report was two years in the making. Under the heading "Trouble Ahead," the report described the Reston emergence as a classic example of "the potential of foreign disease agents to enter the United States." The Reston emergence scared a lot of epidemiologists.

The Institute of Medicine report essentially warns us to stay tuned. It says that not only emerging viruses but also mutant bacteria, such as the strains that cause multidrug-resistant tuberculosis, and protozoans, such as mutant strains of malaria, have become major and growing threats to the American population. The report says, "We can also be confident that new diseases will emerge, although it is impossible to predict their individual emergence in time and place." The Institute of Medicine finds that there has been a general breakdown in the public health system in the United States. We lack the forces to deal with a monster, at the very time when a monster could appear—especially given the emergence of HIV.

In its two years of deliberation, the committee came up with some recommendations: We need to have a national and worldwide surveillance system to identify emergences as they happen. (If we had had such a system in place fifteen years ago, we might have seen AIDS hatching off the river, as it were, perhaps in Central Africa, and we might have been able to save thousands of American lives.) We need a modernized and strengthened vaccine program, which would include a "surge" capacity for vaccine development, to respond to an emergency. We need better preventive medicine, to keep people from spreading emergent infectious diseases. And we need to train more field epidemiologists, since they are the detectives who help us find and know our enemies.

One of the authors of the Institute of Medicine report is a virologist named Stephen Morse. In the course of writing this account, I dropped in on him several times at Rockefeller University, in Manhattan. Morse is a voluble, bearded figure, who inhabits a paper-jammed lair on a hallway that reeks of urine from rabbits and mice. (Viruses need to grow in cells.) One day an unpleasant thought crossed my mind, and I asked Morse if an emerging virus could wipe out our species.

"Isn't HIV enough?" he asked. He said that HIV might actually do 130 the job. There has been some debate, recently, about whether HIV could mutate into an airborne disease, like influenza. Then AIDS would suddenly become AIDS-flu. It would circle the globe in a flash. The case mortality in AIDS seems to be close to a hundred percent. "The HIV particle does get into the lung," Morse explained to me. "There is no reason *in principle* why HIV couldn't spread by the respiratory route. Many viruses that are closely related to HIV, such as the Visna virus, which is a fatal immune-deficiency virus of sheep, do spread through a cough. The sheep cough, and the virus is aerosolized. Indeed, primary HIV infection—when you first get infected—has been associated with a flu-like illness, with upper respiratory system involvement: coughing, wheezing, and so forth." He added that if HIV did mutate into AIDS-flu, the question was whether it would remain fatal. Would it kill its human hosts or would it evolve toward something more benign, something like a nasty but survivable cold? The human population is genetically diverse, and I have a hard time imagining everyone getting wiped out by a virus," he said. "But if one in three people on earth were killed —something like the black Death in the late Middle Ages—the breakdown of social organization would be just as deadly, almost a species-threatening event."

I drove to Reston one day in autumn to see the former Primate Quarantine Unit, and stopped my car in front of the building. A sycamore tree on the lawn dropped an occasional leaf. The place was as quiet as a tomb. "For Lease" signs sat in front of many of the offices around the parking lot. I sensed the presence not of a virus but of financial illness— signs of convalescence from the eighties, like your skin peeling off after a bad fever. I parked beside a school and walked across the grassy area behind the former monkey house until I reached the glass door that had been the insertion point. It was locked. Shreds of silver duct tape dangled from the door's edges. I looked inside and saw a floor mottled with reddish-brown stains. A sign on an inner wall said "CLEAN UP YOUR OWN MESS." I discerned the air-lock corridor—the gray zone through which the teams had passed into the hot zone. It had unpainted cinder-block walls: the ideal gray zone.

My feet rustled through shreds of plastic in the grass. I heard a ball bounce, and saw a boy dribbling a basketball in the school playground. The ball cast rubbery echoes off the buildings. I walked along the back wall of the former monkey house until I came to a window. Inside the building, climbing vines had rioted, and had pressed themselves against the inside of the glass. The vine was Tartarian honeysuckle, a weed that grows in waste places and abandoned ground. I couldn't see through the leaves into the former hot zone. I walked around to the side of the building, and found another glass door, beribboned with tape. I pressed my nose against the glass and cupped my hands around my eyes, and saw a bucket smeared with a dry brown crust. It looked like monkey excrement. I guessed that it had been stirred with Clorox. A spider had strung a web between a wall and the bucket of shit, and had dropped husks of flies and yellow jackets on the floor. Ebola had risen in these rooms, flashed its colors, replicated, and subsided into the forest.

Questions

1. Preston writes, "You might call AIDS the revenge of the rain forest." What does he mean by that statement?
2. Why does Preston list emerging viruses? "Lassa. Rift Valley. Oropouche. Rocio. Q fever. VEE Guanarito. Ross River. Monkeypox. Dengue. Chikungunya. . . . " Why does he tell us that HIV "might have been called Kinshasa Highway, if it had been noticed earlier"?

Four

TRAVELING

*S*uccessful cartography depends on tenacious and curious exploration. The essayists in this chapter are all willing to undergo that journey and to record their discoveries. Their destinations—two small towns, a city, and two foreign countries—are very different, as are, more importantly, the kinds of things that become the objects of their gaze. At least two of these essayists force us to consider the travelers' effects on the places to which they travel, so that the indigenous population's response to the traveler becomes the issue of interest. This inversion of the usual point of view suggests the degree of interplay between all these essayists and their subjects, between the travelers and their destinations, between daily gestures and their implications. No matter how many predecessors have taken the same journey, these essayists map the place anew.

Both Alice Walker and Edward Hoagland are conscious of following well-marked trails. Walker traveled to China with a delegation of American women writers in 1983 and published "A Thousand Words: A Writer's Pictures of China" in 1985. Her snapshots, then, are taken before the Tiananmen Square Massacre; what could be seen of the violence to come? Walker sees fathers out walking with their little girls, and she even carries home icons of that sighting, pictures of the signs posted around the square: "pearl gray against a blue background without letters of any kind, the outline of a father and daughter holding hands, crossing the street." That this relationship is posted, codified into a sign, makes her "incomparably happy," and gives us, at another historical moment, two visions of the same place, neither of them false, neither of them wholly true.

Edward Hoagland sees himself as Alexander Mackenzie's spiritual heir, taking his title from the explorer's "stirring boast: *Alexander Mackenzie from Canada by land.*" Not walking to the Pacific, as Mackenzie did, but taking the train from Prince Rupert to Montreal, Hoagland slides along the shining rails from west to east, "from nature to art." His perennial wish is for that migration to be perpetual. Disembarked, he feels the ground "swing underfoot"; the traveler who peered out of the train to " 'see where we are' " lets us board that train in his essay, so that all of us, now, can join him in seeing what was in the distance.

Like Hoagland, John McPhee understands himself as an explorer, characterized, as are all explorers, by his curiosity. This time, an entry of only seventeen listings in the Fairbanks and Vicinity Telephone Directory has caught his eye, directing his gaze to the hamlet of Circle, Alaska. We come to know individuals in that town, like Carl Dasch and Richard Hutchinson and Albert Carroll, but by the end of the essay, McPhee has linked events in Circle with the spendthrift state dynamics that govern Alaska itself. "Riding the Boom Extension" shakes out any romantic notions we might have attributed to this frontier outpost; no place, it seems, can isolate itself from the empty values that characterize contemporary life.

Most of us would overlook Circle and its small group of inhabitants. Joan Didion charges that Miami's Anglo population is doing just that with the state's Cubans. The Anglos speak of " 'diversity,' " she writes, "and of Miami's 'Hispanic flavor,' an approach in which 56 percent of the population [is] seen as decorative, like the Coral Gables arches." This invisible majority is lauded by the Anglo community only for its dash of culinary exoticism and its desire to assimilate —but the Cubans see themselves as living in exile, in which "assimilation would be considered . . . a doubtful goal at best." Rather, living in Miami is "still at the deepest level construed by Cubans as a temporary condition." Didion measures the distance between two notions of home; although both groups live in the same city, their contradictory assumptions give them no common ground.

The Cubans have changed Miami, despite their feelings that they are just temporary residents. The Hmong and ethnic Laotians that Calvin Trillin looks at, however, are resettling in America as permanent residents. Having traveled from their own country forever, they are embraced by sponsors prepared with all the spiritual virtues, but who know nothing about their new charges. But would the thin "pamphlets on Hmong culture," which the sponsors never knew of or read, have been enough to change the travelers' effects on their new home? Not only is the ancient antipathy between Hmong and Lao reenacted in their new country, but it is also spread to their hosts. By the end of their story and the end of the essay, the immigrants' bitterness has taken root in new soil, contaminating the native townspeople, intensifying the estrangement of the Baptists and Methodists from each other.

In "Resettling the Yangs," Trillin documents old enmities being mapped onto new ground. Although Didion's Cubans make up the majority of Miamians, their narratives are inaudible to the Anglos, who replace the story of living in *exilio* with that of assimilation. Sharing the same place doesn't mean sharing the same geography, which demands sharing the same understanding of the relationship between the center and the periphery. Perhaps only the essay can help remap the geography of the imagination, to allow movement across otherwise guarded borders and boost travelers over the Great Wall without their having to bribe the guards.

Alice Walker

A THOUSAND WORDS:
A WRITER'S PICTURES OF CHINA

Alice Walker is most famous for her highly celebrated novel *The Color Purple* (1982), for which she won the Pulitzer Prize, the American Book Award, and a National Book Critics Circle Award nomination. The novel was made into an Oscar-nominated movie in 1985. She is also a prolific writer of poetry, essays, short stories, and other novels, and her entire body of work serves to justify one reviewer's description of her as "lavishly gifted." Walker writes most often about black women with hard lives, and issues of racism and sexism are of major importance in her work. But her vision is not a bleak or hopeless one. As she has said, her characters are often people "who make it, who come out of nothing." Walker was born in Georgia in 1944 and graduated from Sarah Lawrence College in 1965. Her latest publications are *The Temple of My Familiar* (1989) and *Possessing the Secret of Joy* (1992).

In 1965 I stood next to a fellow American traveler in northern Uganda as he took a picture of a destitute Karamojan tribesman, who was, in fact, dying. The man was a refugee from ancestral lands to the south, now expropriated by another group, and had been forced to eke out what living he could in the barren north. He wore the briefest shredded loincloth, had at most a single tooth, and his eyes were covered with flies. He sat very still for the photograph (he had raised himself at our approach), and as we turned away held out his hand. The photographer gave him a quarter.

No doubt this memory is one reason I never travel with a camera. But another is my belief that human beings are already cameras, and that adding a second camera to the process of seeing (and remembering) shallows, rather than deepens, vision. When the TV commercial declares Kodak "the nation's storyteller," I shudder, because I realize our personal culture is about to become as streamlined as our public. But perhaps only poets and writers feel this.

In June of 1983 I went to China with a group of twelve American women writers that included Paule Marshall (our delegation leader), Nellie Wong, Blanche Boyd, Tillie Olsen, Lisa Alther, and my friend and travel companion Susan Kirschner, who took many beautiful pictures of our trip with a real camera, which she has shared with me, as I wish to share these imaginary or mental "snaps" with her and with the other members of our group.

1

This is a picture of Susan and me at the San Francisco airport en route to China! We are leaning against the ticket counter furiously scribbling notes to our loved ones. I have chosen the same card for my daughter as for my companion. On a white background in large black letters above a vibrant red heart are the words I AM SO-O-O HAPPY WITH YOU!

So why am I going to China?   5

Whenever I fly, I fear I will not return to Earth except in shreds. As the plane lifts off I look at the Earth with longing and send waves of love to cover it as I rise.

How could anyone be foolish enough to leave the ground?

But you, I write to both of them, will also understand this contradiction in me: that I must fly to see even more of the Earth I love.

2

In this one Susan and I are on the plane somewhere over the Pacific reading identical copies of *The True Story of Ah Q* by the immortal Lu Hsun and drinking innumerable cups of Japanese green tea. In this story (1921), by the "father" of modern Chinese literature, a penniless peasant blunders his way into revolutionary pretense among local villagers, who hang him for his troubles. Lu Hsun depicts Ah Q as a foolish, childish person with no understanding of his emotions or his fate. We finish reading it about the same time and look at each other in quizzical disbelief. We feel Lu Hsun has condescended to his character, in precisely the way white Southern writers have condescended to their characters who are black. And as male writers condescend to characters who are women. That he, in fact, cannot believe a peasant capable of understanding his own oppression, his own life. Since the story is also exceedingly dull, we wonder what the Chinese value in it, beyond the fact that it is perhaps the first attempt to portray a Chinese peasant in fiction.

3

This one shows our arrival in Beijing. Not the actual landing and meet-   10
ing with our interpreters and Chinese writer hosts, but the long drive from airport into town. Our first awareness is that though China's

people population is phenomenal, its *tree* population is more so: and they are a kind of planned magic. From the air they're hardly visible because of the dust that sweeps down from the northern desert steppes and turns the landscape dun and yellow. And even when they first appear they seem modest and young, and one thinks of them in future tense. How grand they will look at eighty, and so on. But by the time one arrives on the streets of Beijing and notices veritable layers of trees five and six rows deep lining the broad boulevards a wonderful relief comes over the mind.

For one feels irresistibly drawn to people who would plant and care for so many millions of trees—and a part of this traveler relaxed. Because, for one thing, the planting of trees demonstrates a clear intention to have a future and a definite disinterest in war.

4

In this one, five members of our group are standing around the limited but adequate bar (orange crush, mineral water, beer, Coca-Cola) at the end of our floor in a hotel in Beijing. It is the day of our first long outing through the dusty streets of the city. Everyone is hot and thirsty. They are trying to decide whether to have orange crush, mineral water, or beer, like Americans who know what is going on. The look of dismay on their faces is because I have just walked up to the counter and said to the barkeep: I'll have a Coke.

I take the Coke into the room I share with Susan, drink some, and pour some out the window in libation. I save the bottle cap with "Coca-Cola" written in Chinese. Wherever I go in the world I buy one Coca-Cola in memory of the anonymous black woman who is said to have created it (probably on the theory that if you dope your masters—I have heard that Coke used to have coke in it—they're more pleasant).

I never heard of that, says Susan.

And I tell her it is the one thing I remember from my high-school graduation day. Our commencement speaker, Mr. Bullock, a horticulturist of stature from Atlanta, tried for thirty minutes to inspire pride of heritage in us by listing name upon illustrious name of heroic and creative black folk. People nodded. But when he said: Even Coca-Cola was invented by a black woman, everybody snapped awake. For didn't most of us drink this part of the heritage every day?

I tell Susan that in Collonwalde, the Coca-Cola mansion outside Atlanta, there is a statue of a black woman in the foyer, but nobody I asked about her seemed to know who she was or why she's there.

I laugh. It doesn't matter, really (though what a story there must be behind this story, I think). There's too much sugar in Coke. I'm sure the original was much better. It may even have been created as a medicine.

We run that down a little, start talking about the two most insidious poisons loose in the world today: sugar and cocaine; and soon drift off to sleep.

5

In this one I am wearing a large mulberry-colored coat several sizes too big, a long grape-colored scarf, a Chinese peasant hat the size of an umbrella, and am carrying a cane with a dragon carved on it. We have just stopped twenty miles upriver from the town of Guilin (after a stunning boat ride through mountains that look like stone trees), and the peasant merchants from the surrounding countryside have ambushed us on the shore. Their one American word is "hello," which they say with the same off-key intonation that I'm sure we say "nee-how" (phonetic Chinese for "hello"). In their mouths it becomes a totally different word. It is like meeting a long line of people and each one solemnly greets you with "Elbow." I fantasize that my "nee-how" probably sounds like, say, the Chinese word for "foot" to them. So all during this trip I've been smiling and saying "hello" and they've been hearing "foot, foot, foot."

Looking closely at this picture I see that I am also wearing very baggy pants. In fact, everything I'm wearing is several sizes too large. I realize we were asked by our tour leader not to wear tight, uncomfortable, or revealing clothes, but the overall looseness of my attire appears extreme.

I suspect, looking at this picture, in which I look ridiculous, but regal, that this outsize dressing is typical of people—especially women —who grow up in families whose every other member is larger than they are. Which is true in my family. We can't believe we're as small as we are. And so, we dress ourselves as if we were they. 20

6

This is a picture of a university dormitory in Guilin. It is early evening as Susan and I walk across the campus on our way to visit families of Susan's Chinese acquaintances in Portland. As is true everywhere in China, there is no wasted electricity (lighting is mellow rather than bright; forty watts rather than a hundred) and no unused space. In rooms smaller than those two U.S. college students would share, five and six students bunk. Freshly washed clothes hang everywhere inside the rooms, and outside the windows on long bamboo poles. The students we meet on the path are returning to the classrooms, which double as places of study at night. We watch rows and rows of them bent silently, intently, over their books.

Of course I think of Hampton Institute, Tuskegee, the early days of Morris Brown, Morehouse, and Spelman, black colleges started just after the Civil War in barracks and basements: poor, overcrowded, but determined to educate former peasants and slaves; schools that have also, like the Chinese schools, managed against great odds to do just that.

7

You would never believe, from this photograph, that I am sitting on the Great Wall of China. I look bored. I look unhappy. There is that tense line around my mouth that means I'll never come thousands of miles to see more of man's folly again. What I hate about the Great Wall is the thought of all the workers' bodies buried in it. I hate the vastness and barrenness of its location. I hate the suffering the women and children attached to the builders endured. I hate its—let's face it, I hate walls.

Susan dashes ahead of me looking for the best view. But the wall tires me, instantly. It is the concrete manifestation of so much that is wrong (a kind of primitive MX). What a stupid waste, I am thinking, in the photograph. A lot of flowers never sniffed. A lot of dancing never done.

The brochure about the wall says that the invaders, finding the Great Wall indeed impenetrable, simply got over it by bribing the guards. 25

The Great Wall is redeemed by only one thing: over each battlement portal (through which hand-propelled missiles must have whistled) there is a tiny decoration, serving no purpose whatsoever except to refresh the eye. And here is where the writer could benefit from having had a camera other than herself, because I feel deeply about this decoration, this modest attempt at art. I send mental salutations to the artist(s). But now I cannot remember what precisely the decoration is: is it a curled line, horizontal and short, like those on the windows of brownstones? Is it the missing flower? Or is it two straight lines from a hexagram symbolizing war, which I have mistaken for peace?

8

This one is of me and Susan walking across T'ien An Men Square looking at the many fathers out for a stroll with their female children. They all look interested, relaxed, happy. Susan stops one little girl and her father and asks if she may take a picture. At first he looks suspicious, or, more accurately, puzzled. We begin to ooh and aah over his child, a serene three-year-old with an enormous red ribbon in her hair. He understands. And beams with pride. Then we notice that street signs at crossings between the Forbidden City and the square depict just such a pair as we photographed: pearl gray against a blue background without letters of any kind, the outline of a father and daughter holding hands, crossing the street.

We are made incomparably happy by this: I think of my daughter and her father. Susan, I know, thinks of her husband, John, at home with their girls. We look at each other with enormous grins. Thinking of fathers and daughters all over the world and wishing them luck.

9

This one shows us sitting down in the middle of the square looking dissatisfied. We look this way because we both really like Beijing. Miraculously feel at peace here. It is true that the dust gives us coughing fits and my eyes feel gritty from the smog, but overall we are pleased with the wide, clean boulevards, the rows of linden trees that sparkle like jewels in every breeze, the calm, meditative motion of thousands of bikers who pedal as if they're contemplating eternity rather than traffic. At night we, like the Chinese, are drawn to the streets. There is no sense of danger. No fear. People look at us, mildly curious. We look back. Occasionally there is a spoken greeting. A smile.

What is it about Beijing that is so seductive? Susan muses. We   30
consider the dimness of the lights at night. The way the few cars and trucks do not use their headlights, only their parking lights. The way homes seem to be lit by candles. How there is very little neon. Nothing that blinks, flashes, or winks. The softness this gives the evening. The night. How strolling through this softness and hearing, through an open window, someone practicing cello or flute is a satisfying experience. And how the mind begins to think religious thoughts but in a new way.

When we first arrived, we thought Beijing a drab and ugly city because of the gray buildings and perpetual dust. Now, after six days, we find it beautiful enough not to want to leave, though neither of us speaks more than three words of Chinese.

In the West, Susan says, the cities are built to impress you with *themselves*. They are all-important. Here, the people are most important, and the buildings are backdrop.

10

Something else occurs to me from this next picture—the one of me wearing both the Chinese ring and the cloisonné bracelet I bought at the Friendship Store. People are more important than what they wear. Everyone wears essentially the same thing: trousers and shirt. And everyone is neat, clean, and adequately dressed. No one wears make-up or jewelry. At first, faces look dull, as a natural tree would look if Christmas trees were the norm. But soon one becomes conscious of the wonderful honesty natural faces convey. An honesty more interesting than any ornament. And a vulnerability that make-up and jewelry would mask.

Except in Shanghai, which resembles a large port city of the West, the Chinese do not have the faces of killers we've become used to in America (where the killer look is encouraged and actually desired); and even the soldiers, very young and wearing straw sandals or black cloth slippers, look gentle and relatively content.

11

In all of China there is nothing and no one more beautiful than the 35 writer Ding Ling. She is short and brown and round. She is also "old." But these attributes alone, which connect her to great masses of women throughout the world, do not make her beautiful. It is a puzzle, at first, what does. In this photograph she is listening to Madame Kang Ke Qing tell our group about the Long March and is swinging her foot slightly, as if to keep it awake. Madame has talked for three hours and told us most of the information about the Women's Federation (which she heads) we'd already read (that the Women's Federation "reeducates" those who would practice female infanticide, for instance).

I have drunk so much tea I am afraid to stand up. But Ding Ling? It is not tea she has drunk. She has drunk patience. Imprisoned by reactionaries and radicals, Kuomintang and Communists, presumed dead at least twice, to national mourning, her young common-law husband executed by firing squad two months after the birth of their child, herself locked in solitary confinement for ten months by Mao Zedong's wife, Jiang Qing, imprisoned and separated from her present husband, Chen Ming, for six years, under the Gang of Four, this small brown round "old" woman—who claps her hands like a child when Susan asks if she will be photographed with me—has, through everything (banishment to Manchuria to raise chickens among the peasants, whom she taught, as they taught her), simply continued to write. Powerful story after story, novel after novel, over a period of fifty years. And though beaten bloody by the Red Guards during the Cultural Revolution (for having been, among other things, famous) and forced to parade through the streets wearing a blackened face and a dunce's cap, she holds no bitterness, only saying, of all her travails—illnesses, children lost, books and notes destroyed—mainly, I lost time.

At nearly eighty she says things like: Oh, to be sixty-seven again!

After meeting Ding Ling, who is radiant with life and writing still, it becomes amusing and finally ludicrous to hear one of our American writers complain in city after city, to group after group, that she was unable to write most of her life "because of her children."

12

In this picture I have just been told by an editor of a Shanghai literary magazine that my novel *The Color Purple* is being translated into Chinese. I am delighted. Especially when she looks me warmly in the eye and says, with a beautiful accent, mocking my surprise: But Alice, it is a very *Chinese* story. She tells me further that two of my stories have already appeared in translation and that the woman who translated them (and who will translate the novel) wanted to meet me but was afraid I'd want to talk about copyrights.

I don't. What interests me is how many of the things I've written   40
about women certainly do, in China, look Chinese: the impact of poverty, forced sex and childbearing, domination as a race *and* a caste (before the Chinese Revolution); the struggle to affirm solidarity with women, as women, and the struggle to attain political, social, and economic equality with men.

But I am disturbed that a young Chinese writer of my generation, Yu Loujing, who is writing stories and novels similar in theme to mine in China, is banned. Whenever we ask about her there is a derisive response. She is only "writing out of her own bitter experiences," they say, as if this is a curse. "She is perpetuating bourgeois individualism." One of our hosts even goes so far as to accuse her of libel.

Still, though we do not meet her, and her books (not yet in English translation) can be bought only on the black market, she is the writer in China, next to Ding Ling, who intrigues me. She has written, for instance, about being raped by her husband on their wedding night, and of her hatred of it; an experience shared by countless women around the world (by now we understand there does not *have* to be blood on the sheets). For this bravery alone I feel the women of China will eventually love her. In fact, already do. For though she is scorned by the literary establishment—and by the Chinese Writers Union in particular—all her books are underground best sellers.

13

In this one, one of our hosts is singing "Old Black Joe" under the impression that this will prove she knows something about American blacks. There is deep sadness in this picture, as we realize that the Chinese, because of China's years of isolation, have missed years of black people's struggle in the United States. No Martin, no Malcolm, no Fannie Lou. No us. I want to move closer to Paule Marshall and put my arms around her, and I want her to hug me back. Here we are, two black women (thank the Universe we *are* two!), once again facing a racial ignorance that depresses and appalls. Our singing host was once in America, in the fifties, she says, and was taught this song as part of her English lessons. This is one of the songs U.S.-trained Chinese learned in America and brought back to teach others throughout China.

I explain the reactionary nature of the song. But the energy required to do this nearly puts me to sleep. Nor could I foretell that from this point in the trip everywhere I go I will be asked to sing. To teach the Chinese "a new song." I sing (one of my secret ambitions, actually); the irony of being asked, as a black person, not lost on me for a second. I start out with the Reverend Dorsey ("We Shall Overcome") and end up with Brother Lennon ("Hold On"). But it is really James Weldon Johnson's Negro National Anthem that is required ("Lift Ev'ry Voice and Sing"); and I am embarrassed to say I could not recall all the words. This I consider the major personal failure of the trip.

Lift ev'ry voice and sing
Till earth and heaven ring
Ring with the harmonies of liberty
Let our rejoicing rise
High as the listening skies
Let it resound
Loud as the rolling seas

Sing a song
Full of faith that the dark past has taught us
Sing a song
Full of the hope that the present has brought us
Facing the rising sun of our new day begun
Let us march on till victory is won.

Stony the road we trod
Bitter the chastening rod
Felt in the days when hope unborn had died
Yet with a steady beat
Have not our weary feet
Come to the place, Oh, where our [ancestors] sighed?[*]

*I have replaced the original "fathers" with "ancestors," believing that Brother Johnson, a sometime progressive in his day (1871–1938) and an artist, in any event, would understand that our fathers were not by themselves when they sighed. — Alice Walker

We have come
Over a way that with tears has been watered
We have come
Treading our path through the blood of the slaughtered
Out from the gloomy past till now we stand at last
Where the white gleam of our bright star is cast.

14

In this one, three young men from Africa are talking. They are from   45
Chad, Uganda, and Somalia, and have been studying medicine in
China for seven years. In a few weeks they will be going home.

They teach us, but that is all, one of them says. There's no such
thing as going up to the professor outside the class.

And if the Chinese should invite you to their home, says another,
they make sure it's dark and the neighbors don't see. And the girls are
told definitely not to go out with us.

But why is this? I ask, heart sinking over the brothers' isolation.
But marveling that they all study medicine in Chinese.

Because the Chinese do not like black people, one says. Some are
nice, but some call us black devils. They don't like anyone really but
themselves. They pretend to like whites because that is now the correct
line, and they're all over white Americans because they want American
technology.

As we talk, I am reminded of Susan's face one evening after she'd   50
been talking, for over an hour, with our interpreters. She was happy
because they had appeared interested in and asked innumerable questions about American blacks. Only after I pointed out that they could
have put the same questions directly *to* American blacks (Paule and
me) did her mood change.

That's right, she said. Damn it.

The next evening a continuation of the questions about blacks
was attempted, but Susan was ready, and annoyed. Any questions
about blacks, ask Paule and Alice. Both are black, and Alice is even
a peasant! she said. And that night her face was even happier than
before.

15

This is a picture of our hotel room in Hong Kong. Susan is standing in
the doorway preparing to leave. She is carrying a beautiful cello she
bought for her husband in Shanghai (which she laughingly says is my
color *and* shape). But is it my tone? I reply.

I have been ill the last couple of days of the trip, and she has been mother, sister, and nurse. All of which adds up to: Let's get a doctor up here quick! It is mostly exhaustion and I am spending my last morning in Hong Kong in bed. Later I will get up and catch a plane to Hawaii, where my companion is waiting to meet me.

Now that we are out of Mainland China there is an eagerness to be   55 gone entirely. I look down on the bay and at the hills of Hong Kong and all I can think about is San Francisco. China already seems a world away. And is. Only a few images remain: the peasant who makes 10,000 yuan (about $15,000) a year and has built a nice two-story house that fills his eyes with pride; the tired face of Shen Rong, the writer whose long short story "Approaching the Middle Age" (about the struggle of Chinese women professionals to "do it all") I watched dramatized on Beijing TV; the faces of people depicted in statues commemorating the Chinese Revolution: strong, determined, irresistible; Ding Ling; and the city of Beijing itself, which of all the marvels I saw is what I like best of the New China.

But the finest part of the trip has been sharing it with Susan. Over the years we have incited each other to travel: Let's go to Mexico! Let's go to Grenada! Let's go to China! And now we have. She stands worriedly at the hotel door, now admiring, now cursing the rather large cello that grows larger by the second, that she's not sure she should have bought. Do you think they'll let it on the plane? she frets. Will it need its own seat? And, are you *positive* you're okay? she asks, striding out the door.

Questions

1. This essay was written in 1985; the massacre at Tienanmen Square happened in 1989. There is a grisly kind of irony to reading this essay, especially because of the romantic nature of Walker's impressions of China, most particularly in section 8, which is set in Tienanmen Square. Of course, as readers, our advantage over the writer is that we know what happened, we know the next part of the story; it's always easy to see what happened in the past. However, Walker's view of China is not solely laudatory. What are some critiques of the culture that her essay presents?

2. "A Thousand Words: A Writer's Pictures of China" is unlike most other essays because of its form. Why is it broken into sections? What effect do its fragments create? How do you understand it to be an essay?

Edward Hoagland

FROM CANADA, BY LAND

Novelist and essayist Edward Hoagland often writes about subjects his audience doesn't know they care about until they read his work—subjects
like tugboats and freight trains, turtles and red wolves, juries and go-go
girls. A former circus hand, hobo, and worker in an army morgue, Hoagland calls himself "an observer" and says that in all his books, fiction and
nonfiction alike, "Witnessing things is what counts." Hoagland was born
in 1932 and graduated from Harvard in 1954. That same year his novel
Cat Man earned him the Houghton Mifflin literary fellowship. It was only
the first of many prizes for Hoagland, including an O. Henry Award in
1971 and Guggenheim Fellowships in 1964 and 1975.

I'd been on a cruise from Nome, in northwestern Alaska, through the
Aleutian chain of islands to the extreme southeastern part of the state;
and it seemed a shame, after such a ceaselessly splendid parade of scenery, to hurry my return to what is called civilization. The obvious solution was to take the train, which three times a week, at nine-fifteen
in the morning, leaves for points east from Prince Rupert, the small
Canadian port, located near the Alaskan border, that is a terminus for
Alaska's state ferries.

Canada is wider than the lower forty-eight states, so theoretically
you can ride a full four thousand miles by rail before reaching the Atlantic Ocean at Halifax in Nova Scotia. I planned to get off in Montreal,
a couple of hours' drive from my home in Vermont. I was eager—I'd
traveled parts of this route in 1952 and again on three occasions during
the 1960s—though perhaps it's even better to go westward by such a
relatively slow means. The West has represented hope and change, and
I've always thought it was a mistake to waste a potentially momentous
transition from East to West by whizzing over the whole continent in
just a few hours by plane. Or, to give a more concrete illustration: A
friend of mine, leaving her marriage to a Boston psychiatrist, found it
was just the ticket to catch the sleeper in Montreal and rock for four
days in her berth till eventually she got to Prince Rupert, boarded a
ferry, and got off in an Alaskan island village, where she found a job as
cook on a fishing boat, rooming with the eighty-year-old, one-eyed
Tlingit Indian captain, who hailed the gleam of her bare legs each

morning when she swung down from her upper bunk to put coffee on, and otherwise was her good chum.

I love trains, despite the fact that my earliest memory is of derailing, and in later years I traveled the East and Midwest at night by circus train, with its rumble and natter and jiggle and sway absorbed in my dreams, a safe haven from the zany, more dangerous theatrics of the day.

Prince Rupert is a pulp-mill and salmon-canning city of sixteen thousand people at the mouth of the Skeena River, which is one of the wildest and most beautiful in all Canada. Once called "River of the Clouds" by the Indians, it flows for three hundred sixty miles from sources only recently surveyed. The modest brick station is an easy walk from where my ship docked, and with the sea's tilt still strong in my head and legs, I was soon rattling east.

A Pacific rain was falling, and the ocean bay that the Skeena empties into billowed with fog. Lovely shaggy cedars and hemlocks leaned over the bank. The river was split by numerous sandbars and drift piles and acre-long islands, and the low mountains were decked with clouds, as the train clumped along, never hurrying or varying its pace except for the syncopated jerks, clicks, and creaks that one could absorb soothingly without listening. There were two coaches and two sleeping cars. The stewardess for the latter told me she would be helping to cook the meals in the dining car, as well as doing her regular job, but that nevertheless she liked her work so much she wanted to stay on with the railroad until she wound up maybe as president.

The grayish-green Skeena coiled and swirled through strata-striped canyons, under ampler mountains beaded with waterfalls, or beside gravel beaches and heavy forests. I was glad to see that this valley, after a passage of twenty years, had remained undisturbed except for some patchy logging. Very few places one is fond of do not change in two decades' time, and I doubt that any scenery in America that can be enjoyed from a railway car is more sumptuous, even including the Alaska Railroad's run from Anchorage to Fairbanks. Past mountains like the Seven Sisters, which were still lavishly snow-spread in this first week in August, past Tsimshian Indian town sites like Kwinitsa and Kitselas, and Kitwanga and Kitseguecla, and past other stations, like Usk and Doreen, we saw the skies lift in this interior region. Big riverbank cottonwoods interspersed the spruce, and woods of birch and aspen replaced the rain forest. At Kitwanga, an Indian graveyard and several totem poles are in sight right from the train.

The Skeena poured and purled by our single track. Old-fashioned snake fencing graced the sparse clearings, with aging log cabins or sagging trailers. The train kabumped and harumphed, while the jade-green river turned milky gray wherever glacier meltwater joined it. Underneath Hagwilget Peak, its valley finally turned north toward its headwaters, as remote as any in British Columbia. We then paralleled by trestle and tunnel a narrower tributary, the Bulkley River. As I lunched with a couple from Düsseldorf, Germany, we admired the blue snout of a glacier on Hudson Bay Mountain, which lay suffering in the sun, the closest that glaciers ever come to a rail line in Canada. Though we were drinking British Columbian wine, I told them the local saying about country like this, when summer ends: "Good for Swedes and grizzly bears, but bad for horses and schoolteachers."

The engine wailed solemnly, but the sunshine was white on the aspens. Purple fireweed grew next to the track. After the town of Smithers, the mountains sank to a loaflike form, and there were hay-fields between the black-spruce marshes and white-spruce forests. With Douglas fir and lodgepole pine, every dozen miles a sawmill was operating full blast. We entered a hundred miles of lake country, gazing out at a series of handsome fingery lakes with wooded turtlebacks or hogbacks and brushy streams between them, and sometimes a moose standing in the willows. A woman from Iowa spotted two bears. The train poked along, waiting in dinky stations for its schedule to catch up with it. It had crossed the Bulkley River about a dozen times. Now it crossed the Endako—a heavenly-looking river in the summer—eight times in only ten miles, and then connected with the Nechako River, platterlike and silvery at dusk, following that one serenely for seventy-five miles. We were near the northern edge of the great Chilcotin cattle range, still as open as Montana's was sixty years ago, and we saw herds of Herefords as dark fell.

The train whistle's time-honored blare accentuated the lonesome appearance of lovelorn lights in tiny cabins. When we chugged around a long curve, the headlight in front of the engine made me remember not only riding a flatcar of the circus train across Minnesota when I was in my teens but also watching my little Lionel train rounding the end-less circle of its track in the living room when I was seven. I went to sleep beside the Fraser River outside the city of Prince George—and woke up before 5:00 A.M. at Tête Jaune Cache in the Rocky Mountains (no station buildings at stops like this, just a dirt-road crossing), under Cinnamon Peak. The Fraser, in its infancy here, is eight hundred fifty miles long, one of Canada's great rivers, discovered in 1793 by Alexander Mackenzie during his epic walk to the Pacific (eleven years before Lewis and Clark's), where at tidewater he wrote on a rock the stirring boast: *Alexander Mackenzie from Canada by land*.

We soon saw the snowy reaches of Mount Robson, 13,000 feet   10 high, though the usual disk of a cloud of its own making hid the top thousand feet. There was a cow moose in Moose Lake, under the Selwyn Range, standing with dripping water plants in her mouth. And a corridor of dozens of handsome mountains on either side led us grandly and energetically but much too swiftly through the Yellowhead Pass into Jasper, which is Canada's premier national park. The town of Jasper itself is ringed by panoramic peaks, notably Mount Edith Cavell, with its ice and snow and slanted, colorful strata. Then for an hour eastward, mountains, gray and saw-toothed, or brown-rocked and bulkier, promenaded alongside the train, while a muscular, new, green-glacial river, the marvelous Athabasca, rushed close by.

When we left the brief but momentous majesty of the Rockies, the Athabasca swung north and left us, as if impatient to head for the Arctic. I had lunch with a retired Alberta farmer and his wife. Both said they were happy to have gotten out of the business of farming before the wheat market collapsed. More than five hours' worth of Alberta passed by, much of it totally forested; then patches of farmland in the jack pine. At Evansburg a troop of Cub Scouts got off. Edmonton, Alberta's capital, and a boom city built by oil and wheat money, welcomed us through its back door, past junkyards and grain elevators. We changed trains, from the Via Skeena to the Via Supercontinental (Via being a government rail agency, like Amtrak in the U.S.), which had come east from Vancouver instead of from Prince Rupert and thus was larger and fancier, with a bubble-dome car and a less cheerful, less busy and versatile crew. I was pleased to notice, however, that even in the 1980s, as in the horse-and-carriage era, a man still walks beside the cars at divisional stops, shining a light underneath and tapping with a hammer. No hotboxes, but a steam pipe had broken; we waited an hour.

East of Edmonton, too, this northerly portion of Alberta remains thinly settled. I supped with a pink-faced New Brunswick man and an African-born Canadian and a Jamaican-born Canadian—a brown-skinned man who, because I was wearing a sport jacket, asked me with a laugh, "Are you for or against the establishment?"

"For *and* against."

He asked the black man where he had "originated from."

"Oh, that's getting into a can of worms, to answer that," said our tablemate. "I always say I was born in Churchill, Manitoba, because that makes people laugh: 'the polar bear capital of the world.' It was Ghana." He told stories of arriving in London and how a series of kindly landladies had fed him leg of lamb and lamb chops until "I always throw a stone at a sheep if I see one now."

The Jamaican-Canadian said *his* English landladies had had to light his gas heaters for him, after he had already dropped in several coins and filled the room with gas, and had singed both their hair and his own in the explosions that followed.

"Don't wash the dishes, because we're going to have to; we've got no money," he told the headwaiter. He ordered roast beef but specified, "No blood on the plate, please. I am a coward." He'd been a paratrooper for two years, but nowadays he didn't even care to fly. He said he'd spent four more years as a military policeman in the American army.

"And all that training went right out the window as soon as somebody fired a shot at me." He was trying to stop a barroom brawl and simply froze. "It was the waitress that saved my life. She dove at me and knocked me down before he shot at me again." He said that now he looks up the Red Cross in the phone book before he shaves in the morning; and we all laughed.

The headwaiter, a man for all seasons in the British style, pointed out the window at a beautifully trim little river valley and told us this was Sitting Bull's haven during his exile in Canada. If indeed that was so, it looked so cleanly pristine that it might have been still.

I woke up in Rivers, Manitoba—having slept through most of Saskatchewan—with the train running on Central Time and the scenery substantially greener and more cultivated than Alberta's, though not densely utilized. Plenty of intractable scrub where wildlife could hide stretched out between the wheat farms, the sparse towns and occasional isolated houses built idiosyncratically by hand.

At Winnipeg we changed trains again, to the Via Canadian, which 20 was yet longer and more impersonal in its feel, having traveled east from Vancouver by the most direct, southerly route, through Banff and Calgary. It had separate bar and bubble cars for coach and sleeping-car passengers.

But there were really *green* fields here, from the increase in yearly rainfall, and new-mown hay lay spooled into barrel-shaped bales. Leaning out the open window in the vestibule, I could feel the midsummer heat, see cattails in the ditches, and, when the train slowed, hear grasshoppers sing. An hour past Winnipeg, every acre was plowed for use except for some unimproved glades by the railroad tracks, where beehives were tucked away, and the houses began to have special amenities, such as round-crowned shade trees sheltering a comfortable yard. On feedlots, red-and-white beef cattle grazed. On dairy farms, the cows were Holsteins, black and white.

But then, in two more hours, we crossed the Ontario line and promptly entered a continuous coniferous forest, seeing muskeg again and frequent ledgy outcroppings of the Canadian Shield, which is some of the oldest rock in the world and "the nucleus of North America," as the *Columbia Encyclopedia* claims. The roadbed grew knucklier, as if to convey every bump of the continent. Hawks and ravens sailed by, past dozens of north-woods lakes in twisty, ingenious shapes, with white birch woods, dark tamarack swamps, and a varying succession of white and black spruce, balsam fir, and white pine. Empty grain cars were being pulled past us in lengthy strings, moving westward after having been unloaded at the Great Lakes ports, while our own train careened, swayed, and rocked at a much quicker pace than the ship I'd been on in the Bering Sea, though a speed that is, oddly enough, a good deal easier on the sense of balance of the inner ear than a nautical slow-and-steady motion is.

In the coaches, young kids were crawling over their mothers' laps in a hubbub of discontent, but in the sleeper passengers' bubble-dome car, two retired businessmen with drinks in their hands were talking about "sitting down and working things out" in South Africa, as if the crisis of apartheid were some kind of a union dispute. I had supper with a Swiss economics student who'd been honing his hockey skills at a camp in Brandon, Manitoba, and who in order to save money was limiting himself to one meal a day; and with two Quebec women who had been visiting one's forester son at the Lake of the Woods ("pickerel that melt in your mouth") and were trying not to worry about how his newlywed wife had been shouting at him because their trailer had no running water and electricity.

Strangers do talk on a train; the circumstances are at once venturesome and intimate; and when the drive shaft broke underneath the dining car and we came to a dead stop between towns, we joked about how our hearts would have stopped if an equivalent part had snapped between towns on a plane. For reading, I'd brought *The Portable Elizabethan Reader*, which was the sort of book to dive deeply into in case of an exasperating delay but not so topical it would tempt me away from my window as long as we kept on rolling. Yet stopping at nightfall almost anywhere was exciting. I'd get off the train for a minute and toy with my childish fear of straying too many steps away and being *left behind* if it started suddenly. The wheels and the springs under each car looked gigantic, as I strolled beside them, and the night lights from two shacks nearby had a faint but dubious hue, as though disreputable events were occurring inside.

After seeing the wheat-shipping town of Thunder Bay, on Lake Superior, I slept through eight hours of north-woods wilderness. One of the givens of long-distance travel by rail is that you're asleep for a third of the view, but when I awoke the sights were still so unpeopled it seemed remarkable to think that Ontario is Canada's most populous, prosperous province. After Sudbury, farms with silos, hay meadows, and large barns at last appeared, though there was soon plenty of forest again, less tough—more pines and less rock—and many, many of Ontario's recently dead lakes, still glittering in the sun but fishless and duckless because of acid rain.

Ottawa can make a fair show of pomp when you come in by daylight, but we arrived at ten o'clock on that fourth night, and it hadn't either the loft and the heft or the burly, kinetic magnificence of a major city, which can infuse even the darkest hours with a python presence.

Montreal lay a couple of hours farther east. And that was the high-hearted, complex old East I'd been traveling toward. Not just cosmopolitan, but bilingual, jostling itself with buildings taller than their physical height and with memories of dreams of development that had slammed clear across the continent in the nineteenth century with the torque of an earthquake. The brilliant sculptures of Joan Miró were on special display at the Montreal Museum of Fine Arts — his *Ladder of Escape* and sculptures of shoes often alchemized into birds.

So, from nature to art: from West to East. In North America, we go west with such hope and zest because we anticipate that nature will reinvigorate art and intelligence and patch up their inadequacies and failings. But we come east again, lonely for art, lonely in nature. For me the migration is perpetual: to nature, and then back to big cities filled with people.

Seeing Miró's shoes miraculously alchemized into birds was really an experience I had the next day. That night, it was midnight when we passengers struggled upstairs with our luggage from the station platform into the spacious old terminal building and immediately separated into two rather starkly divergent categories — the travelers who had people meeting them and the travelers who didn't. I was blessedly among the former. But everybody, if they were like me, felt the floor, and the very ground, swing underfoot under them for the next three or four days, and frequently peered out whatever window was near to "see where we are."

Questions

1. Hoagland organizes his essay according to geographical chronology; he boards the train in Prince Rupert and disembarks in Montreal. Along the way, he attributes particular characteristics to the two poles of West and East. What are these characteristics? Does he note these attributes of West and East during the course of his journey?
2. Throughout "From Canada, By Land," Hoagland includes quick sketches of fellow travelers. He doesn't develop these sketches, but merely lets us overhear a few brief words ("pickerel that melt in your mouth"). What are some reasons that a travel essay might include these character sketches? In what ways do they parallel his descriptions of his trip?

John McPhee

RIDING THE BOOM EXTENSION

A staff writer for *The New Yorker* for thirty years, and Ferris Professor of Journalism at Princeton University for nearly twenty, John McPhee has published about a book a year since 1965. Among the many talents he exhibits in his work is a rare ability to make specialized knowledge accessible to lay readers, and to make previously unconsidered topics seem of vital interest. He has written on subjects as small as oranges (in *Oranges*, 1967) and as big as Alaska (in *Coming into the Country*, 1977), as mindless as pinball and as mindboggling as nuclear power (*Giving Good Weight*, 1979). Richard Preston, once McPhee's student, has called that time "a formative intellectual experience." McPhee was born in 1931, graduated from Princeton in 1953, and did graduate work at Cambridge University in 1953–54. Renowned as he is for his nonfiction, he began his professional life as a television writer.

*A*t the end of the day in slowly falling light a pickup truck with a camper rig came into Circle City, Alaska. It had a Texas license plate, and it drove to the edge of the Yukon River. Piled high on the roof were mining gear, camping gear, paddles, a boat, and a suction dredge big enough to suck the gold off almost anyone's capitol dome. To operate a suction dredge, swimmers move it from place to place on floats as it vacuums uncounted riches from the beds of streams. For the moment, though, no one was about to swim anywhere. In the gray of the evening, the Fahrenheit temperature was thirty-one degrees, smoke was blue above the cabins of the town, and the occupants of the pickup— having driven four thousand miles, the last hundred and twenty on an unpaved track through forests and over mountains—were now pausing long to stare at a firmly frozen river. May 4, 1980, 9 P.M., and the Yukon at Circle was white. The river had not yet so much as begun to turn gray, as it does when it nears breaking up.

There was a sign to read. "CIRCLE CITY, ESTABLISHED 1893. . . . MOST NORTHERN POINT ON CONNECTED AMERICAN HIGHWAY SYSTEM. . . . THE END OF THE ROAD." The new Dempster Highway, in Yukon Territory, runs a great deal farther north than this one, but the Dempster is in Canada and is therefore not American. The haul road that accompanies the Alyeska pipeline goes to and over the Brooks Range and quits at the edge

of the Arctic Ocean, and if the haul road is ever opened to the public it
will destroy Circle City's sign, but meanwhile the community maintains a certain focus on this moribund credential. Circle City was given
its name in the mistaken belief that it was on the Arctic Circle, which is
somewhere nearby. The town was established not as a gate to the Arctic, however, but as a result of the incontestable fact that it would stand
beside the Yukon River. This was the trading port that supplied the
Birch Creek mining district, which lies immediately to the south, and
where miners around the turn of the century working streams like
Mammoth Creek and Mastodon Creek—in a country of mica schists
and quartz intrusions, of sharp-peaked ridges, dendritic drainages,
steep-walled valleys, and long flat spurs—washed out in their cleanups
about a million ounces of gold. Circle was for a time the foremost settlement on the Yukon, and proclaimed itself "the largest log-cabin city
in the world." It was served by woodburning stern-wheel steamers.
They ran until the Second World War. In 1896, there were ten thousand miners out on the creeks of the district, with their small cabins,
their caches. The resident population of Circle was twelve hundred, its
all-time high. Works of Shakespeare were produced in the opera
house. The town had a several-thousand-volume library, a clinic, a
school, churches, music and dance halls, and so many whorehouses
they may have outnumbered the saloons. A large percentage of these
buildings have since fallen into the river. Circle is considerably smaller
now and consists, in the main, of two rows of cabins, parallel to the
Yukon and backed by a gravel airstrip. The center of commerce and
industry includes the Yukon Trading Post ("SOUVENIRS, TIRE REPAIRS"),
the Yukon Liquor Cache, and the Midnite Sun Cafe—names above
three doors in one building. The cabins are inhabited by a few whites
and for the most part by a group of Athapaskans who call themselves
Danzhit Hanlaii, indicating that they live where the Yukon River comes
out through mountains and begins its traverse of the vast savannas
known as the Yukon Flats. Circle, Alaska 99733.

   In a thousand miles of the upper Yukon, the largest vessel ever
seen on the river in present times is the Brainstorm, a barge with a
three-story white deckhouse, an orange hull; and on that chill May
night a few weeks ago even the Brainstorm was disengaged from the
river, and was far up on the bank, where it had been all winter, canting
to one side in Circle City. To the suckers in their pickup from Texas, the
appearance of the Brainstorm may have been one more suggestion that
they had come a little early with their dredge. The pickup turned
around, eventually, and moved slowly back into the forest.

   If the arrival was untimely, the rig was nonetheless the first of a
great many like it that would come to the End of the Road in a summer
of excited questing for gold. The price of one troy ounce had gone up so
much over the winter that a new boom had come to a region whose

economy has had no other history than booms. In Fairbanks, a hundred and sixty miles away, dealers in the goods of placer mining were selling their premises bare. Bulldozer parts were going like chicken livers—and whole bulldozers, too, many of them left over from the construction of the pipeline. Placer miners have recently discerned the hidden talents of Astro Turf. They use Astro Turf in sluice boxes—in much the way that the Greeks washed auriferous gravels over the unshorn hides of sheep. Gradually, the hides became extraordinarily heavy with arrested flecks of gold. They were burned to get the metal. What for the Greeks was Golden Fleece for us is Astro Turf. To be sure, the Astro Turf of Alaska is not the puny Easter-basket grass that skins the knees of Philadelphia Eagles. It is tough, tundric Astro Turf, with individualistic three-quarter-inch skookum green blades. In a cleanup, this advantageous material will yield its gold almost as readily as it has caught it. Astro Turf costs about four hundred dollars a roll. Sold out.

People from all over the Lower Forty-eight are fanning into the 5 country north of Fairbanks. As they represent many states, they also represent many levels of competence. The new price of gold has penetrated deep into the human soul and has brought out the placer miner in the Tucson developer, the Denver lawyer, the carpenter of Knoxville, the sawyer of Ely, the merchant of Cleveland, the barber of Tenafly. Suction dredging is a small-time effort made by people without established claims, who move up and down streams sniping gold. The real earthmovers are the Cat miners, with their steel sluice boxes and their immense Caterpillar D8s and D9s. Some people named Green from Minnesota have shipped the family bulldozer to interior Alaska for five thousand five hundred dollars. There are a lot of new people in the country who know how to move gravel but will not necessarily know what to do with it when it moves. Whatever the level of their skills may be, the collective rush of suction dredgers and Cat miners is so numerous that, like their counterparts of the eighteen-nineties, most of them will inevitably go home with pockets innocent of gold. Gold is where you find it, though, and not all of it lies in the beds of creeks. Richard Hutchinson, who has been in the country for sixteen years, knows where the gold is now. He has struck it right here in Circle City.

Three years ago, Hutchinson went down to Fairbanks and returned with a telephone exchange in the back of his pickup. It had been in the Tanana Valley Clinic and was of a size that could deal with only about eighty individual lines, which had become too few for the expanding needs of the Tanana Valley Clinic but would be more than adequate for Circle City. Hutchinson prefers not to mention what he paid for it. He will say that he got it for "a song," but when asked he will not sing it. "The thing is called a PABX. It was on its way to the dump. Luckily, I came along—the big boob at the right time. I got it for next to nothing." Hutchinson is a dust-kicking type, modest about himself and his accomplishments. He is big, yes, six feet one, and trim in form, with blue irises and blond hair, cut short in homage to the Marine Corps. But he is away from the mark when he calls himself a boob, as almost everyone in Circle will attest.

"He gave us lights."

"He gave us telephones."

"He did it all by himself."

Eight hours over the mountains he drove home with his PABX. A   10
tall rectilinear box full of multicolored wires and wafery plates, it might have been a computer bought in an antique store in Pennsylvania. Hutchinson had no idea what its components were, what their purposes might be, or how to advance his new property into a state of operation. Remembering the extent of his knowledge of telephone technology at that time, he says, "I knew how to dial a number." There was a manual, but with its sequence charts and connecting schemes, its predetermined night answers and toll-diversion adapters, its spark-quench units and contact failures, the manual might as well have been for human sex. He had friends, though, who knew the system — telephone technicians and engineers, in Fairbanks, in Clear. They would give him his training, on the job. He emptied his tool shed and put the PABX in there. He strung wires. He sold subscriptions. In July, 1977, he opened his local service.

Carl Dasch was having none of it.

"Would you like a telephone, Carl?"

"No."

"A phone is a real convenience, Carl."

"When I say no, I don't mean yes."   15

Dasch, from Minnesota, has been in Alaska forty years and lives on a pension from the First World War. He trapped for many seasons, and he used to take passengers on the river in his boat. He wears high black shoes and, as often as not, a black-and-red checkered heavy wool shirt. He has a full dark beard. He is solidly built, and looks much younger than his years. His cabin is small and is close to the river. "Why would I need a telephone? I can stand on the porch and yell at everyone here."

The village otherwise clamored for Hutchinson's phones. He soon had twenty subscribers. Albert Carroll, the on-again-off-again Indian chief, speaks for the whole tribe when he says, "I don't get out and holler the way we used to. I call from here to here. We stand in the window and look at each other and talk on the phone. I don't have to walk over next door and ask Anne Ginnis if she has a beer. I call her and tell her to bring it."

The wire cost Hutchinson a couple of thousand dollars. He already had the poles. In 1973, he bought a fifty-five-kilowatt generator and a seventy-five-kilowatt generator to bring light and power to the town. He went to Fairbanks and bought used telephone poles, which he set in holes he dug in frozen gravel, with an ice chisel, by hand. He strung his power line. "When I put it in, I couldn't wire a light fixture. It was comical." He sent away for "The Lineman's and Cableman's Handbook" and "The American Electrician's Handbook." Before he was off page 1 he had almost everyone in town signed up for electricity. The only holdout was Carl Dasch. Soon there was a record-player in nearly every home. There would have been television everywhere, too, but television has yet to reach Circle City.

Hutchinson in his books learned how to install meters. His son, who is called Little Hutch, was five years old when the generators began to operate. He is now twelve and is the reader of the meters. A number of people in Circle have two Mr. Coffee coffeemakers, one for coffee and one for tea, which they brew in the manner of coffee. They have big freezers, in which king salmon are stacked like cordwood. Albert Carroll has at least three freezers, for his moose, ducks, fish, and geese. For four years, Carl Dasch observed all this without a kind word, but then one day he mentioned to Hutchinson that he wouldn't mind a little current after all. Hutchinson dropped whatever he was doing and went home for his wire, and Dasch was on line that day. Dasch has a small freezer, and a single forty-watt bulb that hangs from his cabin ceiling. With the capitulation of Carl Dasch, Hutchinson's electric monopoly became as complete as it ever could be, with a hundred percent of the town subscribing.

At some point early in the history of the company, the thought 20 occurred to a number of customers that plugging in an electric heater would be, as one of them put it, "easier than going out and getting a log of wood." In various subtle ways, they brought heaters into Circle. They did not want Hutchinson to know. They did not understand the significance of the numbers on his meters. Now there are not so many heaters in town. There are wringer-style electric washers but no dryers and no electric stoves, except at the school. The government and the pipeline are paying for the school. Hutchinson charges thirty-two cents a kilowatt hour for the first hundred kilowatt hours used each month, twenty-two cents through the second hundred, and seventeen cents after that—rates that are regulated by the Alaska Public Utilities Commission and are roughly double the rates in New Jersey. There are no complaints, and, according to one subscriber, complaints are unlikely from the present generation—"People remember what it was like to use kerosene lamps." In Hutchinson's electric-lighted home, an old Alaskan kerosene lamp is on display like a trophy: an instant antique, garlanded with plastic daisies.

For about a year and a half, the telephone customers of Circle Utilities, as Hutchinson has named his diversified company, had no one to call but themselves. That, however, was joy enough, and for five dollars a month they were on the telephone twenty-four hours a day, tattling, fighting, entertaining their neighbors. "It's almost like having TV," Hutchinson observed. "They're always on the phone, calling each other. Suddenly they can't live without it. A phone goes out and you ought to hear them squawk." From the beginning, he has been busy with his manual, practicing the art of repair. When conversations turn bellicose, people will rip phones off the wall. They shatter them on the floor. Albert Carroll, one winter night, opened the door of his wood stove and added his phone to the fire. Hutchinson makes cheerful rounds in his pickup, restoring service. The cost to him of a new telephone instrument is only twenty-eight dollars. He says, "Phones are cheap if you own the phone company."

At the end of 1978, RCA-Alascom and the Alaska Public Utilities Commission, the communications powers of Arctic America, completed a long series of discussions about Hutchinson, with the result that Circle City subscribers were let out of their closed circuit and into the telephone systems of the world. There is a white dish antenna outside the Circle City school, facing upward into the southeast toward a satellite in geosynchronous orbit more than twenty-two thousand miles high. When someone telephones a relative in Fort Yukon, which is the next town downriver (sixty miles), the call travels first to the dish antenna, and then up to the satellite, and then down to the Alascom earth station at Talkeetna (beyond the summits of the Alaska Range), and then back up to the satellite, and then down to Fort Yukon. The relative's voice reverses the caroms. The conversation travels ninety thousand miles in each direction, but the rate charge is reckoned by the flight of the crow: Circle City to Fort Yukon, forty-five cents for three minutes.

Alascom allows Hutchinson to keep about eighty percent of the tolls. When someone at Alascom first acquainted Hutchinson with this nineteen-carat percentage, he could not believe what he was hearing.

"That's not right," he said.

"What? You want more?" said Alascom.

"No. That's too much," said Hutchinson.

And Alascom said, "Don't ever say it's too much."

Circle City people are running up phone bills above a hundred dollars a month, calling their kin in Fort Yukon. They call Metlakatla. They call Old Crow. They call Anchorage, Fairbanks, and Chalkyitsik. They call New York, Deadhorse, and San Jose. Albert Carroll's toll calls exceed fifteen hundred dollars a year. "When I'm drinking, I call my brothers in Fort Yukon and my sister in Florida," he says. "Before the telephone, I wrote letters. It took me two years to write a letter. Don't ever take the phone out of Circle City. It's our best resource." When it is suggested to the sometime chief that the dish antenna is drawing out of his pocket thousands of dollars that might otherwise be spent on

25

something solider than words, he says, "Money is nothing. Easy come, easy go. I make good money trapping. I'm one-third partner in the Brainstorm."

Carroll is the captain of the Brainstorm. He goes to Black River, Coal Creek, Dawson, hauling diesel fuel and D8 Cats. He does not resemble Lord Nelson. He is short and sinewy, slight like a nail. With his dark felt eyebrows and black beard, his dark glasses and black visored cap, he is nearly illegible, but there is nothing enigmatic in his rapid flow of words. For the moment, he is not the chief. "Margaret Henry is the chief. But I'll straighten that out when I get good and ready," says Carroll. His wife, Alice Joseph, is the Health Aide in Circle, and school cook. "Her great-grandfather was Joe No. 6," he says, with evident pride. "I am Albert No. 1, you see—Albert Carroll Senior the First." The pelts of half a dozen ermine decorate their cabin wall. Hutchinson and Carroll used to trap together. Sometimes Hutchinson comes into Carroll's cabin, sees only one light on, and asks, "How am I going to make any money?" "He turns on every light there is, inside and out," Albert says. "If a bulb is missing, he'll go and get one."

Alice earns about fifteen thousand dollars a year. A doctor in Fairbanks calls her frequently to discuss the health of Circle. Last year, Albert trapped thirty lynx. A lynx skin was worth thirty-five dollars not long ago and was worth five hundred last year. Meanwhile, the State of Alaska has been making so much money from its one-eight share of pipeline oil that the legislature is in a feeding frenzy. Pending court approval, Alaskans are to receive fifty dollars in 1980 for every year they have lived in Alaska since statehood. Alice and Albert Carroll will together get twenty-one hundred dollars. Next year, they will get twenty-two hundred, twenty-three hundred the year after that. The oil will last about twenty-five years. Easy come, easy go. The state will soon have a surplus in its treasury of nearly four billion dollars. It will cover many calls to Fort Yukon.

Circle is now a part of the Fairbanks and Vicinity Telephone Directory, wherein many businesses stand prepared to serve few people. There are five hundred yellow pages, a hundred white ones. The "vicinity" is about three hundred thousand square miles. It includes communities as far as six hundred miles from Fairbanks. One telephone book. One-tenth of the United States. Only eighteen towns are in the directory, because few villages have a Dick Hutchinson and telephones are little known in the bush. Circle, with its seventeen listings, is not the smallest community in the book. The Summit Telephone Company, of Cleary Summit, Alaska, lists seven subscribers. The Mukluk Telephone Company, an intercity conglomerate, has twenty-three listings in Teller (sixty miles north of Nome), thirty-two in Wales (on the Bering Strait), and fifty-six in Shishmaref (eighty miles up the coast from Wales). Up the Koyukuk, there are forty-one listed telephones in Bettles (Bettles Light & Power). Of course, there is no saying how many unlisted telephone numbers there might be in a given village. In Circle, there is one. Also, there are eight credit-card subscribers—trappers whose cabins are thirty, forty miles up the Yukon. They come into town and use other people's phones.

There is a shortwave transmitter in the Yukon Trading Post. People used to come into the store and call Fairbanks, where they would be patched into the national telephone system. The charge was seven dollars and fifty cents to Fairbanks plus the toll from there. Hutchinson's rate charge for three minutes to Fairbanks is a dollar and ten cents. Two dollars and thirty-five cents to Anchorage. Of course, three minutes mean nothing to an Alaskan. They take three minutes just to say hello. When they talk, they talk. An encountered human being is like a good long read.

When the trappers come in from the country and appear over the riverbank, Hutchinson can be counted on to intercept them with their phone bills. Monthly statements are not mailed out in Circle. They are hand-delivered by Hutchinson in his Chevrolet pickup, a vehicle he starts with a hammer. In it is a gimballed cage in which a glass tumbler swings always level. Levi Ginnis, a hundred and ten dollars. Ruth Crow, a hundred and forty dollars. Albert Carroll, two hundred dollars. Helge Boquist's toll calls come to eight dollars and twenty-three cents. Helge is a Swede and he is married to an Athapaskan. Long since retired, he once worked Mastodon Creek. It is said that his Athapaskan relatives take advantage of his good nature, making free use of his telephone for long-distance calls. At eight dollars and twenty-three cents, he would seem to have the problem under control.

The Reverend Fred Vogel has a modest bill, too. Vogel is more or less a one-man denomination. He holds services in his cabin. The return address he sends out with his mail is "Chapel Hill, Circle, Alaska." He has been in and out of Circle City for nearly thirty years. "He's all bent out of shape because the Episcopals give wine to kids during Communion," Hutchinson says. Once, when Vogel was off doing missionary work, he tried to close the Yukon Liquor Cache by mail from Liberia.

Calvary's Northern Lights Mission, of North Pole, Alaska, near Fairbanks, has a small outpost here in Circle—a young couple, who also have a low-toll phone bill. At its home base, the mission operates a fifty-thousand-watt radio station called KJNP—King Jesus North Pole. A great deal of bush communication is accomplished by a program called "Trapline Chatter" on KJNP—people announcing their travel plans and their babies, people asking favors or offering fragments of regional news, people begging and granting forgiveness. "Trapline Chatter" knits the lives of citizens of the bush, but its audience has declined in

Circle City. As a result, Circle City people are much less current with what is going on around the bush. What they know now is what has been said on their own telephones. And there are no party lines.

From time to time, a bill will become seriously overdue, the subscriber indefensibly delinquent. Hutchinson has yet to disconnect a phone. "I strap their lines," he says, which means that he takes a pair of pliers to the PABX and turns off their access to the satellite.

Gordon MacDonald's aggregate phone bill approaches five hundred dollars a month. He has two or three lines. Young and entrepreneurial, MacDonald and his wife, Lynne, own the Trading Post, the Liquor Cache, the Cafe, and a helicopter-and-fixed-wing flying service, which takes geologists into the country in a three-place Hiller for a hundred and fifty dollars an hour, or twice that in a five-place Hughes. MacDonald carries supplies to trappers in winter and to miners in summer. Hutchinson works for him as a part-time fixed-wing pilot. Certain trappers resist MacDonald, who has been in the country four years. They say that if he brings his geologists around their home streams they will open fire. "Just try that once" is MacDonald's response, "and a fifty-five-gallon drum filled with water will land on the roof of your cabin."

On billing days, Hutchinson does not call on Carl Dasch. Now and again, Hutchinson has renewed his attempts to sell Dasch a phone, but the prospect seems unlikely. "He knows it's no use," says Dasch. "I have no one to call." Living alone in his cabin, with his two rifles above his bed, Dasch has achieved a durable independence that he obviously enjoys. In the nineteen-seventies, Dasch's brother appeared one day in Circle. The two men had not seen each other in forty years. They had a pleasant conversation for fifteen or twenty minutes, and then Carl's brother went back down the road. The brother is dead now.

"This is a good country to get lost in if you want to get lost," says Carl.

"Yes, it is," Helge Boquist agrees. "One guy was lost here three months." 40

"That's a different kind of lost," says Carl Dasch.

Dasch went to Fairbanks last summer, and he has visited Anchorage. "Yes, I was in Anchorage just after the Second World War."

He has found much to interest him here in the country. He used to watch ornithologists from the Lower Forty-eight shooting peregrine falcons off the bluffs of the Yukon. "They were allowed to do this. It was a scientific deal. They wanted to see what the falcons had been eating. All they had to do was look at the bones in the nests to see what the falcons had been eating."

As advancing age increases his risks, would he not be reassured by having a telephone at hand?

"I'm a hard guy to convince. When I say no, I don't mean yes." 45

"What happens if you get sick, Carl?"

"If I get sick enough, I'll die, like everybody else."

Dasch's obstinance notwithstanding, Circle Utilities is in such robust condition that Hutchinson has become deeply interested in the growth of the town. This past school year, he was pleased to note five new first graders. He referred to them as "future customers." Hutchinson is the town welcome wagon. "Circle has plenty of capacity for expansion," he says. "I think it could probably stand a hundred and fifty people and still be comfortable." The new census has amazed and gratified him. "The count was eighty. That really surprised me. I thought there were sixty-five." To prepare himself for the demands of the future, he has bought a Pitman Polecat, the classical truck of the telephone lineman, with a plastic bucket that can lift him forty-one feet into the air and a big auger that can drill holes deep in the ground. While Hutchinson is up in the bucket, Little Hutch is operating the truck below, his hands flying to the levers of the pole-grabber, the outriggers, the load line, the boom extension. It is Hutchinson's hope that one day Little Hutch will inherit the place in the bucket.

Hutchinson's father was a Boston fireman, and Hutchinson grew up in South Weymouth, Massachusetts, where he read a little less than he hunted and fished. He learned offset printing in the Marine Corps, and had been working for a job printer in Los Angeles when he first got into his pickup and drove to Alaska. Unlike most people who experiment with Alaska, he spent no time in Anchorage or Fairbanks but directly sought the country of the upper Yukon. The year was 1964, and he was twenty-three. He lived in the woods some miles from Circle. His adventure ended one day when, just after killing a wolf, he tripped and accidentally shot himself in the leg. After time in the hospital in Fairbanks, he went Outside to recover. It is a measure of his affection for Alaska that he returned as soon as he could, with intent to stay forever. He trapped from a cabin on Birch Creek and, as the expression goes, made his groceries. He worked as "a flunky for a biologist," live-trapping lynx, shooting them with tranquillizers, putting radio collars around their necks, and then tracking their movements. He worked in the Yukon Trading Post, and in Fairbanks printing *Jessen's Weekly*, among other things, while assembling the capital to establish his utility. His flight instruction was under the supervision of the late Don Jonz, who was at the controls when the plane carrying Congressmen Hale Boggs and Nick Begich disappeared over the Gulf of Alaska. Hutchinson has had a commercial flying license since 1972. He also worked as a generator operator on the construction of the Alyeska pipeline, making well over five thousand dollars a month, at Franklin Bluffs and Prudhoe Bay, doing "seven twelves"—twelve hours a day, seven days a week. Hutchinson's wife, Earla, thinks a more accurate translation of "seven twelves" would be "seven days a week, twelve minutes a day," but Earla has the so-called work ethic deep in her fabric. From Standish, Michigan, she came to Circle to teach in a Bible school that was run by the Episcopal Church. The Hutchinsons have two children: Earl Francis (Little Hutch) and Krista, who is ten. For ten years, the family lived in a small cabin that had one bedroom. They now live in a handsome new house that stands eight feet in the air on steel poles like a giant cache. Last year, an ice jam on the Yukon at Circle backed up water until it went over the bank and flooded much of the town. The PABX telephone exchange stood boot-deep in water. So Hutchinson, later constructing his new home, backed the Pitman Polecat up to the site and planted his metallic stilts—ten feet into frozen ground. The house is all second floor—forty-two feet long, three bedrooms, galvanized roof. Temperatures in Circle reach seventy below zero. There's a foot of insulation in the elevated floor. Even the outhouse is raised off the ground on what appear to be short stilts. A chorus of sled dogs is chained in the yard.

Inside, Hutchinson sits back with a contended grin, a Calvert's-and- 50 water. He listens to the static on his radio. "Music to my ears," he says. The static indicates that at least one long-distance telephone call is in progress in Circle City. It is an almost purring static. It stops when the parties hang up. The static caused by a local call is different. Local-call static is staccato, crackly, arrhythmic, and not particularly pleasing to Hutchinson's ears.

He wears a black-and-gold Ski-Doo cap, an elbow-patched canvas shirt, blue jeans, and L. L. Bean's shoepacs, which he calls "breakup boots." In his living room and kitchen, he is surrounded by mementos of life on the Yukon River: the locally obsolescent kerosene lantern, a wolverine pelt, a model of a log cabin (very much like the cabin the Hutchinsons lived in for so many years). There is a model dogsled and a model Yukon River fish wheel. A red fifty-five-gallon drum full of water stands beside the kitchen sink. It is the house water supply, and he fills it from a neighbor's well. There is a tall refrigerator-freezer, a microwave oven, an electric coffeemaker, an electric can opener, a toaster, a washing machine, an electric typewriter, an electric adding machine, and a Sears electric organ. Along a bookshelf are *Livingstone of the Arctic, Cultures of the North Pacific Coast, How to Select and Install Antennas, McGuffey's 5th Eclectic Reader.* Dick and Earla are partners in Circle Utilities, which earned for them about sixty-five thousand dollars last year. Earla now teaches in the public school. With her salary and his income from flying and trapping, their grand total has broken the six-digit barrier and gone into the proximate beyond. Hutchinson tugs apologetically at the visor of his Ski-Doo cap. He says, "Of course, that won't sound like much to people in the Lower Forty-eight."

Helge Boquist remembers that when he came here fifty years ago a telephone line ran from Circle a hundred and sixty-five miles among miners out on the creeks. Galvanized wire went through the forest from tripod to tripod of spruce. It was an all-party line "with one long, three shorts, that sort of thing, a box on a wall with a crank," and everybody heard everybody else, from Circle to Ferry Roadhouse to Central to Miller House, and on Birch and Independence, Deadwood and Ketchum, Mammoth and Mastodon Creeks.

"Helge knows where gold still is," says Carl Dasch. "He should get a skookum young partner and go out there."

"Today, they get five hundred dollars for a teaspoonful of gold" is Boquist's contemplative response. "And the old telephone wires that went out to the creeks are clotheslines now, here in Circle."

Questions

1. "There are no complaints [about the rates], and, according to one subscriber, complaints are unlikely from the present generation — " 'People remember what it was like to use kerosene lamps.' " (para. 20). How does electricity improve the lives of people in Circle City? Does McPhee seem sympathetic to life without these things that we take for granted? How do you compare the first quotation with this one: "I don't have to walk over next door and ask Anne Ginnis if she has a beer. I call her and tell her to bring it"?
2. What does Albert Carroll mean when he says, "Don't ever take the phone out of Circle City. It's our best resource." (para. 28)? What does he mean by "resource"? What is McPhee's definition?

Joan Didion

EL EXILIO AND THE MELTING POT[1]

When Joan Didion won *Vogue's* Prix de Paris contest in her senior year at the University of California, Berkeley, she forwent a trip to France in favor of a cash prize and a job at the magazine. So began a career that has seen her widely hailed for her precise prose and her stunning use of

[1]Editor's title.

detail. Didion's first really successful book was *Slouching Towards Bethlehem* (1969), a collection of essays she had written for the *Saturday Evening Post*. Another essay collection, *The White Album* (1981), was nominated for the National Book Critics Circle Prize and the American Book Award. She is the author of several novels as well, including *Play It as It Lays* (1970), which was nominated for the National Book Award, and *A Book of Common Prayer* (1977). Also, with her husband, novelist John Gregory Dunne, she has written a number of screenplays. Didion was born in 1934 in Sacramento, California, and much of her writing has centered on her native state.

*O*n the one hundred and fiftieth anniversary of the founding of Dade County, in February of 1986, the *Miami Herald* asked four prominent amateurs of local history to name "the ten people and the ten events that had the most impact on the county's history." Each of the four submitted his or her own list of "The Most Influential People in Dade's History," and among the names mentioned were Julia Tuttle ("pioneer businesswoman"), Henry Flagler ("brought the Florida East Coast Railway to Miami"), Alexander Orr, Jr. ("started the research that saved Miami's drinking water from salt"), Everest George Sewell ("publicized the city and fostered its deepwater seaport"), Carl Fisher ("creator of Miami Beach"), Hugh M. Anderson ("to whom we owe Biscayne Boulevard, Miami Shores, and more"), Charles H. Crandon ("father of Dade County's park system"), Glenn Curtiss ("developer and promoter of the area's aviation potential"), and James L. Knight ("whose creative management enabled the *Miami Herald* to become a force for good"), this last nominee the choice of a retired *Herald* editorial writer.

There were more names. There were John Pennekamp ("conceived Dade's metropolitan form of government and fathered the Everglades National Park") and Father Theodore Gibson ("inspirational spokesman for racial justice and social change"). There were Maurice Ferre ("mayor for twelve years") and Marjorie Stoneman Douglas ("indefatigable environmentalist") and Dr. Bowman F. Ashe ("first and longtime president of the University of Miami"). There was David Fairchild, who "popularized tropical plants and horticulture that have made the county a more attractive place to live." There was William A. Graham, "whose Miami Lakes is a model for real estate development," Miami Lakes being the area developed by William A. Graham and his brother, Senator Bob Graham, at the time of Dade's one hundred and fiftieth anniversary the governor of Florida, on three thousand acres their father had just west of the Opa-Locka Airport.

There was another Graham, Ernest R., the father of Bob and William A., nominated for his "experiments with sugarcane culture and dairying." There was another developer, John Collins, as in Collins Avenue, Miami Beach. There were, as a dual entry, Richard Fitzpatrick, who "owned four square miles between what is now Northeast 14th Street and Coconut Grove," and William F. English, who "platted the village of Miami." There was Dr. James M. Jackson, an early Miami physician. There was Napoleon Bonaparte Broward, the governor of Florida who initiated the draining of the Everglades. There appeared on three of the four lists the name of the developer of Coral Gables, George Merrick. There appeared on one of the four lists the name of the coach of the Miami Dolphins, Don Shula.

On none of these lists of "The Most Influential People in Dade's History" did the name Fidel Castro appear, nor for that matter did the name of any Cuban, although the presence of Cubans in Dade County did not go entirely unnoted by the *Herald* panel. When it came to naming the Ten Most Important "Events," as opposed to "People," all four panelists mentioned the arrival of the Cubans, but at slightly off angles ("Mariel Boatlift of 1980" was the way one panelist saw it), and as if this arrival had been just another of those isolated disasters or innovations which deflect the course of any growing community, on an approximate par with the other events mentioned, for example the Freeze of 1895, the Hurricane of 1926, the opening of the Dixie Highway, the establishment of Miami International Airport, and the adoption, in 1957, of the metropolitan form of government, "enabling the Dade County Commission to provide urban services to the increasingly populous unincorporated area."

This set of mind, in which the local Cuban community was seen as   5 a civic challenge determinedly met, was not uncommon among Anglos to whom I talked in Miami, many of whom persisted in the related illusions that the city was small, manageable, prosperous in a predictable broad-based way, southern in a progressive sunbelt way, American, and belonged to them. In fact 43 percent of the population of Dade County was by that time "Hispanic," which meant mostly Cuban. Fifty-six percent of the population of Miami itself was Hispanic. The most visible new buildings on the Miami skyline, the Arquitectonica buildings along Brickell Avenue, were by a firm with a Cuban founder. There were Cubans in the board rooms of the major banks, Cubans in the clubs that did not admit Jews or blacks, and four Cubans in the most recent mayoralty campaign, two of whom, Raul Masvidal and Xavier Suarez, had beaten out the incumbent and all other candidates to meet in a runoff, and one of whom, Xavier Suarez, a thirty-six-year-old lawyer who had been brought from Cuba to the United States as a child, was by then mayor of Miami.

The entire tone of the city, the way people looked and talked and met one another, was Cuban. The very image the city had begun presenting of itself, what was then its newfound glamour, its "hotness" (hot colors, hot vice, shady dealings under the palm trees), was that of prerevolutionary Havana, as perceived by Americans. There was even in the way women dressed in Miami a definable Havana look, a more distinct emphasis on the hips and décolletage, more black, more veiling, a generalized flirtatiousness of style not then current in American cities. In the shoe departments at Burdines and Jordan Marsh there were more platform soles than there might have been in another American city, and fewer displays of the running-shoe ethic. I recall being struck, during an afternoon spent at La Liga Contra el Cancer, a prominent exile charity which raises money to help cancer patients, by the appearance of the volunteers who had met that day to stuff envelopes for a benefit. Their hair was sleek, of a slightly other period, immaculate page boys and French twists. They wore Bruno Magli pumps, and silk and linen dresses of considerable expense. There seemed to be a preference for strictest gray or black, but the effect remained lush, tropical, like a room full of perfectly groomed mangoes.

This was not, in other words, an invisible 56 percent of the population. Even the social notes in *Diario Las Americas* and in *El Herald*, the daily Spanish edition of the *Herald* written and edited for *el exilio*, suggested a dominant culture, one with money to spend and a notable willingness to spend it in public. La Liga Contra el Cancer alone sponsored, in a single year, two benefit dinner dances, one benefit ball, a benefit children's fashion show, a benefit telethon, a benefit exhibition of jewelry, a benefit presentation of Miss Universe contestants, and a benefit showing, with Saks Fifth Avenue and chicken *vol-au-vent*, of the Adolfo (as it happened, a Cuban) fall collection. One morning *El Herald* would bring news of the gala at the Pavillon of the Amigos Latinamericanos del Museo de Ciencia y Planetarium; another morning, of an uncoming event at the Big Five Club, a Miami club founded by former members of five fashionable clubs in prerevolutionary Havana: a *coctel*, or cocktail party, at which tables would be assigned for yet another gala, the annual "Baile Imperial de las Rosas" of the American Cancer Society, Hispanic Ladies Auxiliary. Some members of the community were honoring Miss America Latina with dinner dancing at the Doral. Some were being honored themselves, at the Spirit of Excellence Awards Dinner at the Omni. Some were said to be enjoying the skiing at Vail; others to prefer Bariloche, in Argentina. Some were reported unable to attend (but sending checks for) the gala at the Pavillon of the Amigos Latinamericanos del Museo de Ciencia y Planetarium because of a scheduling conflict, with *el coctel de* Paula Hawkins.

Fete followed fete, all high visibility. Almost any day it was possible to drive past the limestone arches and fountains which marked the boundaries of Coral Gables and see little girls being photographed in the tiaras and ruffled hoop skirts and maribou-trimmed illusion capes they would wear at their *quinces*, the elaborate fifteenth-birthday parties at which the community's female children came of official age. The favored facial expression for a *quince* photograph was a classic smolder. The favored backdrop was one suggesting Castilian grandeur, which was how the Coral Gables arches happened to figure. Since the idealization of the virgin implicit in the *quince* could exist only in the presence of its natural foil, *machismo*, there was often a brother around, or a boyfriend. There was also a mother, in dark glasses, not only to protect the symbolic virgin but to point out the better angle, the more aristocratic location. The *quinceañera* would pick up her hoop skirts and move as directed, often revealing the scuffed Jellies she had worn that day to school. A few weeks later there she would be, transformed in *Diario Las Americas*, one of the morning battalion of smoldering fifteen-year-olds, each with her arch, her fountain, her borrowed scenery, the gift if not exactly the intention of the late George Merrick, who built the arches when he developed Coral Gables.

Neither the photographs of the Cuban *quinceañeras* nor the notes about the *coctel* at the Big Five were apt to appear in the newspapers read by Miami Anglos, nor, for that matter, was much information at all about the daily life of the Cuban majority. When, in the fall of 1986, Florida International University offered an evening course called "Cuban Miami: A Guide for Non-Cubans," the *Herald* sent a staff writer, who covered the classes as if from a distant beat. "Already I have begun to make some sense out of a culture that, while it totally surrounds us, has remained inaccessible and alien to me," the *Herald* writer was reporting by the end of the first meeting, and, by the end of the fourth: "What I see day to day in Miami, moving through mostly Anglo corridors of the community, are just small bits and pieces of that other world, the tip of something much larger than I'd imagined. . . . We may frequent the restaurants here, or wander into the occasional festival. But mostly we try to ignore Cuban Miami, even as we rub up against this teeming, incomprehensible presence."

Only thirteen people, including the *Herald* writer, turned up for the   10
first meeting of "Cuban Miami: A Guide for Non-Cubans" (two more appeared at the second meeting, along with a security guard, because of telephone threats prompted by what the *Herald* writer called "somebody's twisted sense of national pride"), an enrollment which tended to suggest a certain willingness among non-Cubans to let Cuban Miami remain just that, Cuban, the "incomprehensible presence." In fact there had come to exist in South Florida two parallel cultures, separate but not exactly equal, a key distinction being that only one of the two, the Cuban, exhibited even a remote interest in the activities of the other. "The American community is not really aware of what is happening in the Cuban community," an exile banker named Luis Botifoll said in a 1983 *Herald* Sunday magazine piece about ten prominent local

Cubans. "We are clannish, but at least we know who is who in the American establishment. They do not." About another of the ten Cubans featured in this piece, Jorge Mas Canosa, the *Herald* had this to say: "He is an advisor to U.S. Senators, a confidant of federal bureaucrats, a lobbyist for anti-Castro U.S. policies, a near unknown in Miami. When his political group sponsored a luncheon speech in Miami by Secretary of Defense Caspar Weinberger, almost none of the American business leaders attending had ever heard of their Cuban host."

The general direction of this piece, which appeared under the cover line "THE CUBANS: *They're ten of the most powerful men in Miami. Half the population doesn't know it,*" was, as the *Herald* put it, "to challenge the widespread presumption that Miami's Cubans are not really Americans, that they are a foreign presence here, an exile community that is trying to turn South Florida into North Cuba. . . . The top ten are not separatists; they have achieved success in the most traditional ways. They are the solid, bedrock citizens, hard-working humanitarians who are role models for a community that seems determined to assimilate itself into American society."

This was interesting. It was written by one of the few Cubans then on the *Herald* staff, and yet it described, however unwittingly, the precise angle at which Miami Anglos and Miami Cubans were failing to connect: Miami Anglos were in fact interested in Cubans only to the extent that they could cast them as aspiring immigrants, "determined to assimilate," a "hard-working" minority not different in kind from other groups of resident aliens. (But had I met any Haitians, a number of Anglos asked when I said that I had been talking to Cubans.) Anglos (who were, significantly, referred to within the Cuban community as "Americans") spoke of cross-culturalization, and of what they believed to be a meaningful second-generation preference for hamburgers, and rock and roll. They spoke of "diversity," and of Miami's "Hispanic flavor," an approach in which 56 percent of the population was seen as decorative, like the Coral Gables arches.

Fixed as they were on this image of the melting pot, of immigrants fleeing a disruptive revolution to find a place in the American sun, Anglos did not on the whole understand that assimilation would be considered by most Cubans a doubtful goal at best. Nor did many Anglos understand that living in Florida was still at the deepest level construed by Cubans as a temporary condition, an accepted political option shaped by the continuing dream, if no longer the immediate expectation, of a vindicatory, return. *El exilio* was for Cubans a ritual, a respected tradition. *La revolución* was also a ritual, a trope fixed in Cuban political rhetoric at least since José Martí, a concept broadly interpreted to mean reform, or progress, or even just change. Ramón Grau San Martín, the president of Cuba during the autumn of 1933 and again from 1944 until 1948, had presented himself as a revolutionary, as had his 1948 successor, Carlos Prío. Even Fulgencio Batista had entered Havana life calling for *la revolución,* and had later been accused of betraying it, even as Fidel Castro was now.

This was a process Cuban Miami understood, but Anglo Miami did not, remaining as it did arrestingly innocent of even the most general information about Cuba and Cubans. Miami Anglos, for example, still had trouble with Cuban names, and Cuban food. When the Cuban novelist Guillermo Cabrera Infante came from London to lecture at Miami-Dade Community College, he was referred to by several Anglo faculty members to whom I spoke as "Infante." Cuban food was widely seen not as a minute variation on that eaten throughout both the Caribbean and the Mediterranean but as "exotic," and full of garlic. A typical Thursday food section of the *Herald* included recipes for Broiled Lemon-Curry Cornish Game Hens, Chicken Tetrazzini, King Cake, Pimiento Cheese, Raisin Sauce for Ham, Sautéed Spiced Peaches, Shrimp Scampi, Easy Beefy Stir-Fry, and four ways to use dried beans ("Those cheap, humble beans that have long sustained the world's poor have become the trendy set's new pet"), none of them Cuban.

This was all consistent, and proceeded from the original construc-   15
tion, that of the exile as an immigration. There was no reason to be curious about Cuban food, because Cuban teenagers preferred hamburgers. There was no reason to get Cuban names right, because they were complicated, and would be simplified by the second generation, or even by the first. "Jorge L. Mas" was the way Jorge Más Canosa's business card read. "Raul Masvidal" was the way Raúl Masvidal y Jury ran for mayor of Miami. There was no reason to know about Cuban history, because history was what immigrants were fleeing. Even the revolution, the reason for the immigration, could be covered in a few broad strokes: "Batista," "Castro," "26 Julio," this last being the particular broad stroke that inspired the Miami Springs Holiday Inn, on July 26, 1985, the thirty-second anniversary of the day Fidel Castro attacked the Moncada Barracks and so launched his six-year struggle for power in Cuba, to run a bar special on Cuba Libres, thinking to attract local Cubans by commemorating their holiday. "It was a mistake," the manager said, besieged by outraged exiles. "The gentleman who did it is from Minnesota."

There was in fact no reason, in Miami as well as in Minnesota, to know anything at all about Cubans, since Miami Cubans were now, if not Americans, at least aspiring Americans, and worthy of Anglo attention to the exact extent that they were proving themselves, in the *Herald's* words, "role models for a community that seems determined to assimilate itself into American society"; or, as Vice President George Bush put it in a 1986 Miami address to the Cuban American National Foundation, "the most eloquent testimony I know to the basic strength and success of America, as well as to the basic weakness and failure of Communism and Fidel Castro."

The use of this special lens, through which the exiles were seen as a tribute to the American system, a point scored in the battle of the ideologies, tended to be encouraged by those outside observers who dropped down from the northeast corridor for a look and a column or two. George Will, in *Newsweek*, saw Miami as "a new installment in the saga of America's absorptive capacity," and Southwest Eighth Street as the place where "these exemplary Americans," the seven Cubans who had been gotten together to brief him, "initiated a columnist to fried bananas and black-bean soup and other Cuban contributions to the tanginess of American life." George Gilder, in *The Wilson Quarterly*, drew pretty much the same lesson from Southwest Eighth Street, finding it "more effervescently thriving than its crushed prototype," by which he seemed to mean Havana. In fact Eighth Street was for George Gilder a street that seemed to "percolate with the forbidden commerce of the dying island to the south . . . the Refrescos Cawy, the Competidora and El Cuño cigarettes, the *guayaberas*,[2] the Latin music pulsing from the storefronts, the pyramids of mangoes and tubers, gourds and plantains, the iced coconuts served with a straw, the new theaters showing the latest anti-Castro comedies."

There was nothing on this list, with the possible exception of the "anti-Castro comedies," that could not most days be found on Southwest Eighth Street, but the list was also a fantasy, and a particularly gringo fantasy, one in which Miami Cubans, who came from a culture which had represented western civilization in this hemisphere since before there was a United States of America, appeared exclusively as vendors of plantains, their native music "pulsing" behind them. There was in any such view of Miami Cubans an extraordinary element of condescension, and it was the very condescension shared by Miami Anglos, who were inclined to reduce the particular liveliness and sophistication of local Cuban life to a matter of shrines on the lawn and love potions in the *botánicas*,[3] the primitive exotica of the tourist's Caribbean.

Cubans were perceived as most satisfactory when they appeared to most fully share the aspirations and manners of middle-class Americans, at the same time adding "color" to the city on appropriate occasions, for example at their *quinces* (the *quinces* were one aspect of Cuban life almost invariably mentioned by Anglos, who tended to present them as evidence of Cuban extravagance, *i.e.*, Cuban irresponsibility, or childishness), or on the day of the annual Calle Ocho Festival, when they could, according to the *Herald*, "samba" in the streets and stir up a paella for two thousand (10 cooks, 2,000 mussels, 220 pounds of lobster and 440 pounds of rice), using rowboat oars as spoons. Cubans were perceived as least satisfactory when they "acted clannish," "kept

---

[2] *guayabera*: A loose, pleated cotton shirt.

[3] *botánicas*: Stores that sell herbs and potions often used in observing rites.

to themselves," "had their own ways," and, two frequent flash points, "spoke Spanish when they didn't need to" and "got political"; complaints, each of them, which suggested an Anglo view of what Cubans should be at significant odds with what Cubans were.

Questions

1. Why does Didion begin her essay with such a long list of Anglo Miamians? What point does she emphasize by including their achievements in parentheses? How does this list guide us to judge the criterion of its authors?

2. "Fixed as they were on this image of the melting pot," Didion writes, "of immigrants fleeing a disruptive revolution to find a place in the American sun, Anglos did not on the whole understand that assimilation would be considered by most Cubans a doubtful goal at best." Why does Didion begin with the images of the melting pot and immigrants fleeing a revolution? What are the concomitant cultural images that are guiding the Cubans?

Calvin Trillin

RESETTLING THE YANGS

Calvin Trillin was born in Kansas City in 1935 and, after many years of New York life, still values the Midwestern roots that lead him to write small-town, little-people stories. Trillin is a master humorist, as seen in his "Uncivil Liberties" column, originally published in the *Nation*, syndicated since 1986, and collected into two books, *Uncivil Liberties* (1982) and *With All Disrespect: More Uncivil Liberties* (1985). He also writes serious journalism in his "U.S. Journal," a continuing series in *The New Yorker*, where he has been a staff writer since 1963. In *Killings* (1984), a collection based on several of these articles, Trillin writes about ordinary, run-of-the-mill murders in a way that says a lot about ordinary, run-of-the-mill lives. Still, to many people Trillin is best known as a patron of the art of relatively low cuisine. Chicago-style pizza, Kansas City barbecue, Italian sausage sandwiches from Manhattan — these are the heroes of some of his most avidly consumed volumes.

Fairfield, Iowa, March 1980

As a refuge, Fairfield, Iowa, has a lot going for it. To Theng Pao Yang and his wife and their four children, who arrived in Fairfield at the beginning of December from Laos by way of a refugee camp in Thailand, it might have looked like any other frigid and startlingly foreign place, but, as the fortunes of Southeast Asian refugees go, the Yang family could have been considered fortunate. The entire state of Iowa seems to have taken upon itself a special responsibility for Southeast Asian refugees. The one state agency among the American organizations resettling refugees from the camps is the Iowa Refugee Service Center. When the nations of the world were trying to decide what to do about the boat people, the governor of Iowa announced that Iowa would take fifteen hundred of them. Iowa's response to reports of widespread starvation among Cambodian refugees in Thailand was to raise more than five hundred thousand dollars in small donations and dispatch what amounted to an Iowa relief column with food and supplies, accompanied by a *Des Moines Register* and *Tribune* reporter to make certain that it reached the people it was intended for. There are, of course, Iowans who believe that the United States should concentrate on the problems of its own citizens instead of worrying so much about displaced Asians — a *Register* poll last year indicated that a shade over half the people in the state were opposed to resettling more boat people in Iowa — but they have not been outspoken about their reservations. The dominant attitude in Iowa toward refugees seems to combine spontaneous generosity and genuine concern and great pride in the leadership Iowa has taken. Asked to account for all of this, Michael Gartner, the editor of the *Register* and of the *Tribune*, tends to smile and say, "Iowa has a better foreign policy than the United States."

Fairfield is a pleasant town of eight thousand people in the southeast corner of the state. It remains financially comfortable through trade with the area's hog-and-grain farmers and the presence of a dozen manufacturing plants and the official business of Jefferson County — conducted out of a magnificent pile of a courthouse that was built in 1891. Fairfield people are accustomed to strangers. In the sixties, the local college, Parsons, was transformed into an education mill that became known nationally as Flunk-Out U. The campus now belongs to Maharishi International University, where students of Transcendental Meditation are said to be instructed in arts that include human levitation—although, as one of the hog-and-grain farmers might say, not so's you'd know it. When the Yangs arrived in Fairfield, there were already three Laotian refugee families in town—ethnic-Lao families from the lowlands—and another arrived a couple of weeks later. The men in the Laotian families were already employed. The older children were in school. Daily English classes had been established for some time in a room at the First Lutheran church. While the adults learned English, Fairfield volunteers acted as babysitters for their small children.

In Fairfield, it is natural for Christian charity to be channelled through a church. Sponsoring a Southeast Asian refugee family began as a commitment taken on at one church or another, but it quickly turned ecumenical. The sponsorship of the first Laotians to arrive in town—Kesone Sisomphane and his family, who came only last spring—passed from the Episcopal priest to the Lutheran pastor when the Episcopalian moved away. A widower and his children from Vientiane were sponsored by the First United Methodist Church through the Catholic resettlement agency and eventually decided to attend Sunday services with the Lutherans. Sponsors shared ideas and problems, and the refugees seemed as compatible as the sponsors. When congregants of the First Lutheran Church decided to sponsor a refugee family—the family, as it turned out, that arrived just after the Yangs—the Lutheran pastor, Keith Lingwall, specifically asked for lowland Lao in order to preserve the homogeneity of the group.

The Fairfield church that sponsored the Yang family, First Baptist, is considerably smaller than the congregations that were already working together with the Laotians. As an American Baptist rather than a Southern Baptist congregation, it is not opposed to ecumenism. Its pastor, Lynn Bergfalk—who, like Keith Lingwall, is in his thirties and bearded and well educated—has served as president of the Fairfield ministerial alliance. Still, there remain limitations on the Baptists' ecumenical participation, and there remains in the minds of other Fairfield Christians some residue of the old notion that Baptists tend to stand a bit apart. Among the refugees in Fairfield, Theng Pao Yang and his family stood more than a bit apart. Although they came from Laos, the Yangs were not lowland Lao-speakers but Hmong—members of a mountain tribe that has had trouble with the dominant Lao for as long as anybody can remember.

In Laos, the Hmong were always called Meo, which means "barbarians"—a name they understandably despise. The Hmong originated in southern China, and over the past century or so many of them have migrated into the highlands of northern Laos and Thailand. To readers of *National Geographic* articles, they were mountain tribesmen in intricate ceremonial costumes—deft with the crossbow, surefooted on mountain paths, skilled at coaxing a steady opium crop out of the steep hillsides, persistent in their animism despite some conversions to Buddhism and Christianity. To military men in Laos, the Hmong had a considerable reputation as guerrilla fighters; there were Hmong forces in the Pathet Lao and in the Royal Laotian Army and particularly in the secret army financed by the Central Intelligence Agency. In Laos, the Hmong have sometimes been considered naïve hillbillies — people subjected to ridicule or harassment or even extortion.

To refugee workers — such as those in the American Baptist Churches resettlement office, which received the Yangs as part of its refugee allotment from Church World Service — the Hmong are known for being close-knit, even clannish people who seek each other out through a tribal communication system that sometimes seems to work almost as well in California or Pennsylvania as it did in the mountains of Southeast Asia. The Yangs had requested resettlement in Iowa because of a friend they mentioned as living in the northeast part of the state — in a town that did not, as it happened, have a Baptist church to act as a sponsor for the family. In Fairfield, a hundred and fifty miles to the south, First Baptist, which had sponsored a Burmese technician and his wife who immigrated in 1975, was eager to sponsor a refugee family. Although the Baptist resettlement office was aware that some antipathy exists between Hmong and Lao, the antipathy had never been considered serious enough to require segregation. The presence of any Laotians in Fairfield — their ethnic background was unknown to the resettlement office — had been considered an attraction: it meant that the town was used to refugees and had some facilities in place for them.

No one in Fairfield knew much about the Hmong. The Iowa Refugee Service Center, which does employment and social-service work among refugees as well as resettling, had pamphlets on Hmong culture and a Hmong outreach worker on its staff and knowledge of some Hmong families in Ottumwa, only twenty-five miles from Fairfield, but First Baptist was not in touch with the Iowa Refugee Service Center. There did not seem to be any need for out-of-town assistance. Theng Pao Yang spoke and understood some Lao, so communication was possible through the Laotians who were available every day at English class. A lot of communication was possible through sign language. The church installed the Yangs in a small bungalow that was empty while on the market to be sold. The two older children, an eight-year-old boy named So and a six-year-old girl named Bay, were enrolled at Roosevelt Elementary School and given individual tutoring in English. Theng Pao Yang's wife, Yi Ly, was taken to the doctor for a checkup. The Burmese who had immigrated five years ago began taking the family to the supermarket once a week. After a week or two, the main burden of transporting the family and looking after its daily needs passed from Lynn Bergfalk to a warm and cheerful couple from the congregation — John Heckenberg, a recently retired postal worker, and his wife,

Madelon, both of whom had spent the first thirty or so years of their lives on an Iowa farm. John Heckenberg drove the Yangs to English class. Madelon Heckenberg did the Yangs' family laundry in her automatic washer. Even without a common language, Madelon Heckenberg and the Yangs had what she calls "regular laugh sessions."

What Madelon Heckenberg knew about Hmong in general she heard from Kesone Sisomphane, the best English-speaker among the Laotian refugees, who told her that they were rather primitive—a remark she took as "sort of a put-down." Other people active in Fairfield refugee work took similar remarks as a natural enough effort on the part of the Lao to distance themselves from people who might make a bad impression on the hosts—or even as a way of pointing out that adjustment might be more difficult for people who had never driven a car or operated a typewriter or spoken some French. To the English teacher, Barbara Hill, it appeared that the other Laotians were trying to help Theng Pao Yang and his family—trying to include them in the joking that sometimes went on in class, trying to commiserate with them when they were sad. Theng Pao was often sad. In English class, he sometimes began sobbing.

One of the Lao explained to Mrs. Hill that Theng Pao was sad about having to leave his parents behind in the refugee camp. It was apparent that the contrast between life in Fairfield and the life the Yangs had left behind was strong enough to be upsetting. The Yangs had been in a refugee camp for five years. The biographical document that had been sent from Thailand on the Yangs summed up the schooling of all members of the family in one word: None. Mrs. Hill, through Kesone Sisomphane, explained to Yi Ly, through Theng Pao, that nursing a child publicly might be considered provocative rather than natural by some American men—an explanation Kesone Sisomphane carried out with dramatic warnings about locking doors and pulling shades. When So and Bay were being registered in school, Theng Pao seemed bewildered, and eventually walked off to squat silently in the hall. Although So, who was more outgoing than Bay, seemed to be responding particularly well to Roosevelt, the two younger children seemed frightened of everybody except their mother—a fact that made for some disturbance in the English class. At first, Mrs. Hill's main concern was for Yi Ly—who appeared troubled, and burdened with her babies—but gradually it turned toward Theng Pao.

Although Yi Ly began joining in the classroom joking, Theng Pao 10 often seemed to retreat within himself, chewing nervously on his pencil. He sometimes seemed upset by having the members of his family separated for any reason. He said, through the Lao, that he didn't understand why he couldn't have a telephone. (First Baptist had decided that it would be wasteful to pay for installing a telephone in a house that might be sold at any time—particularly considering the fact that the Yangs could not speak English and might even be alarmed by a wrong number.) An attempt to find Theng Pao a job at a local plant that employed two of the Laotians as sweepers proved unsuccessful. The personnel man found him distracted and asked Mrs. Hill if there was anything wrong with him. Mrs. Hill did not believe that there was anything wrong with Theng Pao — or anything serious enough to bring to the attention of Lynn Bergfalk. Theng Pao was, after all, in a difficult position — suddenly placed in a strange country, where he could communicate with his hosts only through a third language. He presumably did have relatives who had been left behind. He was less equipped to deal with the shock of modern America than the urban Lao were. Mrs. Hill simply thought he would be slower to adapt. Lynn Bergfalk had seen Theng Pao cry a couple of times, but why shouldn't a man in his situation cry? With the Heckenbergs, the Yangs seemed all smiles and genuine affection. "They just smiled," Madelon Heckenberg has said. "It was easy to work with them, because they appreciated what you did for them. That family wanted to please more than anybody I ever heard of."

On a cold Thursday in January, Su Thao, the Hmong outreach worker at the Iowa Refugee Service Center, happened to be calling on a Hmong family in northeast Iowa. He was shown a letter from Theng Pao Yang, who had written that he was homesick and wanted to move in order to be with other Hmong. The next day, Su Thao drove to Fairfield to look in on the Yangs. Theng Pao cried when he saw Su Thao. He told Su Thao that he wanted to move to California, where he had a first cousin. Su Thao tried to comfort Theng Pao. He said there were seven hundred and fifty Hmong in Iowa, some of them as close as Ottumwa. He told him that the people at First Baptist were obviously attentive and caring sponsors. He told him that the Yangs would be wise to remain in Fairfield, where there were people committed to helping them, at least until Theng Pao learned some English. Su Thao did not consider Theng Pao's mood alarming. He had seen a lot of homesick refugees. He had seen a lot of refugees who did not have sponsors as attentive as the people from First Baptist. The family he had been calling on when he heard about the Yangs had been brought to Iowa by a man and wife who then decided to get a divorce. Su Thao left Theng Pao his office telephone number and his home telephone number.

The Tuesday after Su Thao's visit turned out to be a day with a lot of changes in the Yangs' regular schedule. The eight-year-old-boy, So, was taken to the dentist to have a tooth pulled. In English class, Mrs. Hill announced that the students would begin coming at two different times so that she could divide up what amounted to the elementary and intermediate speakers. That evening, the Heckenbergs, who had learned of an out-of-town funeral they would have to attend, realized that the laundry they would have ordinarily delivered the next day might be needed before they returned from their trip; John Heckenberg drove over to the Yangs' with it. He found Yi Ly distraught. Her son, So, was lying on the living-room sofa. The boy's eyes were closed. He was cold to the touch. Theng Pao and Bay seemed to be moaning or grieving in the bedroom. Heckenberg, seeing no light on in nearby houses, drove home, and his wife phoned Lynn Bergfalk, who phoned for an ambulance. Theng Pao and Bay turned out to have been moaning not out of grief but because of serious injury. They were rushed to the Jefferson County Hospital and then taken by air ambulance to a hospital in Iowa City. So was pronounced dead at the scene.

It was not at all clear what had happened. Yi Ly, of course, spoke only Hmong. Finally, she pulled Madelon Heckenberg out of the crowd in the bungalow's tiny living room and led her down into the basement. Some of the Yangs' possessions were on the floor: five dollars in American bills that had been cut up with scissors, a Hmong flute that had been shattered, a knife whose blade had been broken. Over a pipe, there were six cords with nooses tied in them.

Yi Ly told two or three stories—in sign language then, in Hmong later to Su Thao, who had hurried down from Des Moines to interpret —but the one the Department of Criminal Investigation and the county attorney came to believe was that the entire Yang family, upon the decision of Theng Pao and with the acquiescence of Yi Ly, had tried to commit suicide—with the parents hanging the children who were too young to hang themselves. Apparently, Yi Ly had changed her mind at the last minute, and had finally managed to cut everyone down—too late for So. If John Heckenberg had not happened to walk in with the laundry, the authorities believed, it might have been too late for Theng Pao and Bay as well.

Theng Pao, rambling and incoherent in his hospital room, had even   15 more stories than Yi Ly. He said that his dead sister had asked him to join her. He said Jesus had given him orders. He said one of the children had broken the case of First Baptist's tape player, and the Yangs were afraid their sponsors would no longer love them. He said that he had read in a book that they would all die anyway. Eventually, Theng Pao and Yi Ly offered a story that caused consternation among the churchgoing people of Fairfield: they said that Theng Pao had acted because of a threat from the lowland Lao. The threat they related was specific. Theng Pao would be killed. The Lao men would sleep with Yi Ly. The children would be divided up among the Lao families. Yi Ly would be married to the widower from Vientiane whom the Methodists had brought to Fairfield.

To Lynn Bergfalk, it was the first explanation that made sense. "The whole situation, from my perspective, is that the hanging is totally inexplicable unless there was an external factor like a death threat," he told the local paper. "They were a happy family, with no reason to do something like this." To the sponsors of the lowland-Lao families, it was an explanation that made no sense at all. The Lao all denied that anybody had said anything that could even have been misconstrued as a threat. Their sponsors believed them. They pointed out that the Lao had visited the Yangs two or three times, that Theng Pao had used the widower's phone to call his cousin in California, that the Lao families had been present, taking snapshots, when the Yangs were visited by friends from northeast Iowa. The Lao's sponsors were concerned that the Lao were being unfairly maligned and perhaps even endangered: a number of out-of-town Hmong, the noted guerrilla fighters, had begun to show up in Fairfield to see if they could be of assistance. Lynn Bergfalk said it was nonsense for anybody to be concerned about the possibility of retaliation, but for a week or so after the hangings Lao women who were alone while their husbands worked night shifts found themselves with visitors from among the sponsors. Some people in Fairfield thought that what the Baptists had found—during a time when they could be expected to be feeling both grief-stricken and guilty—was not an explanation but a scapegoat. Some Baptists thought that the other sponsors were refusing to consider the possibility that their refugees could lie to them—that Theng Pao and Yi Ly had been telling the truth. As positions hardened, Keith Lingwall, a pastor who is friendly by nature and ecumenical by policy, found himself uncomfortable in the presence of Lynn Bergfalk.

The county attorney of Jefferson County, a young man named Edwin F. Kelly, found himself with a complicated legal situation. He was satisfied, after a time, that he knew what had happened that night at the Yangs' bungalow, but he was not optimistic about finding out for certain exactly why it happened. He could find no evidence, other than the story told by the Yangs, that a threat had been involved. That still left the question of whether to prosecute. Theng Pao and Yi Ly—both of whom had presumably tried to hang their children as well as themselves. Some of the people involved in Iowa refugee work contended that, considering the unchallenged authority of the father in a Hmong household, Yi Ly could hardly have been expected to do other than her husband had instructed her to do. Kelly believed that both Theng Pao and Yi Ly were lacking in what lawyers call *mens rea*—criminal intent. There was another consideration that weighed heavily with Kelly. Whatever crime had been committed had been committed against the children, and Kelly believed that the deportation of the Yang family—an inevitable consequence of a felony conviction—would bring the victims not justice but simply more suffering.

Among the material furnished him by the Iowa Refugee Service Center, Kelly came across a paper by a San Francisco psychologist named J. Donald Cohon which dealt with instances of "trauma syndrome" found in refugees throughout the world. Kelly underlined some of the symptoms of trauma syndrome that were familiar from the investigation of what Theng Pao had been like around the time of the hanging—paranoid tendencies, for instance, and inability to concentrate and loss of appetite and fear that something could happen to members of his family. Kelly's presentation to the grand jury stressed the possibility that Theng Pao had been suffering from trauma syndrome, and that, Theng Pao being Yi Ly's only source of information in Fairfield, his version of reality had become her own. The grand jury returned no indictment. The Yangs were resettled among Hmong in another part of the state, in an arrangement that included some outside supervision of their children. It seemed a humane, Iowa sort of solution —what Keith Lingwall has called "a kind door-closing on a sad and tragic situation." There were presumably people in Fairfield who believed that the Yangs had got off too easy, but, like the people in Iowa with doubts about whether refugees should be there in the first place, they did not make a public issue of it. Everybody seemed satisfied. The way some of the Baptists would describe Kelly's solution, though, was not as a kind door-closing but as "a convenient answer that lets everybody off the hook."

"It's easier for everyone else to say 'Let's end this chapter,'" Bergfalk said recently. In the view of some Baptists, the people of Fairfield, comfortable with their humane solution, ended the chapter without investigating thoroughly enough the possibility that Theng Pao Yang was driven to his appalling decision by a threat. Although Lynn Bergfalk has not made any accusations against the Lao families personally, it is apparent to his colleagues in the ministry that he has never accepted Kelly's notion that what Theng Pao did can be explained by a paper written by a psychologist in San Francisco. The reluctance of the Baptists to discount the possibility that the Lao played some role in So Yang's death was bolstered by the Hmong who came to Fairfield just after the incident. To them, the threat Theng Pao described had a dreadful resonance. "It's the sort of thing that would happen at home," Tou-Fu Vang, a Hmong leader, said recently. To Tou-Fu Vang, the fact that the Lao visited the Yang family is not an indication that they were friendly but an indication that they had designs on Yi Ly. Why else would Lao visit Hmong?

Publicly, there is no argument in Fairfield about the Yangs. Privately, there are hard feelings. A Methodist refers to the Yangs' sponsors as "those Baptist people" in the same tone the Lao might use to speak of Hmong. A little girl who goes to the Methodist church is upset because a Baptist friend says. "That old man your church brought caused all the trouble." A clergyman like Keith Lingwall is troubled be- 20 cause he realizes that the door never quite closed. "I need to go visit with Lynn," Lingwall said not long ago. He did, but the visit did not change the views of either of them. "The truth, no matter how unpleasant, has to be faced," Lynn Bergfalk has said. There are expressions of compassion in Fairfield for the anguish the Baptists must have suffered over the death of So Yang, but there is also talk about what the Baptists might have done wrong—the possibility that they "smothered" the Yangs or treated them like pets, the possibility that Theng Pao's self-respect was threatened, the possibility that the Yangs were insulted rather than pleased at, say, having their laundry done for them. There are people in Fairfield who, out of irritation with the Baptists or a paucity of Christian charity or a sincere belief that they are facing an unpleasant truth, say that So Yang would be alive today if the Baptists had been willing to risk having to pay an extra installation charge on a telephone.

Nobody knows, of course, whether a telephone would have made any difference. Nobody knows what caused Theng Pao to decide that he and his family should die. In Fairfield, though, there is no shortage of theories. It may have been, some people say, that Theng Pao, in addition to his other problems, was suffering from an awful failure in communication. What he heard from his hosts, after all, went from English to someone who only began learning English last spring, then into Lao that Theng Pao may have understood imperfectly. Perhaps Kesone Sisomphane's dramatic message about breast-feeding gradually grew in Theng Pao's mind into the impression that his wife was going to be abducted. Perhaps, through the muddle of languages or his own disorientation, what Theng Pao understood from the changes announced in English class that day was that he had somehow been rejected as a student of English. Perhaps the notion that everyone would die anyway had come from a Lao New Testament Bergfalk had given him. It is possible to envision Theng Pao as someone trapped in a horrifying isolation —receiving information only through the short circuits of half-understood languages and his own confusion, communicating only through people he mistrusted. It is possible to envision him entertaining friends or talking to his first cousin in California on the telephone. It may be that Theng Pao Tang, bewildered and unsure of the language, understood a joke, perhaps even a cruel joke, as a threat. It may be that Theng Pao was in fact threatened with death by the Lao. It may be that he was suffering from trauma syndrome.

"We were doing everything we knew how," Madelon Heckenberg said recently. "Maybe we just didn't have the know-how." Lynn Bergfalk has given a lot of thought to what the First Baptist Church might have done differently in its sponsorship of the Yangs—whether finding a Hmong interpreter at the beginning would have made any difference, whether searching out the Hmong families in Ottumwa would have made any difference. He has given a lot of thought to whether or not a tendency to believe in the likelihood of some external factor like a threat is simply a way of dealing with feelings of guilt. National agencies involved with the resettlement of the Yangs are considering the possibility that Hmong ought to be settled only in clusters and that sponsors ought to be more carefully briefed on the cultural background of arriving refugees and that refugee agencies ought to figure out how to communicate with each other more effectively. The people in Fairfield who noticed some signs of stress in Theng Pao wonder what might have happened if they had expressed serious concern to his sponsors, who saw only smiles. "We every last one of us feel guilty about this," Barbara Hill said recently. It may be, of course, that there is no reason for anyone to feel guilty. No isolated Hmong has ever before attempted suicide. What would the Baptists have done differently if they had been experts in Hmong culture? Perhaps what happened to the Yangs was caused by something from their past in Asia. Perhaps it came from a combination of the reasons people in Fairfield have offered — or from none of them at all. Barbara Hill sometimes thinks that the Asians she teaches are not as intent as Westerners on finding reasons for everything. "We can't tolerate a void," she said not long ago. "We have to find a cause. It may be that we're trying to find reasons for something Theng Pao never intended there to be a reason for."

Questions

1. After the family's attempted suicide, Trillin writes that "a number of out-of-town Hmong, the noted guerrilla fighters, had begun to show up in Fairfield to see if they could be of assistance." Has Trillin emphasized guerrilla fighting as the Hmong's primary characteristic before? Why do you think he might do so now? Consider the different ways in which the Hmong are described throughout this essay: by the author, by the townspeople, by the Lao. Discuss some reasons why Trillin might be interested in including so many definitions of the Hmong in "Resettling the Yangs."

2. Trillin notes that "a Methodist refers to the Yangs' sponsors as 'those Baptist people' in the same tone the Lao might use to speak of Hmong." Why might Trillin stress the parallels between divisions between Methodists and Baptists, the Lao and the Hmong? How does this parallel underscore the intractable nature of enmity itself? How does Trillin go on to develop this parallel in his essay?

Five

READING CULTURES

*D*escribing a culture, paradoxically, may depend on one's distance from it, a distance that establishes foreground and background, that enables a particular detail to register, somehow, as typical. Watching and weighing the subtlest gesture, or the almost imperceptible sign, these essayists allow us to recognize that cultures are not simply *there*, available to be read; rather, the very act of reading *produces* a culture and our notion of culture. The essays in this chapter are alert to the tiniest details that, clustered, intimate a larger pattern, a legible constellation. As a group, they suggest the fit between the essay form and the everyday: the limber limits of the genre illuminate quotidian detail so as to trace the long shadow that it can cast.

"I have never looked for utopia on a map," proclaims Richard Rodriguez, in "Late Victorians." A member of the gay community in San Francisco, in this essay he meditates on the idea of paradise within that city, which historically has seen "itself as heaven on earth, whether as Gold Town or City Beautiful or the Haight-Ashbury." Rodriguez lives there as a skeptic; his "compass takes its cardinal point from tragedy." For him, neither utopia nor angels exist. But angels *do* appear on earth, disguised as ordinary people who have learned "the weight of bodies" in AIDS volunteer work. In response to this motley and blessed company. Rodriguez measures his own distance from the lesson that AIDS has taught them: "to love what is corruptible." The disease has created cultural coherence within daily life.

Diana Hume George needed twenty years and "half a continent" to be able to gain enough distance from American Indian culture to come to terms with it. Her marriage to a Native American and their life on the reservation left "wounds" on her mental "landscape." In "Wounded Chevy at Wounded Knee," George comes to see what should be valued in that culture. She teaches her son what to value in a friend whose life on the reservation has left him crippled, alcoholic, diabetic, and dying — yet able still to tell stories about his barroom brawls: "In another time Hank would have been a tribal narrator, a story catcher with better exploits to recount. He would have occupied a special place in Seneca life because of his gifts." In this essay, Hume herself takes on that role, using both the gifts she was born with and the gifts she gathered on the reservation to stand in for the tribal narrator, the all-but-native informant.

The stone horse in "The Stone Horse" tells its own ancient story. Not marked on any map, the horse shows how human history can be inscribed in landscape. For Barry Lopez, this enormous line drawing in stone, this intaglio, bridges both centuries and cultures, an incarnation of the commonalities in the human urge toward art throughout recorded time, to express the "very old desires bearing on this particular animal: to hunt it, to render it, to fathom it, to subjugate it, to honor it, to take it as a companion." This monument is the incarnation of "the history of us all." That history, however, is dependent on the intaglio's isolation and obscurity. Only distance and inaccessibility can protect it from vandals; only in silence will its story be passed on to the next generation of listeners.

In Gerald Early's "Waiting for Miss America: Stand Up and Cheer," it's not ancient culture but contemporary mass culture that becomes the object of knowledge. Early dismantles the iconography of mass culture in analyzing the crowning of the first black Miss America. At first sight, choosing Vanessa Williams seems unproblematic — if not politically progressive. Yet Early sees the pageant from two perspectives, as a black man and as an academic, both of which prompt him to read the cultural conflicts of white America as they manifest themselves within the competition. "It is an oddly bestowed kiss," writes Early, "that white popular culture has planted on black women; it is just the sort of kiss that makes the benevolence of white folk seem so hugely menacing."

In "Sun City—1983," Frances FitzGerald maps the landscape of an almost completely homogenous culture, a retirement community cocooned in sameness and comfort, isolated from children, people of color, poverty, crime, noise, and even grown sons and daughters and grandchildren, a community whose only "real threat" is death itself. "The irony" for those hidden inside this cocoon, writes FitzGerald, "is that their golf courses have been carved out for them from Florida swampland, their artificial lakes have alligators in them, and they live in a town without any history on the edge of a social frontier, inventing a world for themselves." Everywhere they look, the inhabitants of Sun City see their own reflection; the town's boundaries effectively become perfect mirrors.

The curving streets of Sun City, all turning back on themselves, isolate it from the world outside. Geography describes a spiritual condition in Maxine Hong Kingston's essay as well, as the emigrant Chinese community, struggling to keep itself safe in the new land of America, tries to confuse "the gods by diverting their curses, misleading them with crooked streets and false names." Like the streets, the title character has been divested of her name in order to deflect divine retribution from her family. "No Name Woman" offers an elusive portrait of Kingston's aunt, given to her in warning. No Name Woman's story is one of her crime—bearing an illegitimate child—and her punishment. In turning the miniature narrative over and over, examining it from every angle, looking at how every facet reflects a possible meaning, Kingston tries to read her own ancestral Chinese culture, tries to "figure out how the invisible world the emigrants built around our childhoods fit in solid America."

Membership in any culture, it seems, is no guarantee of understanding it. Whether these essays are written by people who identify themselves as insiders or outsiders, they are all trying to discern the shape of the territory under their gaze. Their essays stand not so much as final comments as notes in progress, as dispatches sent back by travelers who have gauged the magnitude of the unmapped land before them.

Richard Rodriguez

LATE VICTORIANS

Born in 1944, Richard Rodriguez began his academic life as an elementary school student unable to speak English. He ended it as a Fulbright scholar studying English Renaissance literature. In between, he earned degrees at Stanford University (B.A., 1967) and Columbia University (M.A., 1969) and did graduate work at University of California, Berkeley (1969–72). Rodriguez ended his studies because he perceived he was benefiting from programs that should be helping disadvantaged students, a category to which he felt he no longer belonged. This belief, that affirmative action tends to help the wrong people, is at the root of his strong opposition to it. Rodriguez is also a firm opponent of bilingual education, which he says can increase children's "sense of alienation from the public society." His deeply felt discussion of language is one of the most praised aspects of the autobiographical *Hunger of Memory: The Education of Richard Rodriguez* (1982), for which he won the Christopher Award. His latest autobiography, *Days of Obligation: An Argument with My Mexican Father* (1992), from which this essay is taken, studies the cultural collisions his life embodies.

St. Augustine writes from his cope of dust that we are restless hearts, for earth is not our true home. Human unhappiness is evidence of our immortality. Intuition tells us we are meant for some other city.

Elizabeth Taylor, quoted in a magazine article of twenty years ago, spoke of cerulean Richard Burton days on her yacht, days that were nevertheless undermined by the elemental private reflection: This must end.

On a Sunday in summer, ten years ago, I was walking home from the Latin mass at St. Patrick's, the old Irish parish downtown, when I saw thousands of people on Market Street. It was the Gay Freedom Day parade—not the first, but the first I ever saw. Private lives were becoming public. There were marching bands. There were floats. Banners blocked single lives thematically into a processional mass, not unlike the consortiums of the blessed in Renaissance paintings, each saint cherishing the apparatus of his martyrdom: GAY DENTISTS. BLACK AND WHITE LOVERS. GAYS FROM BAKERSFIELD. LATINA LESBIANS. From the foot

248

of Market Street they marched, east to west, following the mythic American path toward optimism.

I followed the parade to Civic Center Plaza, where flags of routine nations yielded sovereignty to a multitude. Pastel billows flowed over all.

Five years later, another parade. Politicians waved from white convertibles. "Dykes on Bikes" revved up, thumbs-upped. But now banners bore the acronyms of death. AIDS. ARC. Drums were muffled as passing, plum-spotted young men slid by on motorized cable cars.   5

Though I am alive now, I do not believe an old man's pessimism is necessarily truer than a young man's optimism simply because it comes after. There are things a young man knows that are true and are not yet in the old man's power to recollect. Spring has its sappy wisdom. Lonely teenagers still arrive in San Francisco aboard Greyhound buses. The city can still seem, by comparison with where they came from, paradise.

Four years ago on a Sunday in winter—a brilliant spring afternoon —I was jogging near Fort Point while overhead a young woman was, with difficulty, climbing over the railing of the Golden Gate Bridge. Holding down her skirt with one hand, with the other she waved to a startled spectator (the newspaper next day quoted a workman who was painting the bridge) before she stepped onto the sky.

To land like a spilled purse at my feet.

Serendipity has an eschatological tang here. Always has. Few American cities have had the experience, as we have had, of watching the civic body burn even as we stood, out of body, on a hillside, in a movie theater. Jeanette MacDonald's loony scatting of "San Francisco" has become our go-to-hell anthem. San Francisco has taken some heightened pleasure from the circus of final things. To Atlantis, to Pompeii, to the Pillar of Salt, we add the Golden Gate Bridge, not golden at all, but rust red. San Francisco toys with the tragic conclusion.

For most of its brief life, San Francisco has entertained an idea of itself as heaven on earth, whether as Gold Town or City Beautiful or the Haight-Ashbury.   10

San Francisco can support both comic and tragic conclusions because the city is geographically *in extremis*, a metaphor for the farthest-flung possibility, a metaphor for the end of the line. Land's end.

To speak of San Francisco as land's end is to read the map from one direction only—as Europeans would read it or as the East Coast has always read. In my lifetime San Francisco has become an Asian city. To speak, therefore, of San Francisco as land's end is to betray parochialism. My parents came here from Mexico. They saw San Francisco as the North. The West was not west for them. They did not share the

Eastern traveler's sense of running before the past—the darkening time zone, the lowering curtain.

I cannot claim for myself the memory of a skyline such as the one César saw. César came to San Francisco in middle age; César came here as to some final place. He was born in South America; he had grown up in Paris; he had been everywhere, done everything; he assumed the world. Yet César was not condescending toward San Francisco, not at all. Here César saw revolution, and he embraced it.

Whereas I live here because I was born here. I grew up ninety miles away, in Sacramento. San Francisco was the nearest, the easiest, the inevitable city, since I needed a city. And yet I live here surrounded by people for whom San Francisco is the end of quest.

I have never looked for utopia on a map. Of course I believe in   15
human advancement. I believe in medicine, in astrophysics, in washing machines. But my compass takes its cardinal point from tragedy. If I respond to the metaphor of spring, I nevertheless learned, years ago, from my Mexican father, from my Irish nuns, to count on winter. The point of Eden for me, for us, is not approach but expulsion.

After I met César in 1984, our friendly debate concerning the halcyon properties of San Francisco ranged from restaurant to restaurant. I spoke of limits. César boasted of freedoms.

It was César's conceit to add to the gates of Jerusalem, to add to the soccer fields of Tijuana, one other dreamscape hoped for the world over. It was the view from a hill, through a mesh of tram wires, of an urban neighborhood in a valley. The vision took its name from the protruding wedge of a theater marquee. Here César raised his glass without discretion: To the Castro.

There were times, dear César, when you tried to switch sides, if only to scorn American optimism, which, I remind you, had already become your own. At the high school where César taught, teachers and parents had organized a campaign to keep kids from driving themselves to the junior prom, in an attempt to forestall liquor and death. Such a scheme momentarily reawakened César's Latin skepticism.

Didn't the Americans know? (His tone exaggerated incredulity.) Teenagers will crash into lampposts on their way home from proms, and there is nothing to be done about it. You cannot forbid tragedy.

By California standards I live in an old house. But not haunted.   20
There are too many tall windows, there is too much salty light, especially in winter, though the windows rattle, rattle in summer when the fog flies overhead, and the house creaks and prowls at night. I feel myself immune to any confidence it seeks to tell.

To grow up homosexual is to live with secrets and within secrets. In no other place are those secrets more closely guarded than within the family home. The grammar of the gay city borrows metaphors from the nineteenth-century house. "Coming out of the closet" is predicated upon family laundry, dirty linen, skeletons.

I live in a tall Victorian house that has been converted to four apartments; four single men.

Neighborhood streets are named to honor nineteenth-century men of action, men of distant fame. Clay. Jackson. Scott. Pierce. Many Victorians in the neighborhood date from before the 1906 earthquake and fire.

Architectural historians credit the gay movement of the 1970s with the urban restoration of San Francisco. Twenty years ago this was a borderline neighborhood. This room, like all the rooms of the house, was painted headache green, apple green, boardinghouse green. In the 1970s, homosexuals moved into black and working-class parts of the city, where they were perceived as pioneers or as block-busters, depending.

Two decades ago, some of the least expensive sections of San Fran-   25 cisco were wooden Victorian sections. It was thus a coincidence of the market that gay men found themselves living within the architectural metaphor for family. No other architecture in the American imagination is more evocative of family than the Victorian house. In those same years— the 1970s—and within those same Victorian houses, homosexuals were living rebellious lives to challenge the foundations of domesticity.

Was "queer-bashing" as much a manifestation of homophobia as a reaction against gentrification? One heard the complaint, often enough, that gay men were as promiscuous with their capital as otherwise, buying, fixing up, then selling and moving on. Two incomes, no children, described an unfair advantage. No sooner would flower boxes begin to appear than an anonymous reply was smeared on the sidewalk out front: KILL FAGGOTS.

The three- or four-story Victorian house, like the Victorian novel, was built to contain several generations and several classes under one roof, behind a single oaken door. What strikes me at odd moments is the confidence of Victorian architecture. Stairs, connecting one story with another, describe the confidence that bound generations together through time—confidence that the family would inherit the earth. The other day I noticed for the first time the vestige of a hinge on the topmost newel of the staircase. This must have been the hinge of a gate that kept infants upstairs so many years ago.

If Victorian houses assert a sturdy optimism by day, they are also associated in our imaginations with the Gothic—with shadows and cobwebby gimcrack, long corridors. The nineteenth century was remarkable for escalating optimism even as it excavated the backstairs, the descending architecture of nightmare—Freud's labor and Engels's.

I live on the second story, in rooms that have been rendered as empty as Yorick's skull—gutted, unrattled, in various ways unlocked

—added skylights and new windows, new doors. The hallway remains the darkest part of the house.

This winter the hallway and lobby are being repainted to resemble   30 an eighteenth-century French foyer. Of late we had walls and carpet of Sienese red; a baroque mirror hung in an alcove by the stairwell. Now we are to have enlightened austerity—black-and-white marble floors and faux masonry. A man comes in the afternoons to texture the walls with a sponge and a rag and to paint white mortar lines that create an illusion of permanence, of stone.

The renovation of Victorian San Francisco into dollhouses for libertines may have seemed, in the 1970s, an evasion of what the city was actually becoming. San Francisco's rows of storied houses proclaimed a multigenerational orthodoxy, all the while masking the city's unconventional soul. Elsewhere, meanwhile, domestic America was coming undone.

Suburban Los Angeles, the prototype for a new America, was characterized by a more apparently radical residential architecture. There was, for example, the work of Frank Gehry. In the 1970s, Gehry exploded the nuclear-family house, turning it inside out intellectually and in fact. Though, in a way, Gehry merely completed the logic of the postwar suburban tract house—with its one story, its sliding glass doors, Formica kitchen, two-car garage. The tract house exchanged privacy for mobility. Heterosexuals opted for the one-lifetime house, the freeway, the birth-control pill, minimalist fiction.

The age-old description of homosexuality is of a sin against nature. Moralistic society has always judged emotion literally. The homosexual was sinful because he had no kosher place to stick it. In attempting to drape the architecture of sodomy with art, homosexuals have lived for thousands of years against the expectations of nature. Barren as Shakers and, interestingly, as concerned with the small effect, homosexuals have made a covenant against nature. Homosexual survival lay in artifice, in plumage, in lampshades, sonnets, musical comedy, couture, syntax, religious ceremony, opera, lacquer, irony.

I once asked Byron, an interior decorator, if he had many homosexual clients. "*Mais non,*" said he, flexing his eyelids. "Queers don't need decorators. They were born knowing how. All this ASID[1] stuff— tests and regulations—as if you can confer a homosexual diploma on a suburban housewife by granting her a discount card."

A knack? The genius, we are beginning to fear in an age of AIDS, is   35 irreplaceable—but does it exist? The question is whether the darling affinities are innate to homosexuality or whether they are compensatory. Why have so many homosexuals retired into the small effect, the

[1]ASID: American Society of Interior Designers.

ineffectual career, the stereotype, the card shop, the florist? *Be gentle with me?* Or do homosexuals know things others do not?

This way power lay. Once upon a time, the homosexual appropriated to himself a mystical province, that of taste. Taste, which is, after all, the insecurity of the middle class, became the homosexual's licentiate to challenge the rule of nature. (The fairy in his blood, he intimated.)

Deciding how best to stick it may be only an architectural problem or a question of physics or of engineering or of cabinetry. Nevertheless, society's condemnation forced the homosexual to find his redemption outside nature. *We'll put a little skirt here.* The impulse is not to create but to re-create, to sham, to convert, to sauce, to rouge, to fragrance, to prettify. No effect is too small or too ephemeral to be snatched away from nature, to be ushered toward the perfection of artificiality. *We'll bring out the highlights there.* The homosexual has marshaled the architecture of the straight world to the very gates of Versailles—that great Vatican of fairyland—beyond which power is tyrannized by leisure.

In San Francisco in the 1980s, the highest form of art became interior decoration. The glory hole was thus converted to an eighteenth-century foyer.

I live away from the street, in a back apartment, in two rooms. I use my bedroom as a visitor's room—the sleigh bed tricked up with shams into a sofa—whereas I rarely invite anyone into my library, the public room, where I write, the public gesture.

I read in my bedroom in the afternoon because the light is good 40 there, especially now, in winter, when the sun recedes from the earth.

There is a door in the south wall that leads to a balcony. The door was once a window. Inside the door, inside my bedroom, are twin green shutters. They are false shutters, of no function beyond wit. The shutters open into the room; they have the effect of turning my apartment inside out.

A few months ago I hired a man to paint the shutters green. I wanted the green shutters of Manet—you know the ones I mean—I wanted a weathered look, as of verdigris. For several days the painter labored, rubbing his paints into the wood and then wiping them off again. In this way he rehearsed for me decades of the ravages of weather. Yellow enough? Black?

The painter left one afternoon, saying he would return the next, leaving behind his tubes, his brushes, his sponges and rags. He never returned. Someone told me he has AIDS.

A black woman haunts California Street between the donut shop and the cheese store. She talks to herself—a debate, wandering, never advancing. Pedestrians who do not know her give her a wide berth.

Somebody told me her story; I don't know whether it's true. Neighbor-hood merchants tolerate her presence as a vestige of dispirited human-ity clinging to an otherwise dispiriting progress of "better" shops and restaurants.

Repainted façades extend now from Jackson Street south into what   45
was once the heart of the "Mo"—black Fillmore Street. Today there are watercress sandwiches at three o'clock where recently there had been loudmouthed kids, hole-in-the-wall bars, pimps. Now there are tweeds and perambulators, matrons and nannies. Yuppies. And gays.

The gay-male revolution had greater influence on San Francisco in the 1970s than did the feminist revolution. Feminists, with whom I include lesbians—such was the inclusiveness of the feminist move-ment—were preoccupied with career, with escape from the house in order to create a sexually democratic city. Homosexual men sought to reclaim the house, the house that traditionally had been the reward for heterosexuality, with all its selfless tasks and burdens.

Leisure defined the gay-male revolution. The gay political move-ment began, by most accounts, in 1969 with the Stonewall riots in New York City, whereby gay men fought to defend the nonconformity of their leisure.

It was no coincidence that homosexuals migrated to San Francisco in the 1970s, for the city was famed as a playful place, more Catholic than Protestant in its eschatological intuition. In 1975, the state of Cal-ifornia legalized consensual homosexuality, and about that same time Castro Street, southwest of downtown, began to eclipse Polk Street as the homosexual address in San Francisco. Polk Street was a string of bars. The Castro was an entire district. The Castro had Victorian houses and churches, bookstores and restaurants, gyms, dry cleaners, super-markets, and an elected member of the Board of Supervisors. The Cas-tro supported baths and bars, but there was nothing furtive about them. On Castro Street the light of day penetrated gay life through clear plate-glass windows. The light of day discovered a new confi-dence, a new politics. Also a new look—a noncosmopolitan, Burt Reynolds, butch-kid style: beer, ball games, Levi's, short hair, muscles.

Gay men who lived elsewhere in the city, in Pacific Heights or in the Richmond, often spoke with derision of "Castro Street clones," de-scribing the look, or scorned what they called the ghettoization of ho-mosexuality. To an older generation of homosexuals, the blatancy of Castro Street threatened the discreet compromise they had negotiated with a tolerant city.

As the Castro district thrived, Folsom Street, south of Market, also   50
began to thrive, as if in contradistinction to the utopian Castro. Folsom Street was a warehouse district of puddled alleys and deserted corners. Folsom Street offered an assortment of leather bars—an evening's re-gress to the outlaw sexuality of the fifties, the forties, the nineteenth

century, and so on—an eroticism of the dark, of the Reeperbahn, or of the guardsman's barracks.

The Castro district implied that sexuality was more crucial, that homosexuality was the central fact of identity. The Castro district, with its ice-cream parlors and hardware stores, was the revolutionary place.

Into which carloads of vacant-eyed teenagers from other districts or from middle-class suburbs would drive after dark, cruising the neighborhood for solitary victims.

The ultimate gay-basher was a city supervisor named Dan White, ex-cop, ex-boxer, ex-fireman, ex-altar boy. Dan White had grown up in the Castro district; he recognized the Castro revolution for what it was. Gays had achieved power over him. He murdered the mayor and he murdered the homosexual member of the Board of Supervisors.

Katherine, a sophisticate if ever there was one, nevertheless dismisses two men descending the aisle at the Opera House: "All so sleek and smooth-jowled and silver-haired—they don't seem real, poor darlings. It must be because they don't have children."

Lodged within Katherine's complaint is the perennial heterosexual 55 annoyance with the homosexual's freedom from childrearing, which does not so much place the homosexual beyond the pale as it relegates the homosexual outside "responsible" life.

It was the glamour of gay life, after all, as much as it was the feminist call to career, that encouraged heterosexuals in the 1970s to excuse themselves from nature, to swallow the birth-control pill. Who needs children? The gay bar became the paradigm for the singles bar. The gay couple became the paradigm for the selfish couple—all dressed up and everywhere to go. And there was the example of the gay house in illustrated life-style magazines. At the same time that suburban housewives were looking outside the home for fulfillment, gay men were reintroducing a new generation in the city—heterosexual men and women—to the complaisancies of the barren house.

Puritanical America dismissed gay camp followers as yuppies; the term means to suggest infantility. Yuppies were obsessive and awkward in their materialism. Whereas gays arranged a decorative life against a barren state, yuppies sought early returns—lives that were not to be all toil and spin. Yuppies, trained to careerism from the cradle, wavered in their pursuit of the Northern European ethic—indeed, we might now call it the pan-Pacific ethic—in favor of the Mediterranean, the Latin, the Catholic, the Castro, the Gay.

The international architectural idioms of Skidmore, Owings & Merrill, which defined the skyline of the 1970s, betrayed no awareness of any street-level debate concerning the primacy of play in San Francisco or of any human dramas resulting from urban redevelopment. The repellent office tower was a fortress raised against the sky, against the street, against the idea of a city. Offices were hives where money was made, and damn all.

In the 1970s, San Francisco divided between the interests of downtown and the pleasures of the neighborhoods. Neighborhoods asserted idiosyncrasy, human scale, light. San Francisco neighborhoods perceived downtown as working against their influence in determining what the city should be. Thus neighborhoods seceded from the idea of a city.

The gay movement rejected downtown as representing "straight" 60
conformity. But was it possible that heterosexual Union Street was related to Castro Street? Was it possible that either was related to the Latino Mission district? Or to the Sino-Russian Richmond? San Francisco, though complimented worldwide for holding its center, was in fact without a vision of itself entire.

In the 1980s, in deference to the neighborhoods, City Hall would attempt a counterreformation of downtown, forbidding "Manhattanization." Shadows were legislated away from parks and playgrounds. Height restrictions were lowered beneath an existing skyline. Design, too, fell under the retrojurisdiction of the city planner's office. The Victorian house was presented to architects as a model of what the city wanted to uphold and to become. In heterosexual neighborhoods, one saw newly built Victorians. Downtown, postmodernist prescriptions for playfulness advised skyscrapers to wear party hats, buttons, comic mustaches. Philip Johnson yielded to the dollhouse impulse to perch angels atop one of his skyscrapers.

I can see downtown from my bedroom window. But days pass and I do not leave the foreground for the city. Most days my public impression of San Francisco is taken from Fillmore Street, from the anchorhold of the Lady of the Donut Shop.

She now often parades with her arms crossed over her breasts in an "X," the posture emblematic of prophecy. And yet gather her madness where she sits on the curb, chain-smoking, hugging her knees, while I disappear down Fillmore Street to make Xerox copies, to mail letters, to rent a video, to shop for dinner. I am soon pleased by the faint breeze from the city, the slight agitation of the homing crowds of singles, so intent upon the path of least resistance. I admire the prosperity of the corridor, the shop windows that beckon inward toward the perfected life-style, the little way of the City of St. Francis.

Turning down Pine Street, I am recalled by the prickly silhouette of St. Dominic's Church against the scrim of the western sky. I turn, instead, into the Pacific Heights Health Club.

In the 1970s, like a lot of men and women in this city, I joined a 65
gym. My club, I've even caught myself calling it.

In the gay city of the 1970s, bodybuilding became an architectural preoccupation of the upper middle class. Bodybuilding is a parody of labor, a useless accumulation of the laborer's bulk and strength. No useful task is accomplished. And yet there is something businesslike about habitués, and the gym is filled with the punch-clock logic of the workplace. Machines clank and hum. Needles on gauges toll spent calories.

The gym is at once a closet of privacy and an exhibition gallery. All four walls are mirrored.

I study my body in the mirror. Physical revelation — nakedness — is no longer possible, cannot be desired, for the body is shrouded in meat and wears itself.

The intent is some merciless press of body against a standard, perfect mold. Bodies are "cut" or "pumped" or "buffed" as on an assembly line in Turin. A body becomes so many extrovert parts. Delts, pecs, lats, traps.

I harness myself in a Nautilus cage.   70

Lats become wings. For the gym is nothing if not the occasion for transcendence. From homosexual to autosexual . . .

I lift weights over my head, baring my teeth like an animal with the strain.

. . . to nonsexual. The effect of the overdeveloped body is the miniaturization of the sexual organs — of no function beyond wit. Behold the ape become Blakean angel, revolving in an empyrean of mirrors.

The nineteenth-century mirror over the fireplace in my bedroom was purchased by a decorator from the estate of a man who died last year of AIDS. It is a top-heavy piece, confusing styles. Two ebony-painted columns support a frieze of painted glass above the mirror. The frieze depicts three bourgeois graces and a couple of free-range cherubs. The lake of the mirror has formed a cataract, and at its edges it is beginning to corrode.

Thus the mirror that now draws upon my room owns some bright   75
curse, maybe — some memory not mine.

As I regard this mirror, I imagine St. Augustine's meditation slowly hardening into syllogism, passing down through centuries to confound us: evil is the absence of good.

We have become accustomed to figures disappearing from our landscape. Does this not lead us to interrogate the landscape?

With reason do we invest mirrors with the superstition of memory, for they, though glass, though liquid captured in a bay, are so often less fragile than we are. They — bright ovals, or rectangles, or rounds — bump down unscathed, unspilled through centuries, whereas we . . .

The man in the red baseball cap used to jog so religiously on Marina Green. By the time it occurs to me that I have not seen him for months, I realize he may be dead—not lapsed, not moved away. People come and go in the city, it's true. But in San Francisco death has become as routine an explanation for disappearance as Mayflower Van Lines.

AIDS, it has been discovered, is a plague of absence. Absence opened in the blood. Absence condensed into the fluid of passing emotion. Absence shot through opalescent tugs of semen to deflower the city.

And then AIDS, it was discovered, is a nonmetaphorical disease, a disease like any other. Absence sprang from substance—a virus, a hairy bubble perched upon a needle, a platter of no intention served round: fever, blisters, a death sentence.

At first I heard only a few names—names connected, perhaps, with the right faces, perhaps not. People vaguely remembered, as through the cataract of this mirror, from dinner parties or from intermissions. A few articles in the press. The rumored celebrities. But within months the slow beating of the blood had found its bay.

One of San Francisco's gay newspapers, the *Bay Area Reporter*, began to accept advertisements from funeral parlors and casket makers, inserting them between the randy ads for leather bars and tanning salons. The *Reporter* invited homemade obituaries—lovers writing of lovers, friends remembering friends and the blessings of unexceptional life.

Peter. Carlos. Gary. Asel. Perry. Nikos.

Healthy snapshots accompany each annal. At the Russian River. By the Christmas tree. Lifting a beer. In uniform. A dinner jacket. A satin gown.

He was born in Puerto La Libertad, El Salvador.

He attended Apple Valley High School, where he was their first male cheerleader.

From El Paso. From Medford. From Germany. From Long Island.

I moved back to San Francisco in 1979. Oh, I had had some salad days elsewhere, but by 1979 I was a wintry man. I came here in order not to be distracted by the ambitions or, for that matter, the pleasures of others but to pursue my own ambition. Once here, though, I found the company of men who pursued an earthly paradise charming. Skepticism became my demeanor toward them—I was the dinner-party skeptic, a firm believer in Original Sin and in the limits of possibility.

Which charmed them.

He was a dancer.

He settled into the interior-design department of Gump's, where he worked until his illness.

He was a teacher.

César, for example.

César had an excellent mind. César could shave the rind from any assertion to expose its pulp and jelly. But César was otherwise ruled by pulp. César loved everything that ripened in time. Freshmen. Bordeaux. César could fashion liturgy from an artichoke. Yesterday it was not ready (cocking his head, rotating the artichoke in his hand over a pot of cold water). Tomorrow will be too late (Yorick's skull). Today it is perfect (as he lit the fire beneath the pot). We will eat it now.

If he's lucky, he's got a year, a doctor told me. If not, he's got two.

The phone rang. AIDS had tagged a friend. And then the phone rang again. And then the phone rang again. Michael had tested positive. Adrian, well, what he had assumed were shingles . . . Paul was back in the hospital. And César, dammit, César, even César, especially César.

That winter before his death, César traveled back to South America. On his return to San Francisco, he described to me how he had walked with his mother in her garden—his mother chafing her hands as if she were cold. But it was not cold, he said. They moved slowly. Her summer garden was prolonging itself this year, she said. The cicadas will not stop singing.

When he lay on his deathbed, César said everyone else he knew might get AIDS and die. He said I would be the only one spared— "spared" was supposed to have been chased with irony, I knew, but his voice was too weak to do the job. "You are too circumspect," he said then, wagging his finger upon the coverlet.

So I was going to live to see that the garden of earthly delights was,   100 after all, only wallpaper—was that it, César? Hadn't I always said so? It was then I saw that the greater sin against heaven was my unwillingness to embrace life.

César said he found paradise at the baths. He said I didn't understand. He said if I had to ask about it, I might as well ask if a wife will spend eternity with Husband #1 or Husband #2.

The baths were places of good humor, that was Number One; there was nothing demeaning about them. From within cubicles men would nod at one another or not, but there was no sting of rejection, because one had at last entered a region of complete acceptance. César spoke of floating from body to body, open arms yielding to open arms in an angelic round.

The best night. That's easy, he said, the best night was spent in the pool with an antiques dealer—up to their necks in warm water—their two heads bobbing on an ocean of chlorine green, bawling Noël Coward songs.

But each went home alone?

Each satisfied, dear, César corrected. And all the way home San   105 Francisco seemed to him balmed and merciful, he said. He felt weightlessness of being, the pavement under his step as light as air.

It was not as in some Victorian novel—the curtains drawn, the pillows plumped, the streets strewn with sawdust. It was not to be a matter of custards in covered dishes, steaming possets, *Try a little of this, my dear*. Or gathering up the issues of *Architectural Digest* strewn about the bed. Closing the biography of Diana Cooper and marking its place. Or the unfolding of discretionary screens, morphine, parrots, pavilions.

César experienced agony.

Four of his high-school students sawed through a Vivaldi quartet in the corridor outside his hospital room, prolonging the hideous garden.

In the presence of his lover Gregory and friends, Scott passed from this life. . . .

He died peacefully at home in his lover Ron's arms.   110

Immediately after a friend led a prayer for him to be taken home and while his dear mother was reciting the 23rd Psalm, Bill peacefully took his last breath.

I stood aloof at César's memorial, the kind of party he would enjoy, everyone said. And so for a time César lay improperly buried, unconvincingly resurrected in the conditional: would enjoy. What else could they say? César had no religion beyond aesthetic bravery.

Sunlight remains. Traffic remains. Nocturnal chic attaches to some discovered restaurant. A new novel is reviewed in *The New York Times*. And the mirror rasps on its hook. The mirror is lifted down.

A priest friend, a good friend, who out of naïveté plays the cynic, tells me—this is on a bright, billowy day; we are standing outside—"It's not as sad as you may think. There is at least spectacle in the death of the young. Come to the funeral of an old lady sometime if you want to feel an empty church."

I will grant my priest friend this much: that it is easier, easier on   115 me, to sit with gay men in hospitals than with the staring old. Young men talk as much as they are able.

But those who gather around the young man's bed do not see Chatterton. This doll is Death. I have seen people caressing it, staring Death down. I have seen people wipe its tears, wipe its ass; I have seen people kiss Death on his lips, where once there were lips.

Chris was inspired after his own diagnosis in July 1987 with the truth and reality of how such a terrible disease could bring out the love, warmth, and support of so many friends and family.

Sometimes no family came. If there was family, it was usually Mother. Mom. With her suitcase and with the torn flap of an envelope in her hand.

Brenda. Pat. Connie. Toni. Soledad.

Or parents came but then left without reconciliation, some prefer-   120 ring to say "cancer."

But others came. They walked Death's dog. They washed his dishes. They bought his groceries. They massaged his poor back. They changed his bandages. They emptied his bedpan.

Men who sought the aesthetic ordering of existence were recalled to nature. Men who aspired to the mock-angelic settled for the shirt of hair. The gay community of San Francisco, having found freedom, consented to necessity — to all that the proud world had for so long held up to them, withheld from them, as "real humanity."

And if gays took care of their own, they were not alone. AIDS was a disease of the entire city. Nor were Charity and Mercy only male, only gay. Others came. There were nurses and nuns and the couple from next door, co-workers, strangers, teenagers, corporations, pensioners. A community was forming over the city.

Cary and Rick's friends and family wish to thank the many people who provided both small and great kindnesses.

He was attended to and lovingly cared for by the staff at Coming Home 125 *Hospice.*

And the saints of this city have names listed in the phone book, names I heard called through a microphone one cold Sunday in Advent as I sat in Most Holy Redeemer Church. It might have been any of the churches or community centers in the Castro district, but it happened at Most Holy Redeemer at a time in the history of the world when the Roman Catholic Church pronounced the homosexual a sinner.

A woman at the microphone called upon volunteers from the AIDS Support Group to come forward. Throughout the church, people stood up, young men and women, and middle-aged and old, straight, gay, and all of them shy at being called. Yet they came forward and assembled in the sanctuary, facing the congregation, grinning self-consciously at one another, their hands hidden behind them.

I am preoccupied by the fussing of a man sitting in the pew directly in front of me — in his seventies, frail, his iodine-colored hair combed forward and pasted upon his forehead. Fingers of porcelain clutch the pearly beads of what must have been his mother's rosary. He is not the sort of man any gay man would have chosen to become in the 1970s. He is probably not what he himself expected to become. Something of the old dear about him, wizened butterfly, powered old pouf. Certainly he is what I fear becoming. And then he rises, this old monkey, with the most beatific dignity, in answer to the microphone, and he strides into the sanctuary to take his place in the company of the Blessed.

So this is it — this, what looks like a Christmas party in an insurance office, and not as in Renaissance paintings, and not as we had always thought, not some flower-strewn, some sequined curtain call of greasepainted heroes gesturing to the stalls. A lady with a plastic candy cane pinned to her lapel. A Castro clone with a red bandana exploding from his hip pocket. A perfume-counter lady with an Hermès scarf mantled upon her shoulder. A black man in a checkered sports coat. The pink-haired punkess with a jewel in her nose. Here, too, is the gay couple in middle age; interchangeable plaid shirts and corduroy pants. Blood and shit and Mr. Happy Face. These know the weight of bodies.

Bill died.   130
. . . Passed on to heaven.
. . . Turning over in his bed one night and then gone.

These learned to love what is corruptible, while I, barren skeptic, reader of St. Augustine, curator of the earthly paradise, inheritor of the empty mirror, I shift my tailbone upon the cold, hard pew.

Questions

1. Rodriguez begins and ends his essay by invoking St. Augustine. There are references throughout to Catholic masses and saints. What role does religion play in "Late Victorians"? What is it about the religious impulse that interests Rodriguez?
2. In the final line of his essay, Rodriguez refers to himself as a "barren skeptic." What does he mean by this? Where else does this essay examine the idea of barrenness and how does it seem to understand the term?
3. The idea of paradise keeps resurfacing in "Late Victorians." Rodriguez sees that for some people, it is in San Francisco. For Cèsar, it was at the baths. Where does Rodriguez locate paradise? How does he perceive it?

Diana Hume George

WOUNDED CHEVY AT WOUNDED KNEE

With interests ranging from gravestones to Freud to feminist criticism, Diana Hume George is a professor of English and Women's Studies at The Pennsylvania State University at Erie, The Behrend College, where she has received awards for excellence in teaching and research. But George is also a highly honored poet and essayist, whose work has been widely published in literary as well as academic journals. Her first prose book, *Blake and Freud* (1980), was nominated for the Pulitzer Prize, and the essay that appears here was selected to appear in *The Best American Essays 1991*. George was born in Gowanda, New York, in 1948, and received her Ph.D. from the State University of New York at Buffalo in 1979. She is the author of *Oedipus Anne: The Poetry of Anne Sexton* (1987), as well as two volumes of her own poetry, *The Evolution of Love* (1977) and *The Resurrection of the Body* (1989). Her latest book is a collection of travel essays, *The Lonely Other: A Woman Watches America*.

Pine Ridge Sioux Reservation, July 1989

"**I**f you break down on that reservation, your car belongs to the Indians. They don't like white people out there." This was our amiable motel proprietor in Custer, South Dakota, who asked where we were headed and then propped a conspiratorial white elbow on the counter and said we'd better make sure our vehicle was in good shape. To get to Wounded Knee, site of the last cavalry massacre of the Lakota in 1890 and of more recent confrontations between the FBI and the American Indian Movement, you take a road out of Pine Ridge on the Lakota reservation and go about eight miles. If you weren't watching for it you could miss it, because nothing is there but a hill, a painted board explaining what happened, a tiny church, and a cemetery.

The motel man told us stories about his trucking times, when by day his gas stops were friendly, but by night groups of Indian men who'd been drinking used to circle his truck looking for something to steal—or so he assumed. He began carrying a .357 Magnum with him "just in case." Once he took his wife out to Pine Ridge. "She broke out in hives before we even got there." And when they were stopped on the roadside and a reservation policeman asked if they needed help, she was sure he was going to order her out of the car, steal it, and, I suppose, rape and scalp her while he was at it. As the motel man told us these contradictory stories, he seemed to be unaware of the irony of warning us that the Indians would steal our car if they got a chance and following with a story about an Indian who tried to help them just in case they might be having trouble.

He did make a distinction between the reservation toughs and the police. He wasn't a racist creep, but rather a basically decent fellow whose view of the world was narrowly white. I briefly entertained the notion of staying awhile, pouring another cup of coffee, and asking him a few questions that would make him address the assumptions behind his little sermon, but I really wanted to get on my way, and I knew he wasn't going to change his mind about Indians here in the middle of his life in the middle of the Black Hills.

Mac and I exchanged a few rueful remarks about it while we drove. But we both knew that the real resistance to dealing with Indian culture on these trips that have taken us through both Pueblo and Plains Indian territories hasn't come from outside of our car or our minds, but rather from within them. More specifically, from within me. For years Mac has read about the Plains Indians with real attentiveness and with an openness to learning what he can about the indigenous peoples of North America. He reads histories, biographies, novels, and essays, thinks carefully about the issues involved, remembers what he has read, informs himself with curiosity and respect about tribes that have occupied the areas we visit. For a couple of years he urged me toward these materials, many of which have been visible around our home for years: *Black Elk Speaks, In a Sacred Manner We Live, Bury My Heart at Wounded Knee*, studies of Indian spiritual and cultural life. While we were in Lakota country this time, he was reading Mari Sandoz's biography of Crazy Horse. But he has long since given up on getting me to pay sustained attention to these rich materials, because my resistance has been firm and long-standing. I am probably better informed about Indian life than most Americans ever thought of being, but not informed enough for a thoughtful reader and writer. My resistance has taken the form of a mixture of pride and contempt: pride that I already know more than these books can tell me, and contempt for the white liberal intellectual's romance with all things Indian. But my position has been very strange perhaps, given that I was married to an American Indian for five years, lived on a reservation, and am the mother of a half-Indian son.

I've been mostly wrong in my attitudes, but it's taken me years to   5 understand that. Wounded Knee is where I came to terms with my confusion, rejection, and ambivalence, and it happened in a direct confrontation with past events that are now twenty years old. My resistance broke down because of an encounter with a young Lakota named Mark, who is just about my own son's age.

I grew up in the 1950s and 1960s in a small white community on the edge of the Cattaraugus Seneca Indian Reservation in western New York State. Relations between Indians and whites in my world were bitter, and in many respects replicated the dynamics between whites and blacks in the South, with many exceptions due to the very different functions and circumstances of these two groups of people of color in white America. The school system had recently been integrated after the closing of the Thomas Indian School on the reservation. The middle-class whites wanted nothing to do with the Indians, whom they saw as drunkards and degenerates, in many cases subhuman. When I rebelled against the restraints of my white upbringing, the medium for asserting myself against my parents and my world was ready-made, and I grabbed it.

I began hanging out on the reserve with young Indians and shifted my social and sexual arena entirely to the Indian world. I fell in love with an idea of noble darkness in the form of an Indian carnival worker, got pregnant by him, married him, left the white world completely, and moved into his. Despite the fact that this was the sixties, my actions weren't politically motivated; or, rather, my politics were entirely personal at that point. While my more aware counterparts might have done some of the same things as conscious political and spiritual statements, I was fifteen when I started my romance with Indians, and I only knew that I was in love with life outside the constricting white mainstream, and with all the energy that vibrates on the outer reaches of cultural stability. My heart and what would later become my politics were definitely in the right place, and I have never regretted where I went or what I came to know. But for twenty years that knowledge spoiled me for another kind of knowing.

Whatever my romantic notions were about ideal forms of American Indian wisdom—closeness to the land, respect for other living creatures, a sense of harmony with natural cycles, a way of walking lightly in the world, a manner of living that could make the ordinary and profane into the sacred—I learned that on the reservation I was inhabiting a world that was contrary to all these values. American Indian culture at the end of the road has virtually none of these qualities. White America has destroyed them. Any culture in its death throes is a grim spectacle, and there can be no grimmer reality than that endured by people on their way to annihilation.

I did not live among the scattered wise people or political activists of the Seneca Nation. I did not marry a nominal American Indian from a middle-class family. I married an illiterate man who dropped out of school in the seventh grade and was in school only intermittently before that. He traveled around the East with carnivals, running a Ferris wheel during the summer months, and logged wood on the reservation during the winter—when he could get work. Home base was an old trailer without plumbing in the woods, where his mother lived. He drank sporadically but heavily, and his weekends, often his weekdays, were full of pool tables, bar brawls, the endlessness of hanging out with little to do. He didn't talk much. How I built this dismal life into a romanticized myth about still waters running deep gives me an enduring respect for the mythopoeic, self-deluding power of desire, wish, will.

When I was married to him my world was a blur of old cars driven   10
by drunk men in the middle of the night, of honky-tonk bars, country music, late night fights with furniture flying, food stamps and welfare lines, stories of injury and death. The smell of beer still sickens me slightly. I was sober as a saint through all of this, so I didn't have the insulation of liquor, only of love. I lived the contrary of every white myth about Indian life, both the myths of the small-town white racists

and those of the smitten hippies. When I finally left that life behind, extricating myself and my child in the certain knowledge that to stay would mean something very like death for both of us, I removed myself in every respect. I knew how stupid white prejudice was, understood the real story about why Indians drank and wasted their lives, felt the complexities so keenly that I couldn't even try to explain them to anyone white. But similarly, I knew how bird-brained the lovechild generation's romance with Indian culture was.

My husband went on to a career of raping white women that had begun during — or maybe before — our marriage. When he was finally caught, convicted, and sent to Attica, I was long since done with that part of my life. My son pulled me back toward it with his own love for his father, and I still keep in touch with my husband's mother on the reservation, sometimes helping her to handle white bureaucracy, but that's all. I heard at a remove of miles, of eons, it seemed, about the early deaths of young men I'd known well — deaths due to diabetes, to lost limbs, or to car wrecks at high speed — and I felt something, but I didn't have to deal with it. When I tried to think about that past life in order to put it into some kind of perspective, no whole picture emerged. When I tried to write about it, no words would come. And when I tried to be open to learning something new about Indians in America on my trips, my heart closed up tight, and with it my mind. When I went to Wounded Knee, the wounds of these other Indians half a continent and half a lifetime away were a part of the landscape.

We pull off to the side of the road to read the billboard that tells what happened here. "Massacre of Wounded Knee" is the header, but upon close inspection you see that "Massacre" is a new addition, painted over something else. "Battle," perhaps? What did it used to say, I wonder, and hope I'll run into a local who can tell me. While I'm puzzling over this, an old Chevy sputters into the pull-off and shakes to a stop. It's loaded with dark faces, a young man and an older woman with many small children. The man gets out and walks slowly to the front of the car, rolling up his T-shirt over his stomach to get air on his skin. As he raises the hood, a Comanche truck pulls in beside him with one woman inside. It's very hot, and I weave a little in the glare of sun. Suddenly I see the past, superimposed on this hot moment. I've seen it before, again and again, cars full of little Indian kids in the heat of summer on the sides of roads. I glance again, see the woman in the front seat, know that she's their mother or their aunt. She looks weary and resigned, not really sad. She expects this.

And then in another blink it's not only that I have seen this woman; I have *been* this woman, my old car or someone else's packed with little kids who are almost preternaturally quiet, wide-eyed and dark-skinned and already knowing that this is a big part of what life is about, sitting in boiling back seats, their arms jammed against the arms of their brother, their sister, their cousin. There is no use asking when they'll get there, wherever "there" is. It will happen when it happens, when the adults as helpless as they figure out what to do. In the meantime they sweat and stare. But I am not this woman anymore, not responsible for these children, some of whose intelligent faces will blank into a permanent sheen of resignation before they're five. I am a tourist in a new Plymouth Voyager, my luggage rack packed with fine camping equipment, my Minolta in my hand to snap pictures of the places I can afford to go.

When Mac suggests that we offer to help them, I am not surprised at my flat negative feeling. He doesn't know what that means, I surmise, and I don't have any way to tell him. Help them? Do you want to get anywhere today, do you have the whole afternoon? The young man's shoulders bend over the motor. He is fit and beautiful, his good torso moves knowingly but powerlessly over the heat rising from beneath the hood. I recognize him, as well as the woman. He has no job. He talks about getting off the reservation, finding work, living the dreams he still has. He'll talk this way for a few more years, then give up entirely. He drinks too much. He has nothing to do. Drinking is the only thing that makes him really laugh, and his only way to release rage. I also know that whatever else is wrong with it the car is out of gas, and that these people have no money. Okay, sure, I say to Mac, standing to one side while he asks how we can help. Close to the car now, I see that the woman is the young man's mother. These kids are his brothers and sisters.

The car is out of gas and it needs a jump. The battery is bad. The 15
woman in the other car is the young man's aunt, who can give him a jump but has no money to give him for gas—or so she says. I know her, too. She is more prosperous than her relatives, and has learned the hard way never to give them any money because she needs it herself, and if she gives it to them she'll never see it again. She made her policy years ago, and makes it stick no matter what. She has to.

Well, then, we'll take them to the nearest gas station. Do they have a gas can? No, just a plastic washer-fluid jug with no top. Okay, that will have to do. How far is the nearest gas? Just up the road a couple of miles. But they don't have any money because they were on their way to cash his mother's unemployment check when they ran out of gas, and the town where they can do that is many miles away. So can we loan them some money for gas? We can. He gets in the front seat. I get in the back, and as we pull away from the windy parking area, I look at the woman and the kids who will be sitting in the car waiting until we return. She knows she can't figure out how soon that will be. She stares straight ahead. I don't want to catch her eye, nor will she catch mine.

Right here up this road. Mark is in his early twenties. Mac asks him questions. He is careful and restrained in his answers at first, then begin to open up. No there's no work around here. Sometimes he does a little horse breaking or fence mending for the ranchers. All the ranches here are run by whites who had the money to make the grim land yield a living. They lease it from the Lakota. Mark went away to a Job Corps camp last year, but he had to come back because his twenty-one-year-old brother died last winter, leaving his mother alone with the little ones. He froze to death. He was drinking at a party and went outside to take a leak. Mark said they figured he must have just stopped for a minute to rest, and then he fell asleep. They found him frozen in the morning. Mark had to come back home to bury his brother and help his mother with the kids.

As we bounce over the dirt road, I stare at the back of Mark's head and at his good Indian profile when he turns toward Mac to speak. He is so familiar to me that I could almost reach out to touch his black straight hair, his brown shoulder. He is my husband, he is my son. I want to give him hope. He speaks about getting out of here, going to "Rapid"—Lakota shorthand for Rapid City—and making a life. He is sick of having nothing to do, he wants work, wants an apartment. But he can't leave yet; he has to stay to help his mother. But things are going to be okay, because he has just won a hundred thousand dollars and is waiting for them to send the check.

What?

"You know the Baja Sweepstakes?" He pronounces it "Bay-jah."   20 "Well, I won it, I think I won it, I got a letter. My little brother sent in the entry form we got with my CD club and he put my name on it, and it came back saying that I'm one of a select few chosen people who've won a hundred thousand dollars. That's what it said, it said that, and I had to scratch out the letters and if three of them matched it means I win, and they matched, and so I sent it back in and now I'm just waiting for my money. It should come pretty soon and then everything will be okay." He repeats it over and over again in the next few minutes: he's one of a select few chosen people.

As he speaks of this, his flat voice becomes animated. Slowly I begin to believe that he believes this. Whatever part of him knows better is firmly shelved for now. This hope, this belief that hundreds of thousands of dollars are on the way, is what keeps him going, what keeps him from walking out into the sky—or to the outhouse in the winter to take a leak and a nap in the snow. What will you do with the money, I ask. Well, first he is going to buy his mother and the kids a house.

The first gas stop is a little shack that's closed when we finally get there. Sandy wind and no sign of life. Miles on down the road is a small Lakota grocery store with only a few items on the shelves and a sign that reads "Stealing is not the Lakota way." Mac hands Mark a five dollar bill. You can kiss that five bucks goodbye, I say to Mac. I know, he nods. When Mark comes back out he has the gas, and also a big cup of 7-Up and a bag of nachos. You want some, he asks me? He hands Mac a buck fifty in change. On the way back I hold the gas can in the back seat, placing my hand over the opening. Despite the open windows, the van fills with fumes. My head begins to ache. I am riding in a dream of flatness, ranch fences, Mark's dark head in front of me wishing away his life, waiting for the break that takes him to Rapid. Later I learn that we are in Manderson, and this is the road where Black Elk lived.

Mark is talking about white people now. Yes, they get along okay. For "yes" he has an expression of affirmation that sounds sort of like "huh." Mari Sandoz spells it "hou" in her books on the Lakota. The Lakota are infiltrated in every way by whites, according to Mark. Lots of people in charge are white, the ranchers are white. And there's a place in Rapid called Lakota Hills, fancy houses meant for Lakotas, but whites live in them. Later it occurs to us that this is probably a development named Lakota Hills that has nothing at all to do with the Indians, but it has their name and so Mark thinks it belongs to them. I am angry for him that we borrow their name this way and paste it on our air-conditioned prosperity. I don't have anything to say to him. I lean back and close my eyes. It would be easy to be one of them again. I remember now how it's done. You just let everything flatten inside.

And when we return to Wounded Knee, the pull-off is empty. Mother, children, car, aunt, all are gone. There's nothing but wind and dust. This doesn't surprise me. Mark's mother knows better than to wait for her son's return if other help comes along. Mark means well, but maybe she has learned that sometimes it's hours before he gets back with gas—hours and a couple of six-packs if he has the chance. Now we face the prospect of driving Mark around the reservation until we can find them. I have just resigned myself to this when his aunt pulls back in and says they're broken down again a couple of miles up. We can leave now. Mark thanks us, smiles, and shyly allows us the liberty of having his aunt take a picture of all three of us. I am feeling a strange kind of shame, as though I had seen him naked, because he told us his secret and I knew it was a lie.

Unemployment, high rates of suicide and infant mortality, fetal alcohol syndrome, death by accident, and drinking-related diseases such as diabetes: these are now the ways that American Indians are approaching their collective demise. Over a century ago, American whites began this destruction by displacing and killing the *pte*, the Indian name for the buffalo the Plains Indians depended upon. We herded them together in far crueler ways than they had herded the bison, whose sacredness the Indians respected even as they killed them for food and shelter. The history of our genocide is available in many historical and imaginative sources. What is still elusive, still amazingly misunderstood, is how and why the Indians seem to have participated in their own destruction by their failure to adapt to changed circumstances.

Whites can point to the phenomenal adjustments of other non-Caucasian groups in America, most recently the Asians, who were badly mistreated and who have nevertheless not only adapted but excelled. Indians even come off badly in comparison to the group in some respects most parallel to them, American blacks, whose slowness in adapting seems at first glance to have more justification. Blacks were, after all, our slaves, brought here against their will, without close cultural ties to keep them bound together in a tradition of strength; and on the whole blacks are doing better than Indians. However slowly, a black middle class is emerging in America. What's the matter with Indians? Why haven't they adjusted better as a group?

The American Indian Movement is of course strong in some areas, and Indians have articulate, tough leaders and savvy representatives of their cause who are fighting hard against the tide of despair gripping the heart of their race. But they're still losing, and they know it. Estimates of unemployment on the Pine Ridge and Rosebud reservations run as high as 85 percent. Health officials at Pine Ridge estimate that as many as 25 percent of babies born on the reservation now have fetal alcohol syndrome. This culturally lethal condition cannot be over-emphasized, since it means that the next generation of Lakota are genetically as well as socioeconomically crippled; one of the consequences of fetal alcohol syndrome is not only physical disability but mental retardation. The prospects are extremely depressing for Lakota leaders whose traditional values are associated with mental acuity and imaginative wisdom. Mark is vastly ignorant and gullible, but he is intelligent enough. Many of his younger brothers and sisters are not only underprivileged and without educational advantages, but also—let the word be spoken—stupid. When the light of inquiry, curiosity, mental energy, dies out in the eyes of young Indians early in their stunted lives because they have nowhere to go and nothing to do, it is one kind of tragedy. When it is never present to die out in the first place, the magnitude of the waste and devastation is exponentially increased. Indian leaders who are now concentrating on anti-alcohol campaigns among their people are doing so for good reasons.

Indian leaders disagree about culpability at this point. Essentially the arguments become theories of genocide or suicide. On one end of the spectrum of blame is the theory that it is all the fault of white America. The evidence that can be marshaled for this point of view is massive: broken treaties, complete destruction of the Indian ways of life, welfare dependency established as the cheapest and easiest form of guilt payment, continued undermining of Indian autonomy and rights.

The problem with this perspective, say others, is that it perpetuates Indian desperation and permits the easy way out—spend your life complaining that white America put you here, and drink yourself into the oblivion of martyrdom instead of taking responsibility for your own life. Some Indians say they've heard enough about white America's culpability, and prefer to transfer responsibility—not blame, but responsibility—to the shoulders of their own people. "White people aren't doing this to us—we're doing it to ourselves," said one Pine Ridge health official on National Public Radio's *Morning Edition* recently. She sees the victim stance as the lethal enemy now.

The situation is as nearly hopeless as it is possible to be. Assimilation failed the first time and would fail if tried concertedly again, because Indian culture is rural and tribal and tied to open land, not urban airlessness. The Indian model is the encampment or village—the latter more recently and under duress—and not the city. Even the more stationary pueblo model is by definition not urban. The only real hope for Indian prosperity would be connected to vast tracts of land—not wasteland, but rich land. Nor are most Indians farmers in the sense that white America defines the farm. Though they might be, and have been, successful farmers under pressure, this is not their traditional milieu. Supposing that many tribes could adapt to the farming model over hunting and gathering, they would need large tracts of fine land to farm, and there are none left to grant them.

When the American government gave the Lakota 160 acres apiece 30 and said "Farm this," they misunderstood the Indians completely; and even if Indians had been able to adapt readily—a change approximately as difficult as asking a yuppie to become a nomad moving from encampment to encampment—the land they were given was inadequate to the purpose. Grubbing a living out of the land we have given them, in what John Wesley Powell called "the arid region" west of the one hundredth meridian—takes a kind of knowhow developed and perfected by white Americans, and it also takes capital. It is no coincidence that the large ranches on Pine Ridge are almost entirely leased by whites who had the initial wherewithal to make the land yield.

The Sioux were a people whose lives were shaped by a sense of seeking and vision that white America could barely understand even if we were to try, and we do not try. The life of a Sioux of a century and a half ago was framed by the Vision Quest, a search for goals, identity, purpose. One primary means of fulfillment was self-sacrifice. Now, as Royal Hassrick has written, "No longer is there anything which they can deny themselves, and so they have sacrificed themselves in pity." Whereas they were once people whose idea of being human was bound to creative self-expression, their faces now reflect what Hassrick calls "apathy and psychic emaciation." Collectively and individually they have become a people without a vision.

Why do they drink themselves into obliteration and erasure? Why not? When white America approaches the problem from within our own ethnocentric biases, we can't see why people would allow themselves to be wasted in this way, why they would not take the initiative to better themselves, to save themselves through the capitalist individuality that says, "*I* will make it out of this." But in fact part of their problem is that they have tried to do this, as have most Indian peoples. They've bought the American dream in part, and become greedy for money and material goods. Life on an Indian reservation—almost any reservation—is a despairing imitation of white middle-class values. In this respect Indians are like all other minority groups in ghettos in America, and this explains why Mark has a CD player instead of the more modest possessions we would not have begrudged him. If he is anything like the Indians I lived with, he also has a color TV, though he may well live in a shack or trailer without plumbing and without siding.

Their own dreams have evaded them, and so have ours. Mark and his brothers and sisters have been nourished on memories of a culture that vanished long before they were born and on the promises of a different one, from whose advantages they are forever excluded. Does Mark really believe he has won the sweepstakes? What he got was obviously one of those computer letters that invite the recipient to believe he has won something. Without the education that could teach him to read its language critically, or to read it adequately at all, he has been deceived into believing that a *deus ex machina* in the form of the Baja Sweepstakes will take him out of his despair.

In 1890, the year of the final defeat of the Sioux at Wounded Knee, the Ghost Dance was sweeping the plains. Begun by a few leaders, especially the Paiute seer Wovoka, the Ghost Dance promised its practitioners among the warriors that the buffalo would return and the white man would be defeated. Ghost Dancers believed that their ceremonial dancing and the shirts they wore would make them proof against the white man's bullets. Among the Sioux warriors at Wounded Knee, the willing suspension of disbelief was complete. It made the warriors reckless and abandoned, throwing normal caution and survival strategy to the wind.

A tragically inverted form of the self-delusion embodied in the 35 Ghost Dance is practiced today on the Pine Ridge and other Sioux reservations. The original Ghost Dance has beauty and vitality, as well as desperation, as its sources. Now many Sioux men who would have been warriors in another time behave as though liquor and passivity will not kill them. Mark chooses to suspend his disbelief in white promises and to wait for a hundred thousand dollars to arrive in the mail.

Hank Doctor was my husband's best friend on the Seneca reservation. He was raunchy, hard drinking, outrageous in behavior and looks. His hair was long and scraggly, his nearly black eyes were genuinely wild, and his blue jeans were always caked with dust and falling down his hips. His wit was wicked, his laugh raucous, dangerous, infectious. Hank was merciless toward me, always making white-girl jokes, telling me maybe I better go home to my mama, where I'd be safe from all these dark men. He wanted me to feel a little afraid in his world, told me horrible stories about ghost-dogs that would get me on the reservation if I ventured out at night—and then he'd laugh in a way that said hey, white girl, just joking, but not entirely. He alternated his affection toward me with edgy threats, made fun of the too-white way I talked or walked, took every opportunity to make me feel foolish and out of place. He was suspicious that I was just slumming it as a temporary rebellion—maybe taking notes in my head—and that I'd probably run for home when the going got too tough. Of course he was right, even though I didn't know it at the time. I liked him a lot.

A few years ago, my son Bernie went through a period when he chose to remove himself from my world and go live in his father's, from which I'd taken him when he was three. I didn't try to stop him, even though I knew he was hanging out with people who lived dangerously. I used to lie in bed unable to go to sleep because I was wondering what tree he'd end up wrapped around with his dad. He was a minor, but I was essentially helpless to prevent this. If I'd forced the issue, it would only have made his desire to know a forbidden world more intense. He lived there for months, and I slowly learned to get to sleep at night. Mothers can't save their children. And he had a right.

The day I knew he'd ultimately be okay was when he came home and told me about Hank. He wondered if I'd known Hank. He'd never met him before because Hank had been out west for years. Now he was back home, living in a shack way out in the country, terribly crippled with diabetes and other ailments from drinking, barely able to walk. Hank would have been in his mid-forties at this time. Bernie and his dad took rabbits to Hank when they went hunting so that Hank would have something to eat. During these visits, Hank talked nonstop about the old days, reminding big Bernard of all their bar brawls, crowing to young Bernie that the two of them could beat anyone when they fought as a team, recounting the times they'd dismantled the insides of buildings at four in the morning. He told his stories in vivid, loving detail. His gift for metaphor was precise and fine, his memory perfect even if hyperbolic. He recalled the conversations leading up to fights, the way a person had leaned over the bar, and who had said what to whom just before the furniture flew.

Bernie was impressed with him, but mostly he thought it was pathetic, this not-yet-old man who looked like he was in his seventies, with nothing to remember but brawls. I told Bernie to value Hank for the way he remembered, the way he could make a night from twenty years ago intensely present again, his gift for swagger and characterization, his poetry, his laughter. In another time Hank would have been a tribal narrator, a story catcher with better exploits to recount. He would have occupied a special place in Seneca life because of his gifts.

My son left the reservation valuing and understanding important things about his father's world, but not interested in living in its grip. He lives in Florida where he's a chef in a resort, and he's going to college. A month ago his daughter, my granddaughter, was born. She is named Sequoia, after the Cherokee chief who gave his people an alphabet and a written language. Bernie took her to the reservation on his recent visit north and introduced the infant Sequoia to her great-grandmother. My husband's mother says that big Bernard is drinking again, using up her money, and she doesn't know how much more she can take. I know she'll take as much as she has to. I hope I'll see Bernard someday soon to say hello, and maybe we can bend together over our granddaughter, for whom I know we both have many hopes.

Just before we leave Wounded Knee, I walk over to Aunt Lena's Comanche and point to the tribal sign that tells the story. "It says 'Massacre' there, but it used to say something else." I ask her if she knows what it said before. She looks over my shoulder and laughs. "That's funny," she says, "I've lived here all my life, but you know, I never did read that sign." We're miles down the road before I realize that I never finished reading it myself.

Questions

1. Discuss the different ways of knowing that George brings into this essay. Consider how the essay opens, and why the author might want to begin this way. How does her husband know American Indian culture? How does she know it? What ways of knowing does the author attribute to the Indians in the essay?
2. "My resistance," George writes, "broke down because of an encounter with a young Lakota named Mark, who is just about my own son's age." To what resistance is she referring? How does her encounter with Mark change things?

Barry Lopez

THE STONE HORSE

Barry Lopez was born in 1945, grew up in California and New York, and earned multiple degrees at Notre Dame. Then in 1970, after pursuing more graduate study at the University of Oregon, he gave up the life of a scholar to become a full-time writer. A frequent contributor of articles, essays, and fiction to periodicals and anthologies, Lopez is perhaps best known for two nonfiction books, *Of Wolves and Men* (1978), for which he won the John Burroughs Medal, and *Arctic Dreams: Imagination and Desire in a Northern Landscape* (1986), for which he won the National Book Award. In both of these works, he considers the propensity of human beings to impose themselves upon the natural world, to try to make it into something it is not. In 1986 Lopez received an Award in Literature from the American Academy and Institute of Arts and Letters, and in 1987 he received a Guggenheim Fellowship.

1

The deserts of southern California, the high, relatively cooler and wetter Mojave and the hotter, dryer Colorado to the south of it, carry the signatures of many cultures. Prehistoric rock drawings in the Mojave's Coso Range, representing the greatest concentration of petroglyphs in North America, are probably 3,000 years old. Big-game-hunting cultures that flourished there six or seven thousand years before that are known from broken spear tips, choppers, and burins left scattered along the shores of great Pleistocene lakes, long since evaporated. A burial site in the Yuha Basin in the Colorado Desert may be 20,000 years old; and worked stone from a quarry in the Calico Mountains is, many argue, evidence that human beings were here more than 200,000 years ago.

Because of the long-term stability of such arid environments, many of these prehistoric stone artifacts still lie exposed on the ground, accessible to anyone who passes by—the studious, the acquisitive, the indifferent, the merely curious. Archaeologists do not agree on the cultural sequence beyond about 10,000 years ago, but it is clear that these broken bits of chalcedony, chert, and obsidian, like the animal drawings and geometric designs etched on walls of basalt throughout the desert, anchor the earliest threads of human history, the first record of human endeavor here.

Western man did not journey into the California desert until the end of the eighteenth century, 250 years after Coronado brought his soldiers into the Zuni pueblos in a bewildered search for the cities of Cibola. The earliest appraisals of the land were cursory, hurried. People traveled *through* it, en route to Santa Fe or the California coastal settlements. Only miners tarried. In 1823 what had been Spain's became Mexico's and in 1848 what had been Mexico's became America's; but the bare, jagged mountains and dry lake beds, the vast and uniform plains of creosote bush and yucca plants, remained as obscure as the northern Sudan until the end of the nineteenth century.

Before 1940 the tangible evidence of twentieth-century man's passage here consisted of very little—the hard tracery of his travel corridors; the widely scattered, relatively insignificant evidence of his mining operations; and the fair expanse of his irrigated fields at the desert's periphery. In the space of a hundred years or so the wagon roads were paved, railroads were laid down, and canals and high-tension lines were built to bring water and electricity across the desert to Los Angeles from the Colorado River. The dark mouths of gold, talc, and tin mines yawned from the bony flanks of desert ranges. Dust-encrusted chemical plants stood at work on the lonely edges of dry lake beds. And crops of grapes, lettuce, dates, alfalfa, and cotton covered the Coachella and Imperial valleys, north and south of the Salton Sea, and the Palo Verde Valley along the Colorado.

These developments proceeded with little or no awareness of earlier human occupations by the cultures that preceded those of the historic Indians—the Mohave, the Chemehuevi, the Quechan, and others. (Extensive irrigation began to actually change the climate of the Colorado Desert, and human settlements, the railroads, and farming introduced many new, successful plants and animals into the region.)

During World War II, the American military moved into the desert in great force, to train troops and to test equipment. They found the dry air, isolation, and clear weather conducive to year-round flying very attractive. After the war, the complex of training grounds, storage facilities, and gunnery and test ranges was permanently settled on more than three million acres of military reservations. Few perceived the extent or significance of the destruction of aboriginal sites that took place during tank maneuvers and bombing runs or in the laying out of highways, railroads, mining districts, and irrigated fields. The few who intuited that something like an American Dordogne Valley lay exposed here were (only) amateur archaeologists; even they reasoned that the desert was too vast for any of this to matter.

After World War II, people began moving out of the crowded Los Angeles basin into homes in Lucerne, Apple, and Antelope valleys in

5

the western Mojave. They emigrated as well to a stretch of resort land at the foot of the San Jacinto Mountains that included Palm Springs, and farther out to old railroad and military towns like Needles and Barstow. People also began exploring the desert, at first in military-surplus jeeps and then with a variety of all-terrain and off-road vehicles that became available in the 1960s. By the mid-1970s, the number of people using such vehicles for desert recreation had increased exponentially. Most came and went in innocent curiosity; the few who didn't wreaked a unique havoc all out of proportion to their numbers. The disturbance of previously isolated archaeological sites increased substantially. Many of these early-man sites as well as prehistoric rock drawings were vandalized before archaeologists, themselves late to the desert, had any firm grasp of the bounds of human history in the desert. It was as though an Aztec library had been found intact and at the same moment numerous lacunae had appeared.

The vandalism was of three sorts: the general disturbance usually caused by souvenir hunters and by the curious and the oblivious; the wholesale stripping of a place by professional thieves for black-market sale and trade; and outright destruction, in which vehicles were actually used to ram and trench an area. By 1980, the Bureau of Land Management estimated that probably 35 percent of the archaeological sites in the desert had been vandalized. The destruction at some places by rifles and shotguns, or by power winches mounted on vehicles, were, if one cared for history, demoralizing to behold.

In spite of public education, land closures, and stricter law enforcement in recent years, the BLM estimates that, annually, about 1 percent of the archaeological record in the desert continues to be destroyed or stolen.

2

A BLM archaeologist told me, with understandable reluctance, where to find the intaglio. I spread my Automobile Club of Southern California map of Imperial County out on his desk, and he traced the route with a pink, felt-tip pen. The line crossed Interstate 8 and then turned west along the Mexican border.

"You can't drive any farther than about here," he said, marking a small X. "There's boulders in the wash. You walk up past them."

On a separate piece of paper he drew a route in a smaller scale that would take me up the arroyo to a certain point where I was to cross back east, to another arroyo. At its head, on higher ground just to the north, I would find the horse.

"It's tough to spot unless you know it's there. Once you pick it

up . . . " He shook his head slowly, in a gesture of wonder at its existence.

I waited until I held his eye. I assured him I would not tell anyone
else how to get there. He looked at me with stoical despair, like a man
who had been robbed twice, whose belief in human beings was offered
without conviction.

I did not go until the following day because I wanted to see it at   15
dawn. I ate breakfast at 4 A.M. in El Centro and then drove south. The
route was easy to follow, though the last section of road proved difficult, broken and drifted over with sand in some spots. I came to the
barricade of boulders and parked. It was light enough by then to find
my way over the ground with little trouble. The contours of the landscape were stark, without any masking vegetation. I worried only
about rattlesnakes.

I traversed the stone plain as directed, but, in spite of the frankness
of the land, I came on the horse unawares. In the first moment of recognition I was without feeling. I recalled later being startled, and that I
held my breath. It was laid out on the ground with its head to the east,
three times life size. As I took in its outline I felt a growing concentration of all my senses, as though my attentiveness to the pale rose color
of the morning sky and other peripheral images had now ceased to be
important. I was aware that I was straining for sound in the windless air
and I felt the uneven pressure of the earth hard against my feet. The
horse, outlined in a standing profile on the dark ground, was as vivid
before me as a bed of tulips.

I've come upon animals suddenly before, and felt a similar tension,
a precipitate heightening of the senses. And I have felt the inexplicable
but sharply boosted intensity of a wild moment in the bush, where it is
not until some minutes later that you discover the source of electricity
—the warm remains of a grizzly bear kill, or the still moist tracks of a
wolverine.

But this was slightly different. I felt I had stepped into an unoccu-
pied corridor. I had no familiar sense of history, the temporal structure
in which to think: This horse was made by Quechan people three hundred years ago. I felt instead a headlong rush of images: people hunting
wild horses with spears on the Pleistocene veld of southern California;
Cortés riding across the causeway into Montezuma's Tenochtitlán; a
short-legged Comanche, astride his horse like some sort of ferret, slash-
ing through cavalry lines of young men who rode like farmers. A hoof
exploding past my face one morning in a corral in Wyoming. These
images had the weight and silence of stone.

When I released my breath, the images softened. My initial feeling,
of facing a wild animal in a remote region, was replaced with a calm
sense of antiquity. It was then that I became conscious, like an ordinary
tourist, of what was before me, and thought: This horse was probably

laid out by Quechan people. But when, I wondered? The first horses they saw, I knew, might have been those that came north from Mexico in 1692 with Father Eusebio Kino. But Cocopa people, I recalled, also came this far north on occasion, to fight with their neighbors, the Quechan. And *they* could have seen horses with Melchior Díaz, at the mouth of the Colorado River in the fall of 1540. So, it could be four hundred years old. (No one in fact knows.)

I still had not moved. I took my eyes off the horse for a moment to 20 look south over the desert plain into Mexico, to look east past its head at the brightening sunrise, to situate myself. Then, finally, I brought my trailing foot slowly forward and stood erect. Sunlight was running like a thin sheet of water over the stony ground and it threw the horse into relief. It looked as though no hand had ever disturbed the stones that gave it its form.

The horse had been brought to life on ground called desert pavement, a tight, flat matrix of small cobbles blasted smooth by sand-laden winds. The uniform, monochromatic blackness of the stones, a patina of iron and magnesium oxides called desert varnish, is caused by long-term exposure to the sun. To make this type of low-relief ground glyph, or intaglio, the artist either selectively turns individual stones over to their lighter side or removes areas of stone to expose the lighter soil underneath, creating a negative image. This horse, about eighteen feet from brow to rump and eight feet from withers to hoof, had been made in the latter way, and its outline was bermed at certain points with low ridges of stone a few inches high to enhance its three-dimensional qualities. (The left side of the horse was in full profile; each leg was extended at 90 degrees to the body and fully visible, as though seen in three-quarter profile.)

I was not eager to move. The moment I did I would be back in the flow of time, the horse no longer quivering in the same way before me. I did not want to feel again the sequence of quotidian events—to be drawn off into deliberation and analysis. A human being, a four-footed animal, the open land. That was all that was present—and a "thoughtless" understanding of the very old desires bearing on this particular animal: to hunt it, to render it, to fathom it, to subjugate it, to honor it, to take it as a companion.

What finally made me move was the light. The sun now filled the shallow basin of the horse's body. The weighted line of the stone berm created the illusion of a mane and the distinctive roundness of an equine belly. The change in definition impelled me. I moved to the left, circling past its rump, to see how the light might flesh the horse out from various points of view. I circled it completely before squatting on my haunches. Ten or fifteen minutes later I chose another view. The third time I moved, to a point near the rear hooves, I spotted a stone tool at my feet. I stared at it a long while, more in awe than disbelief, before reaching out to pick it up. I turned it over in my left palm and took it between my fingers to feel its cutting edge. It is always difficult, especially with something so portable, to rechannel the desire to steal.

I spent several hours with the horse. As I changed positions and as the angle of the light continued to change I noticed a number of things. The angle at which the pastern carried the hoof away from the ankle was perfect. Also, stones had been placed within the image to suggest at precisely the right spot the left shoulder above the foreleg. The line that joined thigh and hock was similarly accurate. The muzzle alone seemed distorted — but perhaps these stones had been moved by a later hand. It was an admirably accurate representation, but not what a breeder would call perfect conformation. There was the suggestion of a bowed neck and an undershot jaw, and the tail, as full as a winter coyote's, did not appear to be precisely to scale.

The more I thought about it, the more I felt I was looking at an individual horse, a unique combination of generic and specific detail. It was easy to imagine one of Kino's horses as a model, or a horse that ran off from one of Coronado's columns. What kind of horses would these have been, I wondered? In the sixteenth century the most sought-after horses in Europe were Spanish, the offspring of Arabian stock and Barbary horses that the Moors brought to Iberia and bred to the older, eastern European strains brought in by the Romans. The model for this horse, I speculated, could easily have been a palomino, or a descendant of horses trained for lion-hunting in North Africa.

A few generations ago, cowboys, cavalry quartermasters, and draymen would have taken this horse before me under consideration and not let up their scrutiny until they had its heritage fixed to their satisfaction. Today, the distinction between draft and harness horses is arcane knowledge, and no image may come to mind for a blue roan or a claybank horse. The loss of such refinement in everyday conversation leaves me unsettled. People praise the Eskimo's ability to distinguish among forty types of snow but forget the skill of others who routinely differentiate between overo and tobiano pintos. Such distinctions are made for the same reason. You have to do it to be able to talk clearly about the world.

For parts of two years I worked as a horse wrangler and packer in Wyoming. It is dim knowledge now; I would have to think to remember if a buckskin was a kind of dun horse. And I couldn't throw a double-diamond hitch over a set of panniers — the packer's basic tie-down — without guidance. As I squatted there in the desert, however, these more personal memories seemed tenuous in comparison with the sweep of this animal in human time. My memories had no depth. I thought of the Hittite cavalry riding against the Syrians 3,500 years ago. And the first of the Chinese emperors, Ch'in Shih Huang, buried in Shensi Province in 210 B.C. with thousands of life-size horses and soldiers, a terra-cotta guardian army. What could I know of what was in the mind of whoever made this horse? Was there some racial memory of it as an animal that had once fed the artist's ancestors and then disappeared from North America? And then returned in this strange alliance with another race of men?

Certainly, whoever it was, the artist had observed the animal very closely. Certainly the animal's speed had impressed him. Among the first things the Quechan would have learned from an encounter with Kino's horses was that their own long-distance runners—men who could run down mule deer—were no match for this animal.

From where I squatted I could look far out over the Mexican plain. Juan Bautista de Anza passed this way in 1774, extending El Camino Real into Alta California from Sinaloa. He was followed by others, all of them astride the magical horse; *gente de razón*, the people of reason, coming into the country of *los primitivos*. The horse, like the stone animals of Egypt, urged these memories upon me. And as I drew them up from some forgotten corner of my mind—huge horses carved in the white chalk downs of southern England by an Iron Age people; Spanish horses rearing and wheeling in fear before alligators in Florida—the images seemed tethered before me. With this sense of proportion, a memory of my own—the morning I almost lost my face to a horse's hoof—now had somewhere to fit.

I rose up and began to walk slowly around the horse again. I had 30 taken the first long measure of it and was looking now for a way to depart, a new angle of light, a fading of the image itself before the rising sun, that would break its hold on me. As I circled, feeling both heady and serene at the encounter, I realized again how strangely vivid it was. It had been created on a barren bajada between two arroyos, as nondescript a place as one could imagine. The only plant life here was a few wands of ocotillo cactus. The ground beneath my shoes was so hard it wouldn't take the print of a heavy animal even after a rain. The only sounds I had heard here were the voices of quail.

The archaeologist had been correct. For all its forcefulness, the horse is inconspicuous. If you don't care to see it you can walk right past it. That pleases him, I think. Unmarked on this bleak shoulder of the plain, the site signals to no one; so he wants no protective fences here, no informative plaque, to act as beacons. He would rather take a chance that no motorcyclist, no aimless wanderer with a flair for violence and a depth of ignorance, will ever find his way here.

The archaeologist had given me something before I left his office that now seemed peculiar—an aerial photograph of the horse. It is widely believed that an aerial view of an intaglio provides a fair and accurate depiction. It does not. In the photograph the horse looks somewhat crudely constructed; from the ground it appears far more deftly rendered. The photograph is of a single moment, and in that split second the horse seems vaguely impotent. I watched light pool in the intaglio at dawn; I imagine you could watch it withdraw at dusk and sense the same animation I did. In those prolonged moments its shape and so, too, its general character changed — noticeably. The living quality of the image, its immediacy to the eye, was brought out by the light-in-time, not, at least here, in the camera's frozen instant.

Intaglios, I thought, were never meant to be seen by gods in the sky above. They were meant to be seen by people on the ground, over a long period of shifting light. This could even be true of the huge figures on the Plain of Nazca in Peru, where people could walk for the length of a day beside them. It is our own impatience that leads us to think otherwise.

This process of abstraction, almost unintentional, drew me gradually away from the horse. I came to a position of attention at the edge of the sphere of its influence. With a slight bow I paid my respects to the horse, its maker, and the history of us all, and departed.

3

A short distance away I stopped the car in the middle of the road to   35
make a few notes. I could not write down what I was thinking when I was with the horse. It would have seemed disrespectful, and it would have required another kind of attention. So now I patiently drained my memory of the details it had fastened itself upon. The road I'd stopped on was adjacent to the All American Canal, the major source of water for the Imperial and Coachella valleys. The water flowed west placidly. A disjointed flock of coots, small, dark birds with white bills, was paddling against the current, foraging in the rushes.

I was peripherally aware of the birds as I wrote, the only movement in the desert; and of a series of sounds from a village a half-mile away. The first sounds from this collection of ramshackle houses in a grove of cottonwoods were the distracted dawn voices of dogs. I heard them intermingled with the cries of a rooster. Later, the high-pitched voices of children calling out to each other came disembodied through the dry desert air. Now, a little after seven, I could hear someone practicing on the trumpet, the same rough phrases played over and over. I suddenly remembered how as children we had tried to get the rhythm of a galloping horse with hands against our thighs, or by fluttering our tongues against the roofs of our mouths.

After the trumpet, the impatient calls of adults, summoning children. Sunday morning. Wood smoke hung like a lens in the trees. The first car starts — a cold eight-cylinder engine, of Chrysler extraction perhaps, goosed to life, then throttled back to murmur through dual mufflers, the obbligato music of a shade-tree mechanic. The rote bark of mongrel dogs at dawn, the jagged outcries of men and women, an engine coming to life. Like a thousand villages from West Virginia to Guadalajara.

I finished my notes — where was I going to find a description of the horses that came north with the conquistadors? Did their manes come forward prominently over the brow, like this one's, like the forelocks of Blackfeet and Assiniboine men in nineteenth-century paintings? I set the notes on the seat beside me.

The road followed the canal for a while and then arced north, toward Interstate 8. It was slow driving and I fell to thinking how the desert had changed since Anza had come through. New plants and animals — the MacDougall cottonwood, the English house sparrow, the chukar from China — have about them now the air of the native-born. Of the native species, some — no one knows how many — are extinct. The populations of many others, especially the animals, have been sharply reduced. The idea of a desert impoverished by agricultural poisons and varmint hunters, by off-road vehicles and military operations, did not seem as disturbing to me, however, as this other horror, now that I had been those hours with the horse. The vandals, the few who crowbar rock art off the desert's walls, who dig up graves, who punish the ground that holds intaglios, are people who devour history. Their self-centered scorn, their disrespect for ideas and images beyond their ken, create the awful atmosphere of loose ends in which totalitarianism thrives, in which the past is merely curious or wrong.

I thought about the horse sitting out there on the unprotected 40 plain. I enumerated its qualities in my mind until a sense of its vulnerability receded and it became an anchor for something else. I remembered that history, a history like this one, which ran deeper than Mexico, deeper than the Spanish, was a kind of medicine. It permitted the great breadth of human expression to reverberate, and it did not urge you to locate its apotheosis in the present.

Each of us, individuals and civilizations, has been held upside down like Achilles in the River Styx. The artist mixing his colors in the dim light of Altamira; an Egyptian ruler lying still now, wrapped in his byssus, stored against time in a pyramid; the faded Dorset culture of the Arctic; the Hmong and Samburu and Walbiri of historic time; the modern nations. This great, imperfect stretch of human expression is the clarification and encouragement, the urging and the reminder, we call history. And it is inscribed everywhere in the face of the land, from the mountain passes of the Himalayas to a nameless bajada in the California desert.

Small birds rose up in the road ahead, startled, and flew off. I prayed no infidel would ever find that horse.

Questions

1. Lopez begins and ends his essay by thinking about various kinds of destruction. What is the difference between destruction and vandalism? Which one is worse?
2. Why doesn't Lopez believe "that an aerial view of an intaglio provides a fair and accurate depiction"? What does an accurate picture depend upon? What does Lopez's essay suggest gives someone an accurate view?

Gerald Early

WAITING FOR MISS AMERICA: STAND UP AND CHEER

Gerald Early was born in Philadelphia in 1952 and earned degrees from the University of Pennsylvania and Cornell University. An associate professor of English and African and Afro-American studies at Washington University, he lectures often on literary, cultural, and racial issues. Early is the author of two books — *Tuxedo Junction: Essays on American Culture* (1990) and *The Culture of Bruising: Essays on Literature, Prizefighting, and Modern American Culture* (1991) — and the editor of two more — *My Soul's High Song: The Collected Writings of Countee Cullen* (1991) and *Speech and Power: The African-American Essay, from Polemic to Pulpit* (1991). Although he is most known as an essayist, Early also writes poetry and fiction and has won awards for his short stories.

I'm as good as any woman in your town.

—Bessie Smith, "Young Woman's Blues"

I remember well sitting in a barbershop in the not so once-upon-a-time-long-ago past right after the yearly telecast of the Miss America contest. Most of the patrons, who were black and male, decided that they would not let so insignificant a matter as not having watched the program prevent them from discussing it endlessly. In fact, not having seen the show or having any real idea of what the Miss America contest was about seemed to have fueled their imaginations and loosened their tongues in such a way that, in retrospect, any knowledge of the true proceedings of beauty contests may have been found inhibitive. Most of the men spoke of "white bitches parading their asses across the stage" with much the same expression of mixed desire, wonder, and rage that often characterized the way I heard a good many black men talk about white women in my childhood. As the talk eventually died down, one of the patrons, a black man with a derby and a gold tooth and who looked for all the world like a cross between Lester Young and Stymie from the *Our Gang* comedies, said with a great deal of finality: "You know, there are three things in life you can bet your house on: death, taxes, and that Miss America will always be white." Now that we have a Miss America who is black or who, at least, can pass for a fairly pronounced quadroon, I suppose that the chiliastic inevitability of taxes and death might be called into question.

I use the word "quadroon" because it seems so accurate in a quaint sort of way. When I finally became aware of the fact that our new Miss America is black (something that I was not aware of instantly, even though I watched the pageant on television), I immediately thought of the character Eliza from Harriet Beecher Stowe's famed 1852 novel, *Uncle Tom's Cabin*. Our new Miss America has elevated the image of the tragic mulatto woman from the status of quaint romantic figure in some of America's most aesthetically marginal literature to that of a national icon. I thought of Eliza not only because she was very light but also because she was the essence of cultured black womanhood. Her hands, according to the witnesses in the novel, never betrayed her as a slave because she never, unlike, say, Uncle Tom's dark-skinned wife, Aunt Chloe, performed any hard work. She was shaped in the image of her mistress, Mrs. Shelby, and, like her mistress, possessed little that would have enabled her to escape pious mediocrity. She had simply a desperate love for her son and her husband and a desperate wish to be good despite the odds against it. And I suppose if there has been anything that has characterized the light-skinned black woman as cultured mulatto, it has been that air of desperation that has made her seem so helpless and so determined in the same instant. She showed such incredible strength bottled in a welter of outmoded morality. This desperation is quite important; any black woman who would want to become Miss America or, for that matter, the first black woman to do just about anything in our country (where such "firsts" *signify* so much while they *mean* so little) has to be a bit desperate; and in this culture desperation and ambition have become indistinguishable. Any act of that magnitude is always reminiscent of Eliza, feet bloodied and hair flying, clutching her son tightly as she jumps from floe to floe across the icy Ohio River. When this desperation has combined with bitterness, it has produced the true tragic genius of the mulatto personality (the term "mulatto" having come to indicate a psychological mode rather than a racial mixture) exemplified by such women as Dorothy Dandridge, Billie Holiday, and Josephine Baker.

But our new Miss America is as sweet as any of her sisters before her, so she will not, in the end, bring to mind those great images of the mulatto personality like Holiday, Baker, and Dandridge. Her reign will help us forget them; for while our culture can tolerate desperate black women who want success and love, it cannot tolerate bitter black women who have been denied success and love. Our current Miss America will always bring to mind Eliza and she will clutch her crown and roses in much the same way that Stowe's character clutched her son. She will personify the strength, courage, and culture of black, middle-class womanhood, and all of its philistine mediocrity as well.

Far from being the far-reaching, revolutionary breakthrough in race relations (a new chink made in the armor of the annealed idea of white superiority) that such black leaders as Benjamin Hooks and Shirley Chisholm seemed to have thought, I believe it to have been a quaint joke in much the same way that the flights of the first black and woman astronauts were. Surely, no one really believes that the choice of a black Miss America is comparable to Jackie Robinson breaking into pro ball. Or perhaps it is. Professional athletics have always been, in some sense, the male equivalent of beauty contests; because they are a male province, they always have been considered to possess deeper cultural significance. But, leaving simplistic feminist thinking aside, I believe our new Miss America is a bit too ambiguous a symbol to be as powerful a jolt to our racial consciousness as the emergence of the professional black ballplayer.

Suffice it to say that a black girl as Miss America is a joke but not an insult. In the first place, it is difficult to be insulted by an act that is so self-consciously well-intentioned. Vanessa Williams, the young student who won the contest, is such a radiantly beautiful woman that only black nationalist types would find her to be absolutely bereft of any redeeming qualities. Our black nationalists, who constitute a more important segment of black public opinion than many white people realize, have already proffered their opinion that the selection of a black woman as Miss America is a completely negative, conspiratorial attempt on the part of white America further to degrade black people. One might almost wish this were true. What makes race relations in America such a strange and dangerous affair is that white America—at least, the white power elite—never acts in concert about anything. It would be nearly reassuring to be black if only one could always suspect whites collectively of acting from the most malicious, wicked designs.

I heard several black men on a local black radio call-in program complain rather vociferously the Monday following the Miss America pageant. One caller, who writes for the local black newspaper, thought Ms. Williams to be "politically unaware" because she refused to be a spokesperson for her race, and he considered her "a liability to the black community." Another caller voiced the opinion that the selection of Williams as Miss America was further proof that white America wished to denigrate black men by promoting black women. It is with a great degree of dire anticipation that I await the response from these quarters once it becomes generally known that Ms. Williams has a white boyfriend. She will no longer be simply "politically unaware" or "an insulting hindrance to the ascendancy of black men"; she will be a traitor, "sleeping with the white boy just like the slave women used to do on the plantation." One might almost think Michelle Wallace's contention in her sloppy little book, *Black Macho and the Myth of the Superwoman*, to be essentially correct: the final racial confrontation will be between not blacks and whites but between black men and black women. One hopes that the neurotic concern over miscegenation that seems to bedevil blacks as well as whites will not ultimately display itself in a game of murderous recriminations.

Most black women I know were overjoyed about a black woman becoming Miss America; it was, to their way of thinking, long overdue recognition of the beauty and the femininity of black women. "It might show black men that we're as good as white women," one black woman told me, and, despite the humor that surrounded the statement, it seemed to be, underneath, a deeply distressing appeal. Perhaps —and if this is true, then racial psychopathology is more heartbreaking than anyone remotely believed possible—black women needed some giant manufactured event of American popular culture to make them feel assured that they were and are, indeed, as good as white women. Winning the Miss America contest has become, for at least some black women, American popular culture's fade-out kiss of benevolence.

At a time when the very purpose and motivation of the Miss America contest is being called into question, and rightly so, by feminists of every stripe, and the entire cultural sub-genre called the beauty contest is being seen as, at best, irrelevant to modern women and, at worst, an insult to them, one might find the Miss America title to be a very dubious or ambiguous honor. Furthermore, Vanessa Williams was chosen largely because her good looks are quite similar to those of any white contestant. It will take no imaginative leap on the part of most whites to find her to be a beautiful girl. She does not look like the little black girl of the inner-city projects who reeks of cheap perfume and cigarette smoke and who sports a greasy, homemade curly perm and who has a baby at the age of fifteen for lack of anything better to do. (Whose little girl is she? one wonders.) Vanessa Williams will not even in a distant way remind anyone of *that* hard reality and, in truth, she is not supposed to. Her beauty, if anything, is a much more intense escapism than that of her white counterpart. In effect, her selection becomes a kind of tribute to the ethnocentric "universality" of the white beauty standards of the contest; in short, her looks allow her to "pass" aesthetically. It is an oddly bestowed kiss that white popular culture has planted on black women; it is just the sort of kiss that makes the benevolence of white folk seem so hugely menacing. As a friend of mine said, "When white folk get in trouble with their symbols, they throw 'em on black folk to redeem." To be sure, it is for such reasons that the selection of a black woman as Miss America is much more ambiguous and less effective as a symbol of American racial fusion than the breaking of the color barrier in professional sports. So, with angry black nationalists on the one side, with uneasy white and black feminists on the other, with many adoring young black women asking, "How do you do your hair?" and with many adoring older black women saying, "Child, you sing just like so-and-so at my church. Lord, you got a voice," Vanessa Williams is not expected to have an easy time of it.

I would like to think it was an act of God that I should choose to watch (for the first time) the Miss America pageant the very year that a black woman won the crown. I had never watched the pageant before, partly, I suppose, because as a male I have never found beauty contests to be interesting and partly because as a black I have always thought them to be chilling in an alienating sort of way (I have always found very beautiful white women to be oddly frightening, as if within their beauty resonated an achingly inhuman purity; they have always been in my imagination, to borrow from Toni Morrison's *Tar Baby*, the snow queens of this life) and partly because, in the instance of the Miss America pageant, the contest took place in Atlantic City and as a native of Philadelphia I have always found this shabby playground of the Eastern Seaboard to detract from whatever glamour the contest might have possessed. I remember as a kid buying boxes of St. James's saltwater taffy, the only souvenir that one could ever really *want* from this resort, and wondering if Atlantic City had ever been the happy place that was pictured on the cover of the boxes. I certainly cannot recall its being so when I was a child, particularly since one had to ride through wretched Camden, New Jersey, to get there and then walk through the endless blocks of despair that made up the black neighborhood in this little town in order to get to "chickenbone" beach—where all the black folk were to be found. I doubt if the casinos have, in any wise, improved the place. I understand that the Miss America contest was instituted in 1921 as an attempt by local businessmen to extend the resort season beyond the Labor Day holiday. It was certainly sleazy enough in those early years; no pretense was made that it was anything more than a flesh show: no talent show, no scholarships to the winner and runners-

up. It was simply a parade of white "goddesses" who were being exploited in the worst sort of way, a "clean" peep show that was dedicated
to making money, endorsing white supremacy, and denigrating
women in one fell cultural swoop. It is no wonder, considering what
the contest stood for, that women's clubs were, in part, instrumental in
shutting Miss America down from 1928 through 1932. It is also no
wonder, considering what the contest stood for, that it was recommenced for good in 1935.

I watched the Miss America pageant this year largely because the   10
subject of beauty contests was on the mind of everyone who lives in St.
Louis. The city fathers (and its few mothers, too) decided that St. Louis
should play host to the 1983 Miss Universe pageant in an effort to improve the image of St. Louis and to promote tourism. How much playing host for that beauty contest helped this city remains to be seen. The
immediate returns show that St. Louis, a city that can ill afford such
losses, will have to have a tremendous boost in tourism next summer
to recoup its expenses. What I find most striking is the lack of imagination, the sheer lack of inventiveness on the part of local politicians: to
think that a beauty contest, itself a confession of a dreadful social tact-
lessness, would resuscitate a city where poverty and crime are the un-
redemptive admissions of failures so vast that instead of being frightened *of* the poor, one is frightened *for* them. I have read in the papers
that our fair city may next bid for the Miss USA contest which, for the
last few years, has been held in Biloxi, Mississippi. If the Biloxi Chamber of Commerce is to be believed, this contest has increased tourism so
much that literally countless thousands of Americans now include
Biloxi in their summer vacation plans. I have no idea what staging the
Miss Universe pageant has done for this city's image, but I believe the
gang rape of a teenage girl in broad daylight before a score of witnesses
in one of our public parks made a deeper impression on the national
mind than the wire-service photo of smiling women in hair curlers visiting the Arch (St. Louis's version of a national treasure) a week before
they were to be judged in the pageant.

I had no idea while I watched the telecast that our new Miss America, then Miss New York, was black. I was watching the show on a
snowy black-and-white television and the girls seemed to be either
olive or alabaster. I had, rather uncharitably, assumed all the contestants were white. Actually, I was more curious about the fate of Miss
Missouri who was, like Miss New York, one of the finalists. She was a
blond girl with a somewhat longish chin named Barbara Webster.

It was a very long program, but surprisingly, not a boring one. I can
say this quite seriously even after having watched the talent portion of
the program and after having discovered that those young women had
precious little of *that*. They made up in earnestness what they lacked in
natural gifts, and since they are supposed to symbolize the girl next

door or the boss's daughter (the girl every man wants to marry but no one is supposed—pardon the vulgarity, but it is really quite appropriate here—to screw), it is all right if they seem, well, amateurish, like products of a finishing school. The girls fairly dripped sincerity. As a consequence, one cheered them all and felt embarrassed by their shortcomings; they all seemed to be somebody's kid sister or somebody's older sister doing a parody of an audition. Miss Ohio did a song-and-dance number that was as devoid of skill as, say, a first-grader's attempt to write a novel; she tried to do some Fred Astaire sorts of things with her hat, but simply gave the overwhelming impression that she would have been less confounded had she simply left it on her head. I think it was Miss Alabama who played a Gershwin medley on the piano. It is very difficult to convince anyone that you are a serious musician when you have to grin all the time (consider Louis Armstrong, one of the greatest musicians America has ever produced) and your smiles are not in response to the pleasure you derive from your playing but from an unwritten rule that any contestant in the Miss America pageant must never appear serious for fear that someone might interpret pensiveness as a sullen demeanor. Miss Alabama, we learned, had something like fifteen years of piano lessons and played Gershwin very much like someone who had had fifteen years of piano lessons and never learned to play the instrument. Miss Missouri wound up looking even more ridiculous than Miss Alabama: she played a hoedown number on the violin; she played well, but a toothy grin and a tasseled jumpsuit made her appearance seem so incongruous with the music she was playing that it bordered on being avant-garde. She needed only the Art Ensemble of Chicago playing behind her with tribal face paint and laboratory robes to complete the lunacy of it all. Another young woman, I don't remember which state she represented, did a dance number to the theme song from *Flashdance* that very closely resembled a routine in an aerobics class. This exercise, which is the most apt word for the performance, did not end so much as it petered out. And, of course, there were singers. In fact, most of the talent consisted of singing that sounded very much like bad versions of Barbra Streisand: no subtlety, no artful working of the lyrics or melody, just belting out from the gut with arms flung wide and face contorted with melodramatic emotion. The two numbers I remember most clearly are the medley of "Dixie" and "The Battle Hymn of the Republic" sung by a young woman who represented one of the southern states, and "Happy Days Are Here Again" sung by Miss New York. The medley seemed to me to be as silly as someone singing a combined version of "The Star-Spangled Banner" and "Amazing Grace"; someone might as well do such a medley in a future Miss America contest and neatly tie together all the ideological aspects of being American. To be American has come to mean, in popular culture, not so much being alienated from our history, but insisting that our history is contained in a series of high-sounding slogans and mawkish songs—indeed, that our history resembles nothing so much as the message and the jingle of a television commercial. I suppose that Miss New York was the best singer; surely she was the most professionally fervent. The song she chose was interesting; it reminded me of the little shows put on by the children who were featured on the *Our Gang/Little Rascals* comedy shorts. The song reminded me of those *Our Gang* segments not only because both are products of the Depression and because they are homely and mediocre, but also because they were both designed to make people forget a harder reality, a more painful reality. The Miss America contest has given us a long line of charming Shirley Temples for a number of years, and now that a black woman has been selected we might assume that she, too, can be Shirley Temple. (Now black women too can be sweet and cloying, dancing and singing automatons like Temple, the most beloved of children in her films, and who, always in search of parents, would teasingly ask, "Whose little girl am I?" and would always find an eager audience ready to answer, "Ours!") Or, perhaps, we might assume that it is getting a bit more difficult for the Miss America contest to protect us from our own reality.

Questions

1. The foundation of the Miss America contest, in 1921, rested on local businessmen's desire

   > to extend the resort season beyond the Labor Day holiday. It was certainly sleazy enough in those early years: no pretense was made that it was anything more than a flesh show: no talent show, no scholarships to the winner and runners-up. It was simply a parade of white "goddesses" who were being exploited in the worst sort of way, a 'clean' peep show that was dedicated to making money, endorsing white supremacy, and denigrating women in one fell cultural swoop.

   Early notes that it was no surprise that women's clubs closed down the show for the next five years, and also, that it was "no wonder, considering what the contest stood for, that it was recommenced for good in 1935." Have the offenses for which he criticizes the first Miss America contests changed? Does the crowning of a black Miss America complicate this list of charges?

2. The Miss America contest surely is one of the defining spectacles of American popular culture. What are some other icons of popular culture that Early presents in this essay? How, for example, does Shirley Temple function in the closing paragraph?

Frances FitzGerald

SUN CITY—1983

The daughter of prominent parents, Frances FitzGerald was born in New York in 1940 and grew up meeting people like Winston Churchill, Adlai Stevenson, and Albert Schweitzer. After graduating from Radcliffe in 1962, she began her writing career by contributing articles to the *New York Herald Tribune, Vogue*, and the *Village Voice*. In 1966, she traveled to Saigon to report on the Vietnam War. Her work there led to a series of essays in the *New Yorker* which she then developed, with the help of Paul Mus, into *Fire in the Lake: The Vietnamese and Americans in Vietnam* (1972). For this book, which analyzed the inherent conflict between the Vietnamese and American cultures, FitzGerald won many awards, including the Pulitzer Prize and the National Book Award. FitzGerald is also the author of *America Revised: History Schoolbooks in the Twentieth Century* (1979) and *Cities on a Hill: A Journey through Contemporary American Cultures* (1986).

*O*n Route 301 south of Tampa, billboards advertising Sun City Center crop up every few miles, with pictures of Cesar Romero and slogans that read FLORIDA'S RETIREMENT COMMUNITY OF THE YEAR, 87 HOLES OF GOLF, THE TOWN TOO BUSY TO RETIRE. According to a real-estate brochure, the town is "sensibly located . . . comfortably removed from the crowded downtown areas, the highway clutter, the tourists, and the traffic." It is twenty-five miles from Tampa, thirty miles from Bradenton, thirty-five miles from Sarasota, and eleven miles from the nearest beach on the Gulf Coast. Route 301, an inland route—to be taken in preference to the coast road, with its lines of trucks from the phosphate plants—passes through a lot of swampland, some scraggly pinewoods, and acre upon acre of strawberry beds covered with sheets of black plastic. There are fields where hairy, tough-looking cattle snatch at the grass between the palmettos. There are aluminum warehouses, cinderblock stores, and trailer homes in patches of dirt with laundry sailing out behind. There are Pentecostal churches and run-down cafés and bars with rows of pickup trucks parked out front.

Turn right with the billboards onto Route 674, and there is a green-and-white suburban-looking resort town. Off the main road, white asphalt boulevards with avenues of palm trees give onto streets that curve pleasingly around golf courses and small lakes. White ranch-style houses sit back from the streets on small, impeccably manicured lawns. A glossy four-color map of the town put out by a real-estate company shows cartoon figures of golfers on the fairways and boats on the lakes, along with drawings of churches, clubhouses, and curly green trees. The map is a necessity for the visitor, since the streets curve around in maze fashion, ending in culs-de-sac or doubling back on themselves. There is no way in or out of Sun City Center except by the main road bisecting the town. The map, which looks like a child's board game (Snakes and Ladders or Uncle Wiggily), shows a vague area—a kind of no-man's-land—surrounding the town. As the map suggests, there is nothing natural about Sun City Center. The lakes are artificial, and there is hardly a tree or a shrub or a blade of grass that has any correspondence in the world just beyond it. At the edges of the development, there are houses under construction, with the seams still showing in the transplanted lawns. From there, you can look out at a flat brown plain that used to be a cattle ranch. The developer simply scraped the surface off the land and started over again.

Sun City Center is an unincorporated town of about eighty-five hundred people, almost all of whom are over the age of sixty. It is a self-contained community, with stores, banks, restaurants, and doctors' offices. It has the advertised eighty-seven holes of golf; it also has tennis courts, shuffleboard courts, swimming pools, and lawn-bowling greens. In addition to the regular housing, it has a "life-care facility"—a six-story apartment building with a nursing home in one wing. "It's a strange town," a clinical psychologist at the University of South Florida, in Tampa, told me before I went. "It's out there in the middle of nowhere. It has a section of private houses, where people go when they retire. Then it has a section of condos and apartments; where people go when they can't keep up their houses. Then it has a nursing home. Then it has a cemetery." In fact, there is no cemetery in Sun City Center, but the doctor was otherwise correct.

In his social history of the family in Europe, *Centuries of Childhood*, the French historian Philippe Ariès shows us that "childhood" is a social construct. In medieval France, the concept did not exist, for children were not differentiated from other people. In the twelfth century, children out of swaddling clothes would be dressed as adults, and as soon as they could get about independently they would join the world of adults, participating in their work and their social life as fully as their physical capacities permitted. (The painters of the period depicted children as dwarf adults, ignoring their distinctive physiognomy.) The notion of "childhood" developed very slowly over the centuries. Only gradually did children become specialized people, with their own dress, their own work (schooling), their own manners and games. To travel around Florida these days—and particularly to visit a retirement community such as Sun City Center—is to suspect that a similar kind of specialization is taking place at the other end of the age spectrum: that American society is creating a new category of people, called "the aging" or "senior citizens," with their own distinctive habits and customs. (That the name for these people has not yet been agreed upon shows that their status is still transitional.)

In a sense, the residents of Sun City Center and their peers across   5
the United States are living on a frontier. Not a geographical frontier but a chronological one. Old age is nothing new, of course, but for an entire generation to reach old age with its membership almost intact is something new. Until this century, death had no more relation to old age than it had to any other period of life. In fact, it had less. In seventeenth-century France, for example, a quarter of all human beings died before the age of one, another quarter died before the age of twenty, and a third quarter before the age of forty-five; only ten out of a hundred people reached the age of sixty. In France from the seventeenth century to the nineteenth, the percentage of the population over sixty remained almost constant, at 8.8 percent. In America during the same period, life was probably even shorter for most people, and the population as a whole was much younger. But then in the twentieth century the demographics turned around; they changed more than they had in the six previous centuries. In 1900, the average life expectancy for children born in the United States was 47.3 years. In 1980, it was 73.6 years. This startling increase was due mainly to medical success in reducing the rates of infant, childhood, and maternal mortality. But there was—also as a result of medical advances—some increase in longevity as well. In 1900, white men aged sixty could expect an average of 14.4 more years of life. In 1978, they could expect an average of 17.2 more (And women could expect to do better than that.) As a result of these and other demographic changes, the number of people sixty or sixty-five and over increased both absolutely and relative to the population of the United States as a whole. In 1900, people sixty-five and over represented 4 percent of the population. In 1980, they represented 11.3 percent of it, and there were 25.5 million of them.

The younger generation in this country has grown up with the notion that people should reach the age of sixty-five, and reach it in good health. But Americans now over sixty belong to the first generation to do that. Modern medicine has increased longevity to some degree, but, just as important, it has alleviated some of the persistent, nonfatal maladies of the body. Throughout history, of course, some people have reached their eighties in excellent health, but until this century the majority of Europeans and Americans aged as many people still do in the poorest countries of the world—suffering irreversible physical decay in their forties and fifties. Philippe Ariès reminds us that until recently chronological age had very little meaning in European society; the word "old" was associated with the loss of teeth, eyesight, and so on. The very novelty of health and physical vigor in those past sixty-five is reflected in the current struggle over nomenclature. Since the passage of the Social Security Act, in 1935, demographers have used the age of sixty-five as a benchmark and labeled those at or over it as "the old" or "the elderly." The terms are meant to be objective, but because of their connotations they have proved unacceptable to those designated by them. Sensitive to their audience, gerontologists and government agencies have substituted "older people," "the aging," or "senior citizens." These terms, being relative, could apply to anyone of almost any age, but, by a kind of linguistic somersault, they have come to denote a precise chronological category.

People now over sixty-five live on a frontier also in the sense that the territory is fast filling up behind them. By the end of the century, if current demographic trends hold, one in eight Americans, or slightly more than 12 percent of the population, will be sixty-five or over. The increase will at first be relatively small, because the number of children born in the thirties was a relatively small one; but then, barring catastrophe or large-scale immigration, the numbers will start to climb. In the years between 2020 and 2030, after the baby-boom generation reaches its seniority, some fifty-five million Americans, or nearly 20 percent of the projected population, will be sixty-five or over. How the society will support these people is a problem that Americans are just beginning to think about. Politicians have been considering the implications for Social Security and federal retirement benefits, but they have not yet begun to imagine all the consequences in other realms.

The younger generation assumes that at sixty-five people leave their jobs and spend five, ten, or fifteen years of their lives in a condition called retirement. But here, too, the generation now around sixty-five has broken new ground. Historically speaking, the very notion of retirement—on a mass scale, at any rate—is new, and dates only from the industrial revolution, from the time when a majority of workers (and not just a few professionals) became replaceable parts in organizations outside the family. The possibility of retirement for large numbers of people depended, of course, on the establishment of adequate social-insurance systems, and these were not created until long after the building of industry. In this country, whose industrial revolution lagged behind that of Western Europe, the possibility came only with the New Deal. The Social Security Act of 1935 created an economic floor for those who could not work. More important, it created the presumption that American workers had a right to retire—a right to live without working after the age of sixty-five. This presumption led, in turn, to the establishment of government, corporate, and union pension plans that allowed workers to retire without a disastrous loss of income. But these pension plans did not cover very many people until some time after

World War II. Even in 1950, 46 percent of all American men sixty-five and over were still working or looking for work. In 1980, only 20 percent were.

In *The Coming of Age*, published in 1970, Simone de Beauvoir called the treatment of the elderly in Western societies a scandal. Citing 1957 statistics, she pointed out that in the United States a quarter of all couples over sixty-five had incomes below the poverty level; the scandal was far worse in the case of single people, since 33 percent of elderly men and 50 percent of elderly women had less than poverty-level incomes. The de Beauvoir analysis is now way out of date, however. Since the late fifties, the economic situation of older people in this country has improved dramatically. In 1978, only 14 percent of all non-institutionalized elderly people had incomes below the poverty line—or about the same percentage that existed throughout the society. (Between 1959 and 1978, the numbers of the elderly poor actually declined, not only relatively but absolutely, from 5.5 million people to 3.3 million.) Elderly single women fared far worse than couples or single men (21 percent had incomes below the poverty level), and the older people fared worse than the younger "elderly." But everyone went up with the rising tide. Between 1965 and 1976, the median income for families headed by an elderly person increased by 38 percent in real dollars. In 1960, outlays for the elderly constituted 13 percent of the federal budget. In 1980, the figure was 27.5 percent. This rise reflected not only a growth in the number of elderly people but also a real increase in Social Security and federal-pension benefits. In addition, Social Security benefits and pensions (from the government and also from a few corporations) have been adjusted to the Consumer Price Index. The result is that for the past ten years—the years of high inflation—the economic situation of older people has improved both absolutely and relative to that of younger people. In the seventies, the average Social Security benefit shot up 55 percent faster than the price index, while the average income of wage earners rose less than 2 percent in real terms. Between 1970 and 1976, the median income for younger people increased by only 4 percent, whereas it increased by around 20 percent for those sixty-five and over. Thus, the present generation of people in their sixties and seventies may be the most privileged generation of elderly people in history.

Simone de Beauvoir complained in her book that older people   10
were looked upon mainly as a social problem. In the sense that she was correct at the time, she would be correct today—except that the "problem" has largely reversed itself. In the sixties and seventies, American parents worried about the kids of the Woodstock generation "dropping out of the system"; in fact, as we now discover, it was their fathers who were dropping out, in droves. In 1981, only 68 percent of all men between the ages of fifty-five and fifty-nine had year-round, full-time

jobs; of those between sixty and sixty-four, only 49 percent did. By the end of 1981, more than half of all male retirees — 57.1 percent — had gone on Social Security pensions before they were sixty-five. The fact that the median age of retirement rose slightly after the economic downturn of 1974–75 suggests that not all these men were victims of unemployment or of mandatory-retirement policies. According to a Louis Harris poll conducted in 1981, 60 percent of all retirements were voluntary; of the remaining 40 percent the great majority resulted from ill health or disability, with mandatory-retirement policies accounting for only a fifth. What all these statistics indicate is that people are living longer, and are also retiring earlier by choice and maintaining something closer to their old standard of living. The question is whether the society will continue to be able to support this unemployed population in addition to its children. Projecting current trends into the future, demographers calculate that by the year 2000 there will be only three active working people to support every person over sixty-five; in the year 2030, the ratio will be only two to one. Government planners, adding up the cost of federal benefits for these future generations of retirees, estimate that at current rates expenditures for Social Security, government pensions, and other programs benefiting the elderly would claim 35 percent of the federal budget in the year 2000 and 65 percent of it in 2025. Given these statistical projections, a number of commentators have announced the imminent outbreak of a war between the old and the young.

Americans now in their sixties and seventies are surely the first generation of healthy, economically independent retired people in history — and, in the absence of significant economic growth, they may well be the last one. But, whatever the economic arrangements of the future, this generation remains the cultural avant-garde for the increasingly large generations of the elderly which are to follow them. Already its members have broken with many of the traditions of the past, shattering the conventions of what older people should look like and do. And in the process they have changed the shape of American society. The census statistics describe a part of this transformation. They tell us, for one thing, that this generation has used its economic independence to get out of the house — or to get its children out. In 1900, some 60 percent of all Americans sixty-five and over lived with an adult child. Today, only about 17 percent live with one. The figures do not tell us who initiated the move, but they correlate very well with the increasing wealth of the elderly. Today, a majority of Americans over sixty-five live in the same community as at least one of their children, and live in the place in which they spent most of their lives. However, a significant minority of them have altered the traditional pattern by moving away from their families and out of their hometowns to make new lives for themselves elsewhere. Retired people — so the census shows—have contributed greatly to the general American migration to the Sun Belt; indeed, they have gone in such numbers as to make a distinct impression on the demographics of certain states. New Mexico, Arizona, and Southern California now have large populations of retirees, but it is Florida that has the highest proportion of them. People over sixty-five constitute 17.3 percent of the population of Florida—as opposed to the national average of 11.3 percent. These elderly migrants have not distributed themselves evenly around the state but have concentrated themselves on the coasts and in the area of Orlando. As a result, there are three counties on the west coast where the median age is between fifty and sixty, and eleven counties around the state where it is between forty and fifty.

Before World War II, there was, broadly speaking, no such thing as an age-segregated community and no such concept as "retirement living." Until the mid-fifties, in fact, "housing for the elderly" generally meant church-run homes for the very poor. In 1956, the federal government began to subsidize housing for the elderly in a number of ways —by direct loans to nonprofit developers, by mortgage insurance, by rent subsidies—and the funds translated largely into age-segregated apartment complexes. Around the same time, private developers began to build housing for middle-income retirees. In the early sixties, when credit and housing materials were still relatively cheap, huge developers, such as the Del E. Webb Development Corporation, of Phoenix, began to construct entire new towns for the retired. In the mid-seventies, when housing costs doubled and tripled, the developers grew leery of such grand schemes, but by that time there were—according to one estimate—sixty-nine retirement villages, a number of which had populations of over ten thousand. The sixties and seventies saw a proliferation of mobile-home parks for the elderly—in 1975, one survey indicates, there were 700 of them, housing some 300,000 people—and the creation of various other forms of age-segregated housing, from retirement hotels to luxury condominiums. The most original of these forms was the so-called life-care facility. This offers the buyer a small house or a private apartment, maid service, nursing care, and meals in a common dining room; in addition, it offers nursing-home care when or if it was necessary. Such institutions are expensive, but by the mid-seventies, according to one estimate, some 85,000 Americans were living in them. Gerontologists struggling to create a taxonomy for all these new forms of retirement housing estimate that about 5 percent of Americans sixty-five and over live in age-segregated housing and another unknown but significant percentage live in neighborhoods that are more or less age-segregated.

The twenty-five-year increase in life expectancy, the expansion and growing length of retirement, the migration of elderly people away from their children and hometowns, and the development of age-segregated housing are phenomena that have occurred on a mass scale in such a short time that they are difficult to comprehend, much less to analyze. As Ronald Blythe wrote in the introduction to *The View in Winter*, his book on the elderly in England, "the economics of national longevity apart, the ordinariness of living to be old is too novel a thing at the moment to appreciate." Of course, there are experts, but these experts—the social gerontologists—do not claim to have much information. Social scientists in general have some propensity to conclude articles in academic journals with the announcement that more research on the subject is needed. Social gerontologists often begin and end their articles with this declaration. Robert Atchley, the author of one of the best-known texts on gerontology, concludes his book with the thought that "there is not a single area of social gerontology that does not need more answers to crucial questions."

In the early sixties, the late Professor Arnold M. Rose, a sociologist at the University of Minnesota, published a paper entitled "The Subculture of the Aging: A Framework for Research in Social Gerontology." In it, he listed all the changes in the status and condition of the elderly—greater longevity, improved standards of living, better health, better education, and so on—and deduced from them the growth of a "subculture of the aging." This subculture, according to Rose, would have its own distinctive attitudes toward death and toward marriage, its own style of "interpersonal relationships," its own argot, its own leisure activities, and its own rituals. There was, he said, an "almost complete absence of empirical data" on most aspects of this subculture. But there was evidence that older people were developing "group consciousness" based on "self-conception and mutual identification"; that is, they were beginning to think of themselves as a group and to contemplate group action in social life and in politics. Otherwise, the subculture remained hypothetical.

Since Rose's paper was published, a number of social gerontologists 15 have attacked his thesis, on the ground that race, class, and even generational culture mean a great deal more to people than age, and create more profound divisions in the society. These objections make sense—certainly on a national level. True, organizations representing the elderly—the American Association of Retired Persons, the National Council of Senior Citizens, the National Retired Teachers Association, and others—have combined to fight for Social Security and other federal benefits, and do so most effectively. But these organizations do not always make common cause—and most of them do not take stands—on social, cultural, or political issues. And their lobbying groups do not always speak with a single voice. In St. Petersburg, for example, the oldest retirement town in America, and therefore presumably the most age-conscious, the retired people who live in the old downtown hotels and rooming houses vote differently from those who live in the new high-rise condos on the beach. The first tend to vote Democratic and for government-aid programs; the second vote Republican and against government spending. (Both, however, vote against local bond issues for the schools—this is their only real area of agreement.) Though about three-fifths of the registered voters in St. Petersburg are over sixty, the city has no united "senior citizen" lobby, and it has only one city council member over sixty-five. Furthermore, in all the years that retired people have dominated the city they have not developed a distinctive single "culture." The blacks in St. Petersburg live in neighborhoods segregated by color, not by age, and the white retirees from the North inhabit a variety of different worlds. In St. Petersburg, I met a spry ninety-six-year-old man who was lobbying the city council to build a new auditorium where the state societies could put on dances and minstrel shows without interference from "the colored or the kids." There also, I met a sixty-five-year-old woman who divided her time between teaching holistic health care to the elderly, tutoring disturbed children, and growing organic vegetables and herbs in a garden of a house she shared with her ex-husband. "I'm an aging hippie," she told me brightly. And when I asked her about Sun City Center she said, "I wouldn't think of going to a place like that. What, and live with all those old people? I'm sure it's not good for anyone."

To say that there is no national subculture of "the aging" is not, therefore, to say that subcultures don't exist. Even those gerontologists who have registered objections to Rose's thesis would admit that in certain communities retired people are inventing new kinds of relationships, new ways of spending their time, and new ways of dealing with death. The Sun Cities and Leisure Worlds are without precedent; no society recorded in history has ever had whole villages—whole cities—composed exclusively of elderly people. These communities are not just places where the elderly happen to find each other, as they do in certain rural communities and certain inner-city neighborhoods after everyone else has moved out. They are deliberate creations—places where retired people have gone by choice to live with each other. Most of them, founded in the early sixties, are now old enough to have evolved from mere developers' tracts into communities with traditions of their own. Oddly, however, they remain almost a terra incognita to gerontologists, despite all the research devoted to them.

The appearance of developer-built retirement villages occasioned a great debate in gerontological circles—indeed, one of the greatest debates ever conducted in that field. In the early sixties, opinion was generally ranged against them. Both professionals and laymen—city planners, journalists, and the like—attacked them as ghettos for ill-adjusted, alienated people or as playgrounds that "trivialized" old age. But there were some who heralded them as an exciting new solution to the problems of physical incapacity and social isolation which so often plagued the elderly. All these early opinions tended to be a priori judgments, by those who had spent little or no time in retirement communities. Then, in the mid-sixties, a number of gerontologists went out to the retirement villages with scientific sampling methods and attitudinal charts. Their investigations produced a new welter of articles in the professional journals. One study showed that the inhabitants of a certain retirement village were better educated and better off than the average retired person—a fact that could have been deduced from the price of houses in that development. Another study showed that the residents of Leisure World, in Laguna Hills, California, had gone there because of the golf; their desire for an "easy-maintenance dwelling unit"; the smog in Los Angeles; and the invasion of their old neighborhood by "minority groups." They had, in other words, gone there for all the reasons overtly and subliminally advertised in the real-estate brochures. The gerontologists had so far discovered what the developers already knew. Measuring the attitudes of residents by "life satisfaction" scales and other tests of their own devising, the researchers also found that the inhabitants of retirement communities were generally satisfied with their communities. This discovery was also less than a scientific breakthrough, since the householders clearly had the option of moving out if they were dissatisfied. One of the last of these studies, conducted by Gordon L. Bultena and Vivian Wood and published in 1969, reached the conclusion that these communities provided life satisfaction to that self-selected group of people which chose to live in them. This redundancy has become the final considered opinion of most gerontologists today.

The interesting thing about these studies was the near-exclusive concern of the researchers about the happiness of retirement-community residents. "Are you happy?" the researchers would ask in a dozen different ways, and in a dozen different ways the residents would answer, "Yes." More recently, the gerontologists have got around to asking themselves what they mean by happiness. In *Aging in the 1980s*, a new textbook put out by the American Psychological Association, Dr. Joyce Parr writes of "an increasing awareness of the problem of confusion associated with such global concepts [as] life satisfaction, morale, adjustment, and developmental task accomplishment." Dr. Parr continues:

> George (1979) expressed the need for reexamining the concept of life satisfaction and the psychometric characteristics of the available instruments. Cutler (1979) demonstrated both the multi-dimensionality of the concept of life satisfaction and that the dimensionality differs substantially across age groups. Larson (1978) presented a review of a variety of measures used to investigate the well-being of older persons. [He] cautions that such measures tell us little about individual informants and notes that "we have little idea how the construct permeates ongoing daily experience."

These are the "crucial questions" that are likely to lack answers for some time to come. Or, as Dr. Parr puts it, "there is an increasing recognition that characteristics of environments interact with characteristics of persons to produce behavior. It is also recognized, however, that much work is needed to develop meaningful ways to describe this interaction." The gerontologists may next begin to ask themselves what they mean by "meaningful."

Among developer-built retirement villages, Sun City Center is   20
middle-sized, conventionally organized, and remarkable only for its isolation. It was founded by the Del E. Webb Development Corporation in 1960. Initial plans called for a development of private houses with communally owned public buildings and recreation centers. That same year, Del Webb also began the development of Sun City, Arizona, near Phoenix. But while Sun City, Arizona, expanded to city size and extends almost to the suburbs of Phoenix, Sun City Center grew slowly and experienced a number of difficulties along the way. The first difficulty was its name. Del Webb wanted to call it Sun City, but a tiny town a few miles away already had the name and refused to give it up, claiming to be the chrysanthemum center of the nation. In 1972, Sun City Center had only about three thousand residents, and Del Webb decided to sell. The purchaser, a Tampa real-estate consortium, formed a new management company for the town, the W-G Development Corporation. Impatient with the pace of sales, W-G broke with the original plan and allowed another development company to build condominiums right next to the housing tract. When it was just under way, the 1974–75 recession hit, the Florida condo market collapsed, and the new development came to a dead stop. W-G and the new development company reverted to their mortgage holders. In 1981, both companies were bought by a partnership supported by corporate pension funds and managed by Victor Palmieri and Company, a large assets-management firm. (Palmieri had been an ambassador-at-large and the coordinator for Refugee Affairs under the Carter administration.) Sun City Center now comprises the original housing development, with a population of fifty-five hundred (I shall call it Sun City), and the newer condominium development, called Kings Point, with a population of about twelve hundred permanent and eighteen hundred seasonal residents. According to W-G, both developments are now doing very well, and the town has been growing more rapidly in recent years than it grew in the past. The changes of ownership do not seem to have affected the residents adversely, and while some move out after spending some time there, it is usually for reasons of their own; most residents consider W-G a satisfactory landlord.

Twenty-five miles from Tampa, the nearest city, Sun City Center has become a world unto itself. Over the years, the town attracted a supermarket and all the stores and services necessary to the maintenance of daily life. Now, in addition, it has a golf-cart dealer, two banks, three savings and loan associations, four restaurants, and a brokerage firm. For visitors, there is the Sun City Center Inn. The town has a post office. Five churches have been built by the residents, and a sixth is under construction. A number of doctors have set up offices in the town, and a Bradenton hospital recently opened a satellite hospital with 112 beds. There is no school, of course. The commercial establishments all front on the state road running through the center of town, but, because most of them are more expensive than those in the neighboring towns, the people from the surrounding area patronize only the supermarket, the laundromat, and one or two others. The local farmers and the migrant workers they employ, many of whom are Mexican, have little relationship to golf courses or to dinner dances with organ music. Conversely, Sun Citians are not the sort of people who would go to bean suppers in the Pentecostal churches or hang out at raunchy bars where gravel-voiced women sing "Satin Sheets and Satin Pillows." The result is that Sun Citians see very little of their Florida neighbors. They take trips to Tampa, Bradenton, and Sarasota, but otherwise they rarely leave the green-and-white developments, with their palm-lined avenues and artificial lakes. In the normal course of a week, they rarely see anyone under sixty.

Bess Melvin, a resident of Sun City who works part time in public relations for W-G, took me on a tour the first day of a visit I made to Sun City Center. Our first stop was the Town Hall recreation complex —a group of handsomely designed buildings with white columns and low red-tiled roofs. In front were shuffleboard courts and lawn-bowling greens, and in the center was a large, round swimming pool, surrounded by deck chairs and tables with gaily colored umbrellas. The buildings housed a glass-roofed indoor swimming pool, an exercise room, billiard rooms, card rooms, and studios with all the equipment for woodworking, weaving, pottery-making, ceramics, and decoupage. There were shops displaying lapidary work and shell decorations made by the residents, and there was an auditorium with brass chandeliers, and chairs that could be rearranged for a meeting or a formal dance. That morning, there were three or four people working in each of the studios and several people doing laps in the indoor swimming pool.

"Sun City Center isn't like the stereotype of a retirement community," Bess Melvin explained. "The usual thought is that you lose your usefulness. You sit back and rock in your rocking chair, and life slows to a stop. But the people here aren't looking for that. Sun City Center has a hundred and thirty clubs and activities. We've got a stamp club, a poetry club, a softball club, a garden club—I could go on and on—as well as active branches of the Rotary, the Kiwanis, the Woman's Club, and that sort of thing. The residents form their own clubs and run the

Civic Association, so if you've got a particular talent or social concern you can always find an opportunity to develop it. Many people take up painting, and we have some really fine artists here."

Possibly some people still imagine retirement communities as boardinghouses with rocking chairs, but, thanks to Del Webb and a few other pioneer developers, the notion of "active retirement" has become entirely familiar; indeed, since the sixties it has been the guiding principle of retirement-home builders across the country. Almost all developers now advertise recreational facilities and print glossy brochures with photos of gray-haired people playing golf, tennis, and shuffleboard. The "activity centers" in the various developments differ, but the differences have largely to do with the economics of the community.

According to the W-G real-estate agents, a new two-bedroom   25 house in Sun City costs from $60,000 to $90,000. Some of the older houses—the ones on the prettiest of the lakes—now resell for $100,000 or more, though they cost only $20,000 or $30,000 in the mid-sixties. A homeowner can buy membership in the Civic Association for fifty dollars a year and have the use of all the communal facilities. Golf is extra—$850 a year for a couple—and golf is clearly the main attraction of Sun City Center. W-G not only advertises the town's eighty-seven holes of golf prominently but sponsors national golfing tournaments and offers weeks of golfing instruction for seniors across the country. At Kings Point, the arrangements and the economics are somewhat different. In the early seventies, the developer put up small, flat-roofed buildings with condos costing only about $12,000 each. After the Florida condo bust, however, W-G found that the real market for Kings Point lay among higher-income people. The new condos are thus more luxurious, and cost $40,000 to $60,000 each. Here also golf is the main attraction—that and the huge white Kings Point clubhouse, with indoor and outdoor pools, card rooms, exercise rooms, and so on. The facilities are just as clean and handsome as those in Sun City, but there are certain stylistic differences, in part because many condo owners only winter in Florida. Whereas at Sun City the residents' Civic Association owns and runs the recreational center, at Kings Point these things are owned by W-G and run by a social director. Whereas Sun City has dance clubs and sports clubs, Kings Point has dance and exercise classes.

Bess Melvin took me to the library in the Town Hall complex at Sun City. The small, bright rooms contained displays of periodicals and a collection heavy on histories, biographies, and novels. Her task there was to photograph the president of the Sun City DAR presenting a book on Early American costumes to the library. A svelte woman in her sixties, the DAR representative had for the occasion dressed in a white jersey dress, stockings, heels, and gloves. She seemed to have no further appointments that morning. I wandered outside to watch the parade of golf carts, bicycles, three-wheelers, and wide American cars proceeding rather slowly along the central boulevard. The traffic was heaviest near the entrance to the golf club. Behind the club, twosomes and foursomes were embarking on the course, the women in golf skirts, the men in Bermuda shorts, Lacoste shirts, and narrow-brimmed straw hats.

Anyone visiting a retirement community for the first time would expect to be impressed by a uniformity of age. But Sun Citians have so much else in common in the realm of appearance that age seems the least of it. On the streets, most people wear golf clothes whether they are golfing or not. At home, the women uniformly wear slacks, with blouses hanging loose outside them. At church on Sunday, it's difficult to recognize a female acquaintance from the back, since all the women have the same neat permanent wave; and in the winter about half of them will have on identical blond fur coats. At Sun City Center Inn on a Saturday night, the women lined up at the well-stocked buffet or dancing to organ music with their husbands wear flowered dresses in pink and green, pearls, and low-heeled sandals. On such occasions, the men—all close-cropped and clean-shaven—dress even more color-fully, in checked trousers and white shoes, red or green linen slacks, pink shirts with blue blazers, madras ties, and the occasional madras jacket.

According to W-G statistics, the people now buying houses in Sun City Center have incomes of between $21,000 and $29,000 a year. ("Some of them are millionaires," Bess Melvin assured me.) The in-come level of Sun Citians has shifted upward over the past ten years along with the price of the houses. Still, Sun Citians are a remarkably homogeneous group; in particular, those who live in Sun City proper occupy a far narrower band on the spectrum of American society than economics would dictate. To look at the Sun City membership direc-tory is to see that the men are by and large retired professionals, mid-dle-management executives with large corporations, or small business-men. Among the professionals, there are some retired doctors and lawyers, but these are far outnumbered by school administrators, colo-nels, and engineers. Most of the women were housewives, but a sur-prisingly large number were schoolteachers or registered nurses. Most Sun Citians are Protestants—Episcopalians, Presbyterians, Methodists, Baptists, and Lutherans—but there are some Catholics as well, and a very few Jews. Politically, they are conservative and vote Republican. (The two most prominent visitors to Sun City in recent years were Ron-ald Reagan and Malcolm Muggeridge. The former came to give a speech in the early days of his 1980 primary campaign, and the latter, unbeknownst to most Sun Citians, stayed almost a month.) A great number of them are Masons or members of such organizations as the Kiwanis, the Shriners, and the Woman's Club. They come from the

Northeast and the Midwest, and none of them—it is hardly necessary to say—are black.

One of the earliest settlers in the town, Erna Krauch, a retired schoolteacher, explained the homogeneity of the community by the fact that many Sun Citians came here through personal recommendations. Mrs. Krauch and her husband, being one of the first couples to come, found Sun City Center through an advertisement. They had spent winter vacations in Sarasota for a number of years, but when they came to Sun City, in March 1962, they bought immediately. By October of that year, Mr. Krauch had sold his business, a pharmacy in Brentwood, Long Island, and by Thanksgiving the house was finished and they had moved in. "He wanted a warm climate," Mrs. Krauch said. "And a place to play golf. He never worried, as I did, about leaving everything and coming here. He lived only two years after that. I think he knew."

Most of the Sun Citians I talked to had come here in much the same way. They had wintered in Florida for some years. Around the time of the husband's retirement, they had visited Sun City Center—often on the recommendation of a friend or acquaintance—and had made a snap decision to buy. A few months later, they had sold their house in the North and moved in, with all their belongings. The men had initiated the move, and the women had been less than sanguine about it at first. "In the beginning, the people who came were mostly retired schoolteachers and businessmen looking for summer homes," Mrs. Krauch said. "They were people who didn't put on airs, people you could be quite natural with." She dropped the subject, but came back to it later, saying, "They were doctors, lawyers, and professors—that sort of thing—people you didn't have to prove anything to. The people who buy the houses now are financially better off than we were when we came. They are more affluent. They can afford to retire. Whereas for us it was a kind of summer home." Technically, what Mrs. Krauch meant was a winter home, but she was at that moment waving a hand toward her chairs and tables, of white rattan and her sofas, covered in flowered chintz. Still, the distinction she was making was a curious one, since she and her husband had never had a second house. They had sold their house on Long Island before moving here. Mrs. Krauch had lived in her "summer home" continuously for over twenty years.

When I asked why they chose Sun City Center, most of the men I talked to said, "The golf." Ronald Smith, an engineer retired from Western Electric, told me that he had always wanted to live on a golf course but had not been able to afford it while the kids were going to school. When he and his wife, Lora, first arrived here, they had dropped everything—had not even bothered to unpack—and had played golf solidly for two months. Now, fourteen years later, Ronald Smith was still playing every day, and Lora was recovering from a knee operation she had undergone in order to be able to play again.

But for Lora Smith, as for most of the other women I talked to, the main attraction of Sun City was the people. "It's the people who sell the houses, not the real-estate agents," Mrs. Smith said. The Smiths had come at the suggestion of a couple they had met in Florida — he was a banker, Mrs. Smith remembered, and his wife was a schoolteacher, like her. "When I arrived, I looked at all the manicured lawns, and thought perhaps Sun Citians were a lot of conformists," she said. "But then I knocked at five doors, and five different kinds of people came out — all very generous, very pleasant. I could not believe that everybody was that kind of person. There's such a variety of people here — people of achievement, people who talk about ideas, not about their ailments, because that's the kind of minds they have." Lively and gregarious people themselves, the Smiths had no difficulty finding friends. "No one gives a hang here what you did or where you came from," Mrs. Smith said. "It's what you are now that matters." Later, in a different context, her husband said much the same thing, adding that the colonels refused to be called "Colonel."

Sun City Center has age restrictions, of course. For a family to be eligible to live in Sun City, at least one member must be fifty, and neither there nor in Kings Point can residents have children under eighteen. But with one exception no Sun Citian I talked to said he or she had chosen the town because of the age restrictions. When I asked Mrs. Krauch why she and her husband had chosen an age-segregated community she looked startled. "Oh, I didn't feel I would just be with a lot of older people," she said. "And Sun City Center isn't like that!" Sun Citians would certainly be horrified to know that some retirees in St. Petersburg and Tampa look upon their town as an old-age ghetto. When Sun Citians speak of a "retirement community," what they usually mean is a life-care center or a nursing home. They came to Sun City Center for all the amenities spelled out in the advertising brochures and for a homogeneity that had little to do with age. In a country where class is rarely discussed, they had found their own niche like homing pigeons. And once they were home they were happy. "Lots of fine people," one resident told the community newspaper. "This is a cross section of the better people in the nation."

The notion that Sun Citians do not care about past professional status is a thought often articulated in Sun City. Sun City boosters — and most Sun Citians are boosters when they talk to an outsider — say it almost as regularly as they say that they are always active and on the go. The fact that the Sun City membership directory — it is actually the phone book — list the residents' past professions along with their addresses suggests, however, that the notion is less a description of the community than a doctrine belonging to it. (Some people list the company or service they worked for, others their calling — "educator," say — and a very few put nothing at all.) Most people, like Mrs. Krauch and Mrs. Smith, have a fairly exact idea of the professional standing of their neighbors. The less exacting say, "We have some doctors and lawyers. We have some millionaires, too." Sun Citians will very often praise the company they are in by saying, "They're people of achievement — people with prestige." That most Sun Citians have the same set of achievements and the same sort of prestige does not seem to worry them; indeed, the contrary is true.

A curious thing about the Sun City Center complex is the lack of   35 parallelism in the rules governing the communal facilities at Sun City and at Kings Point. The Kings Point club — owned by the developer — is open to anyone (or anyone within reason) who wishes to purchase membership. The Sun City Civic Association buildings — owned by the residents — are closed to anyone who does not live in that particular development. More than one resident explained to me that the tax laws were responsible for this restriction. But a community-relations executive for W-G told me that the tax laws had nothing to do with it: the restriction was an arbitrary one, made by Sun City residents. Asking around among Sun Citians, I discovered that when Kings Point was founded, in 1972, a number of Sun Citians had objected to the development, arguing that the cheap condos would attract a new element and ruin the community. Failing to stop it, they had refused to open the Civic Association to Kings Pointers. "It's really foolish," Lora Smith told me. "Sun City has all these clubs established — an Audubon Society Chapter, music groups, and that kind of thing — but the people from over there can't join them if they meet on Civic Association property. I mean, a really good musician from over there wouldn't be able to join a chorus or chamber-music group. There's a sort of a wall between us. People here feel — Well, they feel they arrived a little sooner than people over there. It's a matter of snob appeal, you see."
When I asked Kings Point residents what the people there used to do for a living, the answer was initially "We've got some doctors and lawyers — some millionaires, too." But when I pressed them about the differences between the two developments they said, "Well, they're more affluent over there." The fact is that Kings Point has a much greater variety of people than Sun City. It has former doctors and lawyers and perhaps some millionaires, but it also has retired policemen, retired door-to-door salesmen, and at least one retired commercial fisherman. It used to be impossible to discover the extent of the professional variety, since the Kings Point directory did not list the former employment of its residents. One resident told me he considered the Sun City directory a form of boasting. However, professions are now

listed in the Kings Point book. Kings Point also has some Democrats, some Catholics, and some Jews. There are not many Jews—only two hundred in a population of three thousand—but there are more than the handful who live in Sun City. And that is another source of anti–Kings Point feeling. Asked to explain the restriction made by the Civic Association, one long-term resident of Sun City said, "Well, you know, at the beginning some people over there bought six or eight condominiums for speculative purposes, and they rent them out." This woman had told me that she speculated in land elsewhere in Florida, so I thought her objection an odd one to make. But she continued, "I know a lot of Jews I don't think of as being Jewish. But there are just some people I think of as Jewish, because of certain qualities they have."

Dr. Robert Gingery, the pastor of the interdenominational Protestant church in Sun City Center, told me that anti-Semitism was a serious problem in the community. "I do all I can to fight against it," he said. At his invitation, the Jewish congregation holds services and Hebrew classes in the chapel of his church. The Sunday I attended his services, he made a point in his sermon of praising the rectitude and courage of the Jewish people after the Diaspora. "We in the church try to act as a bridge," he said, "but a lot of people were brought up with these attitudes." The Jews in the community are naturally quite conscious of these attitudes, but most of them are anxious to play the issue down. The head of the Jewish congregation said that at Kings Point anti-Semitism was "no worse than it is anywhere in the society"; but he and others admitted that it was one of the reasons for the exclusion of Kings Point people from the Sun City Civic Association.

Kings Point people—Christians as well as Jews—are well aware of Sun City attitudes, and resent them. "There's a strong sense that this is the wrong side of the tracks," one man said. What is more, the Kings Point people retaliate systematically. While I was there, the development voted against sending money and volunteers to the Sun City Emergency Squad, even though the contributions would have meant free ambulance service for Kings Point. Kings Pointers habitually refuse to go along with civic projects initiated by Sun Citians. But they have another, more insidious form of retaliation. At the entrance of Kings Point, there is a large white double archway through which all vehicles must pass. The guards at the gate—some of whom are retired policemen living in Kings Point—will not let anyone though the gate who does not have a sticker or a visitor's pass. The gateway does seem to enhance security in the development. But because the guards are so punctilious about their job, refusing to let even the oldest citizens through without a pass, one function that the gateway serves in the course of a day is to keep Sun Citians out.

What most Kings Point people do not realize is that Sun Citians make distinctions among themselves that are finer but no less finely understood than those between the two developments. Sun Citians are not uniformly "affluent," and people like Mrs. Krauch know exactly where the richer people live and what their houses cost. The newer people have, on the average, higher incomes than those who retired on the Social Security and pension benefits of between ten and twenty years ago. The older people resent this inequity, not only for its own sake but because it makes it seem that the younger people had better jobs than they did. Struggling to make me understand this injustice, one of the older residents said, "No, it's not that the new people are *richer*—it's that they had larger pensions when they retired." There is thus some friction between age groups. But age does not completely determine status; Sun Citians make other distinctions as well. "The golfers are the elite of the community," one man told me. "They're the ones who give the cocktail parties." According to Sun Citians, there are, generally speaking, three social groups: the golfers, the "cultural set," and the people who take craft classes and go to potluck suppers at the Town Hall. The golfers don't mix much with the others. "I went to a party the other day," one of the older residents told me, "and there was a golfer there. He didn't have anyone to talk to. I happened to know him, so finally he came up to me and said, 'I guess golfers are different people.' I'd like to have said, 'Yes, they're the biggest bunch of snobs!'" While the nongolfers tend to categorize all the golfers as "stuffed shirts," the golfers make their own internal distinctions. In 1980, a group of them got together and put up the money for the developer to build a private golf course on the edge of town. Now completed, the Caloosa Club is a private country club inside a semiprivate country club.

In Sun City Center, a few people make serious efforts to break down some of these social barriers. One of them is Lou Ellen Wilson, an attractive and competent woman of forty-four, who is in charge of community relations for W-G. The company has an interest in keeping peace between the developments, and Mrs. Wilson often manages to make them cooperate in spite of themselves. Because of her, the Sun City ambulances do react to emergencies at Kings Point—the fact is simply not advertised. Another such person is Jackie Fenzau, the social director of the Kings Point club. A striking-looking woman of generous enthusiasms, Mrs. Fenzau, who is in her early fifties, has since the beginning organized everything that goes on at the club, including bus trips, classes, and entertainments. She is proudest of her monthly "theme dances," at which people wear costumes and do skits or sing songs. ("You should see the cutups we have!") Her goal is to make people happy with the club and with each other, and in her view the people who are the least happy are the ones who dwell on their past achievements. "Some people are still in competition when they come here," she told me. "A few of the men are very insecure, so they brag about what they have done in their lives. But that doesn't make them any friends. One couple I am thinking about had a terrible time adjusting. He came in here all the time to complain, telling me he was a lawyer. He had a very negative attitude toward everything. With most people, though, you wouldn't know what they did unless you happened to be involved in some activity where their backgrounds could be useful. Most people have reached a time in life when they don't want to worry about what Mr. So-and-So did."

Dr. Gingery has much the same attitude, though he, of course, addresses the problem of community in more global terms. He has served in Sun City Center for over ten years; his church, affiliated with the United Church of Christ, now has over sixteen hundred members and is one of the fastest-growing churches in the denomination. This is something of a personal triumph for Gingery, since there are four other Protestant churches in town and his views are not wholly orthodox for the community. A Methodist by training, he is both a theological liberal, as most Sun Citians are, and a political liberal, as most of them definitely are not. A tall, handsome man of sixty-three, he gives a stylish sermon and could probably get away on charm. But he and his three assistant pastors work very hard. He spends a great deal of time on pastoral work, and he has made his church the cultural and civic center of the town. The most important piece of neutral ground between the two developments, the church has music groups, writing groups, and a "college," which brings in speakers to talk about subjects ranging from medical advances to foreign policy; the "college" also has a weekly forum for the discussion of community affairs. Dr. Gingery worries a good deal about the fact that Sun City Center is an island of wealth in the midst of rural poverty. Recently, he persuaded his church members to put up seed money for a government housing loan so that forty or so very poor families in the area could build houses with indoor plumbing. He is possibly the social conscience of the town. He also likes Sun Citians. "There's a great deal of camaraderie here," he told me. "People know they are in the same boat. When I talk with new arrivals in town, I like to compare them to the Pilgrims crossing the ocean to take up a new life. They have to put their best foot forward, and they do. They work at making friends, and they know what didn't work before."

Dr. Gingery's simile is a powerful one. The story of the Pilgrims' crossing—the creation myth for the United States—suggests an ideal of community, a brotherhood transcending all social distinctions. It evokes the egalitarian strain in the American tradition and the optimism about making a radical break with the past. In the context of Sun City, however, the image is somewhat disturbing, for if Sun Citians were to cast off their past, who or what would they be? They have no jobs, no families around them, and not very much future. Furthermore, the community they have chosen is already so homogeneous as to threaten the boundaries of the self.

Writing of the United States in the 1830s, Alexis de Tocqueville as much as predicted the reaction of Sun Citians:

> In democracies where the members of the community never differ much from each other and naturally stand so near that they may at any time be fused in one general mass, numerous artificial and arbitrary distinctions spring up by means of which every man hopes to keep himself aloof lest he should be carried away against his will into the crowd.

> This can never fail to be the case, for human institutions can be changed, but man cannot; whatever may be the general endeavor of a community to render its members equal and alike, the personal pride of individuals will always be to rise above the line and to form somewhere an inequality to their own advantage.

Dr. Gingery and Jackie Fenzau would surely consider this a gloomy view of human nature. But Tocqueville did not see it that way at all. His concern was for the integrity of the individual. What worried him about egalitarian systems was their tendency to destroy individual differences, dismantle identity, submerge the individual within the crowd. Had he been able to visit Sun City, he might have felt that by making social distinctions Sun Citians were in an existential sense protecting themselves.

Certainly it is fortunate that Sun Citians can discern the differences between the houses in their development, for an outsider walking or driving around Sun City finds the experience akin to sensory deprivation. The curving white streets — with names like La Jolla Avenue and Pebble Beach Boulevard — lead only back upon themselves, and since the land is flat they give no vistas on the outside world. Turning through the points of the compass, the visitor comes to another lake, another golf course, another series of white houses. The houses are not identical — the developer always gives buyers several models to choose from — but they are all variations on the same theme: white ranch house. Then, too, the whole town looks as if it had been landscaped by the same landscape gardener. Every house has a Bermuda-grass lawn, a tree surrounded by white gravel, and a shrubbery border set off by white stones. Some owners have put white plaster statues of cupids or wading birds in the shrubs. In the newer sections, each house has a wrought-iron fixture with a carriage lamp and a sign reading THE JONESES or THE SMITHS (there are twenty-eight Smiths in Sun City Center, and fifteen Joneses), and, under that, "Bob and Betty" or "Bill and Marge." No toys litter the pathways. The streets and the sidewalks are so clean they looked scrubbed.

The developers have created this world, but they have made no mistakes. Sun Citians maintain it, and they like it as it is. One woman told me that she had come there at least in part because of the neatness of the lawns. "But I'm afraid I don't take as good care of my lawn as I should," she said. "When the wind blows hard, a palm frond will often blow down, and the next day my neighbor will be angry at me for not picking it up. He wants me to cut the tree down. I don't think I will." Kings Point people often sit outside their houses; Sun City people rarely do, perhaps because they require more privacy, perhaps because they're loath to disturb such perfection.

Sun Citians keep their houses with the same fanatical tidiness: the   45 fibers in the carpets are stiff from vacuuming; the tables reflect one's face. One woman I visited had put a plastic runner across her new white carpeting; another apologized for the mess in her workroom when there was only a pencil and a sheet of paper out of place. But the interiors of Sun City houses are not anonymous, for Sun Citians are collectors; their houses are showcases for family treasures and the bric-a-brac collected over a lifetime. On the walls are oil paintings of bucolic landscapes, pastel portraits of children, Thai rubbings, or Chinese lacquer panels inlaid with cherry blossoms. Almost every living room has a cabinet filled with pieces of antique china and gold-rimmed glass. On the tables are ship models, sports trophies, carved animals, china figurines, or trees made of semiprecious stones. In a week in Sun City, I visited only one house where there was no bric-a-brac to speak of and where the owners lived in a comfortable disarray of newspapers, usable ashtrays, and paperback books. In most Sun City living rooms, the objects seem to rule. China birds, wooden horses, or ivory elephants parade resolutely across coffee tables and seem to have an independent life and purpose of their own.

For all this cleanliness and order, there is something childlike about Sun City. In part, it's that so many people have collections of puppets, animals, pillows, or dolls. In part, it's that everyone is so talkative, so pleasant, so eager to please. The impression also comes from the warm air, the pastel colors, the arbitrary curving of the streets, the white plaster ducks on the lawns and the real ducks that parade undisturbed among them on their way from lake to lake. The very absence of children contributes to this atmosphere, since the people riding around on three-wheelers or golf carts seem to have no parents. Then, too, one associates uniformity of age with camp or school.

The rhythm of life in Sun City comes in some measure from the weekly schedule of events set by the Civic Association. On Mondays from nine to noon, Sun Citians can choose yoga classes, the Table Tennis Club, the Shuffleboard Club, the Lawn Bowlers' Club, or the Men's and Women's Golf Association matches. The studios for the shell-crafters, needlepointers, weavers, and so on are open most weekday mornings and afternoons. On Tuesday, the Men's Chorus meets from nine to eleven, and the Duplicate Bridge Association meets at one. On

Wednesdays and Fridays, the Potter's Wheel Club meets in the mornings, and there is volleyball at two. The decoupage group meets on Thursday mornings, and the Men's Card Club plays gin rummy at twelve-thirty. Most days, a regular bus leaves for Tampa or Bradenton at ten, but there are special trips for dinner theaters once a week in the winter. The Woman's Club has a luncheon once a month, and so do the Investment Club and the Shriners; the Kiwanis Club meets every week. Most of the card clubs—Ladies' Penny Ante Poker, Men's Bridge, and so on—meet at one o'clock or in the evenings from six-thirty to ten. On Tuesday evenings, there is square dancing, on Wednesday evenings there is ballroom dancing, and on Saturday afternoons Sun Citians can practice their rumbas, waltzes, and cha-cha-chas.

To talk with Sun Citians is—necessarily—to hear a great deal about their schedules. With one or two exceptions, all the Sun Citians I met went on at length about the activities, clubs, civic groups, and cultural events in the town. Not just the public relations people but more than one of the residents reminded me that this was "the town too busy to retire." It was not sheer boosterism, for the same people would go on to tell me what activities they participated in and what busy schedules they had. In preparation for an interview, one man went to the trouble of writing out a list of his activities: Emergency Squad, travel abroad, gardening, bicycling, Photo Club, Radio Club. He also wrote out a list of his wife's activities: library, bicycling, cleaning.

So strongly do Sun Citians insist on their activities that after a while the visitor must begin to imagine that there is some unspoken second term of people who are not active at all. And, of course, such people exist. Sun City has its sick and feeble elderly people. It also has some alcoholics—how many it is impossible to tell. Dr. Gingery's pastors counsel only a handful of them, but one of the pastors, Dr. Mark Strickland, believes that there are many more, who go untreated, since their circumstances permit them to live as alcoholics undetected. (A doctor at the University of South Florida who has researched the subject believes that alcoholism is more prevalent among the elderly than is generally supposed.) In addition, there are people who after the loss of a spouse have simply turned their faces to the wall. These are also people who don't know what to do with themselves, and watch an inordinate amount of daytime TV. And there are a great many people who, while active, are not really very busy. When a golf cart breaks down in some public place, a dozen men will collect around it to kick the tires and trade theories about the electrical connections.

But the fact that this second term of people exists does not, perhaps, provide an explanation for Sun City's insistence on busyness. For to stay around Sun City Center for any length of time is to see that some large proportion of the Sun Citians do lead active lives. The Sun   50

City Town Hall and the Kings Point clubhouse are busy places all day long. The craft studios are perhaps not quite as popular as Sun Citians advertise, but there are usually a few people in every one of them. The organized activities—the bingo games, the bus trips, the dances—are well subscribed, and a lot of people swim, play shuffleboard, and work out in the exercise rooms. The golf course have players on every hole from morning until dusk, and at the Caloosa Club at midday there are sometimes three dozen women playing bridge and gin.

Not all the activities go on at the clubs; many people have private pursuits. The Neubergers, a former meteorologist and his wife, collect replicas of musical instruments of the Renaissance and invite their friends in for musical evenings. (The Neubergers also swim a half mile a day in the lake behind their house. They continue to do this even though Mr. Neuberger was once rather severely bitten by an alligator.) The George Richardses have a dachshund named Gretel who has won numerous prizes for tracking and obedience. Ronald Smith works a ham radio and collects golf balls. (He now has nine hundred golf balls of different makes and markings.) Mrs. Evelyn Schultz swims competitively in the over-seventies division. Colonel Lyle Thomas grows orchids; James Morris carves animals and birds out of wood; and Louis Goodrich collects and rebuilds wall and grandfather clocks. These people are known around town for the interesting hobbies they have.

Frank Minninger is known as the best decoupage artist in Sun City Center. A tall, bronzed, good-looking man in his late seventies, he was wearing, when I met him, red linen slacks and an open shirt. He came here fourteen years ago, when he retired from the Connecticut General Life Insurance Company. Since then, he has made fifty decoupage handbags, half of which he gave away to friends and half of which he could show me, since he had given them to his wife. He had also built five ship models and grown a border of prize red begonias. He had, he said, always loved hobbies. When his boys were growing up, he had built model trains for them. And for some time he was quite serious about photography. He did a series of wildflower photographs which was exhibited around the country. Kodak bought a series of Christmas cards that he and wife did over the years with pictures of their youngest son and their dogs dressed in costume and posed around the fireplace. His wife raised German shepherds, he said, and he was very keen on bird-watching. Minninger described all his hobbies to me in great detail and with enormous pride and enthusiasm. "There's an awful lot of people here who don't do anything," he said. "But if you're not happy it's really your own fault." Frank Minninger seemed to be a happy man. He seemed to be doing what he had wanted to do all his life— and what in fact he might have done for a living if he had not had a certain vision of himself. When I asked why he had chosen Sun City, he said he had come for the golf and the duplicate bridge. "I have all these hobbies," he told me gaily, "but golf is my business."

That many Sun Citians do lead active lives is perhaps not very surprising. Many of them, like Frank Minninger, are not old except by a demographer's measure, and some of the more recent settlers are not old even by that. In the beginning—that is, in the early sixties—most of the people who bought houses were around sixty-five years old. But in recent years people have been coming here in their early sixties and in their late fifties. In 1980, nearly a quarter of the population was under sixty-five. Many of the younger men had been military officers —people who had taken their pensions before retiring. Some of them had been civil servants with similar pension schedules, and some had been executives of companies that, for diverse reasons, encourage retirement before the age of sixty-five. Theodore Peck, for example, a former Air Force Reserve officer and sales manager for a carpet company, bought his house here when he was forty-six and moved in when he reached fifty. (Peck, exceptionally, still works. He deals in local real estate.) Betty Cooper Pierce, the wife of an Air Force officer, has been here almost nine years and is only fifty-nine. To these people, Sun City is certainly not a home for the elderly but, rather, a community desireable for its well-kept grounds, its golf, and its complement of successful people. Furthermore, many of those who are chronologically older have the same attitude. Ronald Smith, for example, plays golf every day, and in the evenings he still has too much energy to sit still for very long. He and his wife told me that they had looked forward to retirement—looked forward to all the things they could do when they were no longer tied down by children and jobs. Now, fourteen years later, they were still enjoying themselves. "It seems as if we'd always been here," Lora Smith said. "It's the long vacation we wished we'd always had."

What surprised me most about Sun Citians was how few of the men seemed to regret leaving their jobs. Civil servants, corporate executives, schoolteachers, independent businessmen—indeed, many of the same people who talked with such pride about the professional success they had had—told me that they had planned their retirement years in advance. A number said they would have retired earlier if they had been able to afford it. One man who had traveled all over the world for the Department of Agriculture, and who appeared enviably fit, said that he had retired at fifty-five, because he was "sick of working." Another man said that he had sold his chemical company "in order to get out of the rat race" and in order to fish and play golf. "I miss the competitiveness of business," he told me. "But I'd hate to go back to work. Pressure, pressure, pressure—I don't want to get involved." He now plays golf five times a week and says, "Don't know what I do but I'm busy all day long." A third man said he had retired from a management position at Kodak. He and his wife had traveled for a year and were now staying in a rented house while deciding whether or not to move to Sun City. "Maybe I shouldn't have retired so early," he said. "But I paid my dues. You work for industry, you work for *x* years, and you retire."

Some Sun Citians told me that they had liked their jobs, and, quite   55 possibly, some who spoke as if they did not miss them were justifying choices that had been made for them. But for many of the men their careers, their professions, seemed only a means of achieving a satisfactory private life—a "life-style," as some put it. And even those who said they had liked their jobs seemed curiously detached from them: they had had jobs, but they had no work in the sense of lifelong interests. There are exceptions. Dr. Harry Skornia, for example, a former professor of communications, is now in his early seventies and continues to read what is being published in his field and to write articles when his health permits. Fred Russell, formerly the president of a construction company and a former city commissioner of public works, has become involved in public works and other civic affairs in Sun City. Then, too, there are some people, such as the Neubergers, who have artistic pursuits or hobbies they care passionately about. But these exceptions were strikingly exceptional. With regard to work, most Sun Citians seemed like castaways on an island of plenty.

Sun Citians' insistence on busyness—and the slightly defensive tone of their town boosterism—came, I began to imagine, from the fact that their philosophies, and, presumably, the beliefs they had grown up with, did not really support them in this enterprise of retirement. Sun Citians are, after all, conservatives and vigorous exponents of the work ethic. They believe that the country is going soft because most Americans don't work hard enough. They complain about the younger generations, and, according to Dr. Gingery, a few of them have threatened to disinherit their grandchildren because "these kids don't know the value of a dollar." Though many of them are former government employees or former executives of large corporations, they believe in free enterprise and rugged individualism. The businessmen quite naturally complain of the "double and triple dippers" in the community, but some of the former government employees—living on indexed pensions—also complain that the government is too big and too paternalistic. A schoolteacher who had taken early retirement in order to move here with her husband told me that she and her friends had backed President Reagan's economic program enthusiastically. "We're old enough and conservative enough to believe that all this spending has to come to a screeching halt," she said. "There are so many boondoggles, so much cheating and crookedness as a result of it. Much of it can be blamed on Johnson and his printing of money. We're just mopping up now after that binge of spending. I can't for the life of me see what's wrong with cutting out the school-lunch program. What's wrong with having a bag lunch from home? We're losing the stuff of which this country was made in the beginning. We want things given to us. We want cradle-to-grave care."

Sun Citians believe in good citizenship, in charity, and in the virtue of volunteer work. They are by temperament joiners, and Sun City has, as Bess Melvin pointed out, a vast array of social, charitable, and civic organizations. Every week, the Sun City Center newspaper announces meetings, fund-raising drives, awards ceremonies, and so forth, held by the Rotary Club, the Woman's Club, the Kiwanis, the Civic and Home Owners associations. The women's groups and national fraternal organizations do raise money for scholarships and other charities; the Shellcrafters and Sawdust Engineers make things to give to the children of the area, or to sell for their benefit. Of course, there is a lot of busywork in these organizations, and a lot of meetings are held for purely social reasons. That is true everywhere. And, as is the case in most volunteer organizations, a few people do the lion's share of the work. What is interesting is that Sun Citians seem to feel somewhat less of a social obligation than they did before they retired. Harry Skornia, who has long been active in community affairs, estimated that only 10 or 20 percent of the Sun Citians took an active role in the various civic organizations. "The rest play golf and bridge, watch TV, and drink at cocktail parties," he said. "They don't come here to be active, they come here to retire." Skornia, being one of the few liberals in the community, had, I imagined, a rather jaundiced view of his fellow citizens. But then Ted Peck, a former president of the Sun City Center Republican Club, told me much the same thing. The club has over six hundred members, but very few of the members are active; they vote in elections but do not otherwise participate. "People are so busy going to cocktail parties," Peck said. "Most of them don't want to work. They feel they've done it all their lives — they feel they've made a contribution." Mrs. Krauch, also a former president of the club and now the head of a cancer drive, gave a similar analysis. "No one wants to take responsibility. They're people who have participated so much that they feel they don't have to anymore. 'I've had it' is what people say. 'I'll help, but I don't want the job.' "

Sun Citians are not Puritans — Dr. Gingery was, in a sense, taking too long a leap with his analogy. "They've never thought their work was socially necessary," Skornia observed. They are private people who enjoy their houses, their friends, their families, and their games. Many of them look upon Sun City as the reward for which they have worked and made sacrifices. Sun City boosters — and there are a lot of them — describe their town as an ideal place to live. But to look upon Sun City Center as an ideal world is to discover something new about the people who live there. Their political philosophy, after all, assumes the wide-open spaces; it is one of unbridled competition, of freedom from social restriction, and even from society itself. Their pleasures, however, are golf and bridge—games for people who love competition but also love rules. They are games for problem-solvers—orderly, conservative people who like to know where the limits are. The harmonious, manmade landscape of a golf course is like a board game writ large—or like Sun City itself. It's not for loners or rugged individualists but for sociable people who value traditions, conventions, and etiquette. It's not "the rat race." There's an aesthetic to it, but it's not that of the open range. Sun Citians think of themselves as quintessentially American, and so, perhaps, they are. But, like President Reagan, they imagine cowboys and live in a world of country clubs. What they value they might themselves associate with the European tradition. What they want is security within a fixed social order. Asked why so many Sun Citians were Republicans, Ted Peck said, "The same reason we feel so comfortable here. It's middle to middle upper class here. There are people who have worked and have prestige. There's comfort in the social status here." The irony is that their golf courses have been carved out for them from Florida swampland, their artificial lakes have alligators in them, and they live in a town without any history on the edge of a social frontier, inventing a world for themselves.

Art Rescorla knows this, but he is an exception, and the organization he heads is also exceptional. The Sun City Emergency Squad is the most important cooperative organization in the town, and the one Sun Citians take most seriously. All those in the housing development contribute to it, and, unlike the Civic and Home Owners associations, it was started by the residents rather than the developers, and has no paid staff. With its fleet of three ambulances, the squad responds to calls for emergency help and drives people to the hospital. For its volunteers— and for many people in the community—the squad has an aura of glamour about it. One woman squad member described it to me in terms of midnight emergencies: a woman with a heart attack, the squad unit responding in five minutes, the victim and her shocked husband being hurried into the ambulance, the rendezvous on the highway with the county paramedical unit, the return home in the middle of the night. And, indeed, the squad does respond to the one real threat to the community—the one thing that bursts through the cocoon of comfort and security.

Art Rescorla spends most of his days in the squad office. When I 60 first went to see him, he was doing the accounts. Excited volunteers kept running in and out of his office with what I first assumed to be emergency business but turned out to be routine bookkeeping questions. Rescorla first referred them to the team head for the day, but they reappeared with the same questions, and then he patiently answered them himself. He described the work of the squad to me in a businesslike fashion. Its main work was transport, he said; only one out of ten calls was an emergency. The squad has 150 volunteers, who go through a twenty-one-hour first-aid course and, in some cases, a driving course; they are then on call for a twenty-four-hour period.

Rescorla had been described to me as "not a very gregarious man," but we talked, initially, for two hours, and he seemed to me to be merely a man who cared less than some others about pleasing. He did not wear resort clothes, and when I went to his house I noticed that he and his wife did not have a collection of animals or dolls. Also, he spoke quite bluntly about the subjects other Sun Citians skirted: illness, old age, and death. He was in many ways the odd man out. He said he had been forced to retire from his job at the American Petroleum Institute when he reached sixty-five. That was in 1975, and he had, he told me, been very resentful—not at the loss of his salary but at the loss of his work. He had taken a volunteer job at the Smithsonian Institution doing research projects, and he had worked without pay for the Virginia town he lived in. But he found that in both places the younger people passed over his ideas and his projects in favor of their own. When I asked him whether this had to do with a lack of respect for age, he said that it had more to do with the fact that younger people were still in the competition—still concerned with furthering their own careers. He could not blame them for that—that was how it was. He had moved to Florida in 1978 because of arthritis. When his doctor told him to go south, he had written away to sixty retirement centers and gone to visit ten or twelve of them. Most of them, he said, were simply apartment complexes or housing tracts built by a promoter and then abandoned with nothing but a sales office. But Sun City Center was a real town, and Rescorla had seen it as an alternative community, a place where he could find work and be useful among his peers.

Rescorla had found work for himself: he served as the managing editor of a publication of the American Chemical Society, he was the academic dean of Dr. Gingery's "college," and he was involved in a number of community projects besides the Emergency Squad. But he had also been in some degree frustrated, because few Sun Citians seemed to share his vision of what a retirement community could be. "What bothers me is that we are losing the brainpower of older people. There's a lot of it around in this area waiting to be tapped. In this job, I look for people with special backgrounds. I found a man who had worked for a telephone company, so I grabbed him, and he helped make a radio hookup for us. He's got the abilities, so I say use them. The trouble is that we push people into senility. A lot of people come here when they're at their peak, and then they drop off." He still, however, believed in the potential of age-segregated communities. "We should put people into areas like this, where they can use their talents. If they're in competition with younger people all the time, they just give up." In his view, what the town needed was a government. It was not likely to get one in the near future, since incorporation would probably mean a rise in the real-estate taxes, but it would have to get one in order to be heard. "When we talk to the country or the state now, we sound like an old-age home," he said.

Rescorla's view of Sun City corresponded to the attitude that the sociologist Arnold Rose labeled "aging-group consciousness." Rose had observed that certain older people were far more conscious than others of their peers; they saw "the aging" as a subsociety and identified with it; they believed that the elderly should organize and demand more rights. These people came from a great variety of backgrounds, but what they had in common was forced retirement. They had not jumped out of the working world and the larger society—they had been pushed.

With the exception of Rescorla, the Sun Citians I talked to had not come here because the town was for older people. On the other hand, they did not seem to object to the age restrictions. When I asked people how they liked living in an age-segregated community, a few said they missed seeing children around. (Some of them then went on to explain that they meant this quite literally: What they missed was seeing children—they didn't miss having them around all the time.) Interestingly, these questions always elicited answers about children—almost never about any other age group. Many Sun Citians, it became clear to me, had simply lost their consciousness of other age groups. They had come to Sun City not to be old but to be young. To put it another way, they were attempting to despecialize old age. "Look at the way we dress," one Sun Citian, a retired minister, said, indicating his own madras shirt. "At a cocktail party the other day, I saw a woman in a miniskirt. She had very nice legs, but she must have been sixty-five or seventy. Her mother would have turned over in her grave!" Paradoxically, the effort at despecialization seemed to work better in an age-segregated community.

On Thursday nights, the Kings Point club holds an informal dance, 65 with music from an amplified sound system. The night I went, about a hundred people had come. I found a seat at a table with three couples. The men were wearing Western shirts with string ties, the women slacks and flowered cotton blouses. The men handed around drinks from bottles they had brought, and all of them were laughing loudly at each other's jokes. When the music started, the women went to the dance floor to join a half dozen other women, some of whom were certainly in their eighties. Led by a tall woman in a tentlike muumuu, they formed a line and did a kick-step routine to a number called, "Bad,

Bad, Leroy Brown." They had learned the routine in dance class, and now they were completely relaxed about performing it in front of an audience. When the dance ended, the men got up, and a few minutes later the floor was filled with couples doing the fox-trot. Through the crowd I could see two diminutive elderly women dancing together.

Actually, there are many ages in Sun City Center. In twenty-some years, the age spectrum has grown almost as large as it is in most new suburban communities: it encompasses four decades, and two generations of certain families. One seventy-three-year-old woman I met had a mother in her nineties living in a house a block away from her. Families with two generations of retired people living in Florida are no longer uncommon; the families tend to consist of a daughter, married or widowed, taking care of her elderly mother. In twenty-odd years, Sun City Center has developed its own life cycle, beginning with people in their fifties and ending with those in their nineties. Carolyn Tuttle, for example, used to be the youngest person on her street when she and her husband moved in, a dozen years ago; now in her seventies, she is, as it were, middle-aged, since some of the earliest settlers are still there and some younger people have moved in. The median age in the whole town is now seventy. When I asked Mrs. Tuttle about age segregation, she told me that she did not miss having young people around. "I love children dearly," she said, "but I don't crave to fall over tricycles on my lawn or see young couples mooning over each other." Later, she said, "When Sun City Center was founded, almost everyone was about sixty-five. Now some of the people are well into their eighties. I know a number of people who are losing their sight, and others who can hardly get about. The next step is the life-care center. I've lost so many friends to retirement homes. It's almost as bad as losing them to death."

Carolyn Tuttle has a bright little dog, a schnauzer, who appears to understand much of what she says. She herself is a greyhound of a woman—tall, lean, attractive, and full of nervous energy. A former English teacher, she uses the language with a playful elegance. Her husband died three and a half years ago. Since then, she has become a member of the Emergency Squad and a vice president of the Civic Association. She does church work, and she directs a poetry workshop, and she belongs to the Woman's Club. A couple of years ago, she took a trip to Australia and the South Pacific with a group. "It's a very fulfilling life here," she said. "Of course, there are people who do nothing but play bridge and golf, but that's their privilege." Though she is a Sun City booster, she finds it difficult to control her irony when she describes the provincial theater groups that come through and the tea-and-cookie meetings of the Woman's Club. She is as demanding of herself as she is of others, and she is also, very obviously, lonely.

In the early sixties, Sun City was a community of couples. The development company pitched its advertisement to couples and built its houses for two. People put up signs that read WORDEN — DOT AND HOW or THE SMITHS — BILL AND MARGE, and the signs signified a good deal. Like many Americans of their generation, Sun Citians had long, stable marriages. On the average, perhaps, their marriages were happier than most, since unhappy couples usually do not decide to pull up roots and leave for a permanent vacation together in a strange town composed of other couples. Then Sun City was a test of these marriages. For social purposes, each couple had to become a united front, an entity. And there were no distractions — no children, no office to go to, no compelling reason for one person to "get out of the house" without the other. Added to that, retirement gradually erased the difference between a man's sphere of activity and a woman's. ("My husband is always the man," one woman told me. "A lot of other men become just people.") Couples that survived these tests grew closer; they became single units, husband and wife joined together like Siamese twins.

But now Sun City is composed of couples and widows. Just how many widows there are it is impossible for a visitor to tell, since most widows do not take down the DOT AND HOW signs or take their husbands' names out of the residents' directory. The 1980 census, however, shows that almost a third of the women in Sun City then were widows living alone. This is about the national average for people their age, since women live an average of 7.7. years longer than men. In Sun City, there are five widows for every widower, which is about the national ratio.

"How," in fact, died three and a half years ago. "Dot" — Dorothy   70 Worden, who is in her seventies and full of life — says she would consider remarrying if she found the right man. But she doubts she ever will, since there are so few men her age around. Of course, she says, some men do lose their wives, and they generally want to remarry, but then there are so many widows with the same thing in mind. "When a man's wife dies, all the widows come around the next day with casseroles," Dot told me. "Some women I know even make a practice of going to funerals. If they like the look of the bereaved husband, they'll go home and make him a casserole even though they've never met him before. Well, it works sometimes. Men aren't very good at living alone. You saw the furniture-sale right down the block? That was put out by a man who just married the widow of a close friend. His wife hasn't been dead a year. That's a fact, but no one really objects. He needed her, and, besides, none of us have all that much time left."

In St. Petersburg, there's a dance hall, called the Coliseum, where for over fifty years retired people have gone to dance to combos and the big bands every Wednesday and Saturday night. Some are couples, but others are single people. The women sit at the tables in groups of four or six with briefcases that open out into bars. The single men stand in a line at the back of the hall, like high-school boys at a prom, passing comments and looking for the prettiest woman to dance with. If a man dances with a woman, and she likes him, she'll invite him for a drink at her table, and sometimes that will be the beginning of something. I asked one man in the line why he came back there night after night, year after year, and he said, "The widows." I said he surely might have found one by then. He turned away slightly and said, "Oh, no, I'm not looking for anything permanent."

At the Kings Point dance, I sat next to a dark-haired woman with dangling silver earrings who seemed to be having a wonderful time. I asked if she and her partner were married, and she said they were not. "My husband died when he was very young," she told me. "He was only fifty-nine years old, but we had been married for thirty-three years. It was shattering. Your friends ask you out, but you're always a fifth wheel. I have children—my oldest son's a doctor in Boston—but I don't want to be a burden to them, so I came to Florida. I met Harry three years ago—his wife had just died, and I adopted him, because I'd been through the same thing. It's like a new life for me. We haven't gotten married, though, because of taxes."

At Kings Point, everyone knows couples like this one, who are not married, and knows the reason for it: if a woman remarries, it is widely (and often erroneously) believed she stands to lose her late husband's pension. Then, too, a couple filing a joint tax return may have to pay more in income tax. The laws are straightforward, but in Florida—particularly in Florida—they have created some strange social circumstances. They have led the most respectable people to the most unconventional behavior. "You can't tell who's married and who's not," a friend of Dot's who lives at Kings Point told me. "People sometimes say they are married, and the woman goes by the man's name. It doesn't matter to us if they're not married, but it seems to bother their children. So sometimes we know and their children don't. Either they tell their children they're married or one of them moves out of the house when the children come down."

Remarriages seem to be more common in Sun City. But then many Sun Citians have enough money to be able to afford the higher taxes. Perhaps for that reason, Sun Citians are far less tolerant than Kings Point people of unconventional living arrangements. Dot, who has lived in Sun City for a decade, knows of only one unmarried couple openly living together there. She does not know of any couples who simply pretend to be married.

Most widows in Sun City Center do not find new partners. The 75 statistics are not in their favor in this town any more than they are nationally. But the statistics are so new that when their husbands die many women face a situation they never anticipated and are not in any way prepared for. According to Dr. Gingery, there are in general two kinds of widows: the dependent ones, who go to life-care centers, and the independent ones, who make a life for themselves. Both Dot and Dr. Gingery know women who actually flourished after their husbands died—who made their own friends for the first time and took up activities they hadn't thought of before. They also know women who do well enough but simply feel that their life has been diminished. Widows at Kings Point seem to be able to have an extensive social life: the neighbors are close, and they can go to dances or on expeditions in groups. Sun City is more of a private place, and thus widows seem to spend more time alone in their houses.

Mrs. Carl Kietzman, who is in her early seventies, has lived alone since her husband died more than three years ago. Formerly an officer in the DAR, she was married to an Army Reserve officer who worked for the automobile insurance division of General Motors. They came here from Ohio, but they had moved around the country a good deal in the course of their lives. A big-boned, strong-looking woman, Mrs. Kietzman has decided opinions on most matters but not on what to do with the stretch of life in front of her. "It's no fun to be alone," she remarked at one point in our conversation, out of the blue. She said it quite simply, and stopped, looking down at her hands. At another point, she said, "This is the first time in my life I've ever lived alone. My family had a big house in Houston. I married young, and I had a happy marriage." When I asked Mrs. Kietzman if she thought of marrying again, she said, "I live on pensions, which would stop if I were married. And I just couldn't live with someone—it's against my principles." Then she said, "But I wouldn't meet anyone here. I don't even see the couples we used to see—or not a lot. You feel like a fifth wheel. I'm in one bridge game because someone's husband died. I miss the company of men. I miss dancing. One night, I went to the singletons thing they have, but I didn't meet any men there. There were so many women. So I ate dinner and I played bridge and I went home." A year after her husband died, Mrs. Kietzman thought of leaving Sun City and going to live with a woman friend who had a big house in Ohio. She liked the woman—she even liked her eight dogs—but in the end she decided against it, because it would have meant selling most of her furniture, and she couldn't bear to do that.

Mrs. Kietzman took me on a tour of her house, pointing out a handsome walnut four-poster bed and a walnut chest of drawers. "They came from Texas," she said, "and they've been in my family for a hundred years." In the study, she apologized for the terrible mess, though the study was almost as painfully neat as the rest of the house. "I don't like to cook," she said as we went through the small kitchen. "My husband always used to do the cooking after he had his heart trouble." The dining table had a lace table-cloth over it and a set of china angels playing around the centerpiece; it looked as though it was never used. "I swim, and I work on committees," she said as we sat down again. "But there isn't much to do at night. There's a bridge game two or three times a month, and sometimes I go out with my girlfriends. If he'd lived, I might have been better integrated into the community. But it isn't good for widows. My neighbors are kind to me, though. They come over when I need something. The man next door says I should lock the door when I go outside through the carport to the utility room to do the laundry."

Security is something of a preoccupation in Sun City, though the town is safe by the standards of most cities and towns. (There are occasional burglaries, mostly of empty houses, and some years ago there was, very exceptionally, a rape.) Sun Citians discuss crime a great deal. A woman in her seventies told me, "I have a gun, and I would use it." In January of 1982, a committee of residents announced plans to create a security patrol, with volunteers driving two radio cars through the streets from dusk to dawn. Major General Joseph (Smokey) Caldara (U.S. Air Force, retired) was selected to head up the patrol. At the time, there was some feeling that elderly vigilantes driving cars would be more of a hazard than a safeguard, but between three and four hundred people volunteered for service, and General Caldara began the operation in April. By July, there had been six burglaries (making a total of eleven for the year), and there had been one patrol-car crack-up. The patrol continues, but the most effective security system in Sun City is still the neighbors. There are Neighborhood Watch Committees in every section of town, but, more important, the residents all notice what goes on in the streets around them. If something looks amiss at a neighbor's house, a Sun Citian will always go and investigate—particularly if the neighbor is a single person with a health problem. This mutual concern often has nothing to do with friendship; it is impersonal, though unsystematic, and it is generally welcomed, because all Sun Citians feel that one day they may require help of some kind. Art Rescorla came to Sun City to find work, but there was another reason he and his wife chose this particular town. "I liked the idea that Trinity Lakes"—the life-care center—"was here," he told me. "It was a place to go if we got into trouble. And if things got real bad, this is a place where people work together. So my wife would always have some companionship."

The developers who built Sun City made no provision for sickness or incapacity. Like builders of retirement villages all over the country, they built recreation facilities, not clinics or nursing homes. (The real-estate people are still reluctant to discuss the problems of extreme age. One man told me that the average age in Sun City Center was sixty-two or sixty-three.) But as the years passed and the first Sun City settlers grew older, medical services were established. Doctors set up offices in the town, the Emergency Squad was organized, and in 1975 an independent developer began to build Trinity Lakes. Residents of Sun

City worked on the feasibility study for the facility, and when it was finished a number of them moved in. Trinity Lakes eventually had 152 apartments and had 60 beds in the nursing home—almost all of both filled with Sun Citians. In a sense, it completed the community, for it offered residents a place to go when they could no longer take care of their houses, and it meant they could stay in Sun City Center or keep their relatives there for as long as they lived.

Recently, however, Trinity Lakes changed hands, after it was al-   80 leged in a lawsuit that several million dollars in membership fees had been used improperly. The suit was eventually dropped, but it shook the faith of Sun Citians not only in Trinity Lakes but in all life-care centers that require a large capital investment in return for lifetime guarantees. There are several such institutions in the Tampa-Bradenton areas, and Sun Citians had heard rumors of financial scandals about some of them. As a result, many Sun Citians, including Art Rescorla, are looking for institutions that do not require an irrevocable commitment of capital. The security they sought has proved elusive.

The fact that many Sun Citians have gone to Trinity Lakes and other such centers in Florida says a good deal about their relationships with their children. Of course, some Sun Citians have no children. (Their age cohort—Americans who came of childbearing age during the Depression—had relatively fewer children, and the Sun Citians probably have even fewer than the average.) And some do rely on their children when they become ill or cannot cope for themselves. But many Sun Citians have made the decision not to depend on their children in sickness any more than in health. In this decision, they are not untypical of middle-class Americans of their generation, and here their generation has broken new ground. Many, perhaps most, Sun Citians took care of their own parents (some of them are still doing so)—and had them living in their houses for years. Art Rescorla was one. "I took care of my mother for fifteen years," he said. "In the end, I had to put her in a nursing home, because it was either her or my wife. My mother took in her sister, and my father his brother. My kids would take care of me if they had to, but I wouldn't impose that on them."

Whether Sun Citians make this decision for their own sake or for the sake of their children is not at all clear, because they tend to describe it in a perfectly ambiguous manner. Art Rescorla, who has thought about the subject a great deal, said, "If I had a heart condition, I wouldn't want to impose it on my kids—at least, as long as I could afford not to. Why hold children down? It would be an interference. I'm not resentful—they have their own lives to lead. Other people— Negroes and Cubans—all live together, but we've reached the point where we don't have to do it." Rescorla had nonetheless imagined what it would be like to live with his children. "Our life-styles are so different it would be difficult to adjust. I wouldn't have any freedom except in my own room, so in practice I'd be confined there. I might just as well go to a nursing home." He spoke without bitterness — indeed, without any particular emotion. "It's heartbreaking to see people here — terminal cases — put into Trinity Lakes to stay until they die. But it doesn't upset their whole families, and they get better service there."

At the bar in the Sun City Center Inn one night, a man sat alone drinking stingers. He said his name was Lewis Fisher. Sixty-three years old and just retired, he had come down to Sun City with his wife to rent a house for the winter months. His wife was sick in bed with a virus, so he had come out alone — suffering, he said, from "cabin fever." He and his wife were trying to decide whether or not to retire to Sun City. "We have two places up north, but we'd like to move to a warmer climate," he said. "We've thought about it for a long time." When I asked if it would be difficult to leave his family, he replied, "My kids have done well, but there are no strings attached. We are as free as birds now." Later, he said, "Do you want to sacrifice five months of good weather for three days — Thanksgiving, Christmas, and Easter? They have a right to their own lives." Fisher seemed glad to find someone younger — myself — to talk to, explaining, "The youngest person I've talked to in months is the bartender. I look at my wife and I say, 'Are we ready for this?' " Turning away, he continued, "Don't like to admit I'm growing old."

Sun Citians often speak of their children with a great deal of respect and affection, but they do not speak as if their lives and their children's were entwined. A sociologist studying retirement communities found that their members had a marked tendency to disinherit their children in favor of friends in the communities. Because these people did not appear to dislike or disapprove of their children, he called this phenomenon "benevolent disinheritance." Sun Citians do not seem to disinherit their children. Rather, they put up with the distance; they exchange visits with their children, but they often make do without family gatherings on the holidays. (Dr. Gingery now has a breakfast party for his parishioners on Christmas morning, because, as one widow told me, "it is the bluest day of the year.") They make their own independence a virtue. "Our children treat us as friends," Lora Smith said. "They see what full lives we have, and they say we're models for them." Similarly, dependence on children is treated as a weakness. A woman going north to be with her children and grandchildren is said to have "gramma-itis." For many, perhaps, the distance is not entirely unwelcome, since it obviates the inevitable tensions between parents and their grown children. "I've noticed that some people here visit their kids out of charity," Rescorla said. "They think they should, because they're blood relations, but they breathe a sign of relief when they get back here. People don't dislike younger people, but they don't want to depend on them. They have more confidence in people their own age —they trust them more." Dr. Gingery also thought there had been a general loosening of family ties, but he had a different view of the causes and consequences. "All this moving around since the Second World War has had its deleterious effects. This age group couldn't follow their children, so the kids lose their grandparents. But it's more than that. Kids lose a sense of responsibility to the extended family— not just their grandparents. And they lose a sense of responsibility to the community."

Sun Citians have taken some steps to create a substitute for the extended family. Neighbors do take care of each other in all kinds of emergencies; when someone falls ill they help out by doing errands, bringing food, or just dropping in for a chat. Sun City Center has its own Meals on Wheels unit; it has a blood bank; and it has oxygen tanks strategically placed around the town. Dr. Gingery's church has a guardianship program to take care of those who cannot make decisions for themselves. (The weakness of the program is that people must sign up for it in advance, and not many are willing to do that.) Professional home nursing is readily available, and the churches have volunteers who take care of shut-ins. Sun City is probably one of the best towns in America in which to be sick. Still, the system of caring for the ill and the feeble is far from perfect, and many people worry what they will do when, as Dorothy Worden said, "this nice interlude is over." Rescorla told me that the squad had recently taken a couple to the hospital because the woman had fallen ill and could no longer take care of her husband, who was blind. The hospital, however, could not keep them, and if their son had not come down to put them in a nursing home, they would have had nowhere to go. Rescorla's immediate ambition is to create a cooperative nursing service for the community—a group of volunteers who would do the housekeeping, get the groceries, and so on, at least on a temporary basis. He and other community activists in town believe in extending the network of volunteer organizations, but they worry that the town is getting too big for that, and they worry that the new arrivals do not understand the problems of the very old—or are so well off that they prefer to have things done for them rather than do the work themselves. "We often bring people back from the hospital who can't take care of themselves," Rescorla said. "It's very sad in most cases. People who can't manage and who haven't prepared for this— they're buried, they just die."

Sun City Center has never had a cemetery. The developers of retirement villages make a point of keeping graveyards at a distance. Not long after Del Webb founded Sun City, Arizona, a speculator bought some land near the development and threatened to turn it into a cemetery. Del Webb bought him out at several times the price he had paid.

As usual, the developer seems to have understood the trend. At any rate, funeral customs have changed a good deal in Sun City over the past ten years. "When I first came here," Dr. Gingery said, "ninety percent of the people wanted a funeral service with a casket, viewing of the body, and burial in a cemetery. Now ninety percent are cremated and have memorial services."

In shifting from burial to cremation, Sun Citians are a part of a nationwide trend—only, they are in the avant-garde. Dr. Gingery told me that the preference for cremation in Sun City was a sign of growing maturity about death. Dr. Strickland explained, more bluntly, that it reflected the decline of pagan thinking about physical resurrection, and this quite naturally took place first among people of a certain class and education. As the ministers suggest, the nationwide trend is in large part a function of changing religious attitudes, particularly among liberal Protestants. It is also, in some part, a judgment on the funeral industry. But Sun Citians have other reasons as well. "I never thought I'd believe in cremation," Verle Modeweg told me. "I'm a Baptist, after all. But we began going to the Presbyterian church down here before the Baptist church was built, and the minister convinced me." Then she said, "Burial is so expensive and such a waste. I'd rather give my money to the church." Cremation is the final act of tidiness, and as such it has appeal for Sun Citians. But it is also quite clearly a function of mobility, of rootlessness. "I don't have anyone," Mrs. Modeweg continued. "And my husband doesn't either, so there's no one to keep up the graves." Many Sun Citians have no hometowns, and their children, if they have any, live in places where they have no attachments. These people ask that their ashes be scattered over the Gulf, or they buy a place for them at Mansion Memorial Park, a cemetery some miles away. Mrs. Modeweg said, "We bought a place at Mansion Memorial, and now friends come up to me and say, 'I've just found out that I'm going to be right next to you!' It seems very neighborly."

Dr. Gingery believes that in ten years Sun Citians have become much more aware of the aging process and much more accustomed to the idea of death than people in general. In this, he is surely correct. Death occurs more frequently in Sun City than it does in most other communities. Yet it is much like death in a wartime army: it is expected, and it happens to comrades, but not (except in the case of a husband or a wife) to somebody one has known all one's life. Sun Citians don't celebrate it with elaborate rituals; they don't talk about it very much, or worry about it in the way they worry about prolonged sickness or incapacity. They are stoics, and they have, in a sense, tamed it.

"Death is less of a tragedy when you're past sixty," Bess Melvin said. She was in her office, but not in her public relations role. "I think people here do have a different attitude toward death from people in a mixed community. There's a greater sense of acceptance. People don't dwell on it so much. They think about how to have fulfilling lives. They say to themselves. 'I enjoy having a big car. I've always wanted a Caddy or a Lincoln. Death—there it is. I'm ready. But in the meantime I'm going to lead the most enjoyable life possible.' "

Questions

1. FitzGerald sees the physical layout of Sun City as a comment on the spiritual geography of its inhabitants. How would you describe the connection she is making?

2. This essay was taken from *Cities on a Hill*, in which FitzGerald takes as her subject four communities: the homosexuals of San Francisco, the fundamentalists of Liberty Baptist Church, the disciples of Rajneeshpuram, and the elderly of Sun City. She describes these disparate groups as being united in "the extraordinary notion that they could start all over again from scratch. Uncomfortable with, or simply careless of, their own personal histories and their family traditions, they thought they could shuck them off and make new lives, new families, even new societies. They aimed to reinvent themselves." After Jonestown, after Waco, we are often suspicious of religious cults that replace the blood family with the ideological family, yet we don't consider age-segregated communities in the same light. What are the ways that FitzGerald finds the Sun Citians making "new lives, new families"? What do you think of the attitudes these elderly hold toward their blood-family bonds?

Maxine Hong Kingston

NO NAME WOMAN

In this selection, Maxine Hong Kingston notes how she grew up trying to figure out what part of her was Chinese, what part was American, what part was simply herself. Similarly, readers of her work may not always be sure what parts are true, what parts are legend, what parts are pure fiction. In the words of one reviewer, Kingston has created "a genre of her own invention." Formally, two of her major books, *The Woman Warrior: Memoirs of a Girlhood Among Ghosts* (1976) and *China Men* (1980) are classified as autobiographical nonfiction, while a third, *Tripmaster Monkey: His Fake Book,* is considered a novel. Kingston's father, who figures largely in *China Men,* immigrated to the United States in the 1920s. Her mother, who plays a major role in *Woman Warrior,* was unable to join him until fifteen years later. Kingston was born in Sacramento, California, in 1940, soon after her mother's arrival in America.

"You must not tell anyone," my mother said, "what I am about to tell you. In China your father had a sister who killed herself. She jumped into the family well. We say that your father has all brothers because it is as if she had never been born.

"In 1924 just a few days after our village celebrated seventeen hurry-up weddings — to make sure that every young man who went 'out on the road' would responsibly come home — your father and his brothers and your grandfather and his brothers and your aunt's new husband sailed for America, the Gold Mountain. It was your grandfather's last trip. Those lucky enough to get contracts waved good-bye from the decks. They fed and guarded the stowaways and helped them off in Cuba, New York, Bali, Hawaii. 'We'll meet in California next year,' they said. All of them sent money home.

"I remember looking at your aunt one day when she and I were dressing; I had not noticed before that she had such a protruding melon of a stomach. But I did not think, 'She's pregnant,' until she began to look like other pregnant women, her skirt pulling and the white tops of her black pants showing. She could not have been pregnant, you see, because her husband had been gone for years. No one said anything. We did not discuss it. In early summer she was ready to have the child, long after the time when it could have been possible.

"The village had also been counting. On the night the baby was to be born the villagers raided our house. Some were crying. Like a great saw, teeth strung with lights, files of people walked zigzag across our land, tearing the rice. Their lanterns doubled in the disturbed black water, which drained away through the broken bunds. As the villagers closed in, we could see that some of them, probably men and women we knew well, wore white masks. The people with long hair hung it over their faces. Women with short hair made it stand up on end. Some had tied white bands around their foreheads, arms, and legs.

"At first they threw mud and rocks at the house. Then they threw   5

eggs and began slaughtering our stock. We could hear the animals
scream their deaths—the roosters, the pigs, a last great roar from the
ox. Familiar wild heads flared in our night windows; the villagers encir-
cled us. Some of the faces stopped to peer at us, their eyes rushing like
searchlights. The hands flattened against the panes, framed heads, and
left red prints.

"The villagers broke in the front and the back doors at the same
time, even though we had not locked the doors against them. Their
knives dripped with the blood of our animals. They smeared blood on
the doors and walls. One woman swung a chicken, whose throat she
had slit, splattering blood in red arcs about her. We stood together in
the middle of our house, in the family hall with pictures and tables of
the ancestors around us, and looked straight ahead.

"At that time the house had only two wings. When the men came
back, we would build two more to enclose our courtyard and a third
one to begin a second courtyard. The villagers pushed through both
wings, even your grandparents' rooms, to find your aunt's, which was
also mine until the men returned. From this room a new wing for one
of the younger families would grow. They ripped up her clothes and
shoes and broke her combs, grinding them underfoot. They tore her
work from the loom. They scattered the cooking fire and rolled the new
weaving in it. We could hear them in the kitchen breaking our bowls
and banging the pots. They overturned the great waist-high earthen-
ware jugs; duck eggs, pickled fruits, vegetables burst out and mixed in
acrid torrents. The old woman from the next field swept a broom
through the air and loosed the spirits-of-the-broom over our heads.
'Pig.' 'Ghost.' 'Pig,' they sobbed and scolded while they ruined our
house.

"When they left, they took sugar and oranges to bless themselves.
They cut pieces from the dead animals. Some of them took bowls that
were not broken and clothes that were not torn. Afterward we swept
up the rice and sewed it back up into sacks. But the smells from the
spilled preserves lasted. Your aunt gave birth in the pigsty that night.
The next morning when I went for the water, I found her and the baby
plugging up the family well.

"Don't let your father know that I told you. He denies her. Now
that you have started to menstruate, what happened to her could happen to you. Don't humiliate us. You wouldn't like to be forgotten as if
you had never been born. The villagers are watchful."

Whenever she had to warn us about life, my mother told stories 10
that ran like this one, a story to grow up on. She tested our strength to
establish realities. Those in the emigrant generations who could not re-
assert brute survival died young and far from home. Those of us in the
first American generations have had to figure out how the invisible
world the emigrants built around our childhoods fit in solid America.

The emigrants confused the gods by diverting their curses, misleading them with crooked streets and false names. They must try to confuse their offspring as well, who, I suppose, threaten them in similar ways—always trying to get things straight, always trying to name the unspeakable. The Chinese I know hide their names; sojourners take new names when their lives change and guard their real names with silence.

Chinese-Americans, when you try to understand what things in you are Chinese, how do you separate what is peculiar to childhood, to poverty, insanities, one family, your mother who marked your growing with stories, from what is Chinese? What is Chinese tradition and what is the movies?

If I want to learn what clothes my aunt wore, whether flashy or ordinary, I would have to begin, "Remember Father's drowned-in-the-well sister?" I cannot ask that. My mother has told me once and for all the useful parts. She will add nothing unless powered by Necessity, a riverbank that guides her life. She plants vegetable gardens rather than lawns; she carries the odd-shaped tomatoes home from the fields and eats food left for the gods.

Whenever we did frivolous things, we used up energy; we flew high kites. We children came up off the ground over the melting cones our parents brought home from work and the American movie on New Year's Day—*Oh, You Beautiful Doll* with Betty Grable one year, and *She Wore A Yellow Ribbon* with John Wayne another year. After the one carnival ride each, we paid in guilt; our tired father counted his change on the dark walk home.

Adultery is extravagance. Could people who hatch their own 15 chicks and eat the embryos and the heads for delicacies and boil the feet in vinegar for party food, leaving only the gravel, eating even the gizzard lining—could such people engender a prodigal aunt? To be a woman, to have a daughter in starvation time was a waste enough. My aunt could not have been the lone romantic who gave up everything for sex. Women in the old China did not choose. Some man had commanded her to lie with him and be his secret evil. I wonder whether he masked himself when he joined the raid on her family.

Perhaps she encountered him in the fields or on the mountain where the daughters-in-law collected fuel. Or perhaps he first noticed her in the marketplace. He was not a stranger because the village housed no strangers. She had to have dealings with him other than sex. Perhaps he worked an adjoining field, or he sold her the cloth for the dress she sewed and wore. His demand must have surprised, then terrified her. She obeyed him; she always did as she was told.

When the family found a young man in the next village to be her husband, she stood tractably beside the best rooster, his proxy, and promised before they met that she would be his forever. She was lucky that he was her age and she would be the first wife, an advantage secure now. The night she first saw him, he had sex with her. Then he left for America. She had almost forgotten what he looked like. When she tried to envision him, she only saw the black and white face in the group photograph the men had had taken before leaving.

The other man was not, after all, much different from her husband. They both gave orders: she followed. "If you tell your family, I'll beat you. I'll kill you. Be here again next week." No one talked sex, ever. And she might have separated the rapes from the rest of living if only she did not have to buy her oil from him or gather wood in the same forest. I want her fear to have lasted just as long as rape lasted so that the fear could have been contained. No drawn-out fear. But women at sex hazarded birth and hence lifetimes. The fear did not stop but permeated everywhere. She told the man, "I think I'm pregnant." He organized the raid against her.

On nights when my mother and father talked about their life back home, sometimes they mentioned an "outcast table" whose business they still seemed to be settling, their voices tight. In a commensal tradition, where food is precious, the powerful older people made wrongdoers eat alone. Instead of letting them start separate new lives like the Japanese, who could become samurais and geishas, the Chinese family, faces averted but eyes glowering sideways, hung on to the offenders and fed them leftovers. My aunt must have lived in the same house as my parents and eaten at an outcast table. My mother spoke about the raid as if she had seen it, when she and my aunt, a daughter-in-law to a different household, should not have been living together at all. Daughters-in-law lived with their husbands' parents, not their own; a synonym for marriage in Chinese is "taking a daughter-in-law." Her husband's parents could have sold her, mortgaged her, stoned her. But they had sent her back to her own mother and father, a mysterious act hinting at disgraces not told me. Perhaps they had thrown her out to deflect the avengers.

She was the only daughter; her four brothers went with her father, 20 husband, and uncles "out on the road" and for some years became western men. When the goods were divided among the family, three of the brothers took land, and the youngest, my father, chose an education. After my grandparents gave their daughter away to her husband's family, they had dispensed all the adventure and all the property. They expected her alone to keep the traditional ways, which her brothers, now among the barbarians, could fumble without detection. The heavy, deep-rooted women were to maintain the past against the flood, safe for returning. But the rare urge west had fixed upon our family, and so my aunt crossed boundaries not delineated in space.

The work of preservation demands that the feelings playing about in one's guts not be turned into action. Just watch their passing like cherry blossoms. But perhaps my aunt, my forerunner, caught in a slow life, let dreams grow and fade and after some months or years went toward what persisted. Fear at the enormities of the forbidden kept her desires delicate, wire and bone. She looked at a man because she liked the way the hair was tucked behind his ears, or she liked the question-mark line of a long torso curving at the shoulder and straight at the hip. For warm eyes or a soft voice or a slow walk—that's all—a few hairs, a line, a brightness, a sound, a pace, she gave up family. She offered us up for a charm that vanished with tiredness, a pigtail that didn't toss when the wind died. Why, the wrong lighting could erase the dearest thing about him.

It could very well have been, however, that my aunt did not take subtle enjoyment of her friend, but, a wild woman, kept rollicking company. Imagining her free with sex doesn't fit, though. I don't know any women like that, or men either. Unless I see her life branching into mine, she gives me no ancestral help.

To sustain her being in love, she often worked at herself in the mirror, guessing at the colors and shapes that would interest him, changing them frequently in order to hit on the right combination. She wanted him to look back.

On a farm near the sea, a woman who tended her appearance reaped a reputation for eccentricity. All the married women blunt-cut their hair in flaps about their ears or pulled it back in tight buns. No nonsense. Neither style blew easily into heart-catching tangles. And at their weddings they displayed themselves in their long hair for the last time. "It brushed the backs of my knees," my mother tells me. "It was braided, and even so, it brushed the backs of my knees."

At the mirror my aunt combed individuality into her bob. A bun   25 could have been contrived to escape into black streamers blowing in the wind or in quiet wisps about her face, but only the older women in our picture album wear buns. She brushed her hair back from her forehead, tucking the flaps behind her ears. She looped a piece of thread, knotted into a circle between her index fingers and thumbs, and ran the double strand across her forehead. When she closed her fingers as if she were making a pair of shadow geese bite, the string twisted together catching the little hairs. Then she pulled the thread away from her skin, ripping the hairs out neatly, her eyes watering from the needles of pain. Opening her fingers, she cleaned the thread, then rolled it along her hairline and the tops of her eyebrows. My mother did the same to me and my sisters and herself. I used to believe that the expression "caught by the short hairs" meant a captive held with a depilatory string. It especially hurt at the temples, but my mother said we were lucky we didn't have to have our feet bound when we were seven. Sisters used to sit on their beds and cry together, she said, as their mothers or their slave removed the bandages for a few minutes each night and let the blood gush back into their veins. I hope that the man my aunt loved appreciated a smooth brow, that he wasn't just a tits-and-ass man.

Once my aunt found a freckle on her chin, at a spot that the almanac said predestined her for unhappiness. She dug it out with a hot needle and washed the wound with peroxide.

More attention to her looks than these pullings of hairs and pickings at spots would have caused gossip among the villagers. They owned work clothes and good clothes, and they wore good clothes for feasting the new seasons. But since a woman combing her hair hexes beginnings, my aunt rarely found an occasion to look her best. Women looked like great sea snails—the corded wood, babies, and laundry they carried were the whorls on their backs. The Chinese did not admire a bent back; goddesses and warriors stood straight. Still there must have been a marvelous freeing of beauty when a worker laid down her burden and stretched and arched.

Such commonplace loveliness, however, was not enough for my aunt. She dreamed of a lover for the fifteen days of New Year's, the time for families to exchange visits, money, and food. She plied her secret comb. And sure enough she cursed the year, the family, the village, and herself.

Even as her hair lured her imminent lover, many other men looked at her. Uncles, cousins, nephews, brothers would have looked, too, had they been home between journeys. Perhaps they had already been restraining their curiosity, and they left, fearful that their glances, like a field of nesting birds, might be startled and caught. Poverty hurt, and that was their first reason for leaving. But another, final reason for leaving the crowded house was the never-said.

She may have been unusually beloved, the precious only daughter, spoiled and mirror gazing because of the affection the family lavished on her. When her husband left, they welcomed the chance to take her back from the in-laws; she could live like the little daughter for just a while longer. There are stories that my grandfather was different from other people, "crazy ever since the little Jap bayoneted him in the head." He used to put his naked penis on the dinner table, laughing. And one day he brought home a baby girl, wrapped up inside his brown western-style greatcoat. He had traded one of his sons, probably my father, the youngest, for her. My grandmother made him trade back. When he finally got a daughter of his own, he doted on her. They must have all loved her, except perhaps my father, the only brother who never went back to China, having once been traded for a girl.

Brothers and sisters, newly men and women, had to efface their sexual color and present plain miens. Disturbing hair and eyes, a smile like no other, threatened the ideal of five generations living under one

30

roof. To focus blurs, people shouted face to face and yelled from room to room. The immigrants I know have loud voices, unmodulated to American tones even after years away from the village where they called their friendships out across the fields. I have not been able to stop my mother's screams in public libraries or over telephones. Walking erect (knees straight, toes pointed forward, not pigeon-toed, which is Chinese-feminine), and speaking in an inaudible voice, I have tried to turn myself American-feminine. Chinese communication was loud, public. Only sick people had to whisper. But at the dinner table, where the family members came nearest one another, no one could talk, not the outcasts nor any eaters. Every word that falls from the mouth is a coin lost. Silently they gave and accepted food with both hands. A pre-occupied child who took his bowl with one hand got a sideways glare. A complete moment of total attention is due everyone alike. Children and lovers have no singularity here, but my aunt used a secret voice, a separate attentiveness.

She kept the man's name to herself throughout her labor and dying; she did not accuse him that he be punished with her. To save her inseminator's name she gave silent birth.

He may have been somebody in her own household, but inter-course with a man outside the family would have been no less abhor-rent. All the village were kinsmen, and the titles shouted in loud coun-try voices never let kinship be forgotten. Any man within visiting distance would have been neutralized as a lover — "brother," "younger brother," "older brother" — one hundred and fifteen relationship titles. Parents researched birth charts probably not so much to assure good fortune as to circumvent incest in a population that has but one hun-dred surnames. Everybody has eight million relatives. How useless then sexual mannerisms, how dangerous.

As if it came from an atavism deeper than fear, I used to add "brother" silently to boys' names. It hexed the boys, who would or would not ask me to dance, and made them less scary and as familiar and deserving of benevolence as girls.

But, of course, I hexed myself also — no dates. I should have stood   35 up, both arms waving, and shouted out across libraries, "Hey you! Love me back." I had no idea, though, how to make attraction selective, how to control its direction and magnitude. If I made myself American-pretty so that the five or six Chinese boys in the class fell in love with me, everyone else — the Caucasian, Negro, and Japanese boys — would too. Sisterliness, dignified and honorable, made much more sense.

Attraction eludes control so stubbornly that whole societies de-signed to organize relationships among people cannot keep order, not even when they bind people to one another from childhood and raise them together. Among the very poor and the wealthy, brothers mar-ried their adopted sisters, like doves. Our family allowed some romance, paying adult brides' prices and providing dowries so that their sons and daughters could marry strangers. Marriage promises to turn strangers into friendly relatives—a nation of siblings.

In the village structure, spirits shimmered among the live creatures, balanced and held in equilibrium by time and land. But one human being flaring up into violence could open up a black hole, a maelstrom that pulled in the sky. The frightened villagers, who depended on one another to maintain the real, went to my aunt to show her a personal, physical representation of the break she had made in the "roundness." Misallying couples snapped off the future, which was to be embodied in true offspring. The villagers punished her for acting as if she could have a private life, secret and apart from them.

If my aunt had betrayed the family at a time of large grain yields and peace, when many boys were born, and wings were being built on many houses, perhaps she might have escaped such severe punishment. But the men—hungry, greedy, tired of planting in dry soil, cuckolded—had had to leave the village in order to send food-money home. There were ghost plagues, bandit plagues, wars with the Japanese, floods. My Chinese brother and sister had died of an unknown sickness. Adultery, perhaps only a mistake during good times, became a crime when the village needed food.

The round moon cakes and round doorways, the round tables of graduated size that fit one roundness into another, round windows and rice bowls—these talismans had lost their power to warn this family of the law: a family must be whole, faithfully keeping the descent line by having sons to feed the old and the dead, who in turn look after the family. The villagers came to show my aunt and her lover-in-hiding a broken house. The villagers were speeding up the circling of events because she was too shortsighted to see that her infidelity had already harmed the village, that waves of consequences would return unpredictably, sometimes in disguise, as now, to hurt her. This roundness had to be made coin-sized so that she would see its circumference: punish her at the birth of her baby. Awaken her to the inexorable. People who refused fatalism because they could invest small resources insisted on culpability. Deny accidents and wrest fault from the stars.

After the villagers left, their lanterns now scattering in various directions toward home, the family broke their silence and cursed her. "Aiaa, we're going to die. Death is coming. Death is coming. Look what you've done. You've killed us. Ghost! Dead ghost! Ghost! You've never been born." She ran out into the fields, far enough from the house so that she could no longer hear their voices, and pressed herself against the earth, her own land no more. When she felt the birth coming, she thought that she had been hurt. Her body seized together. "They've hurt me too much," she thought. "This is gall, and it will kill me." With forehead and knees against the earth, her body convulsed and then relaxed. She turned on her back, lay on the ground. The black well of sky and stars went out and out and out forever; her body and her complexity seemed to disappear. She was one of the stars, a bright dot in blackness, without home, without a companion, in eternal cold and silence. An agoraphobia rose in her, speeding higher and higher, bigger and bigger; she would not be able to contain it; there would be no end to fear.

Flayed, unprotected against space, she felt pain return, focusing her body. This pain chilled her—a cold, steady kind of surface pain. Inside, spasmodically, the other pain, the pain of the child, heated her. For hours she lay on the ground, alternately body and space. Sometimes a vision of normal comfort obliterated reality: she saw the family in the evening gambling at the dinner table, the young people massaging their elders' backs. She saw them congratulating one another, high joy on the mornings the rice shoots came up. When these pictures burst, the stars drew yet further apart. Black space opened.

She got to her feet to fight better and remembered that old-fashioned women gave birth in their pigsties to fool the jealous, pain-dealing gods, who do not snatch piglets. Before the next spasms could stop her, she ran to the pigsty, each step a rushing out into emptiness. She climbed over the fence and knelt in the dirt. It was good to have a fence enclosing her, a tribal person alone.

Laboring, this woman who had carried her child as a foreign growth that sickened her every day, expelled it at last. She reached down to touch the hot, wet, moving mass, surely smaller than anything human, and could feel that it was human after all—fingers, toes, nails, nose. She pulled it up on to her belly, and it lay curled there, butt in the air, feet precisely tucked one under the other. She opened her loose shirt and buttoned the child inside. After resting, it squirmed and thrashed and she pushed it up to her breast. It turned its head this way and that until it found her nipple. There, it made little snuffling noises. She clenched her teeth at its preciousness, lovely as a young calf, a piglet, a little dog.

She may have gone to the pigsty as a last act of responsibility: she would protect this child as she had protected its father. It would look after her soul, leaving supplies on her grave. But how would this tiny child without family find her grave when there would be no marker for her anywhere, neither in the earth nor the family hall? No one would give her a family hall name. She had taken the child with her into the wastes. At its birth the two of them had felt the same raw pain of separation, a wound that only the family pressing tight could close. A child with no descent line would not soften her life but only trail after her, ghostlike, begging her to give it purpose. At dawn the villagers on their way to the fields would stand around the fence and look.

Full of milk, the little ghost slept. When it awoke, she hardened her 45 breasts against the milk that crying loosens. Toward morning she picked up the baby and walked to the well.

Carrying the baby to the well shows loving. Otherwise abandon it. Turn its face into the mud. Mothers who love their children take them along. It was probably a girl; there is some hope of forgiveness for boys.

"Don't tell anyone you had an aunt. Your father does not want to hear her name. She has never been born." I have believed that sex was unspeakable and words so strong and fathers so frail that "aunt" would do my father mysterious harm. I have thought that my family, having settled among immigrants who had also been their neighbors in the ancestral land, needed to clean their name, and a wrong word would incite the kinspeople even here. But there is more to this silence: they want me to participate in her punishment. And I have.

In the twenty years since I heard this story I have not asked for details nor said my aunt's name; I do not know it. People who can comfort the dead can also chase after them to hurt them further—a reverse ancestor worship. The real punishment was not the raid swiftly inflicted by the villagers, but the family's deliberately forgetting her. Her betrayal so maddened them, they saw to it that she should suffer forever, even after death. Always hungry, always needing, she would have to beg food from other ghosts, snatch and steal it from those whose living descendants give them gifts. She would have to fight the ghosts massed at crossroads for the buns a few thoughtful citizens leave to decoy her away from village and home so that the ancestral spirits could feast unharassed. At peace, they could act like gods, not ghosts, their descent lines providing them with paper suits and dresses, spirit money, paper houses, paper automobiles, chicken, meat, and rice into eternity—essences delivered up in smoke and flames, steam and incense rising from each rice bowl. In an attempt to make the Chinese care for people outside the family, Chairman Mao encourages us now to give our paper replicas to the spirits of outstanding soldiers and workers, no matter whose ancestors they may be. My aunt remains forever hungry. Goods are not distributed evenly among the dead.

My aunt haunts me—her ghost drawn to me because now, after fifty years of neglect, I alone devote pages of paper to her, though not origamied into houses and clothes. I do not think she always means me well. I am telling on her, and she was a spite suicide, drowning herself in the drinking water. The Chinese are always very frightened of the drowned one, whose weeping ghost, wet hair hanging and skin bloated, waits silently by the water to pull down a substitute.

Questions

1. Part of the compulsion to read essays comes from their disclosure of lives and people whom we would otherwise never know; the essay gives us access to secrets. Consider Maxine Hong Kingston's opening line: " 'You must not tell anyone,' my mother said,

'what I am about to tell you.' " How does Kingston explore the theme of breaking silence by telling secrets throughout her essay?

2. Scientists refer to possible solutions to an event with no agreed-upon explanation as "competing theories." How does Kingston learn of the event she is trying to explain? Since her knowledge is not firsthand, how can she ascertain the true narrative? What does this essay seem to suggest about the idea of narrative truth?

(*Continued from p. iv*)

Diana Hume George, "Wounded Chevy at Wounded Knee." Copyright © by Diana Hume George. Originally published in *Missouri Review,* 1990. Reprinted by permission of the author.

Barbara Grizzuti Harrison, "Growing Up Apocalyptic." From *Off Center* by Barbara Grizzuti Harrison. Copyright © 1980 by Barbara Grizzuti Harrison. Used by permission of Doubleday, a division of Bantam Doubleday Dell Publishing Group, Inc.

Vicki Hearne, "Lo, Hear the Gentle Pit Bull." Copyright © 1985 by Vicki Hearne. First published in *Harper's.* Used by permission of the Wallace Literary Agency, Inc.

Edward Hoagland, "From Canada, By Land." From *Balancing Acts* by Edward Hoagland. Copyright © 1987, 1992 by Edward Hoagland. Originally appeared in *Travel & Leisure Magazine* as "Three Trains Across Canada." Reprinted by permission of Simon & Schuster, Inc.

Maxine Hong Kingston, "No Name Woman." From *The Woman Warrior* by Maxine Hong Kingston. Copyright © 1975, 1976 by Maxine Hong Kingston. Reprinted by permission of Alfred A. Knopf, Inc.

Natalie Kusz, "Vital Signs" as it appeared in *The Threepenny Review,* Spring 1989, later published in slightly different form in *Road Song* by Natalie Kusz. Copyright © 1990 by Natalie Kusz. Reprinted by permission of Farrar, Straus & Giroux, Inc.

Barry Lopez, "The Stone Horse." Copyright © 1986 by Barry Lopez. Reprinted by permission of Sterling Lord Literistic, Inc.

John McPhee, "Riding the Boom Extension." From *Table of Contents* by John McPhee. Copyright © 1985 by John McPhee. Reprinted by permission of Farrar, Straus & Giroux, Inc.

N. Scott Momaday, "The Horse." From *The Names* by N. Scott Momaday. Copyright © 1976 by N. Scott Momaday. Reprinted by permission of the author.

Richard Preston, "Crisis in the Hot Zone." Copyright © 1992 by Richard Preston. Originally published in *The New Yorker.* Reprinted by permission.

Richard Rodriguez, "Late Victorians." From *Days of Obligation* by Richard Rodriguez. Copyright © 1992 by Richard Rodriguez. Used by permission of Viking Penguin, a division of Penguin Books USA, Inc.

Theodore Roethke, "My Papa's Waltz." From *The Collected Poems of Theodore Roethke* by Theodore Roethke. Copyright © 1942 by Hearst Magazines, Inc. Used by permission of Doubleday, a division of Bantam Doubleday Dell Publishing Group, Inc.

Judy Ruiz, "Oranges and Sweet Sister Boy." First published in *Iowa Woman Magazine,* Summer 1988. Reprinted by permission of the author.

Oliver Sacks, "A Walking Grove." From *The Man Who Mistook His Wife for a Hat.* Copyright 1970, 1981, 1984, 1985 by Oliver Sacks. Reprinted by permission of Summit Books, a division of Simon & Schuster, Inc.

Scott Russell Sanders, "Under the Influence." Copyright © 1989 by *Harper's.* All rights reserved. Reprinted from the November issue by special permission.

Lewis Thomas, "To Err Is Human." From *The Medusa and the Snail* by Lewis Thomas. Copyright © 1976 by Lewis Thomas. Used by permission of Viking Penguin, a division of Penguin Books USA, Inc.

Calvin Trillin, "Resettling the Yangs." From *Killings* by Calvin Trillin. Copyright © 1984 by Calvin Trillin. Reprinted by permission of Ticknor & Fields. Originally appeared in *The New Yorker.*

Alice Walker, "A Thousand Words: A Writer's Pictures of China." From *Living by the Word: Selected Writings 1973–1987.* Copyright © 1985 by Alice Walker. Reprinted by permission of Harcourt Brace & Company.

Index of Authors and Titles

To the Student

We regularly revise the books we publish to make them better. To do this well we need to know what instructors and students think of the previous edition. At some point your instructor will be asked to comment on *Cartographies: Contemporary American Fiction;* now we would like to hear from you.

Please take a few minutes to rate the selections and complete this questionnaire. Send it to Bedford Books *of* St. Martin's Press, 29 Winchester Street, Boston, Massachusetts, 02116. We promise to listen to what you have to say. Thanks.

School _____

School location (city, state) _____

Course title _____

Instructor's name _____

	Liked a lot	Okay	Didn't like	Didn't read
1. Becoming				
Harrison, *Growing Up Apocalyptic*	——	——	——	——
Momaday, *The Horse*	——	——	——	——
Dorris, *Life Stories*	——	——	——	——
Garrett, *Whistling in the Dark*	——	——	——	——
Field, *In the Realm of a Dying Emperor*	——	——	——	——
2. Embodying Identities				
Ephron, *A Few Words about Breasts*	——	——	——	——
Ruiz, *Oranges and Sweet Sister Boy*	——	——	——	——
Kusz, *Vital Signs*	——	——	——	——
Castle, *First Ed*	——	——	——	——
Sanders, *Under the Influence*	——	——	——	——
3. Constructing Nature				
Ehrlich, *Architecture*	——	——	——	——
Sacks, *A Walking Grove*	——	——	——	——
Thomas, *To Err Is Human*	——	——	——	——
Hearne, *Consider the Pit Bull*	——	——	——	——
Dillard, *Total Eclipse*	——	——	——	——
Preston, *Crisis in the Hot Zone*	——	——	——	——
4. Traveling				
Walker, *A Thousand Words: A Writer's Pictures of China*	——	——	——	——
Hoagland, *From Canada, By Land*	——	——	——	——
McPhee, *Riding the Boom Extension*	——	——	——	——
Didion, *El Exilio and the Melting Pot*	——	——	——	——
Trillin, *Resettling the Yangs*	——	——	——	——

	Liked a lot	Okay	Didn't like	Didn't read
5. Reading Cultures				
Rodriguez, *Late Victorians*	_____	_____	_____	_____
George, *Wounded Chevy at Wounded Knee*	_____	_____	_____	_____
Lopez, *The Stone Horse*	_____	_____	_____	_____
Early, *Waiting for Miss America: Stand Up and Cheer*	_____	_____	_____	_____
FitzGerald, *Sun City—1983*	_____	_____	_____	_____
Kingston, *No Name Woman*	_____	_____	_____	_____

Name _____ **Date** _____

Address _____